THE DRAGON AWAKENS

BOOK ONE

THE FALLEN KNIGHT SERIES

PETER WACHT

KESTREL MEDIA GROUP, LLC

The Dragon Awakens
By Peter Wacht

Book 1 of The Fallen Knight Series

Cover design by Ebooklaunch.com

Published in the United States by Kestrel Media Group LLC.

ISBN: 978-1-950236-54-1

eBook ISBN: 978-1-950236-53-4

Library of Congress Control Number: 2024917558

Created with Vellum

ALSO BY PETER WACHT

THE FALLEN KNIGHT SERIES

The Death of the Dragon (short story)*

The Dragon Awakens

Duel With a Dragon (Forthcoming)

Beware the Dragon (Forthcoming)

The Dragon Returns (Forthcoming)

THE REALMS OF THE TALENT AND THE CURSE

THE TALES OF CALEDONIA

(Complete 7-Book Series)

Blood on the White Sand (short story)*

The Diamond Thief (short story)*

The Protector

The Protector's Quest

The Protector's Vengeance

The Protector's Sacrifice

The Protector's Reckoning

The Protector's Resolve

The Protector's Victory

THE TALES OF THE TERRITORIES

Stalking the Blood Ruby (short story)*

A Fate Worse Than Death (short story)*

Death on the Burnt Ocean

Monsters in the Mist

The Dance of the Daggers

Bloody Hunt for Freedom

A Spark of Rebellion

Shadows Made Real

Shadow's Reach

Storm in the Darkness (Forthcoming 2025)

THE SYLVAN CHRONICLES

(Complete 9-Book Series)

The Legend of the Kestrel

The Call of the Sylvana

The Raptor of the Highlands

The Makings of a Warrior

The Lord of the Highlands

The Lost Kestrel Found

The Claiming of the Highlands

The Fight Against the Dark

The Defender of the Light

THE RISE OF THE SYLVAN WARRIORS

*Through the Knife's Edge (short story)**

* Free stories can be downloaded from my author website at PeterWachtBooks.com. My books are also available on Amazon and other online retailers.

PROLOGUE

My Story

It's the powerful people who write the histories.

Why?

So they can say what they want to say. So they'll be remembered as they want to be remembered. So that the story *they* want told becomes reality.

Whether that reality is real or a pile of horseshit.

Control the narrative.

Control the legacy.

They do that, and *they* increase their power. And there's nothing that powerful people like more than more power.

It's a drug. Once given a taste, people want another taste. And another.

People don't want anything else but that.

My father is one of them.

Power drives him.

Power is who he is.

Quite a lot has been written about him.

Libraries worth. And still more books appear. Every year. Hundreds. Maybe even thousands.

I've lost track and interest.

And not just histories. Academic tomes. Historical fiction. Epic fantasy. Urban fantasy. Mythological reworkings.

His story struck a chord.

In fact, he's one of the most popular figures in history.

Some of what's been written about him is justified. Much of it isn't.

For that, all credit to the public relations firms that have molded his story into the history that he demanded. For helping to make him who he's become.

And there's the rub.

Most people don't know that the story about my father was written by him. For him. So that he could do what he believed that he needed to do in our world.

At first, I understood. I saw the value of what he was doing. I believed what he told me instead of questioning him.

My father was a hero. Deservedly so. He earned that title.

At least some of the time.

When he was younger and he did what he thought was right rather than what he thought was necessary.

I remember when he was a hero. When he was my hero. But then he changed.

I've seen him at his best and I've seen him at his worst.

I've seen what he's done because he started to believe the story that he crafted.

I know what he wants to do.

I know the lengths that he'll go to achieve his goals.

I even helped him for a time.

For much too long a time.

Yet as the years passed, and then the centuries, after he turned me into what I became -- what he wanted me to be --

and after I saw what he had become, I realized that he wasn't always doing what he *needed* to do *in* our world. He was doing what he *wanted* to do *to* our world.

I almost didn't realize the distinction between *need* and *want* before it was too late.

That's why I decided that I needed to tell my story. An alternative history of sorts. A different perspective. My take.

Admittedly biased. Although not biased toward my father. Biased toward the truth. Or at least the truth as I know it. As I believe it.

No one likely will read it.

That's all right.

It's not the reading that matters to me so much as the writing.

Because at least what I put on these pages will be my story. Not the story that my father wanted to tell. The story that my father believes he needed to tell.

The story he wants to share is one based on a myth. Some of it true. Much of it lies.

My story is real.

Or at least as real as can be when you're fitting together your own memories with the memories of those who were with you. When you're striving for accuracy and fighting against bias with every keystroke.

So admittedly I offer you a history that's skewed right from the start. But at least in my case anything that I recall incorrectly was done because of my poor memory rather than any desire to mislead or to craft a new and false narrative.

There was another reason as well for sharing my story. Or stories, I should say. Because I've lived through quite a few during my centuries.

One in particular that I wasn't sure that I should share. But at this point, why not.

I've already talked about *need* and *want* and the distinction between the two.

I didn't *want* to do it, but I *knew* that I had to.

I *needed* to kill my father before he killed me.

That's why I wanted to tell my story.

I needed to tell you as much as I could before my father killed me.

So this is my story.

Who am I?

I'm Axel Draig.

And my father?

My father is Arthur Pendragon.

And how did all of this start?

With me already being dead.

I liked being dead.

I still would be dead, in fact, if not for the Witch who brought me back to life.

1

STICKY FINGERS

"Why did I agree to this?" Melissa whispered.

She had told herself that she wasn't going to do this. Never again. Not after what happened the last time.

She should have said no. She should have walked away. She didn't need the money.

Once again, she had ignored her better judgment.

Because here she was. Clad in a black drysuit that allowed her to blend into the night, twenty yards off the beach treading frigid water that threatened to turn her body to ice.

Only her head broke the waves, and that was because she wanted to get a look at what she was up against.

Melissa should have trained more for this job. She would have but she didn't have the time.

That lack of training was why she was so tired. That and the fact that she had already swum a mile along the coast to get to her current position. Actually longer than that. She had to fight the current that kept trying to push her out to sea.

Yet despite all that effort, her work hadn't even really begun.

Getting here was the easy part. Getting past what waited for her on the beach and beyond was the hard part. And, without a little bit of luck, most likely the lethal part.

She tried not to think about that, although it was getting harder to do as the reality of what she was about to attempt struck her. Instead, she forced herself to focus on the plan she had developed that she hoped would keep her alive.

Plans could change. They usually did. But they gave her something to hold onto when everything was falling apart around her.

She had a practical mind. Her mother said the mind of an engineer, in fact, the mind of her father. She used that mind now.

Rather than getting trapped within the many risks that she would be taking, she organized what she needed to do that night into a series of steps. Complete those steps and she completed the job. Simple as that.

And, maybe, just maybe, she would make it out alive.

"You did this to yourself," she muttered as she fit the mouthpiece of her snorkel back into place and ducked below the waves, leaving only a few inches of the tube above the water as she kicked in closer to the shore.

She had seen the movement along the shore. The guards came together on the sand as they passed one another. The two teams then broke away and headed for the far ends of the beach before they turned back around and crossed paths again.

She stopped, still submerged, wanting to confirm that she was in the right spot. The sea was dark but for the gleam of the full moon. Every few seconds she brought her wrist up to her mask. The dull green glow of her diver's watch told her how much longer she needed to wait.

Ten seconds. Twenty seconds. Thirty seconds. Not until the timer had ticked down another sixty seconds did she push her head back above the waves.

She smiled, at least as well as she could without

dislodging her mouthpiece. Her timing was spot on. The two pairs of guards already had met and were well past each other, their backs turned as they made for where the sand curled out into the ocean in both directions, large rocks marking the points of the beach that was shaped like a crescent moon.

She'd make her move the next time the guards came back around and passed one another.

The question of why she had put herself in this position once again popped back into her mind as she glanced at her watch every thirty seconds. It wasn't because of the money. That was true. It wasn't because of the challenge either. No, she was there for a much simpler reason. One that left a sour taste in her mouth.

She didn't have a choice.

That thought filling her stomach with acid while at the same time bolstering her nerve, she kicked beneath the surface, seeing no reason to expend any more energy after her long swim and not wanting to make any noise that would catch the attention of the guards.

The location that she wanted to reach was about fifty yards to her left. Thankfully, the current had shifted and was actually in her favor, giving her a gentle push to get her where she wanted to go.

Once she reached the spot where she was lined up with the flights of stairs that switch backed up the cliff, she focused on maintaining her position. She would need to time perfectly what she needed to do next.

If she didn't, the guards wouldn't just catch her. They'd kill her.

She glanced at her watch. Two more minutes before she needed to move.

Although she had already spent hours studying her target and could recall every detail perfectly in her mind, still she used the seconds that were ticking down to study the landscape in front of her one final time.

At that very moment, the clouds decided to aid her efforts, drifting farther to the east to reveal the full moon. The light gave her an excellent view of what was waiting for her as soon as she emerged from the water.

The sandy beach ran fifty yards up from the surf, the tide currently in. Backstopping the beach were massive sand dunes covered by large swathes of beach grass. There was one path between the dunes that led to the staircase that would allow her to climb the cliff without having to scale it.

If worse came to worse, she could scramble up the rocks, though she didn't want to. The precipice was only one hundred and twenty feet in height, so an easy climb for her. Even so, not using the staircase would cost her minutes she could use elsewhere.

She had built some extra time into her schedule, just in case, and if she had the chance to make use of it, she wanted to use it elsewhere. Not to get off the beach.

Moving her gaze beyond the staircase, just above the cliff she saw a lawn of tightly mowed green grass. Two hundred and seventy-three yards in length to be exact. Melissa had used Google and another program that wasn't readily available on the market to confirm the distance. The grass began at the cliff's edge and ran up to a mansion.

Although mansion wasn't the right word for what dominated the promontory. The mansion more resembled a European castle. Spires rose for several stories, anchoring each corner, each one set to a cardinal point of the compass.

Most impressive was the central spire, which rose for seven stories and was one hundred and thirty-three feet in diameter. Google had helped with that as well. Even more so the construction blueprints filed with the city that she had acquired through illicit means the week before.

The lights affixed to the castle lit up the huge field of green like it was midday. The only shadows to be found ran along the edges where the grass bordered two paths that led from the northern and southern sides of the back patio to gazebos that extended out over the edge of the cliff. Massive oak trees lined both sides of those walkways, their branches twisting and curling above the gravel to create a world of permanent gloom.

She looked at her glowing watch once more even while she counted down the seconds in her head. A habit that she couldn't break.

Looking one more time at what rose before her, she felt as if she had returned to the Old World. Blenheim Palace or Windsor Castle, even the Tower located in central London, only bigger.

Of course, considering who lived here, at least for part of the year, that only made sense. The man oozed an ancient heritage that was almost sickening.

She locked that irritating thought away.

She didn't have time to allow her mental meanderings to cloud her judgment. Upon seeing the movement along the shore, Melissa ducked back beneath the water and stayed there, taking deep, easy breaths through her snorkel. Even though she was counting off the seconds, she checked her watch for what seemed like the thousandth time just to make sure that all was well.

It was. Right on time. Like clockwork.

The two teams of guards approached each other from the south and the north and were about to pass by. They would continue on toward the far curls of the beach that were barely visible now that the full moon had slipped back behind the clouds.

She studied the guards. How stereotypical.

Black tactical pants. Black combat boots. Black t-shirts. Black ball caps.

Not very original, but that wasn't necessarily a bad thing when conformity was demanded by their employer and viewed as a key tool to ensure that they worked together like a team.

After all, they were a military organization of a type.

Paladins.

Getting a closer look at these soldiers soured her stomach, and with good cause. Based on what these mercenaries did and what they'd done, these Paladins had twisted the term beyond recognition, at least in the minds of those forced or unlucky enough to cross paths with them.

The Paladins of the Teg world didn't have the reputation that you'd expect from how that term was applied in classic literature or even in Dungeons and Dragons. And they were definitely a far cry from the Paladins of Charlemagne's court, the twelve legendary knights who fulfilled a similar role as that of the Knights of Arthur's Round Table.

These Paladins had a darker reputation. Much darker. In fact, the blood that they had spilled over the years, most of it unwarranted, likely would overflow the small bay that she was swimming through.

These Paladins functioned as a private army for their employer. The soldiers working for the dirtiest military contracting companies across the world looked like Boy Scouts compared to these men and women.

They had no morals or scruples. They would do whatever was necessary to achieve the objective given to them by their employer. They had been trained that way. Many of them had been raised that way.

Meeting the needs of their employer, their benefactor, essentially their creator, was all that mattered, consequences be damned. Which often proved to be the case since their employer wasn't known for always being of a sound mind, his legendary temper more often than not getting in the way of making sound decisions.

She understood why he called his cutthroats Paladins.

Historically, it was a revered name. Image was critical to him. It always had been. How he was perceived was just as, if not more, important than what he did.

He was also known for having a massive ego, a reality that she had seen firsthand and would have preferred to forget. Of course, it only made sense. He had a unique way of viewing himself in the world, driven in large part by his pathological insecurity and past failures.

That and the fact that he had a bone to pick with one person, and he'd been picking at it for centuries. The Paladins that he had created helped him to do that.

She pushed those thoughts to the side. She couldn't afford to be distracted now. Too much rode on what was being required of her, and she couldn't make any mistakes.

She had to focus on the challenge that she had accepted. The first step of addressing that challenge was getting past these guards without being seen.

The Paladins were not armed with guns or swords of old. They didn't need them. They were trained in the use of some unique weapons that they employed with devastating effect. She could testify to that herself.

Even with the darkness, she caught a few flashes of light off the weapons they held in their hands or carried strapped to their backs, the moon peeking through the clouds every so often. A Paladin had hit her once with one of the flanged maces that they preferred. She never wanted to experience that again.

Made of tungsten steel, the three-foot-long weapons were virtually indestructible, and they packed a vicious punch. Thankfully for her when she felt the unnatural power contained within the weapon it had only been a glancing blow. If it had been more than that, she likely wouldn't be where she was now. She'd be dead.

She had turned her body just in time, taking the brunt of

the blow on her shoulder and arm rather than her chest. The bones in both shattered.

Every time she thought about that she got angry, just as was happening now. She tried to calm herself, seeking her happy place as her therapist called it. It was a struggle.

Because that injury had been her fault. She had allowed herself to be distracted. Taken unawares, she hadn't been quick enough to form a shield with the Grym and deflect the swing.

Thanks to her error, she had been left writhing on the ground in pain, barely able to think because of the fiery agony that began on her right side and burned through the rest of her body, the tainted power contained within the mace increasing her suffering a hundredfold.

The Paladin had approached warily for the kill.

Somehow, she had found the wherewithal to send a blast of energy his way. The Paladin had blocked the attack with his mace, the Twisted Grym infused within his weapon protecting him, giving him the capacity to render the unique power of her people moot.

That didn't stop her, however. She had no desire to die because of a crushed skull. With her strength waning and her pain intensifying, the Paladin grinning at her with maniacal glee as he prepared to swing his weapon down upon her head with all his might, she did the only thing that came to mind, knowing that if she tried to throw another bolt of energy at him, he'd simply block it again.

Melissa did as her mother had taught her while learning how to master the Power of the Ancients. There was a time for strength and there was a time for subtlety. At that moment, when her life hung in the balance, she chose subtlety, sending a spark of the Grym toward the Paladin's black tactical pants.

That was all that was needed for her to shift the dynamic of the combat. The magical fire flashed when it struck the cloth, and in a heartbeat the flames raced up his leg toward the Paladin's chest and face.

The Paladin having forgotten her, beating uselessly at his burning clothes, she sent another bolt of the Grym into the man's chest, killing him instantly.

She hadn't wanted to do that. She took no pleasure in killing. She tried to avoid it when she could.

But when it was a choice between herself and a Paladin there was really no choice at all to be made.

The Paladins did not have the ability to use the Grym themselves, at least not at a significant level. That magical power circulated throughout the world, yet only she and the other Tylwyth Teg could sense and use it. However, with their weapons imbued with the corrupt power known as the Twisted Grym, the Paladins could hold their own against the Teg.

Disappointing perhaps. If nothing else, however, her target was predictable. The leader of the Paladins viewed the world in black and white. There was no room for grey.

He perceived any who chose to oppose him, any who didn't view the world from his perspective, any who didn't believe as he did in the supremacy of the Tylwyth Teg and their rightful place in the world, as an obstacle to be removed. To be crushed. To be made examples of.

Even his own people.

And because of the power and wealth he had acquired, he didn't believe that any of the Teg, except perhaps for a select few -- most of the others who would do so he had eliminated over the centuries -- would dare to challenge him now.

Knowing all that, in addition to seeking to make use of his predictability, Melissa hoped that she would also be able to take advantage of his complacency, or at least that of the Paladins based here.

She looked at her watch one more time, waiting for a few more seconds to pass, using those seconds to keep her nerves under control. It had been almost a year since her last job, and she felt a little on edge. She was worried that her taking a break would affect her work. If it hadn't been for that son of ...

It was time. With several strong kicks beneath the water and careful strokes that didn't give her away in the rough surf, she swam toward the shore, pleased that the moon had chosen that moment to slip back behind the clouds.

Setting her feet into the sand in just a few feet of water, she could feel the power that resonated along the shore and gained intensity the farther her senses extended toward the manor house atop the cliff.

The Grym.

Both active and residual.

Just as she expected.

She was definitely in the right place.

She pulled off her drysuit, revealing the black yoga pants and tight long-sleeve top that was her standard apparel on jobs like this. Pushing her drysuit beneath the water and dropping the weights she had worn around her waist to help keep her submerged atop it, she stepped up onto the beach wearing custom-made molded sport shoes.

So far so good. Still, she had a long way to go before she could breathe easy. Next step? She had to get off the beach, and she had only so much time to do it.

Fighting the urge to sprint up the sand, already sensing what was waiting for her, she used the Grym. Extending her senses, she identified the dozens of magical tripwires that turned the beach into a minefield.

If she set off any of the traps, she could be in for a nasty surprise. Worst case, the Twisted Grym would kill her. Best case, the Paladins would come running, and not just those stomping in the sand.

Those pleasant thoughts dancing in the back of her head, she walked up the beach in a haphazard manner, moving forward for a few steps before jumping to the right and continuing in that direction before walking toward the sand dunes again. She stopped after less than thirty seconds, smiling to herself.

Tricky, but not tricky enough. Some of the traps set on the beach had shifted their position, whether because they sensed the Grym within her or they were supposed to do so at certain times, she didn't know.

No major worries, however. She could deal with that. She just needed to be careful.

Melissa was simply glad that she had noticed in time, as she had almost stepped right where a tripwire was moving. Shaking her head in a mix of amusement and relief, she realized that she was playing the classic video game Frogger.

Her goal?

Crossing the beach without getting squashed.

She skirted the invisible tripwire that had moved in front of her, stepping a few paces to her right, then hustled forward for several dozen feet before the moving tripwires could block her path.

If not for her use of the Grym, she would have been caught or dead the second she walked out of the water. The thin streams of power resembled infrared beams that not only shifted their position but also took on different angles and different heights.

More of a challenge than she had wanted or expected so early on this job, yet there was nothing that she could do other than find the path through a constantly shifting pattern designed to catch the unwary, the unlucky, or the clumsy.

As she navigated her way through the maze, several times she almost missed a step because she was moving too quickly. She knew that she only had so much time to get off the beach, that challenge made all the more difficult by her natural inclination to not rush and make a mistake.

Those two desires warring within her, she stepped to her left and then up, immediately dancing back when a tripwire shifted right in front of her. Sidestepping to her left for twenty feet, she sprinted forward for almost fifty feet before stopping again.

She allowed a tripwire to pass by her. Then she moved to her right ten feet then trotted forward, following the always changing pattern of the living maze.

Several times she had to double back, realizing that she had selected a path that led to a dead end.

Once, she was surrounded on all sides by the magic traps, their height and angle seemingly changing upon a whim. Then, she had no choice but to remain in place and hope that a path would open for her. It did, thankfully, but it forced her to go backward.

That increased the time she spent on the sand, which increased her odds of being seen by the Paladins coming back toward her on their circuit.

Even so, she kept her rising irritation and worry in check, understanding that it wouldn't help her in this situation. She needed to stay calm. Focused. Intent on the magical traps that moved all around her.

She glanced at her watch again, her impatience growing despite her best efforts to keep it under control. Thirty seconds before the Paladins would be in sight again.

If she could see them, then they would be able to see her.

She wanted to move faster, the seconds ticking down much too quickly. She didn't. Instead, she maintained her pace even as a klaxon started to sound in the back of her brain.

She stayed on course, making her way through the maze, knowing that she was almost to the end. There were just a few tripwires still visible to her front.

Finally, she reached the end of the beach. The spot that had been her objective from the very beginning, where the path led up and over the sand dunes.

She stopped abruptly, realizing that she now faced two challenges, and she had little time to address either of them.

The most pressing was the fact that the Paladins guarding the beach were coming back around. They would see her in a matter of seconds. She could already make out their dim shadows at the edge of her peripheral vision.

Adding to her level of difficulty, three tripwires stretched across the path in front of her. The first was placed at two feet, the next at four feet, the third at six feet off the ground, each one separated by three feet of sand. She thanked her luck that at least these three were stationary and not moving like the ones behind her.

Since she wasn't in a position to avoid these traps and she needed to get off the beach swiftly, she took two steps back and then one big step forward, hopping over the first trap. Stuck between the two and recognizing that maintaining her momentum was essential, as soon as her foot hit the sand, she pushed off and leaped over the second tripwire like it was a hurdle.

Two down, the third, the most challenging of them all, still to go.

She understood that if she stopped moving after getting over the second trap she would be stuck with nowhere to go.

Harkening back to her high school days, Melissa planted her right foot in the sand, bent at the knee, and pushed herself up into the air as far as she could, curling her back in the same motion so that she could clear the tripwire just as she had done the bar when she competed in the high jump.

This time, however, rather than allowing herself to fall onto the sand on her back, she continued with her motion. Whipping her legs over the invisible wire so that she flipped backward and landed on her feet, her front facing the surf.

She couldn't stop herself from raising her arms in the air to complete the move, pleased that all the hours she had spent training as a gymnast had paid off.

Not having the time to congratulate herself any further on her success, she turned around and dug her way up the trail, clawing at the sand with her hands before sliding up and over the top. She disappeared from view just a heartbeat before the Paladins appeared below her on the beach.

Sneaking back up to the top of the path, her head barely above the crest, she watched as the two teams passed each other, oblivious to what she had just accomplished.

She remained where she was for several seconds, just wanting to make sure that she had escaped the beach without incident. It seemed that she had.

No alarms were going off. No large, ill-humored, muscular men were running toward her with maces in hand.

Without mercy she crushed the pleasure that she was experiencing at her initial success. That was enough of a celebration.

She had gotten off the beach, or rather behind the sand dunes. Good, the first step in her plan was complete. But only the first step.

Her night was only beginning, and though she was keeping herself on task, for some reason she couldn't get her mother's voice out of her head.

"Don't equate luck with skill."

"Thanks mom, supportive as always," she murmured to herself as she slid back down the path and turned to face the next obstacle, this one hopefully a little easier than the last.

Whether because of luck or skill, she didn't care. Breathing a sigh of relief, she sprinted through the sand and then started to climb the wooden stairs. She needed to be quick, but she also needed to time her climb perfectly. Otherwise, she would be visible to the Paladins below her when they made their way back along the beach.

Yet even here she needed to be careful, because in addition to his predictability and complacency, she also had to take into account her target's anal retentiveness. The magical tripwires on the beach weren't enough for him. They were also set here on the steps, though in a slightly different form.

Using the Grym as her guide as she climbed the staircase, several times she jumped over a step or two, placing any weight on those pieces of wood leading to a nasty surprise and a very loud alarm. Two times she climbed up the side of the cliff in order to avoid an entire flight of stairs set with a lure.

Her mark was definitely *not* a trusting soul.

The entire time she heard the clock ticking in the back of her head, that coinciding with her silently counting down the seconds she had left before she would be spotted by the Paladins who would be coming back around on the beach.

Sprinting up the steps when she could, she felt the burn in her thighs and calves, aggravated when she had to come to an abrupt stop when she had to jump over more than a couple of steps. She cursed herself for not spending as much time in the gym as she should have these last few months.

Still, she kept pushing herself, forcing herself to maintain her pace, knowing what would happen if she got caught.

Right before the Paladins came back into view beneath her, she jumped up the last five steps, all of which had been set with the Twisted Grym, and rolled across the gravel path, coming to a stop just inches from the cut grass that ran all the way up to the manor house.

She closed her eyes in relief. Her left foot had missed the top step by less than an inch, and the slightest touch would have been enough to bring the Paladins running.

She had done it!

"Don't equate luck with ..."

"Enough, mother," she wanted to shout out loud. She didn't give in to the urge, locking away her mother's voice, not needing the distraction when she still had so much more to do.

She had escaped the guards on the beach. However, the change in shift for the Paladins assigned to the lawn and the manor house would take place in fifteen minutes. If she wanted to complete the next step in her plan, the most critical step in fact, then she needed to be in a specific location when the current guards came off duty.

That concern driving her, Melissa pushed herself to her feet. She didn't have any time to waste.

Most thieves seeking to break into the mansion -- although, in all honesty, she doubted anyone but her would be stupid enough to attempt to sneak into this castle knowing who owned it and the likely consequence of doing so, a quick death not the most terrible option -- would select one of the paths running on each side of the lawn to make their approach if they faced the same dilemma she did. They would view the shadows provided by the monstrous live oak trees as their friends, as a means to a quick score.

She knew that selecting that route would be a mistake. Besides, she wasn't most thieves.

Allowing more of the Grym to flow through her, she directed her senses toward all that was around her. As the magical Power of the Ancients filled her, she faded slowly into her environment, taking her time, ensuring that she was thorough in her work, until she blended perfectly with her surroundings.

Now she was invisible even to another of the Tylwyth Teg.

The clock continuing to count down in the back of her head, her window of opportunity closing faster than she would have preferred, she stepped out onto the lawn. As she began to walk across the lush grass cut to the height of a putting green, she sent the Grym out in all directions, wanting to make sure that the way was clear.

She didn't think that there would be any traps here waiting for her. The approach was too obvious.

She was certain that there would be watchers in the manor house who would pick up on any movement.

Even so, that didn't worry her. Any watchers couldn't see her, even if they looked directly at her.

Still, this wasn't the place to make a mistake. Thus, her focus on identifying any tricks or traps that might have been set in the large space to catch the unwary.

Melissa's caution paid off.

She was forced to stop every few seconds. There were tripwires here, although they functioned more like pressure plates as was the case on the staircase.

If she stepped in the wrong place, she was in for a nasty surprise, and assuming she survived the surprise, the Paladins would be on her in the blink of an eye.

Even though she wanted to move faster, she didn't. She was careful with her steps, making sure that she gave those areas of the lawn that were seeded with the Twisted Grym a wide berth.

Every so often she stopped just for the sake of stopping, wanting to ensure that nothing was amiss. Off to each side she caught movement beneath the trees, flashes of light reflecting through the shadows.

That was something she hadn't been made aware of. Paladins patrolling the walkways. A good thing she decided on her current approach instead.

As she got closer to the mansion, she began to see more activity. The first time the Paladins appeared at the back of the castle, always patrolling in twos and threes, she stopped.

She snorted to herself in mild amusement when she did. So long as she maintained control of the illusion she had crafted around herself, she was safe. The Paladins wouldn't have a clue that she was there.

She was strong in the Grym. She could walk right past the Paladins without them even being aware so long as she didn't knock into one of them.

Feeling more confident, when she stepped off the grass and onto the patio that wrapped around the back of the mansion, she walked normally, her illusion concealing her.

She moved silently but swiftly to the south, evading the Paladins as she went. Hugging the stone of the turret, she curled around the corner, then she dodged out of the way with a deft sidestep, avoiding one of the guards who almost brushed up against her as he followed his comrades toward the walkway that led to the gazebo.

With just a minute to spare, she reached the spot that she had been aiming for. She pressed herself against the side of the house between two very large flowerpots, staying out of the way. The entrance to the manor house was on the other side of the flowerpot to her right. The entrance to the guard house, where the Paladins assigned to the castle lived and slept, was on the other side of the patio, no more than twenty feet away.

Now for the tricky part. She needed to select the correct Paladin. It had to be one of the officers. But not just any officer. One of higher rank. One who could give her the access that she required.

At the exact instant that the clock in her head struck midnight, dozens of teams of Paladins emerged from the military barracks, the shift change beginning. At the same time, those Paladins who had just ended their four-hour shifts headed toward the guard house.

It was a scrum of activity. Thus, the perfect opportunity for what she needed to do next.

Identifying her target, and now unconcerned whether she jostled anyone because of all the bodies in the small space between the doors, she stepped out from her hiding place and up behind one of the officers who had just emerged from the mansion. The man made her think that he had just walked out of the nineteenth century, what with his long hair greased back and a curled mustache that would have made baseball reliever Rollie Fingers jealous.

Stumbling into the Paladin's shoulder as he walked past another of the guards on his way to his quarters, she used the distraction to unhook with her deft fingers the laminated keycard hanging from the clip on his belt.

Leaving the Paladin officer to berate the guard he thought had knocked into him, she stepped into the manor house before the door closed.

When the Paladin's keycard touched her fingers, it disappeared from sight, fading into the deception that she had crafted.

Melissa grinned. It was exactly the keycard that she needed. The strip of black running along the long sides confirmed it. This keycard would give her access to every section of the mansion except for the owner's private suite on the top floor.

The power contained within the molded plastic sent a slight tingle up her fingertips and into her arm. The manor house's security system didn't function as the systems in standard mansions or office buildings did. These keycards contained the Twisted Grym, and they were attuned to the magic that guarded every room in the massive house.

The Paladins likely found that surge of tainted energy comforting. She, on the other hand, fought hard to ignore it, knowing what could happen if she started to listen to the Twisted Grym's whispers, faint though they were.

There were no security plates mounted on the walls that required a touch of the card to allow access. Rather, the person who possessed this keycard could walk into a room uninhibited. Knowing that, she slid the keycard into a small velvet bag so that she no longer had to touch the cursed object, the tempting whispers of the Twisted Grym now no more than a buzz in the back of her brain.

Of course, if a person without the appropriate keycard attempted to go where they were not permitted, they were in for an unpleasant shock. Something that she didn't want to contemplate as she moved away from the bustle of activity taking place just beyond the door.

Now all she had to do was find what she had been sent here to acquire. Simple, she thought, her sarcasm evident in her expression if anyone had been able to peek through the illusion masking her. She had only so much time and more than a hundred rooms to search, as well as several rooms that she suspected were never on the construction blueprints.

Still, she believed that she knew where she needed to start.

She walked into the kitchen, which was quiet at this time in the morning. The Paladins heading out for their shifts had left behind a few uneaten sandwiches, power bars, bottled water, Jolt colas, and Mountain Dews.

She considered snatching a sandwich. She was hungry. The swim and then the trek up from the beach had drained her energy. But then she thought better of it.

Hearing the low murmurs of conversation coming from behind her as several of the Paladins who had completed their shifts came into the kitchen for a snack, she ducked through a servant's entrance in the back, then tiptoed down a hallway where the chef and several housekeepers lived.

She came out in the main dining room. Impressive. Actually, more over the top compared to her more practical sensibilities.

Moving away from the swinging door, making sure that it closed before the Paladins entered the kitchen behind her, she leaned back against a wall in a small open space between two freestanding cupboards filled with China plates, silver, and crystal glasses and flutes.

All of it looked to be hundreds of years old. A quick glance told her that it came from just after the French Revolution. She had seen similar ceramics on auction at Christie's just a few months before.

Who knew? Maybe Napoleon had eaten from one of the plates.

On the other side of the room, a table that could easily seat fifty blocked her way. Just above it crystal chandeliers reached down every few feet from the ceiling and several paintings hung from the wallpapered wall across from her.

Every item in this room spoke of wealth. Obscene wealth, in fact. But it was those paintings that piqued her interest the most.

She wanted to take a closer look at them, because she couldn't be sure from where she was standing, the shadows that draped the room hindering her view. They all appeared to be originals painted by the Dutch masters, several of which, maybe all in fact, were said to be lost or stolen. Many of them taken from their Jewish owners by the Nazis, never to be seen again. Until perhaps now.

Despite her building curiosity, she fought the urge for a closer look and remained in place for several minutes. Waiting. Listening. Trying to get a feel for her surroundings during the witching hour.

The voices in the kitchen died down over the next few minutes, the Paladins returning to their barracks to catch some sleep before the shift changed again. Even the officers who had access to the castle were gone.

Once the Paladins had left, the only sounds that she heard were what she would expect from an old house. A squeak here. A creak there. Nothing that gave her any cause for concern.

Nothing to suggest that she would find a squad of Paladins waiting for her just around the corner.

Getting more comfortable in the mansion, while also feeling the press of time, she left the dining room. Walking through the foyer quickly, only glancing at the two staircases -- one that curled to the left and the other to the right that would allow her to reach the second floor, she headed into a living room that contained dark leather couches and chairs set in various configurations that she would expect to see in a men's-only club in New York City.

Every inch of the space suggested opulence, extravagance, and excessive affluence. But not of New World riches as you might expect for this part of the country where the Manhattan financiers preferred to play and celebrate what they perceived as their arrival on a larger stage.

No, the mood of this large, rectangular space that ran for almost the entire length of the western wall, with its dark wood and exposed beams, shadowed carvings in the ceiling, suggested once again the Old World. What she looked at now was what she expected to see in a castle on the banks of the Rhine or the Thames.

The various pieces and design contributing to the mood of the room, with it as well came a hint of darkness.

She couldn't escape the feeling of oppression, of a shade stalking her from just behind her shoulder, always out of sight, yet always there.

It was as if everything in this room, in this castle, had been bought with blood. With pain and terror. With hate.

Knowing who owned the castle, maybe it all had been. The histories certainly suggested as much.

Not wanting to get trapped within her own thoughts, Melissa brought back to mind the plans of the mansion that she had memorized. Already knowing the route that she wanted to take, she walked halfway through the living room before turning right through an open doorway that took her past several closed doors -- storage spaces, a laundry room, and several utility closets, as well as a backup security center if the Paladins ever had to fall back to the castle. She ignored the game room to her left, one wall covered by a huge screen.

She turned left at the end of the hallway, continued down the short corridor without making a noise, then turned right again. Her route took her past several bedrooms that weren't currently in use before coming out in another hallway that connected to the one she was in on a right angle.

Turning right, she made for the gloom at the far end. After one hundred and twenty-two steps -- she was exceedingly precise in her work and was quite pleased that she had estimated correctly -- the dark wood of a cathedral-like door rose well above her.

The scarred wood, the color of cinders, sent a chill through her body. And not just because of what she sensed beyond the door. There was a story attached to the hardened oak that blocked her way. A bloody story, a savage story, and one that at present she had no desire to learn.

Pulling her thoughts from the grim path that they had been following, she took a deep breath to settle herself.

All had gone to plan so far. Better than expected, actually.

Yet the true test still waited for her. Several in fact.

There was no point in feeling any pleasure that she had made it this far without being discovered. She couldn't breathe easy until she was well away from this castle that hid secrets she had no desire to learn.

Not having any other choice based on what she needed to do next, she released her hold on the Grym.

The illusion that had protected her faded, revealing her to anyone who might enter the hallway and look in her direction.

That reality worrying her, she went to work immediately.

She could only hope that the arrogance of the castle's owner played in her favor now.

More important, that the information she received was accurate. Because if it wasn't, her adventure was going to come to an abrupt and likely painful end.

Recalling in precise detail the instructions that Melissa had been given, she didn't touch the door with her hand, knowing that doing so would set off the magical alarm. Instead, she ran her fingers just above the wooden frame bolted to the stone wall, looking for any hints as to how to open it. Anything hidden within the wood. Any secret latches or buttons. Because there was no keyhole visible within the intricate scrollwork that covered the hardened oak.

Nothing. Nothing at all.

She should have assumed as much. None of her other jobs had ever been easy. Why would she think that this one would be?

Her search of the frame complete, she turned her attention to the door itself.

Her breath caught in her throat, her heart beating faster. She heard footsteps coming in her direction from the hallway she had just slipped through, and she had nowhere to go. She was caught at a dead end.

Her first instinct was to hide herself with the Grym again. She didn't. Using so much of the Power of the Ancients where she needed to go would give her away.

She either had to figure out how to open the only door that led into the castle's central turret or prepare for a fight.

Having no interest in pursuing the latter course -- the footsteps, now joined by the approaching Paladins' quiet voices, growing louder -- she concentrated on the door itself. Because she could see barely anything in the gloom of the corridor, she ran her fingers along the smooth, polished wood.

Her client had only so much information to share with her about what she would encounter in the castle. Melissa was on her own now, so she allowed her instincts to guide her.

The intricate design appealed to her. Even better, it was exactly as she thought it would be based on her own research of the owner. At her gentle touch, the carved wood revealed a two-headed eagle.

The sound of approaching footsteps almost deafening in her hyper-sensitive ears, she placed her hand on the chest of the eagle, finding the small piece of the wood in the center that was carved into the shape of a long sword. She then took hold of scarcely a trace of the Grym for just an instant, whispering the old Welsh word her client had given her.

"Medraut."

Hearing a quiet click, she released her hold on the Grym, nudged the door open just enough so that she could sneak through, and then pushed it closed on silent hinges after she climbed onto the first step right behind the oak.

Just in time. But she didn't breathe easier.

Despite the thickness of the wood, she could still hear the footsteps as the Paladins entered the hallway she had been standing in just seconds after she closed the door behind her.

And those footsteps were coming closer. Much too quickly. It was almost as if the Paladins patrolling the inside of the castle knew that she was there.

Did she use too much of the Grym?

She held her breath, hoping that the other piece of information her employer gave her proved correct. Otherwise, she was done for.

The steps that had been chasing her stopped right in front of the door that she was hiding behind. She heard a mumbled conversation through the wood, but because of the thickness she was unable to make out any of the words.

She almost hissed in surprise when she felt a slight pressure on the door, as if the guards were giving the wood a push so that they could enter the turret. But just as quickly, it was gone.

She held her breath for several seconds, listening as the Paladins continued their conversation, their words finally drifting away as they walked back down the hallway and kept to their rounds.

Almost gasping for air when she finally drew breath again, she placed her back against the door, willing her rapid heart rate to decrease. That had been much too close for her tastes.

She would have to thank her client for the accuracy of the information that she provided. Then again, she had no desire to ever see her client again, so maybe just a note slipped under her door, or a dagger in her back Melissa mused with a silent chuckle.

Pushing her brief moment of humor to the side, she climbed the circular staircase that ran along the outside of the wall and took her well up into the tower. She placed her feet on the far edge of each step, careful not to make a sound.

She knew that the owner of the mansion wasn't here. He was away on business.

If he had been here, she never would have agreed to take this job, no matter how much pressure her client applied. She had her own standards to maintain after all.

She stopped when the stairs came to an end, an open doorway beckoning her to brave the darkness beyond.

About to cross the threshold, at the last second she hesitated. She knew that the man living here was conceited in a way that few others could match. He had little concern that anyone would be so foolish as to challenge him. To invade his home. To steal from him.

Yet was she willing to take that risk now?

Because as soon as she stepped into his private sanctuary, there was no going back. Not if she wanted to make it out alive.

What was worrying her?

Maybe it was because she thought it should have been harder for her to reach this point. She had expected to face several unexpected, additional challenges by now. Traps. Alarms. Monsters. Something.

But nothing that she had faced since she stepped out of the water and onto the beach had gone against plan. The most perilous threat she'd overcome so far was the current that threatened to push her away from her designated location.

During her preparations, she had worried more about the traps and wards. About the surprises that her client likely didn't know about.

She had feared the Paladins, and with good reason based on previous experience.

Yet all had gone to plan up until this point.

Maybe that was the problem, she mused. No matter how hard she worked to prepare, nothing ever went to plan.

Something would go wrong. It always did. It was just a matter of when.

She shrugged her shoulders a few times, working out her tense muscles.

She would expect the worst and enjoy her good fortune while it lasted.

A nifty trick if she could manage that.

She stepped into the circular room. As soon as she did, the candles set along the wall and on the desk flashed to life.

Fearing that she had set off a hidden alarm, she stood rooted in the thick carpet, terrified about what was going to happen next.

Much to her relief, nothing did.

She sensed the wards in the room. The power circulating around the chamber. Seeking just the faintest hint of the Grym.

But she wasn't using the Grym, and she wouldn't so long as she remained in the turret.

That made her task more difficult. It would add time that she didn't have to waste to an already tight schedule.

She needed to be away from the castle well before the sun was up. Otherwise, the Paladins patrolling the grounds would have a better chance of catching her.

Even so, the challenge didn't bother her all that much. She had learned her unique skills before she had learned to master the Grym. She would simply put that training to use now.

To do that, she allowed her gaze to travel slowly around the room. Spinning in a slow circle, she took in all that was around her, seeing everything and seeing nothing both at the same time, filing it away, learning more about her target as she did so.

Much of the tower wall was covered by bookcases. She was sure only first editions graced the shelves. Anything else would be sacrilegious to him.

Based on the spines, the range of interests was remarkably wide. *The Iliad, The Odyssey,* and *The Aeneid*. Sophocles and Euripides. Pliny and Virgil and Aristotle and Plato. Hemingway, Twain, and F. Scott Fitzgerald. Dante and Shakespeare. Oscar Wilde and Mary Shelley. The works of Dostoevsky. Adam Smith. Bronte and Tolkien. And so it went. An eclectic mix, but only the classics.

Then she spotted one of her favorites. *Oliver Twist*. That masterpiece had always spoken to her. There were scenes in the text that mirrored her own early experiences in many ways.

She shouldn't have, but she did it anyway. Pulling the book from the shelf, she flipped open the cover. Signed by the author himself in a broad flourish. Charles Dickens. Just as she assumed would be the case.

Ignoring the urge to slip the classic text into her pouch, she returned the book to the shelf. She made sure that it was positioned exactly as it had been before she pulled it free.

She then swept her gaze once more over the artifacts filling the room. Ancient statuary, busts of famous men, Greek philosophers, Roman emperors, and, as she anticipated, not a woman in sight. Jewelry made of gold and silver placed in areas of prominence on open tables, her mark clearly not worried about theft. Behind the desk she glimpsed medieval weapons and maps. She wasn't surprised to see those there. The owner was playing to what he was most familiar with.

Her eyes widened when she saw the paintings on the wall opposite the bookcases, the frames reaching all the way up to the ceiling, which was at least fifty feet above her.

She stepped closer to get a better look. The colors, themes, and brushstrokes all had a Renaissance feel. She understood why quickly.

Michelangelo. Durer. Raphael. Jan van Eyck. Bellini and Botticelli. And below the several dozen paintings, in a position of honor, several sculptures by Donatello as well as Da Vinci.

She had no doubt that these were all the real thing. If any of these pieces were in a museum somewhere, they were counterfeits.

The owner of this castle only wanted the best for himself, no matter the cost. He would never accept anything other than the original. And he would do whatever was necessary to obtain what he desired.

Impressive. Slightly frightening as well.

And another testament to his arrogance. The same arrogance that had allowed her to get this far into his sanctuary without being discovered.

Despite all the treasures that surrounded her, Melissa's eyes were drawn to the massive desk set in the center of the room, the modern Aeron leather chair sitting behind it the only item that felt out of place in this man cave. As she stepped farther into the room and placed herself in front of the desk, which she thought might have been made just before the French Revolution, the resonance of power that she experienced in this section of the tower almost took her breath away.

Her mark wasn't physically in the room, but he was in a way, particularly right here, the residue of his strength in the Grym pervading the turret, suggesting that this was where he spent most of his time. At his desk, managing his various enterprises and interests. Some legitimate, many not.

The ripples of power giving her goosebumps, she was certain that the prize would be here. Just as her client believed that it would be.

But where?

If she used the Grym, she could find it in an instant. But she couldn't. Not if she wanted to make her escape in one piece.

That thought sobering her, she allowed her gaze to search randomly around the room, taking in the history, the presence, the age of what was contained within the turret. Time after time her eyes always returned to the desk, to the sense of power that continued to play across her.

She smiled when it came to her.

He was an arrogant man. He wouldn't expect anyone to make a play for what he was hiding here in plain sight. He wouldn't expect anyone to take such a risk, knowing the consequences of doing so.

His scorched earth approach to insults and perceived slights was legendary.

Did she really want to do this? Did she want to risk his wrath?

After giving those questions some thought for just a few heartbeats more, she shook her head in resignation.

No, she didn't want to do this. But she didn't have a choice.

Her target was bad enough. Her client was even worse.

She was stuck in a no-win situation.

To have any chance of changing the odds, she needed leverage. She needed some way to make those who came after her hesitate. Maybe even make them think twice before doing anything to her.

She needed to find what she was sent here for. As her fears played through the back of her mind, her eyes fixed on and then never left the large humidor that was perfectly centered on the top of the desk.

Her target had many vices. Some she didn't want to think about. But he didn't smoke.

So why would he have cigars sitting in such a place of prominence?

She concentrated more on the humidor, thinking that at the edge of her vision she should see energy radiating from the well-crafted wooden box much like heat rising from a highway on a blisteringly hot day. Yet there was nothing.

Every item in this room carried with it a hint of power, whether because of its age or how it was used. Everything but what she stared down upon.

Smiling, believing that she was right, hoping that she could count on her target's conceit for just a little while longer, she opened the humidor, knowing instantly that a cigar had never graced the interior. The well-built box was similar to a Faraday bag, which was used to block signals from being sent and received by electronic devices, though it functioned in a slightly different way.

The humidor prevented anyone skilled in the use of the Grym from sensing the potency contained within the wood box. As soon as she opened the top, she felt the intense power wafting off the item hidden within.

She stared down at a package that was wrapped in brown wax paper, likely done so to protect it against the rain. It wasn't much larger than a paperback book.

She didn't need to remove the wrapping to know that she

had found what she had come for. The Grym emanating from the package almost took her breath away.

The desire to examine her find more closely intensified when she removed the package from its enclosure and held it in her hands. She didn't know exactly what she had claimed, but she knew that she wanted to learn more about it, and there was only one way to do that.

She stopped herself right before she ripped the wrapping off.

She could think about all that later. When her natural curiosity wasn't threatening to get the better of her. When she had time to think about next steps.

Now, she needed to get out of the turret and the mansion. Then she could focus on what she could do with the leverage she held in her hand.

With an almost palpable level of regret, she slid the package into the specially designed pocket in her top, zipping it closed. The item fit perfectly at the small of her back and wouldn't get in her way as she exited the property.

She could head back the way she had come. But she didn't want to do that if it could be avoided. There were too many opportunities along the way for her to make a mistake or for her luck to run out at the most inopportune time.

Instead, she took a few seconds to study the circular chamber once again. Curious. Hopeful.

Her target spent much of his time here when he was in the castle. The plans she had studied showed that the only means of ingress and egress was the door she had used at the bottom of the stairs.

That seemed out of character for the owner.

He wasn't a man who would allow himself to be cornered. He would never take that risk, whether in a fight or a business deal. He would always have another way out.

Thinking of the design carved into the door just a few flights below, she scanned the room with greater care.

Where was it? It had to be here. It was the only thing that would make sense for someone like him.

He would try to hide it. He would think that no one else would ever be able to locate it.

She had learned that in addition to being arrogant, conceited, and vengeful, he was also not very creative.

So it had to be ...

She smirked as she stepped around the polished wood and approached the wall behind the desk. She shook her head in disdain. How predictable.

She traced her fingers across the carving that mimicked the one in the door at the bottom of the staircase.

Placing her hand just above the double-headed dragon, she whispered the same word she had before.

"Medraut."

There was a soft click, the section of the wall with the carving on it sliding into the darkness. No, her target wasn't very imaginative at all, and she was more than happy to play off that failing.

Stepping into the hidden passageway, she closed the door behind her, hearing the soft click to confirm that she had locked it back into place. As soon as she did, candles set in the walls came to life just as had happened when she entered her mark's office.

She didn't know where this passageway led. She didn't care so long as it took her a good distance away from the castle.

Her smile broadened the farther she went, candles winking out behind her just as the candles ahead of her came to life as she approached. She was walking down a curling ramp that ended at the bottom of the turret. From there, the long and straight corridor continued for more than a thousand yards.

Despite being underground on a path leading below the

estate, she realized that she was heading toward the west. That was good. She knew what she was going to find in that direction.

After she had walked a few hundred more yards, she slowed, sensing that she was coming to the end of the secret corridor. When the darkness just in front of her shifted to a dark grey, she stopped.

For just a second, she considered the risk that she was about to take. She was going to expose herself in a way that she usually tried to avoid.

There was nothing for it, however. She didn't like being in the dark in a place where she didn't belong.

Giving in to the urge, she grasped the Grym, the natural magic of the Ancients sparking to life within her.

She waited, barely breathing for several seconds. Her smile grew broader.

Nothing happened. The restriction of using the Grym in the main turret didn't apply here.

Maintaining her hold on the Grym, she extended her senses down the last few yards of the tunnel. Just as she expected. Another tripwire. Or rather a series of tripwires.

Mapping in her mind the traps that she had discovered, she stepped carefully over, under, and around the strands of energy that stretched from one side of the corridor to the other, not wanting to find out what would happen if she disturbed one.

At the same time, with each step she took, she felt more and more the cool touch of the night air. After just a few more seconds of dodging, ducking, and contorting herself into poses that she hadn't done since her last yoga class, she made her way past the last of the alarms.

She wanted to scream with delight, to punch a fist into the air to celebrate her victory.

Instead, she ducked and rolled across the forest floor. As she emerged out into the bright light of the full moon, a massive claw slashed through the space where she would have been standing, missing her head by a hair and striking the rock at her back, scattering dozens of splinters of stone in the air.

Rather than getting to her feet, she rolled again, this time to her left, feeling another claw scrape through the space just behind her back, her muscles twinging at the thought of those razor-sharp nails digging into her flesh.

Almost recognizing too late the tree that rose up to her front, she tried to change her direction while she rolled, but she couldn't. She was moving too fast. Nevertheless, she was able to protect herself by twisting to the side just in time.

With that slight adjustment, she slammed into the bark with her back rather than her head, knocking the breath from her instead of breaking her neck. Even so, she was well aware that she was still in grave danger.

Gasping for the air that wouldn't fill her empty lungs, she found the wherewithal to dodge to the side.

Her hunter's claw slammed into the tree trunk right where her head had been only a second before, large shards of wood flying up into the air because of the power of the blow.

A howl of rage echoed through the night, her attacker struggling to free his claw, which was now stuck almost a foot into the massive evergreen's trunk.

Taking advantage of the opportunity given to her, she pushed herself up against the bark and made a break for it.

She was too slow.

Her attacker freed himself before she could get her feet back under her and was already turning in her direction.

Because of the dense latticework of wood just above, the darkness was almost complete in this section of the woods, the full moon unable to break through the branches above with much success. Even so, Melissa could see just enough to know what was trying to kill her.

Her terror almost froze her in place. She had never come up

against a monster like this before. Never wanting to. Because the stories she had heard about them suggested that she had little chance of escape.

They were relentless hunters, living for the kill. Living for the taste of their prey's blood and flesh.

The monster's yellowish gold eyes glowed brightly in the gloom. Based on how much she needed to bend her neck to lock eyes with the beast, the monster stood at least eight feet tall.

It was manlike in form, but its arms and legs were elongated, allowing the beast to walk upright or to run on all four paws. Its chest was broad and muscled, suggesting an almost unimaginable strength and stamina. And its body was covered in a thick black fur.

When the monster's eyes flashed, the beast clearly believing that he had his prey cornered, he raised his long snout and, opening his teeth-filled maw to the sky, howled.

She knew for certain that she was about to die, the beast's long, sharp fangs gleaming just like the monster's claws when they caught the few rays of moonlight that broke through the branches for a split-second.

What in all the hells was a werewolf doing here?

Having a Paladin in this section of the wood as a guard to defend against anyone who might try to make use of this secret passageway to gain access to the castle made sense.

Her mark hated any creature of the Teg that he couldn't control, and werewolves were notoriously independent, ferociously so, when it came to interacting with those not of their own kind.

She wanted to scream when the werewolf lowered his head, his howl still echoing through the forest, the monster turning his sharp gaze toward her. But she couldn't. Her recently regained breath caught in her throat.

For just a heartbeat she didn't know what to do, watching in slow motion as the werewolf's claw slashed toward her throat.

At the very last instant she forced down her fear and allowed her instincts to take over. Ducking and rolling toward the beast, the werewolf's claw shot just above her head and slammed into the tree trunk. Sharp chunks of wood cascaded through the air at the exact same moment that she kicked to the side with her foot, catching the beast on the knee and forcing the joint in a direction that it wasn't supposed to go.

The werewolf howled again, this time not in hunger but rather in anger and pain. The monster tried to turn so that he could come at her again, but the injury slowed the beast.

The werewolf stumbled instead, his injured leg giving out beneath him, the monster's claws digging into the soft earth as he fought to keep himself upright.

She was ready for that, forming in her hand a dagger made of the Grym and punching down hard into the back of the werewolf's other leg.

Her action was greeted by another agonized howl as well as a backward swipe of the werewolf's claw that was aimed for her hip. She barely avoided the slash, one of his razor-sharp nails slicing her pants and across her thigh.

A thin, shallow cut, no more than that thankfully. But it was a good reminder as to just how dangerous a werewolf could be, even one hobbled by injuries to both his legs.

Rather than continue the fight and press the advantage she had earned, Melissa left the werewolf where he was and sprinted off between the trees toward the west. Once she lost sight of the beast, she would change direction. She would continue to change direction, zigzagging through the forest, until she found the car she had parked at the edge of the road.

But until she reached her car, until she was miles down the road, she needed to worry about what else might be in the forest with her.

Werewolves were pack animals. They rarely hunted alone.

To prove her point, as she ran, the howls of the injured werewolf followed her, other howls answering the monster's call.

Focused on her escape, she didn't see the shadowy figure standing farther in among the trees who had observed the brief fight and her slipping away.

The figure who was smiling.

2

TURNING THE TABLES

Lost in thought, he walked down Duke of Gloucester Street, heading away from the College of William and Mary and into Colonial Williamsburg. His black tweed overcoat flapped behind him thanks to the strong breeze that gusted down the mile-long thoroughfare from the east.

He ignored the many people enjoying the chilly but comfortable late evening who were partaking of the restaurants, shops, and other holiday attractions that drew tourists to this small college town.

Head down, he watched his steps as he strode past the families and couples who were preparing to brave the ice-skating rink. He appreciated the darkness that wrapped itself around him as he passed the Bruton Parish Episcopal Church on his left. There were few if any streetlights in this section of the historic town, the side streets pitch black.

Even so, the crowds didn't diminish. In fact, there were a handful of large groups meandering up and down DOG Street, often wandering onto a side street before coming back to the main road. One group had stopped on Market Square by the stockade, while two more were coming down the Green from the Governor's Palace. With the darkness and distance, another was barely visible farther down the way by the Capitol Building. All the people on these ghost tours diligently tracking their docents and their handheld lanterns.

One of the more popular activities that could be enjoyed here, the tour guides dazzled the many participants with tales of the dozens of spirits said to haunt the surrounding environs. The ghost stories were quite fun and interesting, many unsettling, and almost all of them true.

Because what the tourists didn't know was how many spirits there actually were flitting about the town at that very moment, several having joined the tours.

As he had learned over the centuries, people preferred to focus on what was, very few interested in what could be. And there was a simple reason for that. What could be often was quite frightening, if for no other reason than it was difficult to understand or didn't fit into their perspective of the world.

As he passed by the group closest to him, he spied one of the spirits following right behind a pair of children, likely brother and sister, who had absolutely no interest in what the guide was saying. The docent had stopped in front of the Magazine, the only all brick building in the town.

The ghost wore a tricorn hat, a blue wool coat, and white linen britches. A powder horn was strapped around his chest and a leather cartridge box hung from his hip, containing the lead balls that he had used with the rifle that he carried when he had walked these very grounds centuries before.

The spirit nodded to him as he passed. He returned the nod out of respect, one soldier to another.

After all that he had dealt with over the years, the ghost tours had lost their appeal. Personally, he preferred the axe throwing. But that undertaking was only open during the day.

Even then, he always had to temper his competitive spirit. He needed to appear just like anyone else when he was away from his home, so he had no choice but to hold back, missing a few of his throws so that he could hide his true skill.

Frustrating at times. Necessary, nonetheless.

He shifted his gaze back toward the Capitol Building down at the far end of the street. He was impressed by the majesty of the structure. The Virginia General Assembly met there until the state capital moved to Richmond in 1780.

He dropped his head again, his eyes tracking the road, the ghost tours behind him now. He didn't really need to see what was around him to know what was around him, so he allowed his thoughts to drift back to what had happened during the last few hours.

He had hoped that the conversation would go better. He should have known that it wouldn't. As his father liked to say, hope had no place in the Teg world.

It had been quite some time since he had visited. And when he last did, they hadn't parted on the best of terms. Terrible terms really, which seemed to be par for the course.

She was angry with him. She blamed him. And he really couldn't blame her for that.

On the plus side, she gave him more time than he thought she would, so there was that.

She had even let him buy her a mocha protein shake from Aroma's coffee shop before walking her back to her place.

Perhaps a slight thaw in their frigid relationship.

He didn't think that he could hope for more than that. At least not yet.

The issue that he was struggling with now was what to do next. He was nervous, a feeling that he was unaccustomed to.

She seemed willing to see him again. Well, that wasn't entirely correct.

When he had asked if he could visit her again, she had grunted. He viewed that as a good sign, because she hadn't told him no.

Besides, last time she had told him that she never wanted to see him again, so he took her noncommittal response as a step in the right direction.

The question was, when should he reach out to her again?

Not too soon, probably. He didn't want her to think that he was trying to smother her.

He would give her some space to process their time together.

But he probably shouldn't wait too long either. He needed to make sure that she understood that he wanted to be a larger part of her life. If she would allow him to be.

On her terms, of course. He couldn't ask for more than that.

He was mulling the approach that he should take when he turned his head to the side just a tiny degree, nodding ever so slightly, his senses coming awake. He never stopped walking, his blackthorn shillelagh, the top knob of which almost reached his chest, continuing to tap lightly on the cobblestones of the sidewalk.

He was being followed, and he didn't want those tracking him to know that he had discovered them.

He considered making a break for it, having no doubt that he would have little trouble evading his hunters. He chose not to.

He was more interested in having a conversation with his trackers. By the scent, he knew what they were, which only served to intensify his curiosity.

He was surprised that they were here. He never expected that his sometimes colleague, oftentimes enemy would take such a risk after all that had occurred between them.

If they wanted to have a conversation with him, then it was going to be at a location of his choosing. And if they wanted to do more than talk, then they risked breaking the agreement he had put in place with their master.

He had a sense of which direction it was going to go.

So be it. He was feeling edgy. It had been weeks since his last scrap.

He turned to the left onto North Queen Street and stepped up to the fence. He took a moment to greet the horses, no more than large shadows in the darkness, that were grazing after pulling carriages for most of the day. He scratched their heads, offering a few soft words, while at the same time allowing his senses to expand around him and give him a view of what his followers were doing.

Satisfied that they had taken the bait, he gave the horses a final scratch and then continued down the dark road, turning right onto East Nicholson Street. Sensing his trackers closing in around him, he crossed North Botetourt Street and passed by the Carpenter's Yard. His pursuers drawing closer, he increased his pace.

He shook his head. Not so much in surprise, but rather in resignation. They were predictable if nothing else. Clearly nothing had changed since he had last come up against these creatures.

As he walked down the slope, the gloom consumed him, the darkness weaving itself around him, becoming a part of the shadow. The only sign of where he was came from the tap of his walking stick on the pavement.

Reaching the spot that he selected upon first realizing that there was a good possibility of trouble, he stopped.

The darkness was almost complete, the Public Gaol at his back, the weathervane rising atop the Capitol Building off to his left flashing briefly as the full moon peeked out from behind the clouds for just a few seconds.

There he waited. He hoped that his trackers didn't take too long to make an appearance. His ride could be testy at the best of times. He doubted that she would wait for him if he was more than just a few minutes late, and he had no desire to take the train all the way back to Kraken Cove.

The Grym surging through him, he pinpointed the location of each of his five trackers. He sensed that they were hesitant, which went against what he knew of these creatures.

They had few natural enemies. Because of that, they usually raced into a situation and worried about the consequences after the fact.

He must have thrown them off by coming this way, expecting him to continue down the main road. Even more concerning for them, they likely didn't understand why he was standing there.

He could imagine the questions circulating through their minds.

Had he made them?

Was that why he stopped?

They hadn't made any mistakes. They never made mistakes. Besides, none of the Teg could track them.

Was he waiting to meet someone?

Was that it?

Should they allow more time to pass before they made their move?

"Come out, come out wherever you are," he said from the shadows that swirled around him, trying to coax his hunters from the gloom.

He allowed a minute to pass, the silence of the dark street complete except for the sound of the small stream murmuring off to his right. Nothing happened. His trackers stayed in place, still unwilling to emerge from the darkness.

Impressive discipline for creatures of their kind. Usually they could barely restrain themselves, their instincts and urges almost too much for them.

Still, he could tell how difficult it was for them to remain where they were. He sensed their unease, all of his trackers tensing upon hearing his words. He was sure they didn't appreciate the gentle taunt.

Apparently, they didn't want to make the first move. Not until they knew why he had stopped.

Fine, he would give them another nudge, this one not so gentle.

"I never took the servants of the Daemon King to be cowards, but I guess there's a first time for everything."

He felt the unease that he sensed shift to anger. He had struck a chord.

That was confirmed just a heartbeat later when a hulking figure stepped out of the darkness, four more shapes following his move. He assumed the leader stood across from him, the others arranging themselves around him so that he was surrounded.

Without the light of the full moon, they appeared to be no more than shadows. He didn't need any light to know what he faced, however. He had known what they were as soon as he latched onto their presence.

Three men and two women. They looked just like anyone else he would see walking on the streets of Williamsburg.

But they weren't human.

They were Daemons.

For those without his skill in the Grym, the only way to know what his trackers were was to glimpse their eyes. Pure black. A natural malevolence burning in the back. Burning with the hope that they could kill and then consume the spirit of a soft human.

"You would say such a thing when you face a fist of our Master's select?" questioned the first Daemon to step out of the gloom. "You must learn your place. You are not what you once were."

He turned to face the monster. The creature that had taken the shape of a man stood well over six feet tall. Perhaps even touching seven. He was quite broad as well.

This Daemon made him think of a professional wrestler.

Not the Rock or John Cena. No, those two were too small. This Daemon reminded him of Andre the Giant. This Daemon would have to duck his head and turn sideways to fit through a doorway.

"I would say such a thing no matter your place with your Master or how many Daemons came for me." He gave the Daemon a flinty expression. "And I still am who I am."

"You are arrogant, Knight of the Round."

"It is not arrogance if it is the truth," he replied, "and you forget yourself. I am no longer a Knight of the Round."

"So you say," said the Daemon, the creature taking a step closer, although not so close as to be within easy reach of the one he had been tracking. "I have heard of you, Fallen Knight."

"Good things, I hope."

"Worrying things."

"And I'm assuming that you're here because of those worrying things," he sighed.

"We are," the leader of the five Daemons confirmed. The creature didn't offer any more than that.

He stood there calmly, holding his walking stick, waiting for the Daemon who spoke for the others to explain more. Because he didn't really know why these creatures had come in search of him. Why they had put in the effort, because he wasn't an easy Teg to find.

Moreover, the agreement was still in place. The past was so supposed to remain in the past, the present governed by the accord earned with blood and death.

Of course with Daemons the accord might mean nothing to them, especially now that they had had a chance to lick their wounds. After all, they were a vindictive lot with long memories.

Maybe these five happened upon an opportunity and wanted to take advantage of the fact that he had left the safety of his home. Maybe they wanted to gain revenge for their many comrades that he had destroyed. Maybe they were here on their own, using their Master as an excuse. Maybe they weren't.

Although he was curious as to why they were here, he didn't have the time for this. His ride would be losing patience with him right about now. And he was much more concerned about angering her than angering a fist of Daemons.

"And what is worrying five Daemons so much that you've left the Daemon Realm to find me?"

"It's gone," the leader of the Daemons hissed, an accusation in his voice.

"You've lost me already." The man sighed again, his patience already wearing thin. "What's gone?"

"The artifact that our Master holds most dear. The artifact that belongs only to us. It has been stolen."

"You're here telling me this why?" he asked, clearly perplexed.

"Few have the power or skill to steal the artifact. And only a handful would take the risk. Of that handful, you are the one who came immediately to mind."

He nodded, understanding dawning within him. "You think I did it."

"We do."

"And why do you think this?"

"You have left your sanctuary," the Daemon replied with a hint of smugness in his tone. "You rarely do. You would only do so for good cause. Also, we have heard rumors."

"There are always rumors," he scoffed, clearly not impressed by the Daemon's reasoning. "That doesn't mean those rumors are true."

"Nevertheless, we are here because of those rumors. As you should know, Knight who is no longer a Knight, in every rumor there is a hint of truth."

"And in every rumor there is also a lie," he countered,

although he knew as soon as he said it that his argument would fall on deaf ears. The Daemon already had made up its mind.

He shook his head in resignation. There was only one direction that this conversation was going to take. The issue now was how hard he wanted to work to avoid that path.

His initial inclination was to let the chips fall where they may. He was edgy after all. Perhaps it was time to scratch that itch.

"Now that you've found me, what are you supposed to do, Daemon? Are you allowed to think for yourself or must you obey your Master to the letter of your instructions."

"Retrieve the artifact that you stole," the Daemon replied, clearly not affected by the insult.

"And if I don't have the artifact? What then?"

"Make you tell us where you hid it. Then we will retrieve it and return it to our Master."

He nodded. Yes, there was little point in trying to avoid what was going to happen next. Besides, it might even be fun. "And if I'm telling you the truth, that I didn't steal it. What happens if I don't have what you want?"

"Then we kill you."

"Despite the agreement that's in place?"

"Our Master will look the other way," the Daemon said without a trace of concern. "He has not said as much, but he has hinted. You are quite a prize, after all. A worthy kill."

"Better Daemons than you have tried to kill me."

"You're wrong there," the Daemon replied harshly. "None of the Daemons you have challenged compared to me and my hunters. We are the Pathfinders. We are the best that our Master has. We are here because no other Daemon can do what is required of us."

"You keep telling yourself that," the man chuckled, enjoying how the Daemon's face twisted into a scowl because of his lack of respect. That and the fact that he didn't display any of the fear that the lackey of the Daemon King expected and craved. If confronted by a Daemon, much less five, most of the Teg would have pissed their pants in fear by now. "You know I don't have the artifact. You and your friends just want to make a name for yourselves."

The leader of the Daemons nodded then, giving him an evil smile. Even with the shadows playing in front of the Public Gaol, he saw how the Daemons around him began to change, their hands elongating into sharp claws, their teeth sharpening to razor-fine points. "We would gain honor in the eyes of our Master. We live only to obey him."

"Are you saying that the Daemon King has sent you here to kill me since I can't give you what you want? That he still holds a grudge against me?"

"He has and he does."

"Grudges can be dangerous things. They poison the heart."

"There are some grudges worth bearing, *Fallen Knight*. You should know that."

It was his turn to nod. He couldn't dispute the Daemon's logic. And he didn't see any way to avoid what was going to happen next. In fact, he didn't really have any desire to avoid the coming confrontation.

It had been a long day, a good day in many respects, but he was getting hungry now, and these Daemons were keeping him from the tapas restaurant just off Jamestown Road that he had heard such good things about.

"If I destroy you and your friends, you all gain nothing. Just like me, your Master has little in the way of mercy. He will not be happy with you when I send you back to the Spirit World."

"We will take that risk. We are not afraid of a Knight who is no longer a Knight, even one of your reputation."

"So be it," he murmured, already moving before he spoke the last word.

He surged to his left, slashing with his walking stick for the

Daemon farthest to his right. In mid-swing, the blackthorn shillelagh shifted into its true form, a blazing white light sparking along the sword, ancient runes carved into both sides of the blade and the hilt flashing at the touch of the Grym.

The unprepared Daemon didn't stand a chance, unable to take anything more than a half-step away before collapsing to the ground, the steel slicing through flesh and bone from his shoulder down to his gut. There was no blood. Daemons were made more of spirit than of substance. Only the skins and frames of their victims remaining. But the steel infused with the Grym had the same effect as if he had struck any living creature.

When he ripped the blade free, the human shell collapsed in the road, the Daemon already leaving the body and returning to its Realm. He barely noticed. Instead of taking on the Daemon closest to him, he decided to keep the remaining hunters off balance.

He attacked the Daemon who was farthest to his left and had the best chance of coming at him from behind.

This Daemon, who had taken the body of a woman, was already rushing toward him, claws extended, seeking to take advantage of his turned back.

Rather than cut with his sword, the Daemon preparing for just such a strike, he avoided her claws and brought his steel in close to his body, slamming into her chest with his shoulder.

Because of the force of the blow, the Daemon skidded across the pavement on her back. Before the monster could rise, he was there, driving the point of his blade through the creature's throat.

The change began almost immediately, the body that the dead Daemon had taken beginning to disintegrate. The flesh and bone flaking away into nothingness. In less than an hour there would be nothing left to suggest that a creature from the Daemon Realm had once walked in the Natural World.

The three remaining Daemons slowly circled their target, no longer certain of their victory. They had heard many stories of this Knight who was no longer a Knight. Of what he could do. Of what he had done. Of the many, many Daemons he had dispatched during the Second Daemon War.

They had believed some of what they had been told, although not all, much sounding exaggerated. Just legends designed to frighten. No more than that.

Until now.

The shillelagh becoming the blazing sword for which he was known was not a surprise. They had expected as much. Rather, they were taken aback by his current appearance, not prepared for what they were seeing.

His eyes burned with a golden flame. His hair stood on end as if he moved in the center of a thunderstorm. Most worrying, sparks of energy flashed all across his body, placing the Knight who was no longer a Knight in the center of an almost blinding nimbus of power.

"Leave now," he said, his voice deep, harsh, as if it wasn't just him who was speaking, as if there was a creature within him that had yet to break free and was striving to do so. "Return to your Master and tell him to keep to the accord. If he doesn't, tell him that I'll finish what I started."

"And if we don't?" asked the leader of the Daemons. "If we choose to fight?"

"Then I destroy you."

For several seconds there was nothing but silent movement, the three Daemons continuing to stalk their prey.

He had no doubt that these assassins were going to ignore his offer, so he was ready when they came for him.

A Daemon in the skin of a man who resembled a linebacker rushed toward him, his right claw sweeping through the air, seeking to slice across his neck.

He didn't bother to attack the creature, instead ducking the strike and spinning around, right leg extended. His boot connected with the Daemon's knee.

He heard the sickening crunch as the Daemon's kneecap shattered and the ligaments in the damaged joint snapped.

True, he was fighting Daemons. Said by some to be the deadliest enemies of the Tylwyth Teg.

But these monsters were restricted by the limitations of the bodies they had selected. They could not function with their full power. That was a weakness that he was more than happy to exploit.

The injured Daemon crashed to the ground, rolling into the legs of the gargantuan leader, taking them both down in a heap.

Leaving the two Daemons in a jumble, he turned swiftly, the female Daemon streaking toward him, hoping that his focus would be on her two remaining partners just a half-second more.

She would soon learn the price for her poor timing.

He raised his sword right before her claws slashed across his face. The Daemon continued with her attack, having no choice, too close, unable to change course, slicing with a blinding speed, desperate to cut into her quarry's flesh.

Every time the Daemon believed that she was going to break through his defenses, he disappointed her, getting his blade in position to block the stab or slash.

He smiled, enjoying the challenge of the combat as they glided across the street, claw meeting blazing steel, ringing like steel striking steel, the Daemon's claws hard enough and sharp enough to cut through brick and stone.

His smile turned to a grimace when he realized what he had allowed. The Daemon was clever. She had maneuvered him so that his back was turned toward the two Daemons who were now back on their feet, although the smaller of the two couldn't put any weight on his injured leg.

A weakness to be attacked, assuming he could escape the

claws of the Daemon who kept him engaged with an unrestrained ferocity.

He could see the delight in the Daemon's eyes, how pleased she was with herself, already thinking of the praise to be showered upon her, the reward to be given to her by the Daemon King, for the part she played in killing the Teg who had pained her Master so greatly. For eliminating, once and for all, the Fallen Knight.

She didn't realize that she was congratulating herself much too soon until it was too late.

When the Daemon again cut for his face with her claw, instead of dodging the slice, he ducked down and rose quickly, his shoulder slamming into the Daemon right below her arms. The shock and power of the blow sent her flying backward through the air, only able to stay on her feet by digging her claws into the pavement.

Sensing the two other Daemons rushing toward his back, he knelt down swiftly, slamming the hilt of his sword against the pavement.

The effect was immediate.

A massive shockwave blasted out in all directions, knocking all three Daemons onto their backs, the monsters sliding across the pavement for several dozen feet, unable to resist the tremendous power that resonated out from the blazing sword.

Feeling the need to even the odds, he focused his attention first on the female Daemon. She made it back to her feet in time, even getting her claws up to block the swing coming for her neck.

He allowed her to deflect the blow. With her attention fully fixed on his blindingly bright steel, he punched with his left hand, striking her in the side. The instant his knuckles slammed into her body, he sent a blast of the Grym into her, the scorching energy surging through the Daemon, burning through her body, the creature's pure black eyes glazing over in an instant.

The Daemon he had already wounded was struggling to rise, his damaged leg and continuing disorientation resulting from the blast making him look like a tortoise stuck on his back.

Not feeling the faintest hint of mercy, he stabbed his sword through the Daemon's chest, the tip appearing for just an instant through the creature's back before he pulled it free.

He took a deep breath then, not so much needing to calm himself as to ensure he maintained control over the power that was racing through him. The power that was desperate to be released. The power that could take him back to a path that he had fought to avoid for a very long time.

Once he was certain that he was himself once more, he turned and faced the leader of the now much diminished fist of Daemons.

"If you want to make a name for yourself, you'll have to kill me on your own."

The surviving Daemon nodded, understanding how drastically his circumstances had changed. The speed of the shift unsettling the predator who was rarely unsettled.

"Or as I said just a few minutes ago, you can take a message back to your Master and tell him that the agreement remains in place. I will forgive this bad decision. If the artifact is gone, I had nothing to do with it. You can tell him that. You can tell him as well that if he comes for me again, then I will come for him."

The Daemon considered the offer, demonstrating a thoughtfulness that usually was lacking in such creatures. "That is fair. I will do as you ask. I will tell my Master to leave you be. I will tell my Master that you say that the accord remains in place."

The Daemon took a step back then, suggesting that he was going to leave the fight, beginning to bend at the waist as if he were preparing to bow in respect to a better and stronger opponent.

The Fallen Knight wasn't taken in by the attempted deception, knowing from hard experience the truth of these monsters. He had fought and killed too many Daemons over the centuries to be fooled now by this one.

Daemons were greedy. They wanted power, and they loved to kill to obtain that power. Even more so, Daemons were fearless, in part because they feared their Master more than they feared being destroyed by someone like him.

So he was ready.

When the Daemon came for him, he pivoted to the left and continued his movement, spinning, allowing the Daemon, claws outstretched, to slide past him. At the same time his blazing sword came around in a backward swing that cut through the creature's neck, the body collapsing to the pavement, the head rolling into the long grass at the side of the road.

"Assassins?" asked a melodic voice from just behind him.

"Yes, but not of our world," he replied, sensing her presence right before the last Daemon attacked him.

He studied the corpses for just a few breaths, the bodies already flaking away, the decomposition process more advanced in those he had killed first. With the surrounding darkness, it wouldn't be long before the evidence of the clash that had just occurred in the very center of the colonial capital of Virginia vanished.

Satisfied that there were no more Daemons skulking about, he released his hold on the Grym, the energy blazing along the blade winking out, the sword itself once more appearing to be a shillelagh.

"You could have helped, Peggy Rose," he said, turning toward the woman who was already walking back down the street from the direction he had come.

"I didn't want to emasculate you," the older woman replied, her hair, frizzy on the best of days, sticking up in all directions as was its wont.

"Seriously," he replied. "That's what you were concerned about while I fought five Daemons? Emasculating me?"

"Well, you were quite sensitive when you were a boy," she replied, turning right when she reached North Botetourt Street.

"I'm not a boy anymore."

"Could have fooled me with your whining now, Draig," she replied.

"I'm not whining," he protested. "I'm trying to make the point that rather than worrying about emasculating me, perhaps you should have worried about me dying."

"I wasn't worried," Peggy Rose replied. "You had everything under control. Having seen you in action before, I didn't think that five Daemons would give you much cause for concern. And I was right."

"Even so ..."

"And if it appeared that you needed assistance ..." she began, cutting him off, not bothering to complete her thought. She knew that he would figure it out.

Draig looked down, seeing the wisps of energy dancing across her palms. He shook his head in amusement. There was no point in continuing the argument when Peggy Rose was like this.

"Have you had dinner?" asked Draig.

"Not yet," she replied.

"How about I buy you dinner?"

"We can go to the tapas place you mentioned?" she asked.

"Of course," Draig replied.

"Then come on," Peggy Rose said, reaching out a hand and

running it through the thick fur of a monstrously large St. Bernard who trotted out from the shadows and forced his way between them.

The dog nudged his nose against Draig's hip, demanding a scratch that he was more than happy to give. He understood now why Peggy Rose had been so confident in his success. She didn't bring Pinkie with her unless she meant business.

When they reached the end of the street, the darkness gave way to the light of the full moon, revealing the motorcycle with the sidecar parked along the road. Pinkie didn't hesitate, the St. Bernard jumping into the sidecar. Familiar with the drill, Draig reached for the two sets of goggles hanging from the motorcycle's right handlebar. The larger pair he placed carefully over Pinkie's eyes. He covered his own eyes with the smaller pair.

Peggy Rose was already in place on the motorcycle's seat, gripping the handlebars. Draig jumped on behind her, raising an eyebrow when she glanced over her shoulder.

"What?"

Draig looked at Peggy Rose, taking in her expression of innocence. He nodded toward the five college students who were sitting against a large tree, hidden within the shadows except for someone like him who could see through such magical deceptions.

"I caught them watching your fight. I didn't want them to interfere and I didn't want them to go running for help."

Draig nodded. "Thank you."

"My pleasure."

"How long will they be out?"

Peggy Rose shrugged noncommittally. "A few more hours at least."

"And after that?"

"The worst hangovers they've ever experienced," she said with a broad smile, "and they won't remember a thing."

"Better than having to kill them."

"Agreed. I always found your father's approach for keeping our secrets from those not of the Teg distasteful."

"I won't argue with you about that."

"How did it go?" she asked as she kicked the engine to life.

"As well as can be expected, I guess," Draig replied, knowing that she wasn't referring to his fight with the Daemons.

"She's still angry with you," Peggy Rose nodded.

"Yes, she made that quite clear. Many times, in fact."

"Even so, I'm sure she appreciated your making the effort to be here with her."

"It didn't seem that way for much of the time."

"All you can do is make the effort," Peggy Rose advised. "It's her choice as to when and how she's willing to interact with you. You have no control over that."

"You think she'll come around?" Draig asked, hope in his voice.

"Maybe. With time. You can be quite charming when you're contrite." Peggy Rose shrugged her shoulders, putting her own goggles in place. "Then again, she does have a stubborn streak that rivals yours, and a mule can be more flexible than you. We'll just have to wait and see."

"We should head back home after dinner." Draig wanted to think some more on what Peggy Rose just told him. As well as about why a fist of Daemons had confronted him. "We've got a long drive."

"A very long drive," Peggy Rose replied.

"I can't believe I agreed to have you come with me."

"I can be very persuasive, you know that. We're family. Besides, with this baby," Peggy Rose said, patting the fuel tank, "we'll make excellent time."

"Just make sure we stay out of sight."

"That goes without saying, but dinner first. I'm starving."

Twisting the throttle, she released the clutch, the motorcycle roaring to life and hurtling down the road, Pinkie's very large tongue flapping in the wind, the St. Bernard enjoying every second of the ride.

3

A SAFE PLACE

Melissa sat in the driver's seat of her silver Toyota Highlander, tapping out a rhythmless song on the steering wheel with her fingers.

She could have afforded a much more expensive ride. She didn't want one.

The Highlander was a popular SUV. Nondescript. A vehicle that didn't stand out in any way and could be lost among the streets of any town or city.

There but not. Forgotten as soon as it passed by. Much like her.

That's why she liked her ride so much. It helped her to hide in plain sight.

Although she couldn't do that now, which was why she had backed in among the trees that grew right next to the road.

She had been sitting there for almost an hour.

Waiting. Thinking. Watching. Worrying.

The darkness was complete except for the full moon that every so often broke through the clouds drifting across the sky.

She hadn't seen a thing since she turned off the engine. Not a car flashing by. Not even a deer or raccoon crossing the road.

She still wasn't sure if that was good or bad. It certainly wasn't what she had expected.

She just knew that she was nervous.

She didn't like being nervous. It was an uncommon feeling for her.

She could handle most anything with aplomb, rarely getting thrown by surprises or when things went off the rails, because that tended to happen frequently in her line of work.

Yet now she couldn't seem to sit still.

Usually when she felt like this it meant that something was wrong. Because every time she felt nervous, something did go wrong. Every time. Never failed.

She couldn't sit here for much longer. She needed to decide. Quickly.

Just then, the theme music for Darth Vader filled her car. She jumped, startled, and then dropped the phone when she reached for it. Cursing, she had to search for it beneath the passenger seat, finally digging it out.

She should have assumed that this was going to happen.

For a few seconds more, she vacillated about answering. She hoped that the caller would disconnect. It didn't happen. The phone just kept playing.

Grumbling to herself, she realized that it would be better to deal with it now.

"You're late." The female voice on the other end was pleasant, though it never failed to send a shiver down Melissa's spine. It wasn't the voice that did it to her. It was knowing what lurked beneath the voice.

"What can I say? The job was more complicated than I thought it would be. I didn't have a chance to call." She tried to keep her own voice light. Make her client think that she was under control. It wasn't an easy thing to do.

"Why was it complicated? It all should have been as I told

you it would be. If you followed my instructions, it should have been a walk in the park."

"It was. Until the end."

"Explain."

"I would, but I need to go. I'm sorry. I can fill you in later."

The pleasantness instantly slipped from the woman's voice, replaced by an acid that made Melissa think of a spitting cobra. She realized that the imagery probably wasn't too far off the mark, which only served to make her even more nervous.

"You need to speak with me. Now. Everything else can wait."

"It's nothing to worry about. Really. The job is done. It's just that I need to go."

"Explain." The woman chewed out the word, the quiet tone of her voice suggesting an almost unfathomable anger.

"I'm sorry, but I need to go. I do have a life outside of my work."

"No you don't."

Silence descended. Melissa's initial reaction had been to agree with her employer, and that instinct burned like nothing else had in quite some time.

She didn't have a life outside her work. It was almost like she was on the phone with her mother, who could see through her just as well. Although her mother didn't have the same reputation as this woman. A reputation for blood, violence, and getting what she wanted at whatever the cost.

"I'm sorry," she said finally, unwilling to allow the silence to drag on any longer. "I need to go. I have a date."

"A date?" The woman's tone suggested that she could smell the lie. "Fine. I will give you the benefit of the doubt. Just this once. I will see you in two days' time. You remember when and where?"

"Of course."

More silence. Longer than the first time. Melissa was sweating now. Her heart was beating fast. She felt as if she was running a marathon, each successive step becoming more of a painful plod.

"Don't do what you're thinking about doing," the woman advised. "You won't like the result if you do."

"What would that be?" Melissa asked, forcing a light tone into her voice, as if she was taking what the woman said as a joke.

"Running."

"That thought never crossed my mind." Her grip tightened on her phone, her breath catching. "I'll meet you in two days, just as I promised."

She placed one hand on the steering wheel, her fingers gripping her phone turning white.

Maybe she should run.

She would be safe. Free. For a time.

She shook her head in resignation, knowing the truth. If she turned the ignition, put her foot down on the pedal, and then drove as fast and as far as she could before she ran out of gas, the woman would find her. Eventually. Probably quite rapidly knowing the resources that she could put to use.

Then her client would make her displeasure known. Painfully so, in fact.

"If you run, I will find you. Be assured of that." The woman laughed for just a few seconds, the sound warm, inviting, until the end, when it turned frigid in a flash. "You know I speak the truth. If I have to find you, the consequences will be less than pleasant."

The line went dead.

Melissa stared at the phone, then dropped it into the seat next to her as if she had been holding a writhing snake. She took a few deep breaths, resting her head on the steering wheel, trying to release the tension that was rolling through her in waves.

Annoyed that the breathing exercises she had learned from

a meditation app weren't working for her, her heart continuing to race, she lifted her head.

She needed to do, not worry.

She chuckled softly. One phone call and she had almost fallen to pieces.

She hadn't. She was proud of that. But she had sweated through her shirt.

She released her grip on the steering wheel, not realizing that she had been holding onto it so hard that her knuckles ached. She reached down, turned off the phone, and took out the SIM card.

She didn't know if the woman had the capacity to track her through her cell phone. She probably could, although Melissa assumed as well that she could track her in other more effective ways.

But there was no reason to take the risk. No reason to make it any easier for her.

Melissa sat in the driver's seat for several more minutes, leaning back against the headrest, letting her mind wander, trying to figure out what to do.

The entire time there was nothing but silence other than the soft murmur of the crickets heard dully through the closed windows of her car. Finally, she found the calm that she had been searching for.

She still hadn't seen anything on the road. If someone was following her, she would have spied them by now.

She cursed softly. There was no easy answer to the problem that she faced. There was nothing to do but keep moving forward. To stick to the plan.

Making a run for it held little appeal, and it ensured only one end. Staying on track gave her more than one option, and she liked having options. She didn't want to be placed in a corner with only one way out.

Pressing the ignition button, the hybrid vehicle came to life.

Looking both ways, she pulled out onto the dark road. The straightaway ran for several miles.

She turned toward the east. Toward the coast. Driving the speed limit. There was no reason to draw any attention to herself.

It wasn't long before she saw the first few houses along the road that marked the town line. A mile farther on, she came to a traffic light. At this time of the night it was blinking red. She turned right, then drove down the road, peeking out of the windows to get a better feel for where she planned to spend the next few days.

It looked like many other New England towns. The buildings were older but well maintained, a church anchoring the town green. Many were old Victorians, painted in bright colors visible even in the darkness. The streetlamps, which made her think that she was driving down an old London street, only offered a dim light that did little to hold back the shadows.

As she crept along, she passed the storefronts that she had researched online. There was the bakery with gluten-free options. Always a must for someone with celiac disease. The bookstore was right next to it. Followed by the pub that also had a coffee bar.

She smiled. She could spend an entire day just on this street moving between the three shops and be quite happy. A book, a pastry, and a coffee. What could be better than that?

Reaching the very end of the street before it twisted down toward the public beach and then to the marina, she read the brightly lit sign that was to her right.

Safe Haven.

She hoped the sign was accurate.

She turned into the long driveway, driving around the curl in front of the bed and breakfast. She looked up at the beautiful Victorian building, this one four stories, with a widow's walk on the very top. The shingles had been painted recently. The color of sea foam that matched the ocean surging up the shore just below the cliff upon which the old house was perched.

She pulled into the one empty parking spot off to the side.

Grabbing her duffel bag out of the back, she closed the car door and locked it. Walking up the staircase, she came to stand in front of an intricately designed glass door.

In the very center was a beautiful mermaid surrounded by waves that rippled across the glass. She was incredibly lifelike, almost as if she was about to step right out of the window and go for a swim. In fact, Melissa thought the mermaid might have winked at her when she approached.

Tired after a very long day, she tried the doorknob. Locked. It was well past midnight after all.

She knocked on the frame of the front door, avoiding the glass. Several minutes passed. Nothing, even though she could see a light on down the hallway.

She was about to knock again when the door swung open.

She was taken aback for a moment, the door seemingly moving on its own. Just then an old woman approached having come down a flight of steps.

"Good evening, love," said the woman. She was wearing a thick white robe, bright pink slippers peeking out from beneath the fringe. Her long grey hair was a wild mess, blue, purple, orange, and green streaks flashing depending on the light. "Can I help you?"

"Yes, I called a few hours ago. I was in need of a room."

"At such a late hour?"

"Well, yes, I'm sorry, but it couldn't be avoided. My plans changed at the last minute and you were my only option."

"This time of year, and all the way out here, love? There's not much around until you get past the national forest, and most people aren't interested in coming this way until the spring."

"That may be," Melissa agreed, not sure what to make of

the old woman. Although the innkeeper's gentle prodding didn't bother her. She simply assumed that anyone opening their door to a potential guest at such a late hour would do much the same. "I spoke with Harriet, I believe?" The old woman didn't say anything, simply staring at her. She appeared to be confused. "I'm Melissa? Melissa Gorgonella."

"Ah, yes," the old woman said, her eyes brightening, giving her a bright smile. "And it's Hestia, dear. Not Harriet. I don't know a Harriet. Or rather I did. But she's dead, so there's no reason to talk about her. Nasty woman, she was. I almost feel bad for all the other residents of where she is now."

Melissa stood there, not knowing how to reply. Although she couldn't help but wonder who Harriet was. Clearly there was a story there.

"Oh, my apologies," she finally said. "When I called I was a bit distracted."

"It sounded like it." Hestia waved away the mistake. "Why don't you come into the foyer." The innkeeper ushered her through the door. "We don't want the gremlins to get you, do we?"

That last statement lifted Melissa's eyebrows. The way Hestia said it made Melissa think that the old woman actually believed that there might be gremlins lurking about.

Despite a brief feeling of concern, she walked passed Hestia, glad to no longer be out in the open.

After Melissa entered the foyer, Hestia took a long look at the shadows playing across the front of the old Victorian mansion and extending down the driveway. The lawn that ran from the house to the trees lining the street was well illuminated by the solar-powered lights placed in strategic locations. And there were a great many lawn gnomes situated around the many garden beds that bordered the mown grass.

Staring out into the darkness a few seconds more, Hestia

ran her gaze over each of the knee-high statues, giving each one a sharp nod.

If Melissa had been standing there with her, she might have thought that the lawn gnomes returned Hestia's nod, as if to say that all was well. But Melissa wasn't there. She had stepped up to the front desk, her exhaustion beginning to hit her hard after such a long day.

Satisfied by her quick survey, Hestia pushed the door closed and locked it. A chime sounded, indicating the door was linked to a security system.

Melissa found that strange since the old house didn't look like it had any modern improvements. She was about to wander into the living room just through the open French doors, curious, her natural instincts pushing her in that direction in search of a security panel, but she didn't get the chance.

Hestia moved with a surprising speed across the carpet and stepped behind the counter.

"What brings you to Kraken Cove, love?"

"I just needed a few days away and my initial plans fell through at the last minute."

"I can understand that," Hestia replied, checking over the reservation form. Seeing that all was in order, she reached for one of the few keys in the dozen cubbyholes behind her. "I came here myself for a few days away and I haven't left since."

"How long ago was that?" asked Melissa, feeling the need to make conversation even though she was swiftly losing what little energy she had left.

"So long ago that I can't even remember." Hestia gave Melissa a mysterious smile. "You wanted some privacy, love, if I remember correctly."

"Yes, I'm a writer." Melissa motioned to her bag, the corner of a laptop peeking out. "I was hoping for a quiet space so that I can get some work done while I'm here. Deadlines and all that."

"Have no fear of that, love. Every room is quiet. I make sure of it."

Melissa didn't know how to interpret what Hestia had just told her. Feeling the need to say something, she responded. "That's good to know. Thank you."

"Let me show you to your room." Hestia stepped out from behind the counter and then walked over to the flight of stairs, beginning to make her way up. Melissa assumed that Hestia was well into her eighties. Nevertheless, she climbed the steps with a sprightly grace that Melissa couldn't match. "You're safe here, love. Nothing can threaten you so long as you stay within the inn."

"Why would you say that?" asked Melissa. Another strange comment that not only got her thinking, but also filled her with a sense of trepidation.

Hestia shrugged. "I just wanted you to understand that you are protected here. So long as you are in the Safe Haven B&B, you're safe. You need not worry about anything coming for you here."

Melissa stared at Hestia for several seconds, feeling a little uncomfortable, not sure what to make of this strange old woman. "That takes a load off my mind." She didn't really know how else to reply, not wanting to continue with the conversation.

Hestia nodded and continued up the second flight of stairs and then the third. On the fourth, she stopped at the only door on the top floor.

She opened it with the skeleton key, walked in, and held it for Melissa. She then handed the key to her newest guest.

Melissa liked the attic room immediately. It was airy, the many windows certain to provide a good bit of light during the day.

And it was renovated. A large, modern space that made her feel right at home the second she stepped over the threshold. It was almost like the room had been put together specifically with her in mind.

"Anything else you need, love? Anything at all?"

Hestia stood there expectantly, as if she could read Melissa's mind.

Melissa didn't reply right away. There was something that she wanted. That she needed. That was true. But it was also something that she wasn't prepared to share.

"No, I'm good. Thank you. I just need to get some rest."

Hestia didn't move, keeping the door open. She sensed that Melissa was worried. Deeply worried. She couldn't divine what it was that was troubling the young woman, although she was fairly certain that it didn't involve any romantic entanglements.

She had figured that out at first glance. No, what was bothering her was another issue entirely.

"All right, love. I'll leave you be. Have a good evening." She turned to go and then just as quickly turned back, hand still on the doorknob. "Breakfast is from six to eight. If you sleep late, the bakery is just a few blocks down the street. Tell Cerridwen that you're staying here and she'll give you whatever you ask for and charge it to my account."

"That's kind of you, Hestia, thank you."

Hestia stared at Melissa for a few seconds more, intrigued by the young woman. She knew what she was, and that didn't bother her. It only made sense that she had come here.

There was more to it than that, however. There was some aspect to Melissa that didn't seem quite right. And Hestia didn't like not knowing what she didn't know.

She shook her head ever so slightly. She needed to remember to rein in her mother hen instincts. Not everyone had need of her.

"Remember, love, you're safe here in the inn. Have no fear of that. Sleep soundly."

Hestia gave her new guest a broad smile and then pulled the door closed behind her.

Melissa stared at the door for almost a minute before pulling her gaze free. Hestia was a nice woman, but strange. And slightly disconcerting.

Melissa sensed that there was something off about her. An energy within her that was rarely found in anyone else that she had never come across before.

Then again, the feeling that something was off had been plaguing her ever since she decided to visit this small town.

She walked over to the large bay window that fronted the room, shaking her head in frustration.

What's done was done. There was no way to go back in time. There was no point in rethinking her decision every waking second.

Doing that would serve no useful purpose. In fact, it would slow her down, and she couldn't afford to allow that to happen.

Taking a deep breath, Melissa closed her eyes.

For the first time in days, she began to feel like herself again.

Maybe Hestia was right. Maybe she would be safe here. There was a feeling of calm and quiet about the room, about the inn, that suggested that she would be. And that appealed to her for a host of reasons.

Melissa's eyes widened. She should have realized it sooner, but she was distracted and tired. It only made sense considering why she was there.

Now that she was fully focused on her surroundings, she sensed the power in this place. That's what had been making her feel a little uneasy, her skin prickling ever so slightly ever since she drove into Kraken Cove.

Her mother had been right to tell her to come to this small town on the coast, the waves of the Atlantic Ocean crashing against the beach far below the bed and breakfast. Her mother hadn't been specific. She had simply said that it was a good place to go for their kind if you needed to disappear for a while. And if you needed to do a little research.

Melissa needed to do both.

She also needed to get some sleep.

However, first she gave into the urge to look out the window. She stepped back quickly, sliding over to the side so that she was behind the curtains.

Taking another deep breath to calm her nerves, she slid between the wall and the curtains, poking one eye out so that she could get a view of the front lawn.

She thought that she saw someone standing near the edge of the driveway in the shadows. Staring right up at her room. Yellowish gold eyes locking onto hers.

She lost track of the person when she stepped behind the curtains. And now she couldn't find him. Or her. She wasn't sure what exactly had been staring back at her.

Whoever it had been, he or she had been there one second and then was gone the next.

She looked out the window a few seconds more, hoping that she could identify the skulker again. But nothing.

All she saw were the many lawn gnomes lit up by the lights placed at various points along the driveway and the lawn.

That was strange. She could have sworn those lawn gnomes had been pointed in different directions when she drove up to the inn. Now, from where she was standing, it looked like they were all facing in the direction that she had been looking. Focused on where the watcher had been standing.

Strange indeed.

She had to have been imagining it.

It was late. She was tired.

She looked out the window one more time.

The lawn gnomes were facing to all points on the compass now.

It was probably just her mind playing tricks on her.

Then again, perhaps not.

4

OLD FRIENDS

It was early, the sun just a thought in the sky, clouds beginning to turn orange and pink, the colors flashing down between the breaks in the branches.

To Draig it was the perfect time of day.

He sprinted through the woods that bordered Kraken Cove, several fingers of forest extending down into the town from the mountains surrounding the bay. It was a cold morning, a light fog wrapping itself around the trees -- the ash, black, green, and white; the aspen; the beech and birch; and the balsam firs, which seemed to be everywhere in this part of Maine -- that he dodged around as he made for the trail.

When he reached the beaten down dirt path ten minutes later, he increased his pace, heading toward the east and the water, the smell of the ocean that grew stronger with every step he took making him smile.

He sped by the trail markers placed there by the town decades before he arrived.

Now on his third mile with just a few more to go, for the first time in days, he was feeling more like himself. This always happened when he left Kraken Cove. This sense of disconnection that stayed with him until he returned and got back into the swing of what had become his routine.

Here, now, running through the forest he knew so well, he felt like he was back where he should be. In a place that he had made his own.

He allowed the quiet and the sense of calm that he found so difficult to attain anywhere else in the world to flow through him. It helped to release the tension that had been building up within him.

He loved being in the Schoodic Forest at this time in the morning, knowing that he was alone. That he could just be.

Finally, after a few more miles, the rhythm of his movement relaxing him, he gained the peace that he had been seeking since he returned home. The clarity that he needed so that he could think about the events of the night before that kept playing through his mind. About what the Daemon had told him while he was in Williamsburg.

He wasn't worried so much about the threats that the Daemon Pathfinder had made. He was used to threats, enduring them all his life. By Teg and monster. None of that ever bothered him.

He found the encounter peculiar, however.

It was as if those foolish enough to threaten him had forgotten who he was. That they believed his time away had changed him.

Not just foolish, he corrected. Potentially suicidal as well.

Rather than be concerned about the Daemon's threat, instead he focused on the thief who had stolen the artifact. It couldn't have been an easy job to accomplish.

He knew where the artifact had been kept. After all, he was the one who placed it there before the protections had been put in place.

In fact, because he knew more about the artifact than most, he was beginning to wonder if two thieves had been involved in the heist. The first stealing the item from where it had been safeguarded for so many hundreds of years. The second stealing it from the first thief.

There were only a few who could have entered the Vault and survived, and he knew them all. Several of them dead.

He knew that for a fact, because he had been the one to kill them. He hadn't wanted to do it, but he hadn't had a choice.

Kill or be killed.

He had chosen to kill.

He had succeeded.

He had survived.

Yet had he?

Because he felt as if a piece of his soul was sliced away every time he was required to kill.

That, in part, was why he was where he was now.

Pulling himself away from what he believed were self-defeating thoughts – he could do nothing to rectify the past, he could only focus on what he did now and in the future – he returned to the clash with the Daemons.

In addition to his curiosity as to who had taken the artifact and how, he was also concerned.

He wasn't afraid of the Daemon King. He had come up against the Master of the Abyss before.

Rather, he was concerned about what the Daemon King might do to reclaim the artifact.

That knowledge driving him, he understood that he couldn't allow that artifact to fall into someone else's hands. Particularly someone with the power and knowledge to use it against him.

That's what had kept Draig up last night. What had gotten him out of his home and into the woods before the sun had risen. He needed to think, and this was the best place to do that.

Besides himself only a few of the Tylwyth Teg had the strength and the knowledge to make use of the artifact.

Of course, he had no desire to do so.

The other members of the Teg who could, though, wouldn't hesitate to use the item that should never have been released back into the world. It was much too enticing, the power it offered almost too much to resist.

That's what worried him. Because he had no doubt as to how those few Teg would employ the stolen item if given the chance.

Increasing his pace as he ran down the trail, he shook his head in irritation.

He was busying himself with issues that were no longer his responsibility.

So why was he making the theft his problem?

Why was his overdeveloped sense of responsibility that had gotten him into trouble so many times in the past telling him that he couldn't allow that to happen? That he needed to reclaim the artifact before one of the Teg tried to make use of it?

He attempted to crush the whisper in the back of his brain that was gaining volume with every step that he took.

This wasn't his responsibility anymore. He had left that world. And for good reason.

Did he really want to return to those heavy, soul-deadening burdens? Knowing what it had cost him? Knowing what it would cost him if he returned to it? If he became once again what he had been before?

And not just him, but his friends as well. The Teg who had helped him. The Teg who had shown him that he was more than what he had been in the world his father created.

A gentle nudge on his leg brought him back to the forest around him. Butch ran right next to him, the dog recognizing that he was distracted and wanting to make sure that he paid attention to where he was going. Cassidy and Sundance ran along his flanks. Their eyes were bright with excitement, all of them enjoying the early morning exercise.

All three were black cockerpoos with flashes of tan and white on their chests and paws. They didn't come up to his knees, yet they all appeared to be larger than they really were.

Maybe it was because of their eyes and the shadows. There always seemed to be shadows dancing around them, and their eyes were similar to Draig's own. A dark orange red that appeared almost black.

Unless he got angry. Then those dark orbs flashed with a fire that promised an unending pain to those who caused them to burn so brightly.

More often than not, the three dogs sprinted off in different directions, checking the scents of the forest, looking for anything that might capture their interest, always coming back to check on him before scampering off again.

Every so often he used the shillelagh that he was never without to move out of the way a branch that extended onto the trail so that he didn't need to slow down.

Still concentrating on what he had learned the night before, it took him a few seconds to realize that Butch, Cassidy, and Sundance were nowhere to be found.

One of them was always close to him, but not now.

That could mean only one thing. And it was never good.

Draig stopped, taking hold of his shillelagh with both hands, thinking that perhaps what happened last night was about to happen again this morning.

He extended his senses with the Grym. He didn't sense anything around him for five leagues. Nothing gave him any cause for concern.

Feeling more comfortable with that knowledge, he waited, listening. Almost a minute passed. Still no sign of the dogs. He was about the reach once more for the Power of the Ancients to locate them when he realized he didn't have to.

He sprinted off the trail and between the trees toward the sharp bark that drifted through the wood. Two more barks directed him to where he needed to go.

He stopped when he reached a small glade that was just off the trail that had taken him closer to town. The dogs were sniffing around the edge of the clearing, staying off the grass. Every so often one of the cockerpoos growled, teeth bared, a deep rumble that seemed out of place from such small dogs.

Draig understood why. They had a good reason for being on edge. A very good reason.

He knelt down, staring at the mud. It had rained the night before. If not for that, he would have had a hard time picking out what were now quite clear tracks.

If he had been home last night, he would have sensed these unwanted visitors to Kraken Cove, but he hadn't been. Having already extended his search with the Grym to more than thirty miles around the town, he wondered where the beasts had gone. He wondered as well if they had come here last night specifically because they knew that he wasn't here.

He wouldn't put it past them.

Draig pushed himself back up. He saw where the tracks led. Either the beasts were clumsy or unconcerned about the prospect of being discovered.

There was another alternative as well. Maybe they wanted to be found out. Perhaps they wanted to send a message.

Draig wasn't sure what it could be if the latter was the case. Either way, this was just something else for him to worry over, as if he didn't have enough already.

Thinking about it a few seconds more, he knew the answer to his question. They weren't that cunning.

These beasts always were very direct in their approach. They preferred to rely on their brawn rather than their brains, believing that no one could challenge them. Not even a Teg strong in the Grym. At least not one in their right mind.

They'd made a mistake. He was sure of it. Which meant they probably had been in a rush.

That was useful information that he filed away.

"Well done, boys," Draig said to the three cockerpoos. "Well done, indeed. Let's see where these tracks take us. Quietly though."

Butch, Cassidy, and Sundance bolted down the trail, focused on their assignment. Draig was right behind them, although at a slightly slower pace.

For the most part, the beasts had stayed at the very edge of the wood, although they did leave a print on the trail here and there, usually when a tree or a root that extended onto the path forced them to reveal their passage.

The tracks continued unerringly along the trail for several miles, past the outskirts of the town and all the way down to the harbor where both the tracks and the path stopped and the town green began.

The dogs trotted out onto the freshly cut grass, satisfied that their quarry had not left the wood. Even so, they remained wary. They had little liking for beasts such as these.

Trotting across the green, Draig stopped when he reached the gravel walkway that tracked the waterfront and connected the public beach to the harbor. The trail continued from there for several miles until it connected to one of the paths that led into the state park.

He walked past the beach to the harbor, the dogs following him, all three on alert, their eyes always focused on the wood that fronted the green. Draig continued to search around the town with the Grym, just to make sure that he wasn't missing anything. That he wasn't being deceived.

The beasts could try to hide in plain sight, but they couldn't hide from the Grym.

Nothing.

He was certain.

He assumed that would be the case.

They had been here when he wasn't, and then they had left just as quickly as they had come.

When he stopped in front of one of the charter yachts, stern facing the path, the dogs settled down in the grass.

Butch, Cassidy, and Sundance were certain that the cause of their unease was gone. Even so, they paid little attention to the water. Instead, they remained focused on the tree line that was just a hundred yards distant.

The dogs knew just as Draig did that they had nothing to worry about. Still, it was a hard habit to break. To always be looking for the next threat.

Because based on experience, there was always another threat to be concerned about, just as Draig had learned last night ... again. A lesson that he had learned a long time ago that kept coming back around to remind him, much like a broken record.

He could understand why his dogs were acting the way they were. They didn't like the tracks that they had found any more than he did.

They understood what the tracks meant.

They already had guessed at the trouble and danger that they would bring.

"You're up early," he said as he continued to stare at the woods fronting the green. He knew that he wasn't going to see anything.

Still, something wasn't right. He could feel it in his bones. And when he got a feeling like this, nothing good ever came from it.

"So are you," grumbled the man standing above him on the stern of the charter boat.

The crusty sailor was carrying a very large cooler, his arms corded muscle. He placed the heavy container against the rear gunwale and then shoved it beneath the bench. It took him a few pushes. The heavy weight made the movement awkward.

"You're looking more presentable than usual."

"Meaning?"

Draig believed that the man standing above him was a dead ringer for Randy "Macho Man" Savage, a 1980s wrestling star. The only pieces missing from his attire were the kerchief tied around his forehead and the eye-catching sunglasses that were part of the wrestler's persona. Draig had told his friend that once. Only once.

"You got a haircut and you trimmed your beard. It's just a compliment. You remember what those are, right?"

The man's hand came up, his fingers scratching the whiskers on his face. He shook his head and offered Draig what was an infrequent smile.

"It was time," he replied vaguely, shrugging his shoulders. His hair used to be in dreadlocks that ran all the way down his back. Now it was neatly cut and kept in check with a ponytail.

"Let me guess," Draig offered. "A charter. You need to look presentable for a business deal that you're working on. Am I close?"

The man's smile broadened. "Something like that."

"Permission to come aboard?"

"This early in the morning? It can't be good if I'm seeing you now, Draig."

"If I wasn't around to bring a little excitement into your life, you'd grow bored, Seamus. Even when you're taking a bunch of women who have no business being around you out on the water to drink."

Seamus chuckled at that. "You know me too well, Draig. Although nothing like that today." He sighed. "Unfortunately." He nodded toward the ladder leading up from where the water kissed the stern. "Permission granted."

Draig jumped the gap between the dock and the stern, then pulled himself up the ladder that took him to the main deck of the *Kraken*. Right beneath the cursive script of the boat's name was the name of Seamus' company in bold black letters.

McCracken Expeditions.

"How's business? I didn't expect to see you getting ready to go out when I came by this morning."

"Better than you'd expect for this time of year."

Draig nodded. Then he pointed to the cooler stowed beneath the stern bench. "So what's in there?"

Seamus was about to reply, but then he closed his mouth quickly and gave his friend a sly smile. "Would you believe wine coolers and beer for a bachelorette party?"

"No."

"Wine coolers and beer for a gathering of sorority sisters?"

"No."

"Beer and hard liquor for a fishing charter made up of high-powered business executives with too much money and too much time on their hands?"

"No."

"Well, it doesn't matter what you believe," Seamus said. "If anyone else asks, I'm using one of those three stories." Seamus shrugged. "But I doubt anyone is going to ask. It's quiet this time of year. And it will remain so if I stay under the radar."

Draig nodded. He assumed as much. During the summer, Seamus specialized in deep sea fishing charters and the occasional stag or bachelorette party, emphasis on the bachelorette. However, at this time of year, to make ends meet – and because it was fun for him -- on occasion he made runs up and down the coast, often crossing into Canadian waters.

He argued that he was performing a needed service. He was bringing expensive and rare goods to Teg who couldn't acquire them in any other way.

Draig called it what it was.

Smuggling.

It didn't bother Draig so long as Seamus stayed out of trouble and didn't bring any unwanted attention to Kraken Cove. So far, so good. Because Seamus was a very skilled smuggler.

"Were you here last night?"

"Why do you want to know?"

"Why are you worried that I'm asking?" questioned Draig.

Seamus usually wasn't this squirrelly, so clearly he had been up to something last night. Probably preparing for today's run, which would explain his veiled agitation.

"No reason," Seamus replied quickly -- too quickly in Draig's opinion -- realizing that how he responded had put him in a bad light. "Was I here last night?"

"That was my original question," Draig confirmed.

"I was," Seamus nodded, giving his friend a very broad and very fake smile. "I was working on a few things so that I'd be ready for today."

Draig nodded, expecting as much. "Did you see anything strange? Out of the ordinary?"

Seamus snorted, then laughed softly. "There's always something strange going on in this town, Draig. You know that better than anyone."

"You know what I mean, Seamus. Anything that gave you pause?"

"I was on the *Kraken* most of the night, making a few repairs for today's charter." Seamus shrugged again. "I didn't see anything that worried me. Not really, anyway."

"But?" Draig knew that tone. He had known Seamus for quite a long time. He also understood that he was going to have to work for the information that he wanted, because that's just how his friend was.

"I sensed something."

"Care to explain in more detail?"

"Do I have to?" asked Seamus, almost petulantly. "If I'm going to get back before dark, then I need to leave the harbor soon."

Just as Draig thought. Seamus was heading up to Canada. What he might be transporting, picking up, or exchanging he really didn't want to know. "I'm not going anywhere until you do."

Seamus frowned at him, obviously grouchy. "You know you're bad for business, right?"

"I know."

"Why are we friends anyway? All you do is aggravate me?"

"I didn't kill you when I was supposed to and when the opportunity was there. Because of that, you keep telling me that you're indebted to me."

Draig's eyes flashed, warning his friend that he was losing patience with him. Seamus nodded and then sighed.

"Good point." Seamus concluded that it was better just to tell Draig what he had seen so that his friend would leave and he could get on with his day. If he was going to make his rendezvous in time, then he needed to be out of the cove within the hour. And he still had a lot to do. "I had just finished fixing a faulty valve, and I was having a cup of tea as a reward."

"Tea? Really? That's what we're calling it now?"

Draig knew that Seamus couldn't stand the taste of tea. He needed a stronger drink to sleep at night. Just to take the edge off. Sometimes memories became nightmares if you thought about them too much and nightmares became something more. Something real. Something worse.

"That's what we're calling it, yes," Seamus confirmed with a touch of heat in his voice.

"All right. While you were drinking your tea ..." Draig prodded.

"While I was drinking my tea, I was standing on the stern and enjoying the breeze. I was looking at the woods at the edge of the park, just as those terrors that you call dogs are doing right now."

Seamus nodded toward Butch, Cassidy, and Sundance. The three cockerpoos were searching for any hint of movement coming from that direction, their heads drawn even to a leaf being pushed across the ground by the breeze that was picking up.

"They're not terrors. They're very friendly once you get to know them. And you don't piss them off, of course."

"I've seen what they can do, Draig. They're terrors." Seamus swiped his hand through the air as if to say it wasn't really important. He needed to conclude this conversation so that he could be on his way. "Anyway, back to last night. I was looking at the wood. I sensed movement. It was coming down the trail toward the town, skirting along the border of the copse, then back the way it had come."

"Fast movement?"

"Very fast."

"For how long?"

"No more than a minute. Maybe two at the most. Whatever was in the wood was in and out quickly. Silently as well, but not so silent that I couldn't sense them and hear them. Still, they didn't want to risk being discovered. That much was obvious."

Draig wasn't surprised by what Seamus was telling him. It was just as he thought based on the tracks his dogs had found.

"Are you sure you didn't see anything? You're not holding out on me?"

"Nothing that I thought was worth mentioning until I just saw that expression on your face." Seamus nodded. "You're not going to do that thing that you do with your walking stick, are you? Because if you are, I don't need to be here for that. I'd prefer to be out on the water if you're going to get angry."

"You have nothing to fear, Seamus. Now what was it that you saw?"

"Again, I can't be sure," Seamus hedged.

"Seamus, spit it out or I will do the thing that I can do with my shillelagh that'll make you piss your pants."

"Your what?"

"My shillelagh." Draig waved his walking stick in the air.

"Why do you call it a shillelagh? Why not just call it a walking stick? It would make things simpler all the way around if …"

"Seamus, are you done?"

Seamus stared hard at Draig. This was another look that Seamus was quite familiar with. Painfully so, in fact. And it was telling him to get to the point as fast as he could because Draig was losing patience.

"I didn't really get a good look at anything, Draig. But because I thought that there were shadows moving in the wood, I grabbed a flashlight and shone it in among the trees. Mind you, I never left the boat. So there was only so much to see from here."

"And?"

"Again, I didn't see much."

"But …" Draig motioned with his hand for his friend to get to the heart of the matter fast.

"But I did see a few flashes of yellowish gold. There for just a heartbeat. Then gone just as fast. Several flashes, actually, all in different locations within the wood."

"They didn't leave the wood?"

"No. They stared at me and then moved on. Either they didn't view me as a threat or they didn't have the time to bother with me."

Draig nodded. His theory was gaining more substance. He wasn't pleased by that. He didn't like the path his thoughts were taking him.

"If this happens again, give me a call, all right?"

"Of course," Seamus replied.

"How's the weather for today's run?"

Seamus didn't bother to try to dispute what he was preparing to do. "Smooth sailing so long as I get back before dark."

"Then you better get going," suggested Draig, who turned for the ladder so that he could climb down from the main deck. "You've got a long way to go."

"Care to stay aboard as a deckhand?"

Draig looked up when he reached the bottom of the ladder. "You want me to meet with one of your buyers? Do you really think that's a good idea?"

"Sellers, actually."

Draig nodded. "Why? Usually you don't like it when I get involved in your business dealings. In fact, you just said that I'm bad for business."

"This seller can be difficult. You might be able to distract her so I can negotiate a better deal."

"Why would you say that?" asked Draig, who jumped back across the water to the dock.

"I have a feeling that she would be taken by that sullen ruggedness of yours."

"I don't know if you're insulting me or complimenting me, Seamus."

"Whatever floats your boat, Draig."

Draig smiled at that. If nothing else, interacting with Seamus always was a lively experience. "Tempting, but no. Have fun. Try to stay safe."

Draig walked down the path that tracked the harbor toward the far end. Just a mile farther on the trail came to a stop where the national forest began.

Butch, Cassidy, and Sundance kept with him step for step, although the three cockerpoos stayed on the grass, ensuring that they were always between him and the wood that grew all along the cove.

"You're going to regret it," Seamus called after him. "She really is quite the looker." He then turned away, mumbling under his breath, "When she's not trying to kill you."

Draig waved a hand over his shoulder, not bothering to turn around. He definitely wasn't going to regret it.

He had been on several of Seamus' charters to Canada, usually when his friend was concerned about what might be waiting for him there. Draig had enough to worry about now as it was. He didn't need to take on Seamus' challenges as well.

Besides, his friend could handle himself in a tight spot. He had proven that time and time again.

Draig was about to cut off the trail, taking the staircase that led up the cliff and behind the Safe Haven. He wanted to check with Hestia about last night. She rarely slept, and she was innately aware of everything going on in and around her inn.

He only made it up the first few steps before he stopped, his three cockerpoos growling softly behind him.

He turned, the first of what were becoming many faint wisps of grey drifting in over the harbor and sliding around him. It was not uncommon for a fog to blanket the harbor, although usually at this time of year the worst that they had to deal with were the patches of grey that tended to settle between the many small islands just a mile out from the shore that protected the small bay from the worst of the northeasters that cut up the coast.

Draig stepped back down onto the trail and stood there for several minutes, the mist thickening. Then he walked a little farther to the south. Reaching the breakwater that extended for several hundred yards into the harbor, he stepped carefully out onto the rocks, walking toward the small lighthouse at the far end that was no larger than a buoy.

The dogs didn't follow him, instead turning and keeping their focus on what could come at them from the shore. They seemed to have little concern about where Draig was going, even though he was concerned.

The fog moving into the cove wasn't coming in this direction because of the wind. The gentle breeze should have been pushing the grey mist that was swiftly enveloping the harbor and town back out to sea.

That could mean only one thing.

A Teg was guiding it.

And Draig had a fairly good idea as to who was behind it.

There were few among the Teg who had the strength to do what was happening now. There was one in particular who enjoyed doing this when he wanted to visit here and there without being seen. And when he wanted to show off. Or remind you of the power that he wielded in an obvious way.

As the grey blanket descended, limiting Draig's visibility to no more than a few feet in any direction, he reached for the Grym. Extending his senses around him, he continued down the breakwater, seeing everything around him as if the fog wasn't even there.

The dogs settled on the trail. Nothing would get by them.

That meant that he could focus his full attention on the figure who stepped out from behind the lighthouse and waited for him at the very tip of the breakwater.

It had been a while. But after last night, Draig should have expected this visit.

"You didn't bring those monsters of yours, did you?"

Draig thought the man looked like Bill Gates except with a long beard that ran halfway down his chest. He was wearing corduroy pants and a cardigan sweater underneath an olive Barbour jacket. He covered his wild hair with a Scottish tweed flat cap.

Many people mistook him for a college professor. Those who did, did so at their own peril. Because he was anything but.

"They're waiting on the trail. They had just as much desire to see you as you do to see them."

"You need to be careful of those three. Vicious animals. They'll turn on you in a second."

"They're just protective. Sometimes they see threats that I might miss. Threats that I should see but I don't because against my better judgment I trust them."

Merlin's expression hardened, not missing the not-so-subtle dig. "That wasn't my fault."

"It never is, is it?"

Merlin glared at Draig, then snorted more in resignation than humor. There was really no point in getting into a battle of wills. He hadn't been able to cow Draig since he was a child, and even then his attempts rarely worked.

Merlin had learned much to his detriment that Draig wasn't afraid of anything. One of his most admirable traits, in the old man's opinion, and also one of his greatest weaknesses. A belief with which Draig likely would agree.

"That's not fair," Merlin replied.

"As you told me long ago, Merlin, the world isn't fair," Draig replied. "The sooner I learned that, the better. So what's on your mind?" His friend, mentor, and sometime reluctant adversary didn't look any different than the last time he saw him, and that had been more than a decade before.

"It's been a while," Merlin said with a shrug of his shoulders and a small grin. "I wanted to check in. See how you were doing."

"You wanted to check in because of what happened in Williamsburg," Draig corrected. He should have assumed that this visit was coming, but he had allowed his worries to distract him.

"You're right." Merlin understood that trying to deny that fact was a waste of time and would only sour the mood between them, which was tenuous to begin with.

"Well, I'm sure you already know what happened in Williamsburg. So there's not much for us to discuss."

"You don't have to be difficult, Axel."

"Draig."

"I will always call you Axel. You know that."

"I wish you wouldn't, Merlin."

"I've known you too long to change now."

"You just do it to keep me on my toes."

"Maybe."

"It's not a maybe," Draig replied, a small smile breaking out on his usually grim visage. In only minutes they had both returned to the banter that had been so much a part of their relationship in the past. Before all the trouble. "You don't do anything unless you do it for a reason, Merlin."

"That's a bit of a harsh statement."

"A true statement, however."

"Maybe," Merlin shrugged again, not wanting to admit to Draig's claim.

"You're here because of what happened in Williamsburg and who decided to visit with me."

"I'm here because I wanted to see you. It's been too long."

"You're here because you know why the Daemons came after me."

"Maybe," Merlin replied noncommittally, shrugging again.

"You know who stole the artifact."

"Maybe."

"Then what do you want from me? Because you know that I didn't."

"Why would you ask that question? Can't I just visit with a young man I've known since he was born?"

"Because I know you, Merlin." The old man was about to protest his innocence. Draig didn't give him the chance to do that. "Every time I see you, you want something."

"I don't want something from you. I just wanted to see how you were."

"And ..." Draig prodded.

"And to satisfy my curiosity."

Draig stared at Merlin, the wisps of grey playing between them. Then he smiled, giving the old man the shit-eating grin that never failed to irritate him. "You think I took it. That's why you're here."

"That thought had crossed my mind," Merlin admitted, his eyes sparking with an almost unrestrained power that would have frightened most any other Teg. Not Draig, of course. He had experienced Merlin at his worst, and he had survived.

"Why would you think that I would take the artifact? I was the one who put it in the Vault in the first place."

"Which means that you know how to retrieve it with a minimum of fuss." Merlin grunted, then pulled his hands from his coat pockets, rubbing them together. Draig translated the habit as a sign that his friend and mentor was getting agitated. "I'm not accusing you of anything. I'm simply stating the obvious. That's all."

"You know I don't want to return to that world, Merlin. You know what it cost me to ..." Draig closed his eyes, an impish smile curling his lips. "You think that I want to use the artifact to challenge my father."

Merlin shrugged, his most common method for communicating when he was trying to put forward an air of disinterest. "The thought had crossed my mind."

Draig laughed softly, shaking his head in amusement. "I thought you knew me better than that, Merlin. You should know me better than that."

"I just wanted to check. There's nothing wrong with that, is there?"

"Did you come here because of your own curiosity or that of my father?"

"My own, of course," Merlin supplied quickly. "You know, he still wants Excalibur returned to him."

"I thought he thought I was dead, Merlin," Draig said in a frigid voice. He had been living with that belief for quite some time now. If that was no longer true, then he needed to think about making some unwanted but necessary changes. Swiftly. He couldn't afford to be caught by surprise.

"Your father can be blind at times, but he's not stupid, Draig. I haven't said anything to him, and we haven't spoken about it, but I have no doubt that he knows that you're still alive. Even if he doesn't want to admit that to himself."

"That's really not something I wanted to hear this morning, Merlin. Does he know that you're here?"

"No, he doesn't," Merlin replied, slightly insulted by Draig's question, "and he wouldn't be able to find me even if he wanted to. Besides, do you know how many times I've put him off your scent? He's been looking for you under the radar ever since he convinced himself that you survived the combat."

"Why did you do that? Why expend that effort to keep me safe from him?"

"Because against my better judgment, Axel, I still see something in you," explained Merlin with more fire in his voice, that heat revealing the person beneath the staid image he was presenting. "I still believe that you have a larger role to play. A larger role you must play. It's the only way."

"This again. Even after all this time." Draig kept himself from shouting, though it was a challenge. Even with the fog, his voice could still carry. He didn't need someone like Seamus listening in on this conversation inadvertently. "I'm done, Merlin. My decision stands. I've had enough."

"Yes, this again," Merlin hissed in exasperation. "Have you ever thought, just once, that perhaps the Teg aren't done with you yet?" Merlin stepped in close, placing a surprisingly strong hand on Draig's shoulder. "We need you, Axel. You can't escape that truth no matter how hard you try."

"Don't call me, Axel," Draig grated, shrugging Merlin's hand off his shoulder, his eyes beginning to blaze with the fire that was never far from the surface. Merlin took a step back as a result, understanding that the power that Draig wielded in many ways matched his own and not wanting to get into a contest of wills at the very end of a breakwater. "Only Lilliana can call me Axel. Only her."

"Now you're just being childish. Stop thinking about what happened and start thinking about what could be. The past doesn't matter. Only the future. And the future is grim if you don't step up."

"You told me when I was growing up that the past always mattered, Merlin," Draig said in a quiet voice, working hard to keep his rising anger in check. "You said that the past was our connection to the present and would provide us a glimpse of the future."

"You're right, lad, I did tell you that," Merlin admitted, "and I still stand by that. Because if you don't come out of your self-imposed retirement, the past is going to repeat itself."

"That's someone else's problem, Merlin. That was made abundantly clear when my father tried to kill me."

"Axel, I understand why you did what you did. I understand why you're angry. But we need you. The Teg need you. Your father needs you even though he's too blind to see it."

"My father doesn't need anyone, Merlin. He's made that abundantly clear as well. He needs only himself."

"I'm asking you to be the bigger man, Axel. You know your father can't do that. But you can. Events are moving in a direction that I hadn't expected. A dangerous direction. We're at the tipping point. Once we slide over, there's no chance to make the world as it was."

"Events are always moving in a direction that you don't

expect, Merlin. You've been telling me that ever since I was a child."

Merlin shook his head in frustration. Why couldn't the lad just listen to him? Life would be so much easier for everyone if he did.

But he already knew the answer to his question. In many ways, Axel was just like his father. Stubborn. Implacable. Not someone easily persuaded.

"Well, one thing hasn't changed since I saw you last."

"What would that be?" Draig asked, although he really wasn't curious about the answer. His thoughts had moved down a different path.

"You're still a pain in the ass."

"Much in the world changes, Merlin. Much doesn't. You know that. In fact, you're the person who taught me that."

"And a smart ass," Merlin grumped.

"I do my best," Draig replied, his shit-eating grin back in place.

"Which in this moment isn't good enough." Merlin gripped Draig's arm tightly. "This isn't arrogance, Axel. I came here to warn you. I'm here because our world is moving down a road from which it may never recover. Please, just think about what I said. That's all I ask."

For several seconds, Draig stared at Merlin, his expression cold. Then he nodded.

"Thank you," Merlin sighed as he stepped back. "And be careful. Please. You've vanquished anyone who has challenged you. Yet this threat who comes our way ... this threat, not even I can defeat."

5

CINNAMON ROLLS

The wonderful smells that drifted down the street never failed to make Draig smile, his grave countenance fading for a few seconds as thoughts of his mother danced through his mind.

Tia's Bakes.

That's what he had named the shop that was just a door down from the bookstore he owned, his pub right next to that. Bagels and scones, rolls and breads, freshly made cream cheese, different types of coffee and shakes, fruit and protein. Gluten free and vegan options.

He owned the bakery. The recipes belonged to his mother.

He hadn't met his mother until he was older. They had both struggled to connect when they finally came together. Not because they didn't want to. But rather because they didn't know how to.

He had bonded with his mother while baking with her when he visited her at her home in the mountains. At first, he didn't want to bake. He wanted to keep exploring the peaks even after the sun had dropped beneath the horizon.

She had convinced him to give it a try. Then he had discovered that he enjoyed it. The baking, yes, and even more so the opportunity to spend time with the woman he had barely known while growing up.

They had learned a great deal about one another. While mixing, rolling, and proofing, they talked and it helped to give them some peace during what had been a turbulent time for them both. It had also set the foundation for their relationship, which only had grown stronger.

That's why he was headed toward his shop. He always felt calmer when he was rolling out some dough. In a better position to think. His focus on the dough allowed his mind to drift, which helped him to work through the challenges that plagued him.

Which was a good thing, because at the moment, he was worried. Very worried.

The last few years had been relatively calm, that calm shattered in just a matter of days.

The beasts that had made the tracks in the wood weren't an immediate concern since they had left the area. But they'd be back. Of that, he had no doubt.

The conversation with Seamus had played out as he had expected. Seamus was a cranky sort, so any engagement with him tended to be difficult.

But that was just Seamus. He liked being difficult. And despite being difficult, he had proven useful, confirming what Draig already had surmised.

It was the conversation with Merlin that weighed on him most heavily.

"Yet this threat who comes our way ... this threat, not even I can defeat."

Ominous, even for Merlin, who liked to play up the drama any chance he got.

What threat was coming his way? And what possible threat could have any chance of defeating Merlin?

The Sorcerer was one of the strongest of the Tylwyth Teg. Perhaps even the strongest.

Few, if any, could challenge him in the use of the Grym.

"Head up, Draig, before you run someone over."

Draig looked up sheepishly, realizing that he had been reaching for the door to his bakery at the same time that one of his friends was leaving.

"Sorry, Brigid." Draig stepped out of the way, holding the door for her.

"Lost in thought again?"

"My apologies. Unfortunately, yes. Lost in thought."

"Well, that's never a good sign," said the attractive woman whose head barely reached his chest. She was wearing overalls, her hair wrapped in a kerchief and an eyepatch hanging around her neck.

"What do you mean?" asked Draig, slightly confused. He assumed that the bag she was carrying contained the blueberry and lemon scones that she liked so much.

"You know exactly what I mean," Brigid replied, giving him a light punch on the arm, almost as if she was trying to wake him up from wherever his worries had taken him. "When you're distracted like this, it usually means there's a problem. That's never a good thing. I know that just as well as you do."

"It's not always a problem," he protested, although not very strongly because he couldn't deny the truth in her words.

"Really?" Brigid asked, her tone making clear that she disagreed with him. She nodded her head, an amused smile creasing her lips. "You were much the same right before you learned what those Paladins were up to. The ones who thought they could eliminate most of the vampires in North America through a single play."

"The tainted blood," Draig murmured, remembering.

That had occurred several decades before. Brigid had played an instrumental role in helping him to stop that plot.

And his efforts on behalf of the vampires had earned him the trust of most of the covens. So much so that they now shared information when that information proved useful to both.

"Yes, you were just like this, off in your own little world."

"That was just one time."

"And then when the fire giants got into it with the frost giants."

"That was a bit of a dilemma," Draig admitted. "Giants do like to hold grudges."

There were several different types of giants in the world. They tended to get along, until they didn't. Usually, the bad blood resulted from a territorial dispute.

With global warming, the boundaries between the fire giants and the frost giants, usually so distinct in the past, were becoming less so. In many places the boundaries were disappearing entirely. Thus, more conflicts. It was inevitable. It was also dangerous.

Draig had no choice but to step into the middle of that disagreement. Otherwise, several volcanos long thought dormant would have blown, all at the same time, all of them in high population areas.

"It was," Brigid agreed. "It was also exciting. I haven't had so much fun in years."

Draig chuckled. "You have a strange definition of fun, what with the end of the world a very real possibility if we didn't get the fire giants and frost giants to play nicely together."

"I have a strange definition for a lot of things," Brigid admitted. "And then there was the time those Warlocks ..."

Draig held up his hands in surrender. "All right, all right. You've made your point."

"I usually do, don't I."

"You do. Quite emphatically."

"So you *are* dealing with some new challenges," Brigid said, pleased to confirm what she suspected.

"Not dealing with, just worrying over some *possible* challenges," Draig explained.

Brigid nodded again, not taken in by his attempt at nuance, glad that she finally had gotten to the heart of the matter. "If you need any assistance, you know where to find me. I've been getting bored lately. I'm in need of some excitement."

"If there's a chance that the world as we know it is going to end, you'll be the first person I call."

"I certainly hope so. I wouldn't want to miss it."

Draig nodded toward what Brigid was wearing. "What are you working on now?" He could tell that she had started a new piece. She was always in a good mood when she did.

"A metal sculpture. I started it late last night. Finally, I was hit with some inspiration." She sighed. "You know how that goes. When it comes, you've got to go with it. Otherwise, it's like the wind. Slips right through your fingers."

"I do," Draig admitted. He had watched Brigid many times, at all hours of the day and night, once for a stretch of thirty-eight hours straight. She was an artist who didn't stop until she was done, because if she did, she risked losing her inspiration somewhere along the way. "What's this piece going to be?"

"Poseidon parting the waters with his trident," Brigid replied with a wicked grin.

Draig gave her a look that only made her grin even wider. "I thought that after what he tried to do to you that you hated Poseidon?"

"I do hate Poseidon," Brigid replied. "He's a scummy bastard. If I had the chance, I'd take that trident of his and stick it right up his ass." She gave Draig a wink. "I'm putting my own twist on this piece. A twist that he deserves."

Draig chuckled softly. He could tell by the roguish gleam in Brigid's eyes that Poseidon definitely wasn't going to like what she came up with. "I'm looking forward to the finished product."

"You'll have to wait. A few weeks most likely. I got the basics down last night. I'll finish the frame later today. Then I'll move on to the more intricate work. The much more revealing work, if you catch my meaning. I'm going to take my time with that. Make sure that no one can miss the message I'm sending."

"Is this something that's going to become another problem?" asked Draig. He had a few too many concerns already this morning. "I don't want to censor your artistic license, but if you really piss off Poseidon ..." He left the rest unsaid.

Brigid knew where Draig was headed. The last time she had done this, her fool of an angry lover challenged Draig to a duel, thinking that he was the reason that she had broken up with him.

It hadn't been the reason.

Yes, she was attracted to Draig.

How couldn't she be?

There was a hidden fire within him that she had to work hard to resist. But it was also because of that hidden fire that she knew she needed to stay away from him, at least from a romantic perspective.

She had warned Narky that he was making a very serious mistake. He had ignored her, feeling the need to defend his honor no matter the cost. Until Narcissus realized exactly who it was he was challenging.

Thinking back on that, she felt a twinge of disappointment. That would have been a fun combat to watch. Quick, yes, of that she was certain, but still fun to watch.

Returning to the ex in question, she responded. "With that god's ego, he won't see what's really there, Draig. You have nothing to worry about. He'll only see what he wants to see."

Draig nodded. Brigid probably was right. "And if he does see what he's intended to see?"

"Then what's he going to do? The last time he tried to challenge you ..."

"All right, all right. We don't need to take a walk down memory lane."

"But Draig, that was so much fun. Just think of what ..."

"I'd rather not," Draig replied. He grimaced inside, having heard much the same before. Just another worry to add to the rest. "I really don't want to get involved again. Doing so defeats the purpose of why we're here."

Brigid was doing it again. He knew what that meant.

She was between boyfriends. Or girlfriends. It was hard to know because she went through her lovers so quickly. She fell in love at first sight, but her desire disappeared swiftly, much like a burning match, more interested in the heat of the initial strike than the enduring flame.

Brigid was looking for something unique in her relationships. Something that none of her former lovers had been able to give her.

Draig wasn't even sure if she could tell him what it was that she was searching for if he asked her. And he certainly wasn't going to ask her.

Just as she burned hot, she could also be quite testy. And she did work with a blowtorch quite a bit, so better to steer clear.

All he could do was hope that when Brigid was done with her piece, Poseidon proved to be just as clueless as he had been when he had started up his affair with her. If he challenged her on it, he'd find out very quickly that Brigid was much more than just a pretty face.

"All right, all right," grumbled Brigid. "I'll tone it down or mask it even more than I was going to or figure out some other way to get my point across."

"Thank you." Draig gave Brigid one of his rare smiles. "I do appreciate it."

"I know you do," Brigid said, returning his smile. He assumed because she was already thinking about how she would refine the piece. In addition to growing bored swiftly, she did like a challenge. “But I’m only doing this because it’s you. I wouldn’t do it for anyone else.”

“I know, Brigid. Again, thank you.”

She turned to go, then just as quickly turned back. “I almost forgot. Even though I’ll be busy for much of the day, do come by later this afternoon or tomorrow morning. I have those garden ornaments that you requested.”

“Excellent. Any problems?”

“No, nothing that I couldn’t handle. They all came out exactly as I wanted. Just one more coating after lunch today and they’ll be good to go.”

“I’ll come by tomorrow. My day is getting busier than I anticipated.”

“I’ll see you then.” At least that’s what Draig thought Brigid had said. It was difficult to tell. She couldn’t wait any longer, taking a bite out of one of the scones, her chewing muffling her words.

Giving Brigid a wave, he walked into Tia’s Bakes. Before he even closed the door behind him, he spun around.

A flash of movement from across the town green made him frown. Whoever it was already had turned the corner, the church now blocking his view. For just a second, he thought he had glimpsed a man wearing a well-cut suit. Not strange in and of itself if someone was in town for business. It was the fedora on his head that caught his eye.

A fedora was a rare thing these days. Most of the people walking the streets of Kraken Cove wore baseball caps or knit caps, depending on the time of year.

It couldn’t be, could it?

Draig shook his head in resignation as he closed the door. With the way that his day had begun, why couldn’t it?

He nodded to many of the people seated at the tables and waiting in line, friends with all of them, stopping to talk with several before moving on. Draig still didn't know what to make of the somewhat surreal experience, so many of the Teg not cringing, or running away from him, in fear.

Before he made the decision to break away from his past and moved to Kraken Cove, he was a man who no one ever wanted to come face to face with. Just the mention of his name terrified most of the Teg. Because they knew that there was only one possible reason as to why he had come calling. A very final, irreversible reason.

But here, in this small town on the Maine coast, he felt at home, as if he belonged here. And, although he thought it would never be possible, the Teg living here accepted him. They didn't fear him, either having forgiven or, barring that, made peace with his past and what was demanded of him by his father when he was younger.

He might make some of the Teg nervous from time to time. Teg had long memories after all. Still, as the years passed, he had become more a part of the community, something that he had never thought would be possible.

Having finally reached the display cases, he walked around the counter and passed by the woman taking orders at the register.

"You could have showered," she murmured, wrinkling her nose as she said it.

"Sorry, didn't get the chance," replied Draig.

Cerridwen stared over her shoulder at him. Then she smiled and chuckled softly. This was so like Draig. She could tell that he was distracted, and she knew what he planned to do so that he could work over whatever it was that was stuck in the back of his brain.

"Then stay in the back. I don't want your stench scaring away any of our customers."

"As you command, my lady," Draig replied with a smile of

his own, his response, which earned a stuck-out tongue from Cerridwen, not entirely a joke.

Before he pushed his way through the swinging door that led to the kitchen, he looked around the bakery. What he saw sent a wave of satisfaction through him. Every seat was taken, the counter was full, and the line to order was almost to the door.

Business was good. Even better, he didn't see any men in the shop wearing a sharply cut suit, a crisp white shirt, and a fedora.

Maybe he had been imagining it. Then again, maybe not.

Draig pulled an apron from the pegs by the back door.

"Argue if you dare." Cerridwen read silently the words on the front of his apron as she walked into the kitchen and watched him loop the tie over his head. "Problems, Draig?"

"No, nothing to be concerned about."

"You mean not yet," Cerridwen corrected, ignoring the irritated glance that he gave her. She could tell quite easily that he wasn't telling her everything.

"There's nothing to be concerned about," repeated Draig.

"Then why are you baking?"

Draig shrugged his shoulders. "Because I like to bake. It's very relaxing."

"Draig ..." Cerridwen's tone suggested that she was done with his dissembling.

"All right, there's nothing to be concerned about. Yet."

"That's better," replied Cerridwen. She pulled up a stool and sat down across the table from where Draig stood. "You'll tell me when I need to know something? Yes?"

"Of course," Draig replied quickly. Probably too quickly based on the expression Cerridwen gave him.

"Draig?" Cerridwen challenged.

"Yes, I will tell you when you need to know. But first I need to know."

"You're not sure what's going on?"

"Only bits and pieces," Draig replied, sighing in frustration. "That's all I have right now. Once I've got a better picture of it all, you'll be the first to know."

"Sounds like you're back at work. Never being told the full story. Having to figure it all out on your own."

"Better this than that," Draig countered. "At least I have some control now."

"I won't argue with you about that," Cerridwen replied, then nodded toward the apron that Draig was wearing. He looked down, then couldn't help but smile. She was quick. That's why he liked spending time with her. Her wit kept him smiling and on his toes. "What were you going to make as you start putting the pieces of this puzzle together?"

"Since you think you know me so well, why don't you tell me."

"I've got a hankering for some cinnamon rolls."

"As do I," admitted Draig with a quiet laugh. Apparently Cerridwen really did know him.

"Gluten free?"

"Of course," confirmed Draig.

"Good." Cerridwen nodded in appreciation. "Sounds delicious."

"I had a feeling that you'd want them."

"Why would you say that?"

"Because they're your favorite," Draig said. "You know me, I know you."

"Fair enough," laughed Cerridwen, pleased that she made Draig smile as he started pulling out measuring cups and a rolling pin from beneath the table. "I was speaking with Hestia this morning, getting her order for tomorrow."

"How's Hestia doing?" asked Draig. "I went by this morning to talk with her about something but she had gone out for her walk."

"About what's worrying you?"

Draig's first instinct was to answer in the negative, but he realized that would be wasted effort. Cerridwen did indeed know him much too well. "Yes. I was hoping she might be able to provide me with some information."

"Maybe I can do that."

"How so?" asked Draig, not understanding.

"I must have caught her when she came back from her walk."

"And?"

"And what?"

Draig tapped the rolling pin lightly on the counter. "You know what. You're just doing this to get back at me."

Cerridwen laughed, enjoying the give and take with Draig. "You're right. You know me just as well as I know you."

Draig waited, then motioned with his free hand, still tapping the pin on the counter. "And?"

"And what?" asked Cerridwen innocently.

"Really? This is how we're going to be this morning?"

Cerridwen laughed again. "Sorry, I couldn't resist. Getting under your skin is much too easy."

"And much too fun," Draig sighed in exasperation.

"That too," Cerridwen agreed. "A new guest arrived late last night."

"And that's important because ..." There were always new guests arriving at the Safe Haven.

"This new guest is one of us."

"She's one of the Tylwyth Teg?"

"She is," Cerridwen confirmed, "and from what Hestia said, quite powerful in the Grym."

That caught Draig's attention. He stopped tapping with the rolling pin, his expression becoming pensive. "When did she arrive?"

"Last night," Cerridwen replied. "I told you that."

Draig tried not to allow his irritation to show, knowing that if he did, Cerridwen would continue to make this conversation more difficult for him than it needed to be. "Do you know what time specifically? It might be important."

"Around midnight. Maybe a little after from what Hestia said. Why?"

Draig nodded, thinking, not really sure if the arrival of a Teg at that time, even one strong in the Grym, was important or even relevant. Of course, he couldn't rule out that it wasn't. That there wasn't the possibility of a connection.

The tracks weren't too far from the Safe Haven. Based on how he read them, and what Seamus had said, the beasts deciding to scout Kraken Cove could be connected to this Teg, particularly if these beasts were hunting for her.

"Just curious, that's all. You know I like to know what's going on in Kraken Cove."

"Right," Cerridwen said, not believing that was the only reason for his interest. She let it go, nonetheless. "You look more worried than when you came back into your favorite place to get away."

"I'm just trying to remember the recipe," Draig replied with a big grin that earned a snort of annoyance from Cerridwen. The pieces that were flitting about in his head were becoming larger in number, and he still had no idea how to complete the puzzle.

"Draig, we've known each other a long time."

"That we have."

"You do realize that I know when you're full of it."

Draig's smiled broadened. "I know."

"And still you're going to be difficult?"

"I'm not being difficult. I just don't have anything to share yet."

Cerridwen stared at Draig for quite some time. He tried to look as innocent as possible and assumed that he was failing miserably. Still, he kept at it, refusing to break. Even so, he was glad when Cerridwen let him off the hook … for now.

"You'll tell me when you're ready?"

"I'll tell you when I'm ready," Draig promised. After tightening the straps across the back of his apron, he walked toward the shelves on the other side of the kitchen, turning on three of the commercial ovens along the way.

The movement, the doing, helped him.

He was feeling a stress that he hadn't experienced in quite some time. Not even when he was fighting the Daemons in Williamsburg.

That clash had been relaxing. It allowed him to release some of his suppressed energy. But now the stress was building.

And with good reason, he believed. He had a lot on his mind.

Who had taken the artifact? Who had the artifact now? What were they going to do with it? Were the beasts who left the tracks in the wood here because of the artifact and him or because of the Teg who had shown up late the night before? Was this series of events going to bring in other players who could put at risk all that he had built in Kraken Cove?

He didn't know, but he really wanted to find out. And as swiftly as possible.

Another question popped into his mind. It was probably the most important question of all the ones bouncing around in his head at that moment.

How was he supposed to find the answers that he needed?

"Do, don't just think. That's how to answer the hard questions."

His mother had taught him that. Many times. And she had been right.

Staring off into the distance, thinking about how to solve a problem, usually didn't lead to a good solution. To any solution, in fact. But doing something else, allowing your mind to wander on its own, often did. Hopefully that would be the case now.

Draig grabbed a bin and started filling it with some of the ingredients that he would need, pulling it all out from the cupboard and the industrial refrigerator next to it. Gluten-free flour. Salt. Sugar. Lactose-free milk. Butter. Eggs. Yeast. Gluten-free baking powder.

"Nuts?" Draig asked over his shoulder.

"No nuts. Not for Hestia." Cerridwen pushed herself up from her stool and walked toward the swinging door. "I'll leave you be. Just remember that I'll need four dozen."

"Four dozen cinnamon rolls! Are you serious? That'll take most of the morning."

"Do you have anything better to do?"

"Well, no, not at the moment, but I ..."

"Then four dozen. Hestia wants a dozen for the Safe Haven tomorrow morning, and we just got an order for a dozen from the fire station. What's left will be sold before the early afternoon once word spreads that you're in the kitchen."

"Fine," Draig grumbled. "Four dozen it is."

As he started measuring out the flour and the baking powder, then the salt and sugar, his mind began to drift, just as he wanted it to. Thinking about the Daemons. The artifact. The thief. Perhaps the thief behind the thief. The tracks and what made them. This new Teg.

Draig could feel the trouble brewing, the hair on his arms standing on end, and he had no doubt that it was only going to get worse.

Because it always got worse when Merlin decided to stop by.

6

SMELLS LIKE HOME

Melissa walked down Market Street, the main drag that connected the Safe Haven to the center of the town. Diagonal parking spaces lined both sides of the two-lane road. At this time of the morning, the bulk of the traffic centered on the bakery that was just a few storefronts down from where she was standing.

Tia's Bakes.

The smell of freshly baked goods wafting down the street made her mouth water. She ignored her grumbling stomach, her attention focused on the Book Nook.

She had another hour to kill before the store opened.

She liked the look of the Book Nook. It was an independent bookstore, and from what she could see, it had a good bit of history to it.

Peeking in the storefront window, she could see that the old wooden shelves ran all the way into the shadows that hid the back of the store. There were wheeled ladders on both sides of the shop, the bookcases extending up to a second story.

If you braved the ladder, you could step onto the walkway

that curled around the shop or you could continue climbing to the third level.

Even more impressive, in the very center of the shop, there were two wooden circular staircases that also allowed access to the floors above. They resembled two snakes curling around one another. It made her think of the Caduceus. A symbol associated with Hermes, not only a messenger of the gods but also the patron of commerce.

She couldn't wait to get inside, the design and the many eclectic titles teasing her through the window.

There wasn't a current *New York Times* bestseller to be seen, which was exactly how she liked it. There were several books that she hadn't read since she was in school and a few that she had always wanted to read but had never been able to find.

She was familiar with *Mages of the Past*, *Witches of Salem: The True Story from a Survivor*, and *Runes for Beginners*. She had never gotten around to *Arthur and Charlemagne: Friends and Rivals?* or *Mythology: Timeless Tales of Gods and Heroes*.

But *Circe's Complete Book of Witchcraft*?

That was out of print. It had been for centuries.

How had that text found its way to this shop in a quiet town on the Maine coast?

Seeing that book gave Melissa hope that she would find what she needed here. Because she was getting even more anxious.

If she couldn't locate the text that she was looking for in the Book Nook, she didn't know where else to search for it. In fact, she didn't think that there was anywhere else to look.

Her eyes sparkling with delight and just a hint of worry, Melissa walked down toward the bakery. Food first, then the bookstore.

She had already explored much of the town. It hadn't taken her long.

And she had enjoyed the experience. She liked the feel of Kraken Cove along with the look of it.

All of the stores were well maintained. A good number of modern designs were mixed in with the Victorian homes, though nothing that would ruin the aesthetics of the coastal enclave.

A large gazebo sat in the center of the town green, which was anchored on the north by a church, its steeple reaching for the sky. From where she was standing she couldn't tell which denomination the church served.

The fire and police stations were directly opposite the church.

The street she was walking on served as the western border of the green. On the far side were the cliffs, a fenced trail along the ledge leading down to the harbor and the beach a hundred feet below.

It resembled many of the other New England towns that she had visited. Although Kraken Cove was unique in several respects compared to those others.

There was a strange though stimulating undercurrent here that made her skin tingle, and not in an unpleasant way.

She corrected herself quickly as she thought about that faint buzz of electricity that was teasing her. Studying that power a bit more closely, she realized that it wasn't really a strange energy.

It was only strange because it was rare to find such a strong and welcome concentration of power like this in any town or city in the world.

The power that flowed through Kraken Cove was familiar to her. Very familiar. She hadn't experienced it for quite some time, and she realized that she had missed it.

This little town made her feel like she was home. Like she was supposed to be here.

It seemed that her mother was right, which irritated Melissa just a little bit. A remnant of her time as a teenager.

Kraken Cove was a place where she wouldn't stand out. She fit in here.

Hopefully this also was the place where she could find what she needed.

She was about to pull open the door to Tia's Bakes when Melissa stopped abruptly on the street. Cursing her ineptness, she forced herself to start moving again.

She reached again for the door handle, but then stepped back quickly. She allowed a gaggle of twenty-somethings to scramble out of the store, coffees and bags of goodies in hand, all of them obviously in a rush to get to work.

She knew better than to reveal herself in such a way. Still, she had given in to the urge.

She had acted just like a novice. Completely forgetting her tradecraft.

The hair on the back of her neck had prickled when she approached the bakery. Just as it always did when she sensed that someone was watching her.

Maybe it was because of where she was. The energy coursing through Kraken Cove lulling her into a false sense of security.

Before she stepped into the bake shop, she glanced behind her swiftly, then studied the reflection in the front window.

She didn't see anyone who gave her any cause for concern.

Her failure irritated her to no end.

She was better than this. She was alive because she hadn't been caught out like this since her mother had started training her.

Melissa didn't know if she was more angry with the fact that she had screwed up or because she had failed to identify her watcher. If she was honest with herself, it was probably a mixture of both.

Closing her eyes for just a moment, she pictured her mother standing in front of her, her usually gentle face marred by an angry expression.

Melissa had made a very similar mistake when her mother decided that she was ready to join the family business. A mistake that she hadn't made since her first day of instruction.

Her mother had expected more from her than she had expected from herself.

She had hated that face when she was a child. Her mother's look of profound disappointment. She valued it now.

"Staying alive means staying aware" was all that her mother had said.

She had taken that message to heart, and doing so had served her well over the years.

Melissa needed to stop focusing on what felt right about Kraken Cove and instead concentrate on what didn't.

That was the first step. Because she wouldn't be able to forgive herself for quite some time for missing the watcher. If she ever did.

Her mistake and failure irritating her, she promised herself that she would find him or her or them.

And she kept her promises.

The smells that assaulted her when she walked toward the counter helped her to release her anger, if only for a time. She had overslept because she had been on the go during the last few days and Hestia had been true to her word.

The owner of the Safe Haven had put the breakfast away at eight sharp. When Melissa had come down to the dining area ten minutes after that, Hestia had sent her to the bakery. The challenge now was to decide what to get, because everything smelled delicious.

"What can I help you with, love?"

Melissa smiled. The woman staffing the counter had a

slight British accent, which was likely the cause of her word choice.

She was very attractive, almost in an otherworldly way that Melissa found quite arresting. The best way to describe her was pixielike, petite, entrancing.

Yet there was something about the woman that put Melissa slightly on guard as well. Just behind the woman's eyes was a wariness that suggested to Melissa that she was more than what she appeared to be.

"What would you recommend? Everything in here smells and looks wonderful."

"Anything you buy you're going to like, love. I promise you that. But, I can sense that you have a very particular taste."

Melissa's natural caution immediately reared its head. "How so?"

"Just a knack I have after running the bakery for so long."

Cerridwen stared at Melissa for several seconds. Staring back, Melissa couldn't figure out the color of the woman's eyes. It almost seemed as if she was looking at a kaleidoscope, the colors always changing. Intriguing. Unsettling as well. She was glad when Cerridwen told her what she wanted.

"Cinnamon rolls would be my guess. They're freshly made."

Melissa smiled. "You have quite a talent."

"Not really," the woman replied with a short and sharp laugh. "Draig's cinnamon rolls are a favorite of everyone in town. So they're usually a safe bet for anyone visiting us for the first time." The woman raised a finger, as if she had just figured out something else about her. "But with you there's more than just a sweet tooth. Am I right?"

"You can tell that with just a glance?" Melissa asked a bit nervously.

"I can tell quite a lot with just a glance, love," the woman replied, giving her a knowing look. "I see as well that you're a bit more traditional than some."

"How do you mean?"

Melissa couldn't pull her eyes free from those of the woman standing across the counter from her, her nerves beginning to tingle. She didn't know if the woman was referring to her favorite baked goods or something of a more personal nature.

She had sensed the power in the woman when she walked in. That in itself hadn't made her uncomfortable. What made her uncomfortable was just how strong the woman seemed to be. Almost on a par with her mother.

"The scones, love," the woman replied with a laugh, clearly trying to make Melissa feel more comfortable, sensing her unease. "I get the feeling those would be to your liking as well."

"You could tell all that with just a glance?"

"A talent of mine as I said. Would you like a taste? The scones are to die for."

The woman's turn of phrase made Melissa's breath catch. "Sure, sounds good. And the cinnamon roll as well if you don't mind. If they're the town favorite after all ..."

The woman smiled then slid two small plates toward her. She took a small piece from each. The cinnamon roll first. Both of the pastries tasted just as good as they smelled.

Melissa's face scrunched up in thought, a habit when there was a puzzle for her to solve. A habit that her mother had tried to break in her.

Habits were predictable. They could get you killed.

Her mother hadn't wanted her daughter to give anything away because of a habit. Nevertheless, this mannerism had stuck with her despite Melissa's best efforts to eliminate it.

The scone. What was it about the scone?

Her eyes widened when she figured it out.

Melissa looked at the woman behind the counter with a more careful eye. Her smile changed just as Melissa's expression did.

The baker knew what Melissa had just concluded. Rather

than being worried or angry at her discovery, the woman actually appeared to be pleased.

Melissa was certain. There wasn't a hint of doubt in her.

The woman was a Witch. Perhaps even a Sorceress. She mixed the Grym into her pastries.

"You can tell," Cerridwen said, nodding ever so slightly with approval. "That's well done. Most Teg can't after just a single bite."

Melissa realized from her brief taste that she had nothing to fear from the Grym infused within the scone. She had analyzed the properties of that tiny amount of power and determined how it was used. Rather than being upset, she was curious instead.

"That's really quite impressive what you're doing with the Grym. If I'm not mistaken, the power is latent until one of the Teg takes a bite."

"Correct."

"So it doesn't affect anyone not of the Teg."

"Correct again." The woman on the other side of the counter clearly was enjoying the interrogation.

"It works differently with each Teg who takes a bite."

"Yes, it's designed to affect each Teg in a specific way because each Teg is distinct," the woman confirmed, her smile broadening as Melissa worked out the details of what the baker was doing on her own.

"It's like taking a natural supplement. The tiny amount of the Grym adjusts to what the person needs whether they know it or not."

"Right again," confirmed the woman, her eyes, Melissa still unable to determine their actual color, sparkling with delight. "The Grym reads the person eating the pastry or the scone or whatever baked item they purchase. It then gives them whatever they might need. If the Teg isn't in the right place mentally, the Grym helps give them a little boost in that department. If the Teg is experiencing some aches and pains, the Grym helps ease what's ailing them. And so it goes. A personalized prescription to help them get through the day if indeed they have such a need for assistance."

"A cure all." Melissa said it with delight. She could already think of a host of other uses for applying the Grym in this manner, although not all of them would be viewed as altruistic.

"A temporary aid," the woman corrected. "It's a small amount of the Grym as you can tell. It'll keep working for most of the day, fading over time."

"So they need to keep coming back." A good business tactic, Melissa believed, if that indeed was the case.

"It's not addictive in any way," the woman explained, although she didn't appear to be offended by the comment. "If the Teg return for more, it's because they want to. Not because they have to."

"How does it work?" Melissa asked, obviously intrigued. "I'd really like to know." She then ordered a large coffee, one blueberry scone, since Maine was known for its blueberries, and a cinnamon roll.

"It's a fairly simple process once you learn how to do it. It just takes a little practice." The baker flipped the iPad around so that Melissa could pay for her selections.

"Any chance you might be able to show me how to do it?" asked Melissa, the hope plain in her voice.

Cerridwen stared at her for several seconds. To Melissa it felt like she was being weighed and measured just as the woman probably did when she was preparing the ingredients for her bakes.

"You want my corporate secret? We haven't even slept together yet."

Melissa's face flushed red. She had never expected such a direct response.

She tried to stammer out an apology and something else

besides that, but she couldn't find the words. She had been caught out a second time in just the last few minutes. That had never happened before. Clearly she was off her game.

The woman on the other side of the counter saved her, reaching across and patting her hand warmly. "I'm just teasing you, love. Sorry. It's been a long morning, and I just wanted to have a little fun."

Melissa laughed nervously. "Right. Sorry. I shouldn't have asked in the first place."

"It's not a problem, love. You just need to be careful."

"What do you mean?" asked Melissa. The woman's eyes had hardened just a bit, although not in anger. Rather in warning. And, still, she couldn't figure out what color they were.

"You've heard the saying I'm sure."

"Saying?"

"How curiosity killed the cat?"

Melissa laughed genuinely then. "More times than I'd care to remember. It was one of my mother's favorites."

"Your mother is a smart woman."

"Among other things," Melissa replied almost too softly to be heard. "It's just that I like to learn ..."

The woman reached out and patted Melissa on the hand again, laughing softly, wanting her to know that all was well. "Don't worry, love. As I said, I was just having a little fun with you. My apologies for that."

She handed Melissa the blueberry scone and cinnamon roll in a small box, the sticker keeping it closed confirming it came from Tia's Bakes. Melissa wondered who Tia was until the woman put the large coffee on top of the counter. After her last few days, that's what she really needed.

"I'd be happy to show you," the woman continued. "I just can't do it now. We're about to get busy. The late morning rush. So I need to get ready. Come back in the late afternoon and I should have time to take you through it."

"Thank you," Melissa replied, thrilled by the opportunity that the woman offered to her.

"And you are?" asked the woman.

"Melissa."

The woman waited for Melissa to provide her full name. She didn't.

"I'm Cerridwen. As I said, feel free to come back later and I can show you how to do what I do."

"Sounds good. I will. Thank you." Melissa reached into her bag and pulled off a piece from the cinnamon roll. Just as delicious as the sample. Better, actually, because this one was still warm. She looked up at Cerridwen. "The cinnamon roll doesn't have the Grym like the scone does."

"No, I didn't make the cinnamon roll." Cerridwen nodded toward the back of the shop. There was a large open window that revealed what was going on in the kitchen. "Our itinerant baker made it. That's why I'm expecting the late-morning rush. Word will spread that he's back there. Whatever he makes always disappears faster than a memory."

Once again Cerridwen's phrasing put Melissa on guard, if only briefly. But not as much as the man in the back of the shop wearing the flour-covered apron.

He was always on the move. Pulling ingredients. Measuring. Rolling. Mixing. It was almost as if he was gliding. Dancing even, his actions so precise, seemingly choreographed.

Still, she was able to get a good look at him for a few seconds. And a few seconds was all that was needed for a prickle of warning to surge down her spine.

He certainly didn't look like a baker. In fact, he looked like the fittest baker she had ever seen.

He had looked up briefly, meeting her eyes, then he had looked down just as quickly, the muscles in his arms straining as he rolled out the dough he had just pulled from the proving drawer.

There was some quality to his eyes that didn't so much upset her as make her nervous. That and the shiver that she had felt suggested to her immediately that this Teg was someone to be wary of. Perhaps even someone to stay away from.

She didn't want to look at him again, but she couldn't stop herself.

What was it about this baker that kept her eyes locked onto him despite the way he made her feel?

She had always been attracted to men who were better avoided. Maybe that was it. Her usual bad taste in the opposite sex.

There was a sense of menace surrounding him. That and a feeling of a restrained power that she couldn't quite comprehend.

Who was this baker?

He looked up for just a split-second, once again catching her eyes. She saw the fire there. The energy.

That second glance made her feel distinctly ill at ease. It also made her feel slightly tingly, but in a good or bad way she couldn't decide.

There was a fire in him.

A power.

She was sure of it. She could sense it.

But unlike the Grym that she had identified in the scone, this was a power that no matter how much it attracted her, she wanted no part of.

"Thank you, Cerridwen. For breakfast and the offer of help."

Before Cerridwen could reply, Melissa turned and walked right out the door just as a woman walking a dog was pulling it open.

Melissa would eat in the park down by the harbor. Then she would head to the bookstore.

Once she found what she was looking for, assuming she located it, she would need to make a decision.

Stay or go?

She already knew the right answer to that question.

The problem was she rarely did the right thing.

DRAIG FOCUSED on his baking as much as he could. However, it had proven difficult as soon as he sensed the woman enter the shop.

Try as he might, he couldn't ignore his curiosity.

The woman was remarkably strong in the Grym. Stronger than most of the other Teg living in Kraken Cove, in fact.

That, in itself, was cause enough to focus more of his attention on her. Yet he hesitated to do that, and he didn't know why.

Every once in a while, he looked up from rolling out and then cutting his dough. Never for long. Just catching glimpses of the woman while she spoke with Cerridwen.

After catching her eyes twice, something that he had wanted to avoid, he kept his head down. There was no reason to make her more uncomfortable than she already was. No reason to give her any cause to suspect him.

She had been studying him regularly.

He ignored her.

It wasn't until he sensed that she was leaving the shop that he looked up.

He was curious about her. More than curious, actually.

The question now was whether he should give in to his curiosity.

He had sensed the power in her before she even came into his bakery.

The woman had been trying to hide the Grym flowing through her. Masking the power to a large extent.

It would work with most of the Teg. Not with Cerridwen, however. And certainly not with him.

He knew in an instant what the woman was.

So he assumed that this was the guest who had arrived at the Safe Haven late last night.

That only added to his worries.

The Daemons. Merlin. Tracks in the wood that he never liked to see.

Now her.

She was beautiful, yes. Was she dangerous as well?

Perhaps.

He had a good idea as to what she could do with the Grym.

Was she here in Kraken Cove by happenstance? Someone of her power and skill?

Probably not.

None of the Teg came to Kraken Cove unless they had a reason for doing so.

Did she work for his father? Had he sent her here to find him? Maybe even try to kill him?

Draig didn't know.

All the questions that had been running through his mind now all dissolved into a single one.

What would it cost him to gain the answers to all of his questions?

7

LONG TIME NO SEE

Deep in thought, Merlin walked back in the direction from which Draig had come, head down, hands in the pockets of his jacket. When he reached the harbor, he watched a single charter boat dare to head out toward the deeper water through the fog that still blanketed the cove.

The lack of visibility didn't seem to bother the captain, who steered with a sure hand. Merlin smiled thinly, shaking his head more in amusement than surprise.

Little bothered Seamus McCracken on the water. It was when he was on land that he tended to get himself into trouble.

Merlin continued farther along the trail, disappearing within the woods. The fog faded away to no more than a few thready wisps when he reached the location that had caught Draig's interest not too long before.

He stared down at the tracks for quite some time. Not moving. Not even blinking.

Those prints were unmistakable.

They didn't bode well for Draig if he was the reason these creatures had decided to hunt in Kraken Cove.

And if they hadn't come here for Draig, it still didn't bode well.

Draig didn't like it when uninvited Teg came to Kraken Cove.

Whether it was his business or not, Draig would feel the need to ensure that the residents of the small town had nothing to fear. By any means necessary.

But Merlin wasn't too concerned about Draig. He could handle himself. The Fallen Knight had proven that time and again.

What bothered him was the fact that there was a scheme in play that he didn't understand. Merlin didn't like it when he didn't understand what was going on in the Teg world.

It made him feel uncomfortable. Itchy. Like he had a rash that he couldn't scratch.

"You shouldn't be here, Old One."

"Who are you calling old?" Merlin asked, his eyes twinkling with delight.

When he turned away from the tracks, a woman stood before him just between the trees bounding the trail. She carried a long walking stick carved from a deep auburn ash, and she wore a cloak around her shoulders to ward off the chill of the morning. She looked like any other hiker, except she was barefoot.

"We are both old, Old One. But you are older than I am."

"Not by much."

"By enough," the woman replied in a voice that suggested that continuing to protest was a waste of time.

"I take it that I'm not going to win this argument."

"You won't. So better just to let it go."

"It's been a long time, Leya. You look no different than when last I saw you."

"Not long enough," Leya replied, ignoring the compliment Merlin offered her.

"I thought we were friends, Leya," Merlin said with a touch of hurt in his voice.

"We are," Leya replied, understanding that Merlin's tone was feigned. "However, our friendship works best when you're not here. Trouble follows you, Merlin. We have no need of it here."

"Trouble is trouble, Leya. Best to deal with it head on rather than try to avoid it." Merlin shrugged as if to say that was just the way of the world. He didn't make the rules. And he preferred not to follow them if he could avoid it. He nodded toward the drying mud. "You saw these?"

"Of course," Leya replied, her tone hinting that she took his question as an insult. "I tracked them here."

"That's why you came down off your mountain?" Merlin nodded to himself. "That certainly makes sense."

"Among other reasons, Merlin. Don't start thinking that you've got it all figured out." Leya shook her head as if she were examining a young boy who had disappointed her. "I thought that you would have learned by now. Whenever you're so sure of yourself you tend to be wrong. That's gotten you into some tight spots in the past."

"No fear of that now," Merlin murmured. "Because, at this very moment, I am consumed by doubts. I have no idea what's happening here, and I don't like that one bit."

Leya smiled and shook her head again. "We have known each other too long, Old One. You are consumed by doubts because you know some of what's going on, but not all. That's what's bothering you. You like to know everything, never satisfied even though you realize that you will never know everything."

"You're right." Merlin's eyes crinkled, a bit of fire appearing in the back of his blue orbs that in the shade of the wood appeared almost black. "I'm beginning to remember why we don't spend too much time together."

Leya laughed at that, her voice melodic, sending a welcome warmth through Merlin's body, just as it always did.

She was right, of course. It was better if they didn't spend too much time together. It often led to difficulties between them that he would prefer to avoid if he could. Still, speaking with her for a few minutes more wouldn't cause any harm.

Besides, he was enjoying himself. Leya kept him on his toes in ways that others couldn't.

He studied her openly then. Unperturbed, Leya stared right back at him.

Usually, anyone else he put under that gaze wilted. Except for Draig, of course. Nothing ever affected Draig.

Leya was the reclusive type. It was simply who she was. She rarely left her home and the forest surrounding it because she didn't need to in order to meet her obligations.

Whatever had drawn her out must have been important. And he had a feeling that the cause was more than just the creatures who had left their tracks in the mud.

"He's well?" Merlin finally asked, not wanting to allow his mind to wander down a path better left untrodden.

"As well as can be," Leya replied with a shrug.

Merlin nodded, expecting just that answer. Leya was reclusive, yes, but even more so she was protective. Of Draig in particular.

She wouldn't tell him anything about Draig unless she believed that it was absolutely necessary that she do so.

"Not much has changed between me and the lad."

Leya shrugged. Merlin's relationship with Draig really wasn't her business or her concern. "It isn't easy for Draig. You know that. You demand too much from him."

Merlin nodded, not feeling the need to revisit that path either. "I understand that he was away from town for a few nights."

"I don't know anything about that."

Merlin hmphed loudly, letting her know that he didn't believe her. Clearly, based on how her expression hardened, she didn't care for the gentle jab.

"You shouldn't be here, Merlin. He came here for a reason. He's not ready."

"I wanted to see him." Merlin lifted his arms as if to say his appearing in Kraken Cove for the first time in a decade was of little concern. "Besides, whether or not he's ready might not be up to him."

Leya's eyes sparked at that. "Your presence here draws too much attention."

"No one knows I'm here, Leya. You have nothing to fear."

"Are you sure about that, Merlin? As I said, what you believe and what is aren't always one and the same, no matter how much you might want it to be that way."

Merlin bit back a sharp retort. Angering Leya now would be of little value. He looked back over his shoulder at the tracks again.

Leya might have a point. She did have a point, actually. But he didn't feel the need to admit it to her. "You're keeping an eye on him?"

"He really doesn't need looking after, Merlin. He's proven his competence more times than anyone has a right to expect."

"And he's proven as well that he can be a major pain in the ass."

"That he has," Leya admitted, and then with a mischievous smile finished her thought. "But then again, so can you."

Merlin's eyes flashed once more, his amusement obvious. He really did enjoy engaging with Leya. Just in spurts, however. "But you are keeping an eye on him?"

"When I need to," Leya admitted.

"Good," Merlin said with a nod. "There are rumblings beyond Kraken Cove."

"What kind of rumblings?" Leya's concern was plain.

"Some of what we buried so long ago might be coming back to life."

Leya stared at Merlin's ageless eyes, recognizing the power behind them. Such a display would frighten most any other of the Teg. Not her, however. She had seen and dealt with far worse in her life than the likes of him.

"Make sure it stays buried, Merlin. That's not a request."

"And if I can't?"

"If you can't, you know what will happen. You know what will be required." Leya's expression changed. She was beginning to understand now. "That's why you're here."

Merlin ignored her last comment. "Can he manage all that? If he's required to do what he doesn't want to do."

"You're asking me?" snorted Leya. "You should already know the answer to that. You helped to raise him."

"You've been closer to him than I have since he came here."

Leya took her time before responding, mulling his question. Knowing what the consequence could be based on how she answered. "He can. If it proves necessary."

"That's good."

"Not for him," Leya replied. "I don't want him to have to go through that if it can be avoided."

"Neither do I, Leya. Neither do I. But some things are beyond my control."

"Nothing is beyond your control," countered Leya. "You've said that many a time." It was her turn to give him a sharp gaze, and he remembered then just how powerful she was. "Keep it buried, Merlin. It shouldn't be too difficult for you. Burying secrets is one of your specialties."

In a flash, Leya disappeared. She was there one moment, gone the next.

Merlin snorted and smiled. Impressive.

Leya always was one for the drama. Then again, so was he.

8

WE MEET AGAIN

The jingle of the bells set atop the door sent a warm flush through Melissa as she stepped into the Book Nook. It brought back a flood of memories. Her mother taking her and her sisters to a bookstore just a few blocks from their home when she was younger.

Every Saturday morning they would go there. Bound Books. Without fail. She could select as many books as she wanted. Her mother didn't care. So long as she read them.

With everything else Melissa's mother had been much stricter. But never books.

She was grateful for that.

For Melissa, books provided an escape, knowledge, instruction, power.

Whatever she might need. So long as she had the correct text and she knew how to crack it.

After Melissa closed the door behind her, she stood still for a few heartbeats, taking in the welcoming space.

It was just like the bakery a door down. Every aspect of this store felt right to her. She could lose herself here, and she wouldn't be concerned if she never found her way out again.

The book titles she perused through the window had piqued her interest in an instant, confirming that she had been right to take her mother's suggestion and detour to Kraken Cove. That sense of excitement only intensified as she began to walk along the outside aisles, wanting to get a sense of where everything was before she began her search.

She felt like a kid in a candy store. Not knowing what to try first.

When she completed her circuit, she examined the books set out on the tables at the front of the store. Many of them appealed to her. If her mother had been with her, she would have scooped up every last one to add to her collection.

Unfortunately, none of these books was the one she was looking for. That didn't surprise her. She didn't believe that she would find what she was looking for easily. The text was too rare.

Next, Melissa began to work her way slowly down the aisle to her left. Taking her time. Her eyes sweeping up then down then up again, pulling out from the shelves any book whose spine she couldn't read clearly.

Not one of the books she examined was the one that she needed, even though one title after another called to her. It was almost as if each book demanded that she pull it off the shelf and start flipping through its pages.

In other circumstances she would have done just that. She could have whiled away the entire morning and early afternoon in this shop and then come back tomorrow to start again.

But she didn't have the time. And she couldn't afford to be distracted.

She picked up *Ars Notaria*, said to be written by King Solomon himself. Melissa believed that it had been. The argument one of her professors made about that claim had resonated with her.

Right next to that ancient tome, and also supposedly by

King Solomon, she found *The Grand Grimoire*, a collection of invocations, spells, and basic use of the Grym.

She, like many other Teg, doubted the authenticity of this text. Not the knowledge that it contained. The spells in the book, if you followed them closely and had the skill and strength necessary to control the power required, did exactly what they were meant to do, often with astounding results.

No, rather the doubt came down to attribution. Most academics believed that although that text was said to be from King Solomon, it likely was written in the sixteenth century by some forgotten Teg who had affixed the name to increase the popularity of the tome.

If so, all credit to that unknown Teg. Because *The Grand Grimoire* was a godsend for Melissa. Once she began working with that book, her ability to finetune her control over the Grym had grown by leaps and bounds.

The *De Nigromancia*, or, in English, *Concerning the Black Art*, was fairly common among her people.

Le Dragon Noir, a scarce French text, and its companion, *Le Dragon Rouge,* contained instructions, the first for making a daemonic pact and talismans, and the second a primary source for the Twisted Grym and evoking Daemons.

Some in her community argued that the texts should be banned. There was no reason to make knowledge of the Twisted Grym available to anyone. Those with a calmer – and in her opinion more expansive – perspective understood that if you needed to combat the Twisted Grym then you first needed to understand how that dark power actually worked.

Melissa allowed her fingers to drift across the spine of each book. *The Malleus Maleficarum*, *The Discoverie of Witchcraft*, and so many more.

Her fingers were getting itchy. She really wanted to take a closer look at several of the texts that she passed.

She controlled herself, however, despite how hard it proved

to be. She had to stay on task. Finding what she needed was all that mattered. Because if she didn't …

Well, she didn't want to think about that.

The Book Nook housed all these rare texts and so many more, no other store she had visited so far devoted to the works of the Teg having even a quarter of this shop's inventory. That gave her hope that the tome she required would be here as well.

It had to be.

If the primer wasn't here, then she didn't know where to go to continue her search.

She pushed those negative thoughts from her mind. If she was going to do what she needed to do, then she had to stay positive.

It was just a matter of locating the work that had been described by many scholars as the most important and powerful text ever written by a Teg. The most dangerous as well, depending on who you might be.

Not really that big a deal, she tried to convince herself.

Her mother had told her that only thirteen copies had been published, and those secretly. They were given to the most powerful Teg of that era for safekeeping, all of those masters of the Grym understanding that these books held the key to their people's survival from an unimaginable threat.

Those Teg entrusted with a copy had done what was required of them for as long as they could. In the end, however, the threat against which the original book had been written had found them all.

All of those guardians, the strongest Teg of their time, were now dead.

The Teg's greatest enemy had burned all the books. Except for one. The story said that the last Teg sent the resource to a safe place before the threat could acquire it.

A safe place that few if any Teg knew about.

A flash of worry shot down Melissa's spine. What was she supposed to do if the last remaining copy wasn't here?

Because if that was the case none of the options that remained appealed to her. None of them guaranteed that she would continue to draw breath.

And if she instead simply completed the deal that she had been forced to make?

That appealed to her the least of all. If she did that, she'd be signing her own death warrant.

She couldn't think like that. Bad thoughts led to bad results. She had seen it too many times not to believe another of her mother's maxims.

She couldn't afford to fall into that trap. Not now.

Her spirits lifted as she moved deeper into the store toward the twisting staircase at the back of the shop. She wasn't having much luck with the books on the shelves, but there was a great deal more to this bookshop than just what met her eye.

She could sense it now. The power infusing this place. More muted when she first entered the store, as if it were just an afterthought, becoming stronger the longer she stayed in the shop.

The Grym.

And not just because of the many texts lining the shelves. The entire store radiated the Power of the Ancients.

Closing her eyes, she allowed her mind to wander. Using a small quantity of the Grym, her senses extended around her, giving her a feel for her surroundings in a way that simply looking with her eyes couldn't.

When she came back to herself she broke out into a broad smile. Maybe the information that her mother provided her with was correct.

There was more to this shop than just the books and shelves she took in while slowly spinning around in a circle. Much more.

In fact, if her assessment was correct, then she was standing atop the tip of the iceberg. The trick was finding a way to get to what was secreted beneath the waves.

Assuming that what she wanted was being hidden from her, of course. She suspected, but she didn't know for sure. She needed to confirm her theory first.

To do that, she started meandering through the shelves again. Taking her time. Making sure that she didn't miss anything.

Looking not only for the text she needed, but also for a way to get past the glamour that prevented her from seeing all that there was to see in the rest of the shop.

Melissa smiled in appreciation as she used a faint thread of the Grym to ensure that she wasn't being deceived in any way.

She had yet to find the key that would unlock the Grym protecting this shop. Not expecting that it would be such a challenge, she concentrated on the books instead. She allowed her senses to continue to drift. Believing that eventually she would find what she was looking for. Because she always did.

Clever, she thought.

Several of the books resting on the shelves were not actually the books the titles on their spines said they were. More often than she would have anticipated, the letters of the titles shifted as her thread of the Grym drifted over them, revealing their true content.

All of them caught Melissa's attention. All of them were of interest. None of them was the specific book that she was looking for.

Just as she thought. She shook her head, grumbling softly. She hated when she was right. Then again, she should never have assumed that this would be easy. Doing that was the mistake of a novice, and she was far removed from being that.

After working her way through the shop from front to back, walking slowly down all the aisles, even climbing the ladders and searching along the terraces, two more floors that she hadn't seen when she looked through the window hidden in the shadows above -- how that was possible since from the outside it looked like a three-story building she wasn't quite sure, but she didn't have the time or the brainpower to ponder this new challenge -- she could say definitively that the text was not here.

Or rather not in this section of the bookstore, where anyone could walk in and peruse its offerings.

That didn't really surprise her. It only made sense, considering how important this text was.

If it was here – and she really hoped that it was -- it was hidden away.

Melissa's smile became more wolfish. She was used to facing challenges like this in her line of work.

Because of her skill and, just as important, experience, she was very good at finding items that didn't want to be found.

"Anything I can help you with, Melissa?"

Melissa almost jumped off the floor, the pleasant voice behind her startling her. She was able to control the impulse, although just barely, not wanting to demonstrate weakness to this woman who appeared to be a wolf in sheep's clothing. She took a second to fix a more appropriate smile on her face before she turned around.

Cerridwen had snuck up on her. How had Melissa not heard the woman come into the shop with the bells on the door?

"What are you doing here?" Melissa asked, working hard to keep the irritation rising within her out of her voice, instead infusing it with the anxiety that had surged through her upon being surprised. She hated being surprised. "Why aren't you over at the bakery?"

"The bakery and bookstore are owned by the same person," Cerridwen explained, her eyes sparkling with delight. It was clear to Melissa that the woman had intended to catch her here, and she was quite pleased with herself for doing just that. "I usually come over here after the morning rush to make sure the shop is ready when Seshat is away."

"Seshat?" asked Melissa, not understanding the reference.

"Seshat is the lib ..." Cerridwen caught herself at the very last second, holding back whatever she wanted to keep to herself. "Seshat runs the bookshop for the owner, but she's out of town for a few days. When she's away, I keep an eye on things."

"Out acquiring more masterworks, I assume," Melissa replied in a joking tone.

"Exactly that," Cerridwen confirmed with a small laugh of her own that didn't match her gaze, which was now as hard as granite. "She has an excellent eye, and we want only authentic works here in the shop. There are many forgeries out in the world. Seshat has a unique ability to identify them. With just a glance, she can tell the real from the fake. Always. Without fail."

Cerridwen paused then, making sure that she caught Melissa's eyes, wanting to emphasize her point. "That's in large part why the Book Nook is so successful. Her ability to sniff out the original from the ones pretending to be what they aren't."

"A unique skill to have," Melissa agreed, forcing herself not to gulp, not really sure how to answer, not with the look that Cerridwen was giving her now.

A look that wasn't as friendly as the one the woman had given her in Tia's Bakes. A look that was making her feel distinctly uncomfortable.

"It is indeed," Cerridwen nodded. "I have no doubt that Seshat would enjoy meeting you just as much as you'd enjoy meeting her. Assuming that you're still in Kraken Cove at the end of the week."

"If I'm still here, that sounds lovely," replied Melissa. "I'd love to pick her brain about some of the titles she has here on the shelves. I'd really like to know how she found some of them. I'm sure she has some wonderful stories."

Based on the look that Cerridwen was giving her, Melissa had no intention of being in Kraken Cove at the end of the week. Worse, the woman had just made Melissa's task all the more difficult. Cerridwen had imposed a time limit on what Melissa needed to do, and she probably didn't even realize it.

"And I'm sure that she'd like to pick your brain as well."

Cerridwen's statement caught Melissa off guard, sending a buzz of worry through her brain. She used every ounce of self-control to maintain her composure. She had been in similar situations before, and she sensed an opportunity.

Rather than bending at the veiled threat Cerridwen had just offered her, she chose to ignore it, her resolve strengthening. Instead, she hoped that the woman might be able to help her, unwittingly of course.

As she had learned when she was younger, another lesson from her mother, sometimes demonstrating little to no ability to read a situation could go a long way when faced with a challenge.

"You know, since Seshat isn't here, perhaps I could pick your brain instead."

"Really," nodded Cerridwen, a spark of interest appearing in the back of her flinty orbs, her expression becoming uncomfortably intense. "What can I help you with?"

Melissa noted the way the woman's personality had changed drastically from one extreme to the other in the time it took her to walk over from the bakeshop. Like Jekyll and Hyde, only faster. The issue she needed to remain wary of was that she didn't yet know how dangerous the Jekyll in Cerridwen could be.

Melissa decided to dive right in, pretending not to feel the distrust emanating from Cerridwen, even as it worked its way beneath her skin. "You have a truly remarkable collection here."

"We like to think so," Cerridwen replied evenly.

Clearly, the woman didn't want to make this easy for her. "All credit to Seshat for her excellent work. She truly is good at what she does."

"You have no idea," Cerridwen replied, her many-hued eyes flashing brightly. "I'm sure you'll have the chance to tell her that when she returns. She certainly would appreciate it."

"And I will. But since Seshat isn't here, I was hoping that you could help me."

Melissa stepped in close to Cerridwen, trying to give the impression that she was about to share a secret only for her even though there was no one else in the store. "What I'm seeing on the shelves really is quite impressive. There's so much to choose from that I feel a little lost."

"You didn't find what you were looking for?" asked Cerridwen, already getting a sense as to what Melissa was trying to do. She was willing to play along. For now.

"Unfortunately not," Melissa admitted. "I was wondering whether all the works available in the store were on the shelves. That maybe there was an archive that was only made available upon request. I've run into similar circumstances in other bookstores."

Cerridwen gave Melissa that predatory smile again, failing to hide the fact that she believed that she had finally figured out why she was really there. Melissa didn't care.

She had revealed a part of her reason for being in Kraken Cove. She needed to if she was to gain anything of use from Cerridwen. But she hadn't revealed all, and Cerridwen could do very little with what Melissa had given her.

As her mother liked to say, when you were fishing for an answer, you needed to offer some bait.

"What is it that you're looking for, Melissa? I can't really help you if I don't know why it is that you came here."

Melissa laughed softly, trying to play off the intensity of Cerridwen's gaze. "Nothing in particular. I was just curious. I just didn't get the sense that the entire inventory was on the shelves."

"Right." Cerridwen's tone confirmed that she didn't believe her. "I'm sorry, but in the Book Nook what you see is what you get." Cerridwen crossed her arms as if to emphasize her point. "Seshat doesn't maintain a very large inventory because she can obtain requested resources remarkably fast. Only what you see here on the shelves is available to you. But if there's a specific text you're hunting for, I can pass the title on to Seshat and she can see what she can do. If she can find it, she will. And if she can't, then she'll let you know ... personally."

"I'll keep that in mind, thank you," replied Melissa, working hard to maintain her poise in the face of Cerridwen's spinning and swirling kaleidoscopic eyes, as well as the woman's words, which she interpreted as another veiled threat. She was certain now that Seshat was a woman that she wanted to avoid at all costs. "But I'm not looking for anything specific. I was just curious. Really, it's just that I was told that you carried some older texts that weren't available to the usual crowd. That special requests often were honored."

Cerridwen's hard eyes somehow became even stonier. Cerridwen stepped even closer to Melissa, who wanted to step back. But she had nowhere to go. The table at her back prevented it.

"For someone who's been in Kraken Cove for such a short time, less than a day, you certainly do seem quite familiar with our town. Very well informed."

"Just what I learned on Google, really, and what a few friends told me," Melissa replied quickly, offering Cerridwen a big smile, realizing much to her chagrin that Cerridwen was unlike the marks she was used to playing. "They said it was a good town to visit for a few days if you wanted a break from the real world. No more than that."

Cerridwen snorted softly, hearing the lie although not taking issue with it. Yet.

"You said that someone told you that we carried some older texts that didn't appear on the shelves."

"I did," Melissa confirmed, beginning to think that she might have made a mistake. "But I was really only listening with one ear at the time. Most of what she tells me she usually just makes up. She's a little off, if you know what I mean." Melissa raised a hand and pointed to her head with her finger to make her point.

"I just figured that I would ask since I was here and you're such a friendly face." Melissa almost bit her lip. Now was not the time for sarcasm, something her mother hated. But what Cerridwen was doing to her now felt exactly like what her mother used to do to her when she was younger. Interrogating her when Melissa went off for days on end without a hint as to where she was before returning home in the middle of the night. "No more than that."

Cerridwen leaned in even closer, hands moving to her hips, her nose just a few inches away from Melissa's. "Even so, what's the woman's name. It will point me in the right direction so that I can help you find what you're looking for."

"I don't know why that would be important. As I said, she's not all there."

Melissa tried and failed to sound casual. She was better than this. She had been in much more dangerous situations. Yet this woman had the uncanny ability to see right through her, and that was making her uneasy to the point that she feared she was making mistakes.

"If I know the name of the person who told you, I might be able to help you find whatever it is you're looking for. That much faster. That's all. It's something that I learned from Seshat. There is always more than one link to every chain. Find all the links and you can find the answer."

"You mean here in the store?" Melissa blurted out. She tried to appear confused by what Cerridwen had just told her, even though she understood full well her meaning. The threat, though veiled, was unmistakable.

Cerridwen smiled and stepped back then. Melissa could tell the woman had gotten what she wanted from her, and she hadn't gotten anything in return, other than the warning that she really didn't want to be in Kraken Cove for very much longer.

"No, not here in the store," Cerridwen replied, once again willing to play along. Cerridwen could take more direct measures to find out what she wanted but she refrained. Draig frowned upon that, and she had no desire to rile him up unnecessarily. Besides, she already had dug out some useful nuggets. "If you can't find it on the shelves, Seshat should be able to find it for you. But before I can ask her to do that, I need to know the name of the woman who told you about our knack for acquiring texts that are no longer a part of mainstream reading."

Melissa stared at Cerridwen. She didn't know what to do. She didn't know how to extricate herself from the mess she had created.

"It's only fair, of course," continued Cerridwen. "We'd want to thank your resource for mentioning the store. It's only good for business, after all."

Her mother had told her of this bookstore and how unique it was. That this shop might be the key to gaining the information that she needed. That whoever owned the store could acquire virtually anything of importance to the Teg, but that such a search would only be undertaken if the bona fides of the person making the request could be established.

Cerridwen was confirming what her mother had told her.

Why was she hesitating?

Melissa could reveal her mother's name, but the voice in the back of her head that warned her of danger was beginning to whisper to her. She studied Cerridwen more closely. She sensed the power within her. There was something there as well that she couldn't identify, and that's what worried her.

That and Cerridwen's eyes boring into hers convinced her that giving the woman her mother's name wasn't the right thing to do.

She hadn't wasted her time coming here this morning. If nothing else, she knew now that she wasn't seeing all that there was to see. It was just a matter of figuring out how to lift the curtain hiding the rest of the shop.

To help with that, she decided to take a risk and throw out a name that might mean something to Cerridwen, but it never left the tip of her tongue.

Out of the corner of her eye, Melissa caught a flash of movement in front of the store.

A man was standing outside. He was wearing a pressed suit, the lines in his pants razor sharp.

Normally that wouldn't have bothered her.

What bothered her was that he wasn't looking at the books in the window.

This man whose face was partially obscured by the fedora he was wearing was staring right at her.

This man, who hadn't said a word to her, who was only staring at her through the window, was making her feel more than uncomfortable. He was frightening her. It was as if he could freeze her blood with just a glance, just as he was doing now.

Melissa was rarely frightened, but it seemed that it was becoming a regular occurrence these last few days. Ever since she had decided to go for that midnight swim. Ever since she had answered the call that she should have ignored.

Just then, the man moved away from the window and pulled open the door. He stepped over the threshold, his well-cut grey suit and polished black leather shoes appearing out of place in this small town.

Seeing that the man had caught Cerridwen's attention, and not in a good way, the woman tensing as if she were preparing herself for a fight, Melissa decided that now was the perfect time to make her escape.

"Thank you for your time, Cerridwen," Melissa said as she pushed past her and hustled through the quickly closing door. "I'll check back with you later. I've got to make a call."

Cerridwen was bad enough with the pressure that she had been applying. Melissa had absolutely no desire to have a conversation with the man she brushed past. She had only glanced at his face, but what she saw only intensified the feeling that something was terribly off about him.

Yet strangely, even though she passed right by him as he held the door for her, no more than a foot between them, she couldn't picture exactly what he looked like. A dozen different faces passed before her eyes as she tried to recall the memory. It was almost as if all those disparate images merged into one during her single glance at him.

She walked across the street and then headed past the fire station, the large doors raised. It looked like it was going to be a beautiful day now that the fog was lifting. Past the station, she walked by several restaurants that led toward the trail at the far end of the green. When she came to the end of the block, she slipped into a small space between the buildings and peeked back around the corner.

What had started as a good morning had quickly gone downhill. She felt like she did when she was hunting for a mark, but right then she couldn't get past the feeling that she was the prey.

She waited for several minutes, eyes scanning the green, Market Street, the side streets leading away from the center of the town, always returning to the Book Nook to see what the man would do.

He stayed in the shop.

If he was going to follow her, he would have come after her by now.

Sighing with relief, she started to walk back toward the restaurants. There was a narrow street between them that would take her where she wanted to go.

She had only gone a few steps when she stopped abruptly. Her mind had already begun working on the challenge of how to get what she needed from the bookstore, so she had an excuse as to why she didn't see the other man, dressed exactly like the first, sitting in a car parked on the other side of the street, his face hidden by his fedora.

Just like the man from the bookstore, this one did nothing more than stare at her.

She fought hard not to give into her fear, trotting down the path then slowing to just a fast walk when she reached the fork that allowed her to walk down to the beach and harbor. After the glances the two men had given her, she felt the need to be anywhere but where she was now.

Realizing how alone she was with no one else in sight, she gave into her fear that was rapidly becoming terror. When she reached the end of the path, she picked up her pace, staying right beneath the cliffs. Feeling the need to keep out of sight.

If she followed this route, she would reach the steps that would take her back up the cliff and leave her at the back door to the bed and breakfast.

Safe Haven.

Her terror making her body begin to shake ever so slightly,

she was about to reach for the railing of the staircase and run up the steps that would take her to safety when she stopped, her hand held out in front of her.

She whipped around, her back to the cliffs.

She swept her gaze along the harbor front. With the fog dissipating, she didn't see anything. There was no one about. Nothing that should give her any cause for concern.

But she wasn't alone. She was sure of it.

The skin on the back of her neck was prickling and the hair on her arms was standing on end.

She scanned her surroundings again, her body turning to ice.

Still nothing.

What was going on?

Consumed by her fear, she never saw the shadows detach themselves from the rocks behind her.

9

POOR IMPRESSION

Melissa stared out at the harbor.

Her eyes were wide.

Her breathing ragged.

Her nerves on edge.

The fog was fading, leaving just as swiftly as it had drifted in, revealing the boats, piers, and water that had been hidden from her just minutes before. Yet despite the larger world opening up to her once again, despite having a better awareness of her surroundings, her terror only increased.

She didn't understand why. She didn't see anything that should give her any reason to fear, to make her feel so afraid that she could scarcely move.

She was alone. There wasn't a soul to be seen.

Nevertheless, she was so scared that she needed to exert almost all of her will to prevent her hands from shaking. To prevent her entire body from shivering.

It was the almost uncontrollable terror that surged through her that caused her to step back toward the cliffs. She needed to feel something solid at her back. Firm. Unyielding.

Just as important, it meant that whatever was causing her to feel this way could only come at her from one direction.

One step back and another. Then a few more smaller strides all at once.

Melissa reached back with her hand, seeking the rough surface of the rocks, beginning to breathe easier for the first time since she left the bookshop.

Right before her fingers grazed the rockface, however, her eyes widened as the terrible realization struck her.

A presence. More than one.

She was being hunted.

Even worse, a trap had been set for her, and she had walked right into it.

Her fear had guided her. Pushing her in this direction.

Melissa tensed.

There was a brief moment of stillness, as if whatever was waiting behind her couldn't believe that she had seen through the deception.

Then she caught a flicker of movement out of the corner of her eye. A flash streaking out of the gloom.

Allowing her instincts to take hold, she ducked, at the same time reaching for the Grym and crafting a small shield of energy that she fixed to her forearm and used to protect her right side and back.

She watched with both a good deal of fascination and trepidation, and then satisfaction, as a steel rod three feet in length with a spike at the end slammed against her magical barrier. There was a sharp crackle when the metal and magic met, a flash of blinding white light erupting.

Although her shield absorbed the blow, Melissa wasn't strong enough to stand against it. She danced backward, allowing the force of the heavy strike to push her away from the cliffs and whatever it was that had lain in wait for her.

She was inordinately pleased that she evaded the worst of

the strike. Her focus on defending against the attack helping her to crush her fear. Lock it away.

Nevertheless, she realized quickly that this was only the beginning of the assault.

She hadn't escaped the trap. She had only made it more difficult for whomever was trying to kill her.

She continued to glide away from the rockface, keeping her shield in place, twisting and turning, blocking strikes just as frequently as she dodged them. When she could, she used the power of each blow that connected with her shield to move more swiftly onto the grass and toward the harbor, using the momentum of the assault to push her where she wanted to go.

She barely had a heartbeat to glimpse her attackers, needing to concentrate on the grey streaks that shot toward her with a frightening rapidity.

The only thing that she could tell with any certainty was that her initial assumption had been correct. More than one person was attacking her.

Despite the challenge she faced, Melissa was quite pleased with herself. She was still standing, she was putting up an effective defense, and she was buying herself time to think about how to get out of this mess.

Unfortunately, because of her assailants' speed, nothing was coming to mind other than to continue to get her shield where it needed to be before one of those steel rods knocked her out cold or cracked her skull.

A legitimate threat. The flashes of light that accompanied each strike against her shield were coming with greater frequency. In fact, it seemed like she was playing the role of a punching bag in a mixed martial arts gym.

Taking nothing but abuse. Not having the chance to strike back.

Although her shield protected her, it didn't weaken the

power of each blow. Her arm and shoulder ached. She was tiring. And even worse, she was slowing down.

Several times she barely got her shield in place before another forceful blow sent her stumbling back toward the harbor.

She couldn't believe how fast her attackers were. All she glimpsed, and poorly at that, were streaks of color surging toward her.

She was certain that she was facing off against several attackers, but she didn't know exactly how many.

That would have been nice to know. It might have given her some ideas as to how to defend herself in a way that didn't leave her battered, bruised, and vulnerable.

But it wasn't just that she couldn't see her attackers with any clarity, it was that they were so damn fast. Faster than anyone she had ever come up against before.

And that was saying something. She had gotten into many a nasty scrape because of her line of work.

Clearly, her attackers were quite skilled in their work. As the assault continued, her efforts to defend herself becoming more frenetic, she realized that they were trying to take her.

If they had wanted to kill her, they could have done that already. Much too easily, in fact.

No, they were tempering their blows. Knocking her around. Looking for that crack in her defenses that would allow them to snag her.

She doubted it would be much longer before they succeeded. Because they were maneuvering her exactly where they wanted her to go.

If she didn't find some avenue for escape, she was engaged in a fight with only one conclusion. One that didn't favor her.

Eventually, her attackers would get past her shield.

She didn't relish the thought of what it would feel like to be hit with one of those rods, cringing at the prospect.

Raising her shield once again to defend her left side, her exhaustion threatening to get the better of her, knowing that if the rod struck her cleanly it would crack if not break several of her ribs, she used the force of the latest blow to roll backward across the grass. As she did so, she swept behind her with her leg.

She hoped to catch the attacker who was coming at her from the right side. Unfortunately, despite timing her swipe almost perfectly, at least in her own estimation, she missed.

The shadowy figure actually flipped backward in the air to avoid her kick.

She didn't have time to applaud, instead pushing herself back to her feet and raising her shield just in time. The steel rod scraping off the edge made her teeth hurt, the flash of light leaving spots dancing before her eyes.

Melissa kicked forward then, thinking that she might finally get in a blow of her own since her attacker was so close to her.

No such luck.

She was fast. She had proven that time and time again. Nevertheless, she wasn't as fast as her kidnappers.

This time the shadow simply pivoted to the side, then swung back down with the rod as soon as she pulled back her leg.

She barely avoided the blow, needing to scamper several more feet toward the trail circling the harbor to evade the strike.

It was then that she began to understand the severity of her predicament.

She had been such a fool!

A rush of embarrassment ran through her, but then, going against her character, she gave herself a break.

She was under attack against she didn't know how many foes she couldn't see with any clarity and she could barely keep up with.

She could focus on little else other than defending herself. She hadn't had the time to confirm the suspicion that had been lurking in the back of her mind.

She sensed the presence of the Grym right before she almost stepped back into the arms of whoever it was that was seeking to capture her.

The Grym had been the cause of her terror. That was also why she couldn't see her attackers now. That was why she could see nothing more than shadows and streaks of grey steel.

If she was going to have any chance against her kidnappers, she needed to change the dynamics of this clash. She needed to see what she was up against.

While continuing to dance away from the cliffs and closer to the water, trying as much as possible now to avoid the powerful strikes rather than deflect them with her magical shield, she shifted a tiny part of her focus to her attackers.

Using a thin thread of the Grym, she sliced apart the shadows dancing in front of her and on both sides.

It was like scissoring through a veil to reveal what was hidden beneath.

Finally!

Without the Grym cloaking them, she identified three gigantic men moving incredibly fast, almost impossibly so.

They each had to be close to eight feet in height and were broader than a doorframe.

That mystery solved, her primary dilemma still stared back at her.

Every muscle in her body ached. She was exhausted. She was slowing down. And the three men swinging their hellish rods at her hadn't even broken a sweat.

It had to be her breakfast, she grumbled to herself. She should have stayed away from the scone and the cinnamon roll and selected the parfait with granola instead.

For the next several seconds, she had no time for her foolish musings. The pace of the combat intensified, her three attackers trying to break through her defenses, sensing that she was weakening.

Melissa wanted to disabuse them of that notion as she ducked and dodged, rolled and dove out of the way. But she was finding it more and more difficult to do that.

When the truth struck her, it was like one of the sledgehammer blows that she was defending against.

She had little chance of escaping.

She had attempted to break free from them several times, but they always adjusted their positioning quickly and with little effort. Always keeping her exactly where they wanted.

Right in the middle of their noose, which was slowly and relentlessly closing around her.

Having trapped her, they were probably enjoying themselves immensely.

That thought helped to rebuild her fire, pulling her free from the tight grip of despair that threatened to engulf her.

Melissa redoubled her efforts as her three attackers continued to push and prod her, herding her toward the trail that ran along the harbor, the water just beyond it.

It wasn't until her feet touched the gravel path, one of the men standing in front of her, one on each side, that they finally halted their assault.

They had cornered her. She had nowhere to go but into the drink.

Irritated that she had failed to get away from these three behemoths who were so deceptively fast, she used the next few seconds to catch her breath and get a better sense of just how much trouble she was in.

She could finally see the trio clearly, the towering figures standing there calmly, rods held in hands that looked to be the size of catchers' mitts. Most galling to her, none of them were breathing heavily or even sweating after the last few minutes of exertion.

That just wasn't fair. She was drenched.

The men took a step closer, looming over her even more.

She had nowhere to go, so she stood ramrod straight, giving all three the harsh look that her mother had taught her to use in situations such as this. A look that had intimidated many a Teg in the past.

Unfortunately, her effort had no effect on these giants whatsoever, one of the men actually smirking slightly, clearly amused.

She was about to offer a few choice words when her eyes swept over their beards that ran down to their belts, all three intricately braided.

Interesting. Even more so, concerning.

She had never come up against Teg such as these before.

Who were they? What were they?

"Give us what we seek," the Teg in the center ordered.

She hesitated before replying, her eyes drawn to the man's beard. The whiskery creation made her think of a snake. She glanced briefly at the beards of the other two.

The same design.

It appeared as if the snake was biting its own tail.

For some reason – maybe it was their blondish almost white hair that was slicked back off their scalps -- Jormungandr, the World Serpent of Norse mythology, said to be coiled around the earth beneath the seas, immediately came to mind as the most obvious representation of the design.

If she looked closely enough and squinted, it appeared as if the weave moved, although she chalked that up to the shadows that still flitted about her three assailants and a quirk of the light.

"What do you seek, beard boy?" demanded Melissa. She tried to instill as much venom in her voice as she possibly could, having lost what little patience she had left after her fight to stay alive. She hoped to push them into a rash decision if she could.

Her insult did nothing for her. The three blonde giants took a step closer to her, tightening the semicircle, rather than giving her the space that she desired.

"You know what we seek, thief," stated the one facing her. "Give it to us. We will not hurt you if you do. But we will do more than hurt you if you do not obey us. Obey or feel the pain that we can and will inflict upon you with our rods of power."

"Your rods of power," snorted Melissa, unable to contain herself. She couldn't ignore a comment like that, laughing softly. "That's what you call them?"

"You dare to scorn us!" the leader roared, clearly not pleased by her insult.

"I have no idea what you're talking about," Melissa replied, her venom and humor gone, replaced by a hint of uncertainty.

How could those hunting her possibly have known where she was? She had been exceedingly thorough while making her escape.

"I'd be happy to help you, but I don't know what you want," Melissa explained. "What is it that you want?"

"Give us what we seek!" The fighter in the center gripped his weapon a bit more tightly, his knuckles turning white, lifting himself up onto his toes, his two companions doing the same. Clearly, the leader of the trio was preparing to finish this encounter in a way that Melissa preferred that he wouldn't.

"I don't know what you want!" Melissa shouted, getting angry now, hoping that her show of emotion might make them hesitate.

The fury that was rising within her was all too real. At these men who had located her so easily. At herself for obviously making a mistake.

She didn't do mistakes. Ever.

But apparently she had. And that really pissed her off.

"You know what we seek! Give us what you stole!"

"I can't give you what I don't have!" shouted Melissa, beginning to realize that unlike all the other difficult situations that she had faced in the past, in which she had found some way to extricate herself, now no means of evasion came to mind.

She was stuck. At the mercy of three large, muscular men who likely used a great deal of hair product.

She would fight, of course. But she wouldn't win.

Beyond that, she didn't know what was going to happen next. Although she could imagine a whole host of possibilities, none of them appealing to her.

"Then you will pay for your insolence," the towering hulk intoned, almost as if he were about to begin an ancient rite.

As one the three men took a step forward. They got no farther. A voice from behind them stopped them in their tracks.

"Really? Three of you to do this job? Aren't you embarrassed?" The voice was mild, almost amused. However, it contained a hard edge as well. Harder than steel. "I would be embarrassed if I were in your shoes. Three big fellas like you being shown up by a woman who barely comes up to those beards of yours."

Melissa's eyes widened.

What in all the hells was the baker doing here? And why was he carrying a walking stick?

As the faces of the three men turned red with rage, the color made even brighter because of their pale skin, she took a closer look at the man she had first seen in the kitchen of Tia's Bakes. He was wearing running clothes, his shirt spattered with several splashes of flour.

Involuntarily she took a step back, which brought her closer to the water lapping against the harbor's retaining wall.

Those eyes.

They were burning so brightly that it was like staring into

the flames of a bonfire. Yet instead of warming her, they chilled her to the bone.

"Leave, little man," said the bearded fellow on Melissa's left side. "You have no place here. The woman is not your concern."

"Actually, it is my place," the baker replied, his eyes flashing dangerously, the bright orange becoming a fiery red. "Although you're right. The woman isn't my concern. But you ... you are."

"Why would that be?" asked the hulking fellow who was the leader of the three, giving in to his curiosity rather than indulging himself and crushing the interloper.

"It's pretty obvious, don't you think?"

"Tell me, little man. I'm losing patience."

"Well, clearly you're insecure because you've got two friends with you to harass this woman -- you can't manage that on your own, which isn't all that surprising -- and you're overly aggressive because you're compensating for something that you find quite embarrassing." The baker held up his hand, thumb separated from his forefinger by only a few inches.

Silence descended around them for just an instant. It took some time for the trio to understand what the smaller man was referring to. Although Melissa understood immediately, and she unavoidably snorted out a laugh behind them.

Her reaction helped the three to make sense of the slight.

The giants' faces, already a bright red, soon resembled volcanos about to blow. Without saying another word, the three rushed toward the baker, steel rods raised above their shoulders so that they could give their tormentor a quick killing blow.

Melissa grinned in delight. This was her chance to make her escape.

But she didn't.

Instead, she stayed rooted to the spot, transfixed by the scene that was playing out before her.

The baker whipped his cane around in a blur, knocking the

steel rods away from him with little trouble. Even more impressive than his speed was his composure. He barely moved while the three hulking men demonstrated a feverishness to their actions that had been missing when they attacked her.

It was almost as if the trio of giants had been consumed by a frantic desperation just seconds after engaging with the baker. Realizing that they had little chance of defeating him, they were allowing their emotions rather than their instincts to rule them.

As she observed the clash for a few seconds more, she couldn't tell for sure, but it almost seemed like the baker's walking stick was more than just a cane.

Every so often, as the baker whipped the length of wood through the air, not only blocking the steel rods, but also slamming the walking stick into the men's guts, kidneys, backs, shoulders, even groin – the last of which elicited a high-pitched hiss from the unfortunate recipient that made Melissa think of her grandmother's tea kettle – it resembled a sword instead.

She had to be mistaken. If the baker was fighting with a sword, the three men who had so stupidly attacked him would be bloody messes by now, nothing more than crumpled masses staining the green grass.

Melissa pulled herself free from the trance the baker's smooth movements had put her in. She didn't understand why, but she continued to ignore the instinct to run that had grown stronger and stronger since the baker first appeared.

It was the smart thing to do. It was what she had been trained to do.

Of course, when had she ever done the smart thing?

In fact, she was in this very predicament now because she hadn't done the smart thing to begin with.

Shaking her head in disbelief at what she was about to do, rather than running, she used the Grym to reform the shield on her forearm. Then, for her free hand, she crafted a rod that resembled those being used by her assailants.

She sprinted toward one of the men who was swinging at the baker. Taking advantage of the fact that the giant didn't realize that she was behind him, Melissa brought the magical rod back behind her ear, then swung down with all the strength that she could muster.

The rod slammed against the man's broad back, sending shockwaves up her arm. However, instead of falling to his knees as she expected that he would, the blonde-bearded giant slowly turned. When her eyes caught his, he gave her a disappointed look that suggested that she had just made another mistake.

A very bad mistake.

In a flash, the man charged her, swinging with a power that she couldn't match.

She deflected the blow. Barely. Then another. And one more.

Despite the difficulty of the combat, Melissa believed that she stood a better chance against one of these hulking blond behemoths than she did against three. More confident in herself, she began to answer his attacks with some of her own.

With her rod crafted of the Grym, she gained a few oomphs and umphs when she struck true, focusing on his joints. Elbow. Knee. Wrist. A few times even targeting his groin.

Although never in a position to deliver a knockout blow, she certainly was able to distract her adversary by focusing on his more vulnerable body parts.

For the next several minutes she was quite pleased with herself, giving as good as she got. She lost herself in the combat, reveling in the motion, the immediate decisions that she needed to make, the look of anger on her adversary's face that slowly transitioned to concern as he began to comprehend that she was a much better fighter than he had given her credit for.

A loud cry from behind her broke her concentration. Another one followed immediately after the first.

Distracted, her hulking adversary stopped and took a few steps back, putting some space between them.

She used the break to catch her breath.

Looking over her opponent's shoulder, she saw that the baker stood over one of the giants. He was pressing the point of his walking stick against his throat, a small trickle of blood leaking down the giant's neck. The other attacker was several feet away, rolling around on the ground.

The injured giant was holding his knee, obviously in agony, revealing a strong will by not screeching at the top of his lungs as he so clearly wanted to do.

She certainly wanted to shriek for him. His lower leg and foot were bent in the wrong direction, a long sliver of bone slicing through his Carhartt work pants.

Melissa was impressed. She had seen the baker's skill at the beginning of the fight. Even so, she had never imagined that the combat would come to an end so quickly or with such finality.

Yet what she found most shocking and inexplicable was that somehow the baker had cut off several inches of his adversaries' beards. Wisps of smoke drifted up from what was left of their whiskers, the smell of burnt hair permeating the space until the breeze coming off the water swept it away.

"Yield," the baker said calmly, pressing down a bit harder with the sharpened tip of his walking stick.

"We cannot yield!" the wounded man hissed between clenched teeth. "We do not yield. Ever!"

"You can, and you have. Others of your people have yielded to me before, and they have done so with their honor intact."

"We are not like the others."

"You will be if you make the right decision," the baker replied. "They're still alive. If you don't yield, you'll be dead. That's a significant difference."

"We cannot …"

"I suggest you yield now," the baker said, pressing down harder on the top of his staff. "Don't let your pride get in the way of reality."

"You don't understand," the man lying at the feet of the baker choked out, speaking a bit more easily when the baker relented just a touch with his walking stick. "We cannot break the contract. It is a matter of honor."

"If you don't break the contract then it's a matter of your life. Is it really worth that to you?"

"We cannot," the man repeated miserably. "Our enclaves are no longer safe. There are those among us who have forgotten the traditions. Who would sell us out if it benefits them."

"Do you have families that you need to worry about?" the baker asked.

"No, we are orphans, trained to this work by a despicable Were."

"One who has forgotten the traditions of your kind."

"Exactly," the large man lying at the baker's feet confirmed. "Yet there is no other path for us among our people. And if there is, we have yet to find it."

The baker nodded slowly, understanding. "Then I offer you a choice, Were. You and your blood brothers. You can return to your employer, who will likely kill you, or I can kill you with less pain than you would suffer otherwise and ease your passage from this world."

Melissa couldn't believe what she was hearing. Less than an hour before the man was wielding a rolling pin. Now, he appeared to be brandishing a blazing sword when the light struck the walking stick in just the right way.

She knew then to keep her mouth shut. To wait to see how this scene was going to come to a close.

"Neither appeals to us," the man bleeding from his throat

whispered.

"Then a third option," the baker offered.

"What would that be?"

"I offer you sanctuary."

"Sanctuary? Here?"

Melissa didn't fully understand what was happening now, even as she listened intently.

"Sanctuary here," the baker confirmed.

Melissa saw that the baker's response immediately caught the attention of her three attackers. The trio looked at one another, trying to judge where their brothers stood on the offer as they thought about what it might mean for them.

The baker didn't seem to mind, giving them all the time that they needed.

"What is the price that must be paid if we were to accept your offer of sanctuary?"

"You renounce the contract and I'll help you and your wounded brother. I'll make sure you both get the medical attention you need."

"You have still not told me your price."

"You work for me." The baker's voice was calm, assured. Also cold, which was a contradiction to the fire in his eyes. "Only for me."

"For you? Doing what?"

"Whatever I require," the baker replied, not feeling the need to offer any details.

The large man lying on the grass didn't respond. The baker, comprehending the source of his hesitation, looked down at him and finally gave him a smile.

"Don't worry, I wouldn't ask you to go to the grocery store or pick up my dry cleaning." The baker's expression became serious once more. "Or perform a task that chafes at your honor."

"What would you require of us?" the man who stood across from Melissa asked, entering the conversation.

"For you to do the work that you're good at. But only for me."

"And you are?" asked the man bleeding from his throat.

The baker leaned down then, removing the tip of his cane as he did so. "If I tell you, then you are bound to keep my name secret, whether you accept my offer or not. You are bound to never reveal where I am."

The man stared into the baker's eyes, startled upon seeing a flaring reddish orange that reminded him of a dragon's fire. "I am so bound."

"Your brothers as well."

"We are so bound," the other two hulking fellows said in unison, the one with the badly injured knee struggling to get the words out because of the pain radiating out from his injuries.

"I am Draig."

The breaths of all three men caught in their throats upon hearing that. The one who had been at Draig's mercy glanced at the other two. They both nodded. Apparently, the three had decided.

"You are the fallen one."

"I'm Draig. No more. No less."

"Many of the Teg say that the Fallen Knight will rise once again," murmured the fellow closest to Draig. "That would be a sight to see."

"Just because some of the Teg say something doesn't mean it's true," Draig replied softly, even as his eyes blazed a bit more fiercely.

"We know you even though we shouldn't," the leader of the trio said cryptically. "We are honored." Then he nodded. "We accept your offer."

"So be it," Draig said with a heavy seriousness. To Melissa it seemed as if an unbreakable bargain had just been struck.

Draig pulled the man to his feet. "Your names?"

"I am Ragnar. The one behind me rolling around on the ground is Urs. The other is Thorsen."

"Ragnar, Urs, Thorsen, I grant you sanctuary in Kraken Cove," intoned Draig. They bowed their heads upon hearing that.

Melissa had no clue as to what was happening, but she was more than just a little intrigued. It was like watching a scene from *Outlander*, her latest streaming binge.

"Your problems are my problems," the baker named Draig stated clearly and in a strong voice, as if what he was doing was part of a sacred ceremony. "You will answer my call just as I will answer yours. Always. Loyalty and faith before all else."

"Loyalty and faith before all else," the trio murmured. "So be it."

Melissa watched, not quite understanding what had occurred, as the three hulking men lifted their heads, even the one with the sickeningly twisted leg, and smiled like giddy schoolboys.

They had just bound themselves to the baker? To Draig? And who was the Fallen Knight?

She cursed under her breath. Another part of her Teg education that she had missed because her mother had raised her away from her people when she was younger.

Draig? Despite her lack of knowledge that name sounded familiar. Had her mother ever mentioned him before?

"Your brothers can help you up the cliff," Draig said to the man with the badly broken leg. He then returned his attention to the leader of the three. "Find Cerridwen at the bakery. Tell her what we have agreed. She will do what needs to be done. She will provide food and shelter until we can speak again."

The hulking fellow who towered over Draig nodded, then offered a short bow. "Thank you for your generosity."

"It will be repaid. Of that have no doubt. Remember that."

"Gladly."

Melissa watched as the three giants shuffled off. Still not comprehending what she had just witnessed, she approached the man who had helped her.

"Your name is Draig."

"And your name is Melissa."

There was something about him that immediately rubbed her the wrong way. Maybe it was how he replied to her statement with a smirk curling his lips.

She couldn't figure out exactly what it was for sure. Maybe it was the certainty with which he spoke that aggravated her.

"There is no way that you're a baker."

"I'm many things," he replied enigmatically.

"Who were they?" she asked, nodding to the three big fellows, two struggling to help the injured one up the staircase that led to the Safe Haven.

"You don't want to know."

"I do want to know. I wouldn't have asked otherwise."

Clearly irritated by her sharp insistence, he told her in a tight voice. "Berserkers."

Berserkers? She shook her head in disbelief. Why would Berserkers come after her?

Then she thought about it a little bit more, locking away her shock. The better question was why wouldn't Berserkers come after her?

If those three really were Berserkers, then that certainly explained the terror that had almost immobilized her at the worst possible moment. That was one of the key traits of Berserkers. They used the fears of those they hunted against them. Freezing them. Taking away their ability to think and move.

"You can't be serious?" she said with a laugh.

"Believe what you want," he replied with a shrug. "I'm just answering your question."

Draig waited for Melissa to think through what three Berserkers coming for her might mean. Any conclusion she reached couldn't be good. Furthermore, the appearance of these hunters hinted that his initial concerns regarding Melissa arriving in Kraken Cove were justified.

Berserkers were Norse warriors, the name used because centuries before these fighters often wore a bear's skin as a coat. The stories told that they fought in a trancelike fury. They were incredibly violent. They were incredibly effective in a battle.

They fought barefoot, bare-chested, and without armor. They were absolutely fearless.

They were said to draw their power from a bear they killed when they were barely out of their mother's womb. They were said to howl like a bear, foam at the mouth, and gnaw the edge of their shields before a battle.

A lot was said about them in the histories. Barely any of it was correct.

Draig knew the truth.

Berserkers actually were members of the Tylwyth Teg.

Werebears.

Although they only shifted to their natural form when there was a dire need to do so. Which was rare, because their size, strength, and speed usually was more than enough for them to get past whatever challenge was placed before them.

"You can't be serious?" Melissa said again, still finding it hard to believe.

"Are you talking to me or to yourself? Because you already said that."

Melissa gave him a sharp look. "Are you always this smug?"

"You know, I did just save your life."

His comment stopped her short again. She held back the

pointed words she wanted to shoot his way. "You did no such thing."

"Really? Then how would you describe what just happened?"

"You were kind enough to help me deal with these Berserkers," Melissa said with an imperious expression.

"Oh, so that was how it went down," Draig interjected, his voice containing a hint of amusement, although very faint. Irritation was more prevalent.

"Which I was managing quite well on my own until you decided to intervene."

"Really? Selective memory, I take it?"

"Yes, really," Melissa replied with a harder edge, her own aggravation increasing. "I allowed you to help me even though I didn't need your help. I had everything well in hand before you complicated matters."

Draig smiled then, although it didn't reach his eyes, which continued to flash a fiery red. "Believe what you want, but we both know the truth."

"I thought you were going to kill him." Melissa ignored his comment, seeking to turn the conversation back toward the end of the fight, curious about the conclusion and knowing that if she continued down the current path she had no chance of winning the argument that she had started.

Yet even as she did so, a key question continued to plague her. Why did he feel the need to involve himself? Especially against Berserkers.

She wasn't used to getting help from someone else. She was used to looking out for herself.

His stepping in to defend her confused her. She didn't know what to do with this baker who apparently was her unwanted knight in shining armor. Or Fallen Knight as the Berserker had said. She would need to learn more about that reference.

"I was."

He said it coldly, as if it was of little concern to him.

"Why didn't you?"

"Because I didn't have to."

Melissa stared at him then as he stood there calmly, his walking stick leaning against his shoulder. Even though she couldn't do it in the bakery, she forced herself to do it now. She really needed to see him.

She had sensed the power within him while he battled the two Berserkers. An almost frightening amount.

"Can I ask you a question?"

"Sure, but no promises that I answer."

She bit back another sharp response. He seemed to specialize in irritating her. "Who are you Draig?"

He smiled then. A real smile. She didn't know what to make of it.

"You already know the answer to that."

He was staring at her so hard that she could feel the pressure building up in the back of her eyes. Her nerves began to fray. She was on edge again. She hated that he could do this to her so easily.

He broke the tension that had been rising between them with a response that made her snort again with reluctant laughter.

"I'm a baker."

"You keep telling yourself that and I guess you might actually believe it."

"It's the truth. And what of you?"

"What of me?"

"Who are you Melissa?"

That question stopped her short. His eyes were still locked onto hers, that reddish orange flaring. She couldn't pull her gaze away from his. And she knew, she *knew*, that he knew who she was.

He knew every aspect of her, even those parts she didn't

know of herself. That realization made her feel naked under his gaze.

It wasn't a good feeling. It wasn't an entirely bad feeling, either. Because she felt drawn to those blazing eyes of his.

With an almost visible effort, she ripped her gaze away from his, finally able to breathe again.

"I'm going to head back to the inn."

She started walking up the steps that led to the Safe Haven's backyard garden.

"A word of advice?"

She stopped, but she didn't look back. "Whatever you're involved in, Melissa, be smart. If they can send Berserkers after you, they can send someone ... or something ... much worse, and they probably will."

Melissa didn't say anything for quite a long time, a chill running down her spine. Then she nodded and continued up the stairs.

At that very moment, she wanted nothing more than to get to her attic room, lock the door, and crawl under the covers.

Draig watched her go, his expression thoughtful. He had sensed it in the bakery and confirmed it on the green.

Melissa was trouble. And that trouble would pull in anyone stupid enough to get involved.

Someone like him, who had a knack for getting caught in someone else's web of difficulties.

He didn't want to become a part of Melissa's problems, but his sense of honor, of right and wrong, had brought him down here.

After seeing the two men wearing fedoras, he couldn't stay at the bakery. He needed to find out what was going on. If for no other reason than to ensure that it didn't risk what he had built here in Kraken Cove.

At least that's what he told himself. Even though he knew that wasn't the entire truth.

Reluctantly, he admitted to himself that there was something about Melissa when he glanced at her in the bakery that had resonated with him.

A familiarity, strange as that may seem. A reminder of his past.

There was another variable that led him to engage with the Berserkers. He sensed that her problems were connected to his larger concerns. That maybe the tracks he had found on the trail were here for her, not him, although he wouldn't accept that conclusion until he had real evidence to back it up.

While he had been studying Melissa just a moment before, he had already known of her conversation with Cerridwen in the Book Nook. From that it didn't take much for him to figure out why she might have come to Kraken Cove.

But there was another piece to this puzzle as well. Maybe that's what resonated with him the most.

He could understand a person's desire to disappear.

Draig had come here to escape his father. Even more so, he had come to Kraken Cove to escape the burden of being his father's son.

He couldn't fault Melissa if that's what she was trying to do.

Evade what was hunting her.

He would fault her if trouble continued to follow her to Kraken Cove.

10

SEVERE CONSEQUENCES

Shri didn't want to be where she was. She didn't have a choice, however.

Usually when she had news, good or bad, she told her client over the phone.

She preferred to keep her distance.

If any of her clients asked why, she told them it wasn't a lack of trust, but rather a matter of efficiency.

She could get more done faster if she wasn't traveling around the world holding their hands.

Well, she didn't say it like that. When she explained her approach, she focused on the efficiency part of her explanation.

In truth, she didn't mind the travel. She could conduct her business from anywhere. So long as she had a wi-fi connection. And even without one she had the capacity to keep her business running. It was one of her unique skills as one of the Teg, a benefit of being who she was. It just took a bit more effort on her part.

No, her hesitation at meeting with her clients came down to self-preservation.

Many of her clients weren't considered the most stable of

Teg. They were prone to erratic behavior. Often violent. Sometimes murderous.

Of course, if they weren't they wouldn't be seeking to hire the men and women she represented.

With this client, however, with the news that she had to give him, she needed to do it face to face. No matter how much she didn't want to. No matter how much the thought of being in his presence made her want to run and hide.

She tried to stay still in an attempt to hide her growing uneasiness. She sat in a chair facing the long, rectangular desk that was placed in the middle of the circular chamber. She had been led up the stairs that wound around the outside of the turret by four Paladins and then told to take a seat with a barely perceptible nod from the leader of the squad.

The four men, all wearing black Polo shirts and khaki pants, steel rods held easily in their hands, hadn't said a word when she arrived at the entrance to the estate, the sound of the ocean pounding against the coast audible even though she was on the other side of the sprawling property that best resembled a castle.

She was nervous, which was rare for her. She usually handled the worst stress with little trouble by internalizing it. Of course, that stress played havoc on her digestive system, thus the antacid she always carried with her and the fact that she drank just as much if not more Maalox with her dinner than she did wine.

Yet, she wasn't edgy because of the Paladins who were arrayed behind her. It was because of the person she was there to meet.

She could handle four Paladins if that proved necessary. She hoped that she wouldn't have to.

It could get messy.

For them.

No, she feared that when word got out, if she engaged in a

combat here, it likely would affect some of her current contracts and eliminate her ability to obtain any more in the future.

She didn't think it would come to that. Her client appreciated discretion and self-control just as much as she did.

Then again, based on his reputation, he wasn't known for his patience or understanding.

Just then a man wearing tan slacks and an untucked light blue button-down shirt strode soundlessly past her, revealing only his broad back and a shock of wavy dark hair before he slipped behind his desk. The shadows growing in the chamber thanks to the sun dropping in the sky made it impossible for her to get a good look at his face.

Probably by design, she thought. A power play on his part. Which only made sense.

She knew that with this client everything he did, everything he said, was about enhancing his power. For him, there was nothing else.

"Why are you here?" he asked after he leaned back in his modern, ergonomic chair, which clashed with everything in the turret, and placed himself in even more shadow, crossing his legs and resting his loafers on the desk.

"I thought that you would want to hear the information I have in person. It's also time sensitive."

"Tell me."

"The three we sent to take the Witch are missing."

"What do you mean that they're missing?" he asked in a deceptively quiet and calm voice.

"That's all I can say, lord. That's all I know. They're missing."

"Three Berserkers don't just go missing. Three Berserkers don't do anything that they don't want to do."

"They've missed four check-ins." She shrugged. "I've heard nothing from them. They're always prompt. They're always meticulous. That's all I can tell you with any certainty."

"The answer is really quite simple," he said, his tone suggesting that there was no doubt to the conclusion that he had reached after barely giving the matter any thought.

"You believe he killed them."

"You don't?"

"Three Berserkers? That's asking quite a lot from a dead man."

"Three Berserkers are nothing to the Fallen Knight."

She didn't respond to his comment, offering him a half-hearted shrug instead as if to say that his guess was as good as any other. "What would you like me to do?"

The man stared at her. Despite the lengthening shadows, she still could feel the iciness in his gaze. Then she thought she caught the flash of a bright smile, although she couldn't be sure.

"Nothing, nothing at all. I'll deal with the Witch in another way."

"So you won't require my services any longer?"

She had expected as much. And truth to tell, losing this contract really didn't bother her. She had hesitated to take it in the first place, only doing so because of the exorbitant fee attached.

"No one will be requiring your services any longer."

The woman reached for the Grym before her client had even completed his sentence, sensing his intention as soon as he had made up his mind.

She believed that she was ready for anything he might try, having been in similar situations before.

Yet she was shocked to discover that she wasn't fast enough. Worse, she wasn't strong enough to break through the shield that he had crafted with the Grym that not only prevented her from reaching the power that she could have used to escape her predicament, but also froze her in place. She could move her eyes and nothing else.

She tried to shudder but she couldn't when she felt a meaty hand tighten around each shoulder, pushing her deeper into her chair.

Two of the Paladins approached, one from each side, preparing to carry her away, chair and all.

11

MAKING HER ESCAPE

Melissa had spent the better part of the day in her attic room. She enjoyed the calm and comfort the Safe Haven offered her. The sense of security that she had never experienced anywhere else but here.

Yet as each hour passed she grew more restless.

There were things that she needed to do, and she couldn't do them from her room.

She wanted to go back to the bookstore. If she timed it right, maybe Cerridwen wouldn't be there. Maybe she would be busy in the bakery and Melissa would have more time to search for what she thought was there but hadn't had the chance to confirm.

The man wearing the fedora scared her, and her need to get away from him had set in motion a series of events that made what had begun as a relaxing morning anything but.

Because of her desire to get moving again, she had stood at the door to her room eight times, willing her hand to reach out and turn the knob.

Instead, rather than take the risk, she retreated to her bed or the very comfortable couch placed in front of the large window that allowed her to look out onto the inn's front lawn.

She couldn't ignore the truth no matter how much she wanted to.

She was afraid.

What happened to her that morning had more than unsettled her. The two men in the fedoras and then the three Berserkers were bad enough.

Meeting Draig, who presented himself as a baker but clearly was so much more, was worse. Of all of them, he was the one who scared her the most.

Draig was a unique name. That's what had stuck with her ever since she met him.

That and those eyes of his that burned like they contained a dragon's fire.

That only made sense, didn't it? Since Draig was the Welsh word for dragon. At least she had figured out that much about him.

She felt like she should be more familiar with his name, but for the life of her she couldn't understand why.

It had to be because of her mother. Thinking about it for much of the day, she was certain that she had mentioned the name, although Melissa couldn't recall when or the circumstances. In passing. Otherwise she would have remembered.

She hoped it would come to her.

Besides his very distinctive eyes, there was something off about her rescuer. She was sure of it.

All right, yes, she could admit it to herself even though she would never admit it to him.

Draig had saved her from the three Berserkers.

If not for him, she would be ...

She didn't know where she would be, and that thought chilled her. Being tortured that very second? Already dead and dumped by the side of the road? Her body floating out of the cove and into the Atlantic Ocean?

She couldn't say, although she was certain that considering who it was who wanted her, whatever might have happened without Draig's timely intervention, it wouldn't be pleasant.

Draig.

Why did he feel the need to intercede on her behalf? How did he even know she was down by the harbor and in danger?

For Hades' sake, he was a baker!

Who was she kidding?

Just because she had seen him baking in the kitchen didn't mean that he was just a baker.

After the display he had put on with the Berserkers and that weird ceremony at the end, he clearly was much, much more than that. He probably could have used a rolling pin rather than that walking stick of his and done just as well against her would-be abductors.

Draig.

Images of the baker wearing a suit of shining armor with an apron wrapped around his waist popped into her mind every time she thought about him, which was more than she wanted. It was beyond irritating now, yet she couldn't seem to turn the imagery off.

Growling in frustration, she tried to concentrate. She couldn't afford to let her mind wander in that direction now. Not with so much at stake. Too much depended on the decisions that she needed to make.

She didn't know what to think of Draig. He frightened her in a way that no one else had in quite some time.

In fact, she couldn't think of anyone else who had made her feel so uncomfortable just with a look. Even the two men wearing the 1950s fedoras and the three Berserkers had nothing on Draig and his dead-eye stare.

Yet now, after spending most of the day telling herself that it was all right to stay in her room because she was using the time to search the Internet for more information on Kraken Cove and Draig in particular, she felt like a failure and a coward.

There was little to be found on Kraken Cove other than what was provided by the town's own website and a few sparse references on Tripadvisor.

And with respect to Draig, there was nothing at all. Not even a connection to the bakery where he worked. In fact, the only success she had was learning what his name meant.

Worse, she had completed her research, or lack thereof, in less than an hour, doing nothing more than wasting time after that.

She couldn't escape the truth. Once she was done with her searches, she had chosen to hide. She hated having to admit that to herself.

Not able to stand it any longer, Melissa decided that she was going to head down to restaurant row and get dinner. And, instead of doing takeaway and bringing it right back to the safety of her room, she was going to force herself to eat in the restaurant.

No more hiding.

Yet she had been standing in front of her door for several minutes now having this conversation with herself. For the ninth time. Her hand was poised above the handle, not yet having touched the brass knob.

Cursing in anger, less at herself and now more at what had sent her fleeing back to the Safe Haven, finally she twisted the knob and stepped out into the hallway.

Although nervous, Melissa smiled. The air smelled fresher out here. Not rank with her fear that permeated the attic.

Pulling the door closed behind her, she trotted quickly down the stairs, wanting to build up her momentum so that she couldn't heed the urge to turn, run back up the steps, and return to her room. When she reached the front desk, Hestia stood there, leaning over the counter, almost like she was waiting for her.

"Heading out, dear?"

"Yes, I'm going to get some dinner," Melissa replied with another smile. Judging from Hestia's expression and slight nod, the older woman clearly could tell that it was forced.

"Restaurant row?"

"That was the plan."

"All the restaurants there can offer you a good bite to eat, dear. And you look famished." Melissa assumed that was Hestia's indirect way of telling her that she knew Melissa had stayed in her room almost the entire day, not bothering to get lunch. "Do you like Italian? You really look like you need to put some meat on your bones."

"I do," Melissa replied, unable to prevent herself from glancing in the mirror behind the innkeeper. "Did you have a suggestion in mind?"

Was Hestia telling her that she was too thin? Melissa didn't think she looked any different as she gazed at her own reflection. She did look tired, but after all that had occurred during the last few days that only made sense.

"In that case, I'll call ahead for you. You'll love Renzetti's."

"Thank you, Hestia. I appreciate it." Melissa sensed that Hestia was trying to be helpful.

Although she got the impression as well that there was more going on with her offer than just that. It was almost as if she was trying to direct Melissa in a certain direction so that the innkeeper could keep tabs on her.

She wondered why Hestia would want to do that. Maybe Draig had mentioned to her what happened.

Draig!

She couldn't seem to go more than a few minutes without his face popping into her mind. And now he wasn't wearing the suit of armor with the apron wrapped around it. He was wearing the apron and nothing else.

This was becoming more than just irritating.

"Also, I would suggest not staying out too late, dear. So I'll make sure they have a table for you as soon as you arrive."

"Why shouldn't I stay out too late?" Melissa asked.

It was only a few minutes after six. She had wanted to swing by the bookstore one more time, just to see if she might be able to escape Cerridwen's attention, before getting a meal. Or perhaps the shop after dinner, employing her unique skills.

"It's a full moon, dear." Hestia's eyes hardened, a warning contained within. "We've been having some trouble around the outskirts of town during the full moon, so better to be safe than sorry. If you need someone to walk you back once you're done with dinner, just give me a call."

Melissa kept her eyes on Hestia. The person she saw standing before her now wasn't the welcoming, mild-mannered innkeeper she had met late the night before.

This woman looked like an angry grandma ready to walk into the ring and go ten rounds with the world heavyweight champion. Not knowing what to say, Melissa nodded in thanks and then stepped outside.

After she closed the door behind her, Melissa stopped on the top step. She looked out across the lawn. The sun was going down and the lights had come on, illuminating the grounds of the inn.

That, in itself, wasn't unexpected. What surprised her were the gnomes.

A quick survey told her that all the garden gnomes were facing away from the Safe Haven. The last time she had looked from her attic room just an hour before she could have sworn that they were positioned differently.

There were at least a hundred of the colorful stone statues, so she doubted Hestia had come out here and moved them all by herself, though Melissa had no doubt that she was right.

Somehow someone even had placed a few of the gnomes up in the trees lining the driveway. The lowest one was at least thirty feet off the ground.

Was someone playing with her?

SEAMUS KEPT the motor close to idle as he backed the *Kraken* into his slip. He wasn't surprised to see Draig waiting for him on the dock.

"I'm glad to see you're still alive," Draig called.

"So am I," muttered Seamus.

"What happened?"

Draig examined the several long scratches across the port-side hull. To his keen eye, it appeared as if a creature with very sharp claws had tried to climb aboard and then, unable to make it all the way to the deck, had hung on for as long as it could before Seamus dislodged it.

The three-foot piece of missing railing, obviously cut free, suggested that last part. Probably with an axe.

"It's a long story," grumbled Seamus. "Before I tell you I need a drink."

Draig caught the line that Seamus threw to him and tied off the stern. Then he trotted down the pier and took the line Seamus tossed to him for the bow.

"That can probably be arranged."

Seamus jumped down onto the pier. "You see the moon?"

"Hard to miss."

"You remember what we were talking about this morning?"

"Hard to forget."

"Why are you so difficult all the time?"

"It's a gift," Draig shrugged.

"You're not down here just to check on me, I take it."

"Of course not, although I did want to make sure you got back safe. Did the deal go bad?"

Seamus shook his head. "No, the deal went down fine. The problem was the third party who tried to force himself into the mix after the exchange had taken place."

"Those are from the third party?" Draig nodded toward the rips and scratches in the fiberglass hull.

"They are."

"Will this third party continue to be a problem?"

"Most definitely not," Seamus stated with a distinct pleasure. "I can tell you that with complete confidence."

"Good to hear."

"So what's the other reason you're here? I know it's not just to check up on me."

"I was hoping that you could help me with something." Draig gave his irascible friend a broad grin and a lift of his eyebrows.

"Now?"

"Now. I wouldn't be here otherwise."

"What about that beer?"

"Later."

~

"WAS it all to your liking, Ms. Gorgonella?" The owner and chef had come out from the kitchen to see her off, the clatter of pots and pans audible until the swinging door closed behind him.

"It was, Joseph. I've never had a better meal. Thank you. I won't need to eat for the rest of the week."

It had taken two busboys to clear all the dishes. The food had kept coming even though Melissa hadn't asked for it.

Insalata verde. Risotto alla salsiccia. Branzino al forno. A tasting menu to be sure. Still, it had added up to a meal that could feed a family of six and still require three or four containers to bring home the leftovers.

Despite the quantity she couldn't help herself. It had been so good that she had eaten every bite. And before she could push herself up from her table, the coffee and cannoli that she hadn't ordered appeared.

She didn't need to eat the dessert. But she had. It was too hard to resist the wonderful smells, and she didn't want to upset Joseph. Even though her stomach protested, she demolished the cannoli in three bites.

She hadn't ordered any of her dinner. Hestia had called ahead and suggested to Joseph that he should get started before his guest arrived. The first dish was coming out of the kitchen as soon as Melissa walked through Renzetti's door, the waiter already pouring wine into her glass.

Melissa reached for her cell phone and the cash she kept in the protective case to pay the bill. Joseph waved her off.

"A special deal with the Safe Haven," he explained. "The dinner comes with your room."

"It seems that Hestia is looking out for me even when I'm not at the inn."

"In more ways than you might think," Joseph confirmed under his breath as he gave Melissa a broad smile and held the door open for her. Speaking more loudly, "Enjoy your evening, Ms. Gorgonella. A good night for a quick walk back to the inn."

She couldn't say that she was surprised by Joseph's comment, although it did remind her of what Hestia had told her before she left the inn.

Shaking off the unease that sought to take hold within her, when she stepped outside, Melissa felt as good as she had after she ate Cerridwen's scone that morning.

Strangely, she didn't feel as stuffed as she thought she would. Perhaps Joseph did much the same with his food as

Cerridwen did with hers, using the Grym to give it a little something extra based on what the diner might need.

A question for Hestia, perhaps, when she returned to the Safe Haven. Until then, Melissa wanted to walk and work off some of her dinner.

Melissa enjoyed the cool breeze coming off the water as she headed out of restaurant row and onto the town green. The sky was clear, not a cloud to be seen, the full moon shining down brightly.

Even so, it was dark in among the streets of Kraken Cove. The streetlights, crafted to look like what you might find in nineteenth century London, gave off a dim glow that barely penetrated the light fog drifting up and over the cliffs.

It was also quiet. It seemed that the only action in Kraken Cove after the shops closed took place at the restaurants, and on this Wednesday evening they weren't too busy. There had only been a handful of people in Renzetti's. And there was no one on the street with her now.

That in itself didn't worry her. She knew how to take care of herself.

Rather, it was the premonition that surged through her that put her on edge. The sense that all wasn't as it should be.

She couldn't ignore it now. Not after her experience from earlier that morning with the Berserkers.

Giving in to the increasingly demanding urge to get out of sight, Melissa decided that it would be best to return to her room in the attic as quickly as she could. She could try again at the bookstore tomorrow when the sun was up.

She began to walk toward Market Street, Tia's Bakes growing larger with each step she took. Once she reached the end of the green, it was just a right turn and then a straight shot for five short blocks back to the Safe Haven.

She stopped abruptly, not yet even to the fire station. Looking to the other side of the green, her eyes were drawn to the pale light hanging above the front doors of the church. She thought she had heard a scuff along the sidewalk just a little farther down the street. But she couldn't see anything in the gloom that would tell her what it might have been.

The noise might not have caught her attention if not for the fact that it hadn't sounded like a shoe. Instead, she likened the faint scrape to fingernails being dragged across a chalkboard. Softly, though. There, than gone just as fast.

She started to walk again. This time at a brisk pace, glad that she was wearing her sneakers rather than a pair of heels so that she could move quietly and with greater speed.

Melissa was almost to the fire station when she stopped again, her edginess making the skin on her arms prickle.

Out of the corner of her eye, she thought that just for a heartbeat she glimpsed a handful of large shadows flashing past the storefronts close to where she had heard the scrape. When she looked in that direction, however, there was nothing except darkness.

She was about to start walking again, wanting to turn the corner and get out onto the main drag as fast as possible, when a soft growl just a few hundred feet in front of her held her in place. It was coming from the narrow alley that ran along the other side of the fire station.

She had noticed the alley on her way to dinner. It was barely large enough for someone to walk through.

She whipped her head back toward the church upon hearing another scrape along the sidewalk.

Definitely not a shoe.

She couldn't believe that this was happening.

How could they have found her?

She had been so careful not to leave a trail after what had attacked her when she made her escape during her last job. The job that had brought her here to Kraken Cove.

She didn't know how they had tracked her, but they had.

She couldn't deny that now when she saw a few more large shadows flash across the storefront windows at an astounding speed.

One of those shadows stopped for just a split-second before streaking off into the darkness. She hadn't gotten a good look, but it had been enough to confirm her worst fears.

On that last job, she had barely gotten away from that single beast. Even with her use of the Grym she didn't stand a chance against a whole pack.

Another growl emanated from around the corner. The corner that she needed to turn if she were to take the most direct route back to the inn ... and safety.

The frightening sound drew Melissa's gaze to several more towering silhouettes in the gloom. Then she heard the scrape of a few more sharp nails across the concrete when they passed beneath the streetlight just past the Book Nook.

They were looking for her. They knew she wasn't at the inn. But they didn't know where she was exactly.

That might be enough for her to get away. If she was fast enough.

Her first instinct was to go back to Renzetti's. She ignored that urge. She'd be trapped there.

The only place where she would be protected from what was stalking her was the Safe Haven. The fastest route to get there required that she go right past several of her hunters.

That wasn't going to work.

She'd be slipping the noose over her head all on her own.

She did have another option, however. She just hoped that it wouldn't be a repeat of her harrowing experience from that morning.

Stepping as quietly as she could down the sidewalk, Melissa fast walked back to restaurant row. Once there, she sprinted past Renzetti's, ignoring Joseph staring at her through the plate glass window, to the path that ran along the top of the cliffs.

She stopped for just a second. Catching her breath. Listening. Wanting to get a sense of where her hunters were.

She didn't hear anything. That didn't mean anything, however, certain that her stalkers had picked up her scent.

At that very instant several of the shadows she had seen on the other side of the town green appeared at the entrance to restaurant row. Hidden in the gloom except for the golden glow of their eyes.

Her hunters had narrowed down their search, but they still didn't know exactly where she was.

Unfortunately for her, it wouldn't be long before they did. These beasts specialized in tracking prey, and they rarely failed when sent out for the kill.

She needed to get away. Fast!

Melissa took a few steps farther down the path, tracking those golden eyes.

She stumbled, letting out a muffled curse. Glancing down, she realized that she had knocked into one of the benches that lined the walkway.

When she looked up again and back toward restaurant row, all of those golden eyes that she was seeking to evade were staring directly at her.

They had her dead to rights.

Racing away from the entrance to the alley, she sprinted down the path. She only had to go twenty yards before she reached the top of the steps that switch backed their way down the cliffs to the harbor below.

It didn't matter.

She wasn't going to make it. Her heart racing, she realized that there was no way that she was going to escape these beasts.

The monstrous shadows were coming from both directions along the path, soft growls preceding them, their clawed feet digging into the gravel of the trail.

There was only one thing that she could do. Try to delay

and use whatever time she earned to find some solution to what appeared to be an unsolvable problem.

Refusing to give in to her fear, she reached for the Grym, threads of white energy dancing across her fingers. Stepping onto the staircase, she wove a web of magic across the entryway.

The barrier of energy was thinner than a piece of paper. Nevertheless, she hoped that since it had proved effective against the Berserker she had fought that morning, it would do the job against these monsters as well.

It had to.

At least for a time.

Otherwise, she was dead.

Done in just a few seconds, the magical barricade glowing brightly, she glanced quickly to both sides of the trail. The shadows were almost upon her, only twenty feet away.

Not knowing how long her defense would hold, she jumped more than raced down the stairs, often missing entire flights.

She didn't think that what she had done with the Grym would stop the monsters pursuing her. She just hoped that the magic would last long enough for her to get down the staircase to the bottom of the cliff.

She could make her escape from there. Maybe even back to the Safe Haven if she was lucky.

Maybe.

And if not?

Well ... better to not think about that.

~

"WHAT DO you think of my new guest?" asked Hestia.

She sat in the back garden of her inn enjoying the touch of the crisp night air. The full moon gave them more than enough light to see by.

Draig had brought with him the cinnamon roll that he had saved for her, all the others selling out in less than an hour once word spread that he was in the kitchen.

She had been diagnosed with Celiac disease later in life, just like Draig. And just like Draig, she also had not lost her sweet tooth or her desire for baked treats. So he always did his best to look out for her, because she always looked out for him.

"To put it mildly, she's a handful."

"Because she drew the attention of three Berserkers?"

"In large part, yes."

"What was the small part?" she asked, her curiosity plain in the sharpness of her gaze.

"Her ability to hide her skill with the Grym."

"That worries you more than three Berserkers coming for her?"

"It does," Draig confirmed, who leaned back into his chair, legs crossed.

"Why? I would think the Berserkers would be of greater concern."

"For some, yes, probably."

"But not for you."

"No, not for me." He held up his hands to hold off what Hestia was going to tell him next, knowing that it likely wasn't useful to the conversation. "And I don't say that to come across as being arrogant."

"It does sound like that though."

"I know, but that's not my intention. The Berserkers are blunt instruments. If you see them coming, you know how to deal with them."

"But if you don't see Melissa coming, you're in for a world of trouble ... or hurt ... depending on the circumstances. Is that what you're saying?"

"That's the feeling I got," Draig confirmed with a nod. He

had already told Hestia of his encounter in the park that fronted the harbor.

"Cerridwen was telling me about her." Hestia let Draig's explanation percolate, her words somewhat garbled as she took another bite from her cinnamon roll. "I have to agree with her. Ms. Gorgonella is here for a reason, and she seems very determined to do whatever it is that she means to do."

"That's what I thought as well."

"Any idea what she was looking for in the bookstore?" Hestia gave Draig a big grin as thanks for the treat he had brought her, wiping the cinnamon and sugar from her mouth with the back of her hand before licking her fingers clean of frosting.

Draig couldn't help but smile. Even at Hestia's age, she still acted the young girl when the mood struck her, which was often.

"A couple possibilities came to mind."

Hestia nodded. She had known Draig for quite a long time. Since he was a child, in fact. She knew that look of his.

She assumed that he had cracked the code. He just wasn't ready to share it with her until he had the evidence to back it up. "Anything that we need to worry about?"

Draig hesitated before responding. "Possibly." He shrugged. "I'm not sure yet. But once I know for certain, you'll be the first to know. After I tell Cerridwen, of course."

"Could it affect us here in Kraken Cove?"

Draig stared at Hestia for quite some time, his expression shifting from one of relaxation to a flintiness that few people cared to see, because when Draig looked like that, nothing good ever came from it. "It could affect all of the Teg. In a very bad way."

Hestia leaned back into her chair then, thinking about what Draig had just revealed. There was only one artifact that came to mind that could have such an impact on their world. That thought immediately brought to mind a topic that Cerridwen had raised with her.

"You heard about what happened a few days ago?" asked Hestia.

"You'll need to be more specific. I was in Williamsburg a few days ago."

"Right, sorry. The break-in. Or at least the rumored break-in. It's all very hush-hush, but too many Teg are talking about it to believe that it's just a rumor."

"Break-in where?"

"At the home of one of our favorite people," Hestia replied, although her tone suggested that she was talking about someone who clearly wasn't one of her favorites.

"You'll need to be more specific. As you know, I have several favorites."

Hestia smirked, appreciating Draig's sarcasm. "After seeing you so relaxed here in Kraken Cove, I keep forgetting how many enemies you have among the Tylwyth Teg."

"A consequence of my previous profession," Draig replied with a shrug.

"That and your unerring need to do what's right," Hestia murmured, giving him a cunning look that carried the faint odor of castigation.

He didn't take the bait, not having the energy to engage in this same conversation with her again. "Which I am trying to get past." He pushed himself up so that he was sitting on the edge of his seat rather than leaning against the backrest. "You just said it yourself. I'm more relaxed in Kraken Cove. I try only to apply my unerring need to do what's right, as you called it, here in town and in the immediate surroundings."

"You'll leave the rest of the world to someone else," Hestia said, nodding slowly. Her eyes sharpened. She knew Draig too well. He was telling her the truth as he saw it, but not the entire truth.

"That's the plan."

"And how's that going for you?"

"Why do you ask?"

"Because Peggy Rose told me what happened to you in Williamsburg."

Draig shrugged, trying to suggest that it really wasn't worthy of discussion. "Just some old animosities rearing their ugly heads. I dealt with it."

"Really? Daemons attacking you on the street. That goes against the compact. I'm supposed to believe that's all that was? A quick attempt at revenge?"

Draig gave her another grin, although the smile never reached his eyes. "For now."

Hestia studied him for a time. Few could maintain eye contact with Draig because of the flames that always seemed to flare in the back of his eyes.

Not so for Hestia. She had seen Draig at his worst and at his best. There was nothing that he could do now that could shock her ... or loosen the bond between them.

"So you have no interest in returning to the larger Teg world?"

"None at all," Draig quickly replied. Perhaps too quickly.

"A pity," Hestia murmured softly.

"Why do you say that?"

"Because I get the sense that the world is changing. That maybe the world needs you to leave Kraken Cove and pick up where you left off."

"Where I left off? I have no desire to go back to that."

"It might not come down to what you want to do. It might come down to what you need to do." It was Hestia's turn to shrug, although her eyes burned brightly with purpose when she did it. "That unerring need of yours to do what's right."

Draig stared at Hestia for quite a long time, not knowing what to say. Hestia had joined him in Kraken Cove within months of when he moved there what seemed like a lifetime ago.

During that entire time, she had never once suggested that he had made the wrong decision. And she had never once suggested that he might want to rethink that decision.

Until now.

"Back to the break-in," Draig finally said, having no desire to follow the path that Hestia had set out before him. "Who are we talking about?"

"The jackbooted thug you should have killed when you had the chance."

"Couldn't have happened to a nicer person," Draig replied with a pleased smile, leaning back into his very comfortable lawn chair, ignoring the accusation in her voice.

Although she was right. He probably should have killed him when he had the chance. It would have made his life much easier.

But it hadn't been the right thing to do at the time.

And there it was again. His almost sociopathic need to do what was right after all those years of doing what someone else told him was right ... and rarely was.

He really needed to break himself of that habit. If he could, it would help to reduce his stress and make his life much more enjoyable. Maybe he should try the meditation app that Cerridwen had suggested.

"I couldn't agree more," confirmed Hestia. "Of course, it is somewhat suspicious, don't you think? Our new friend shows up just days after that? Primarily interested in something that she believes is hidden away in your bookstore?"

"Not very trusting of you, Hestia," teased Draig.

"When have you ever known me to be very trusting?"

"Good point," Draig replied. "Now tell me the other point that you're not sure you want to share with me."

"I don't know what you're talking about," Hestia murmured, even though her expression said otherwise.

"You know very well what I'm talking about. You wouldn't have taken our conversation in this direction if you weren't debating whether to tell me what was really on your mind."

"You know, you really need to come over more frequently, Draig. I always enjoy these discussions of ours."

"As do I," Draig admitted, getting the feeling that Hestia was using some of the sarcasm that was so much a part of his personality against him. "I'm assuming that the next time I do I should bring something with me."

"Perhaps one of those pumpkin chocolate chip muffins that you make when the mood strikes you?"

"Maybe more than one?"

"That would be lovely."

"Now that we've got the most important matter out of the way, what else did you want to tell me?"

"Don't trust her."

"Why would I trust her? After bringing three Berserkers into town?"

"Because no matter how hard you can be, you still have a soft heart. Thankfully, after all the crap you've been through, that hasn't changed."

"Now that's a mean thing to say." Draig sounded slightly offended even though he gave Hestia another smile.

Hestia reached across the glass-topped table that separated them, patting him on the arm. "I'm sorry, but it needed to be said."

"You're worried, aren't you?" asked Draig.

"Why do you say that?" Hestia tried to project a tone of innocence, despite knowing that never worked with Draig.

"Because you think that she's ..."

Draig pushed himself out of his chair, his eyes burning even more brightly. His expression had changed. The sharp angles to his face had become more prominent, revealing a cold purpose.

Hestia knew what that meant. Trouble.

"What's the matter?"

"They're back," Draig replied. "We'll have to continue this later." He reached down and picked up his walking stick.

Butch, Sundance, and Cassidy, who had been lying down behind him, hidden in the shadows, were already standing up, ears perked. Their eyes burned just as brightly as Draig's.

Several low growls emanated from deep within their chests. A sound that Hestia always found disconcerting since she associated their rumbling timbre with a breed like a Rhodesian Ridgeback rather than a mix between a cocker spaniel and a poodle.

"I'm assuming you don't want to do this in town," said Hestia. "Cerridwen and I can help -- we'd be more than happy to, in fact -- but it could get messy and we'd have to deal with the cleanup."

"I'd like to avoid that for now. I might be able to learn more if I handle this on my own."

"What are you going to do?"

"Don't worry. I'll take care of it."

Draig walked toward the back gate, holding it open so that his three dogs could trot through. They immediately set up a perimeter, eyes trained on the park and harbor below them.

"You'll take no unnecessary risks?" asked Hestia, her concern obvious.

"When have I ever taken any unnecessary risks," he called to her as he disappeared into the darkness.

"When haven't you?" Hestia muttered quietly to herself.

She stared up at the full moon for a few heartbeats. Then she shook her head.

The beasts who entered Kraken Cove without permission were either foolish or arrogant.

Probably a bit of both, she decided. Probably desperate as well. And desiring to make a name for themselves while earning some good money.

Not a good blend.

For them.

Because she had no doubt that with the mood Draig was in, the night was going to get bloody.

And she had no doubt as well that the blood spilled would not be Draig's.

MELISSA RACED down the last few steps, almost tripping when she rounded the final corner, gripping the railing just in time to steady herself, before running out onto the grass.

She cursed herself for being a nitwit. The barrier she had crafted with the Grym barely delayed her hunters. And with good reason.

She should have extended it all along the edge of the cliff. She knew that now. But she had been in a rush and it was too late to do anything about it.

Her hunters didn't require the use of the steps to follow her along the escarpment. With their claws they were having little trouble sliding rather than climbing down the crag.

Sprinting across the small park toward the harbor, she realized that they would be on her in just seconds. As soon as they reached the green she was done for.

Understanding what fate held in store for her if they caught her, she was about to turn so that she could defend herself when she noticed that the scrabbling along the ridge had stopped.

Confused, she kept running, wondering why the beasts chasing her had chosen that moment to halt their descent.

Then she saw Draig with three dogs walking by his side. With the darkness she had almost missed them.

Draig didn't seem to have a care in the world.

The dogs stayed between him and the park, their heads turned toward the cliffs.

Did those little dogs see the monsters hanging from the rock?

The brightness of their gazes suggested that they did, their eyes never leaving the cliff.

Although the dogs had identified her pursuers, she didn't think the trio of cockerpoos had seen her yet.

Hoping that was true, Melissa used the Grym to hide herself in plain sight, her application of the Power of the Ancients blending her into her surroundings so that if anyone looked in her direction they would see what they expected to see and not her.

At the same time, she removed her scent. She worried that the dogs would find her out even though she was invisible.

That done, and not knowing how long her hunters were going to remain clinging to the precipice, she continued at a fast clip across the park until she was standing right next to the stern of the antique cabin cruiser that Draig had climbed onto with his groceries. The dogs stayed on the path, their eyes never leaving the cliff.

The cruiser appeared to be a restored classic right out of the 1920s with its hull mahogany on oak and gleaming brass railings and cleats. It was at least sixty feet long. A fully extendable awning covered the aft deck.

There were several cabins beneath the front deck. How many there were, she couldn't tell. But she meant to find out.

Why her hunters weren't coming after her ...

Based on what Draig had done to the Berserkers, she could understand their hesitation if they had some knowledge of him. Or perhaps they were just surprised and didn't want any witnesses. Regardless, she had little doubt that it wouldn't be long before they resumed their hunt, Draig or no.

"STAY," Draig commanded as he jumped down from the boat and walked back toward the parking lot and his pickup truck, the back gate open and revealing several more bags of groceries.

The three dogs didn't respond. Instead, they remained right where they were. Their eyes glittered in the darkness, and they never shifted their gaze away from the crag rising above the harbor.

With the dogs distracted, Melissa walked silently down the trail behind them and then climbed up the ladder on silent feet. Stepping onto the deck, she snuck below right before she heard Draig shut the tailgate.

He was on his way back.

Not wanting to risk giving herself away, she hustled through the narrow galley and then pushed open the first door she came to. Perfect. A small cabin.

She stepped inside and shut the door quietly behind her, sitting back on the bed. Waiting.

For almost a minute, she didn't hear anything. Then the silence that had settled over the harbor was broken when she heard the dogs bark with a ferocious anger. That was followed by some very loud growls. Clearly, Draig's friends were not happy.

Were her hunters coming down the cliff face?

"Butch, Cassidy, Sundance!" Draig called. "Not now. Time to go."

There were a few more angry growls followed by some irritated huffs, the dogs apparently disagreeing with Draig's decision. Still, they obeyed, because next Melissa heard the patter of their paws on the deck above as the trio came on board.

She heard Draig speaking to them again, although she wasn't certain what about. "I know. I know. Later. I promise."

The rumble of the motor starting drowned out all the other noises. Not long after, she felt the boat pulling away from the dock and she assumed that Draig was guiding them out of the harbor.

To where, Melissa had no clue. But it had to be better than where she had been.

Finally, after several minutes of terror, Melissa breathed a sigh of relief.

She was safe.

A liquid cold ran through her just a second later, hearing over the roar of the motor a very loud, angry howl coming from the direction of the marina that carried well across the cove.

A warning perhaps.

She forced herself to start breathing again after almost a minute passed, realizing that she had been holding her breath. She felt the need to clarify if only to confirm for herself where things stood.

She was safe.

For now.

Because clearly her client either was angry, desperate, or both.

Neither boded well for her.

12

AN UNREAL DATE

Draig pulled the last few bags of gear off the boat, dropping them onto the dock. Butch, Cassidy, and Sundance waited for him there.

They were highlighted by a faint light that Melissa could just make out through the porthole.

What was she supposed to do now?

Her watch told her that Draig had piloted the boat out into the cove for more than thirty minutes. Where they could be she had not a clue because she didn't know what direction he had taken.

Before she had come to Kraken Cove she had studied a map of the town. But she hadn't paid much attention to the many small islands just off the coast.

She was stuck here for she didn't know how long.

Safe from her hunters. But was she safe from Draig?

That question suggested to her that she should stay in the cabin. Hide out here until he went back to town.

"Can you grab those last few bags of groceries?" he called over his shoulder as he walked down the dock.

Melissa stood behind the door, her mouth opening in shock.

She had been as quiet as a mouse. She had even taken the precaution of hiding herself with the Grym. Just in case he peeked into the cabin.

How could he have sensed her?

She had masked her use of the Power of the Ancients.

Who was this guy?

Melissa didn't have a choice now. She opened the door and stepped out into the galley. Grabbing the grocery bags, she climbed up the steps and onto the deck.

She needed to figure out who this mystery man really was now that she was stuck on an island with a baker who could have killed two Berserkers without breaking a sweat.

The guy had to be a psycho. She was sure of it.

Her last few boyfriends had been psychos so she knew the warning signs.

And that was bad news for her.

~

"Have you lived here long?"

"Since I came to Kraken Cove."

"When was that?" asked Melissa as she wandered through the first floor of the lighthouse. Pretending that she had been invited rather than barging into his home.

She had been trying to dig out what information that she could from her host ever since she walked over the threshold.

She enjoyed little success. Because he said very little when he said anything at all, offering only brief responses and not a single detail.

It was like trying to crack open a nut. Every time she struck it with a mallet, instead of splitting open, the nut just skittered away.

She needed to hit it head on. But she was finding it very difficult to do.

In addition to Draig being skillfully evasive, she was distracted. Every few seconds she had to stop and look twice at some unique item in the house.

A statue. A sculpture. A painting. A tapestry. Jewelry. Ceramics. A very, very old book written in an ancient script, Latin she believed, although it looked more like Aramaic, that was in perfect condition.

It was like walking through a museum without the guards and glass cases.

She had an almost uncontrollable urge to reach out and run her fingers across every one of the ancient artifacts. And not just because of her professional curiosity.

Nevertheless, she refrained. She knew herself too well. If she touched them, it would only increase her desire to slip one or two items into a pocket.

She hadn't asked her host but she had little doubt that all the artifacts that she was perusing were originals. If that was the case, then they were priceless ... or close to it.

In her line of work, she had learned that there was a price for everything. Even when there supposedly wasn't.

What really caught her eye, however, were the medieval weapons displayed on the wall closest to the front door.

It was almost as if Draig had placed them there so that they would be within easy reach if he needed to rush out for a fight. Which, as Melissa thought about it, wasn't all that farfetched after what had happened on the green.

Several spears were fixed to the brick like billiard cues. There was a halberd as well as a pike. Also two English long-bows, six feet in length, which if she remembered her history had proven incredibly effective during the Hundred Years War.

Right below them two quivers full of arrows leaned against the wall. A smaller quiver right next to the larger two contained bolts for the crossbow perched just above and hanging from a hook.

There were more swords than she could count. In addition to the handful hanging from the wall, right next to the front door there were many more sticking hilt up out of what looked like a couple of umbrella stands.

Just above the swords and given a place of prominence on the wall were two long shields that would easily protect her from head to toe. Shaped like isosceles triangles, they tapered down to a sharp point at the very tip.

Those two shields held her attention for several minutes. Surprising even herself, she knew the sigil on the first. She was a fan of English football, and she had gotten hooked on the FX documentary *Welcome to Wrexham*, which was about a Welsh football club purchased by two American movie and television stars.

The first shield displayed the Welsh Dragon in bright red.

That image was unmistakable.

A symbol of a country. A people. A way of life. A history.

The design on the other shield she didn't recognize. It made her think of the Three Lions of England, an emblem she was familiar with after watching the most recent World Cup. Of course, the English flamed out before the final just as they always did. To the hated French of all opponents.

This sigil was much the same as the one on the players' jerseys, except for a few distinct features. The colors were different. The background was green, and in the place of three lions there were three dragons, all the color red.

Curious. Something to do with Wales, she assumed, because they were the spitting images of the Welsh Dragon portrayed on the shield next to it.

But she didn't know for sure.

And that's what bothered her. Because she should know.

The symbol seemed so familiar to her. Had she seen it somewhere else before? If so, where?

She couldn't recall, and that was driving her crazy. She shook her head in annoyance, feeling as if the answers to her questions were taunting her from the shadows.

She hated when this happened. A mystery like this would tease her, becoming more and more annoying, until she found the answer. A puzzle that she couldn't ignore.

"Not so long ago," Draig replied.

His response pulled Melissa from her thoughts to the puzzle who stood in the kitchen, wearing an apron and oven mitts as he put a vegetable lasagna back into the oven to cook. He then pulled a cast-iron skillet from the rack above his head and placed it on a gas burner, stirring in some butter, garlic, and shallots.

Her mouth began to water as the wonderful smells coming from the kitchen permeated the lighthouse. The sizzle of the steak as he seared it in the pan made her stomach growl even though she was only a few hours removed from her earlier dinner at Renzetti's.

Not wanting to embarrass herself with any more inappropriate noises, she turned her attention back to what felt like a very comfortable home despite some of the jarring adornments.

He didn't seem to mind that she was there. He also didn't seem to mind that she was studying everything she found in his house.

She was categorizing all that she learned but was frustrated that she still didn't *know* much about him, other than perhaps the fact that he was likely just as good a cook as he was a baker.

Not the most useful finding considering her current circumstances.

She was usually much better at breaking open a mark.

Her lack of success should have aggravated her.

But strangely, she was becoming more amused than anything else. Then she smiled as an unexpected thought passed through her mind.

This had to be the weirdest first date that she had ever suffered through.

She stopped herself then. Thinking back, she had been on worse first dates, including the one where the guy decided to bring his mother to dinner.

No, as more of her dating disasters played through her mind, she reminded herself that this was definitely not a first date. That was the only aspect of her being in Draig's home that was crystal clear to her.

"Are you always this vague?" asked Melissa.

"Yes," Draig replied unashamedly and without a hint of mischief in his voice.

She snorted softly. She was very good at reading people. Most people. Apparently not him, however.

But from what she could tell, he was simply stating the truth. And clearly, he didn't care how she took it.

It was a welcome change. She wasn't used to dealing with Teg who spoke plainly.

And she was grateful that he hadn't raised any of the several uncomfortable issues that she thought he would.

Draig hadn't said a word about her sneaking onto his boat when she walked through the door carrying the grocery bags. He had simply nodded in the direction of the counter.

As soon as she put them down, he had gotten to work on dinner. Cleaning and slicing vegetables. Dropping gluten free noodles into the boiling water to cook. Breaking down tomatoes over a slow heat with garlic, oregano, and a handful of other spices to make his own sauce.

He wouldn't reveal to her everything that he put into it, which for some strange reason annoyed her. When she started to press him, he told her to take whatever she wanted from the industrial grade refrigerator at his back if she was thirsty.

Realizing that she could only push him so far, and not knowing what else to do, she had grabbed the iced tea and lemonade, made an Arnold Palmer for herself and also for him, then she left him to the cooking. She got the sense that he didn't need and didn't want her help with the main course.

The kitchen was Draig's space, and she didn't want to intrude.

She also needed some time to think about how to manage her new reality. She was stuck on this island until Draig brought her back to the mainland.

She didn't know how long she would be here. Assuming he didn't try to poison her or suffocate her while she slept.

She was certain that Draig had a reason for allowing her to come out to his island home. But for the life of her, she didn't know why he had taken the risk.

She assumed that it was because he wanted something from her.

Before she could give much thought as to how she wanted to handle what she assumed would be an interrogation during dinner, the uniqueness of Draig's home distracted her again.

Approaching the house from the outside, she had walked across a narrow length of steel and wire that resembled a modern-day drawbridge. Because of how the cottage was positioned in relation to the beacon, the house appeared to be a separate structure from the lighthouse.

Once Melissa stepped through the door, she realized that wasn't the case. Perhaps at one time the cottage and the lighthouse had been distinct buildings, but no longer.

Clearly, Draig had done a good bit of remodeling when he bought the property and assumed responsibility for maintaining the beacon, since this was still a working lighthouse.

It wasn't at all what she had anticipated it would be, initially envisioning something out of *The Ghost and Mrs. Muir*, one of her favorite classic movies that she had first watched with her mother.

No ghosts, at least as far as she could tell. Not yet anyway.

A combination of rustic and modern. A lot of open space. A lot of light. And no emphasis on maritime design with the requisite harpoon and framed picture of the various nautical knots.

Draig had opened up the inside of the structure so that the circular steel staircase that led four storeys up to the top of the beacon was the centerpiece of his home.

The living space was on the ground level. The bedrooms, four in total, were one floor above, each door set to a cardinal point on the compass.

She couldn't tell what might be on the floor just below the beacon. Storage maybe? There was a narrow steel walkway that branched off from the center staircase and led directly to the only door on that level.

Its unique design, what she thought more resembled an entrance to an ancient vault, kept drawing her eyes. Her fingers were getting itchy just looking at it.

She really wanted to know what was up there. To control her impulses, she shifted her attention to everything else that caught her interest on the bottom floor.

Strangely, despite Draig continuing to make her nervous, the space itself felt quite comfortable and welcoming. It made her think of the Safe Haven, a feeling of calm mixed with security resonating throughout his home just as it had the inn.

That and the décor certainly appealed to her. Soft leather couches faced one another not too far away from the circular staircase. An office with a desk, computer, and several screens was set off in a nook where the cottage and the lighthouse came together. The placement allowed Draig to look out through a large window that wrapped around much of the base of the lighthouse on its eastern side, providing an excellent view of the Atlantic Ocean.

There was no entertainment area. Although she did see a long credenza off to the side that contained a television that looked like it was from the 1950s with an old-fashioned record player right next to it.

She found that strange. No large flat-screen TV. No speakers or sound system.

Draig didn't seem to have an interest in any of that. Rather, it appeared as if he was more taken with the unique design of the furniture than anything else. She wondered if he kept any records in the cabinet beneath the player.

She was curious about that. However, it wasn't very hard to identify his weakness, and it certainly made sense based on the store that he owned in Kraken Cove.

Built-in bookcases lined the wall farthest away from the door. On those shelves were books, manuscripts, even some scrolls. All of them beckoned to her, begging her to run her fingers over their spines and pull them from their position on the shelves so that she could flip through the pages or unroll the lengths of parchment.

She would have, if not for Draig working behind her in the kitchen.

The shelves continued up the wall for thirty feet, a wheeled ladder attached to the top of the bookcases so that the texts at the very top were accessible. From what she could tell, Draig had as large an inventory here as he did in the Book Nook.

That made her wonder if the text that she was seeking was hidden away somewhere on those shelves.

Under normal circumstances she would reach for the Grym so that she could do a quick search. She didn't, instead wrapping the fingers of her left hand over those of her right just to make sure that she didn't give in to the urge. She knew without a doubt that if she did that, Draig would sense her use of the Power of the Ancients.

She didn't know how he'd react. And after his display against the Berserkers, she concluded that discretion was required.

Besides, she doubted that he would leave an artifact so important and so valuable to the Tylwyth Teg lying about on a shelf in a lighthouse at the very edge of the Atlantic Ocean. The manuscript she wanted would be secreted away and heavily protected.

She was sure of that.

Disappointed though not surprised, she stared wistfully at the books and scrolls for several seconds more before finally turning away.

And just in time to watch Draig put the finishing touches on dinner. He had taken the steak from the skillet and placed it on a cutting board, letting it sit for a few minutes.

Besides going with an open floor plan, she noticed that he had put most of his remodeling work into the kitchen.

A long, curling counter with a half-dozen barstools separated it from the rest of the first floor. Stainless steel appliances lined the wall behind it.

An old-fashioned six-burner gas stove sat in between the refrigerator and dishwasher. There was a wood-fired oven, cold at the moment, off to the side.

And right next to the farmhouse sink was a long counter that based on the various flours and other ingredients shelved just above it confirmed that was where Draig did his baking.

"Dinner should be ready in a few minutes," Draig said as he left the kitchen and walked past her. "Would you mind preparing the salad? I've left everything on the counter."

"Of course," Melissa nodded, feeling a tingle as he brushed past that she did her best to ignore even as it made her smile.

She tried not to chuckle as he pulled his apron from around

his neck and threw it over a chair. Master Baker was scrawled across the front. Either he was unaware or he didn't care about how that phrase could be construed.

She studied Draig as he set the silverware on the long table that was not too far away from the couches. She shook her head, still having a difficult time reading him. Nothing about him added up. Nothing.

Draig was a baker, a lighthouse keeper, and he carried a walking stick that she didn't think was actually a shillelagh, it's true essence hidden with the Grym.

In fact, his use of natural magic was so good, so refined, that it was completely undetectable.

That intrigued her.

She had never known any of the Teg who could do such a thing.

That suggested a great deal of skill and likely a great deal of experience with the Power of the Ancients. Even so, he didn't appear to be much older than she was.

There were some streaks of grey in his hair, but those didn't make him look older. If anything, they made him appear more distinguished. She hated that, because when it came to grey in a woman's hair, the most common adjective associated with that natural development was old.

She watched as Draig returned to the kitchen and pulled the lasagna from the oven. Right at that moment, he appeared quite normal.

But he wasn't. He was anything but.

He had sensed her on his cabin cruiser even though she had concealed herself with the Grym. No one had ever seen through her illusion before. Not even her mother, who was one of the strongest practitioners of the Grym among all the Teg.

Oh, and what about those cute, cuddly dogs that weren't afraid of Weres?

That was uncommon behavior. Most dogs ran from Weres,

recognizing them as dominant predators. But not those three. And they barely reached her knee.

Speak of the devils.

The three furry cockerpoos burst into the lighthouse when Draig opened the back door.

What was going on?

Draig was staring at the dogs and they were staring right back at him. It was almost as if they were having a private conversation.

Could he communicate with animals through the Grym?

Was that even possible?

She wasn't sure. She had never heard of it being done before. But based on what she was seeing, she was beginning to believe that it was a skill that the strongest of the Teg could employ.

Because clearly Draig was one of the strongest of the Teg.

After a few more seconds passed, Draig nodded at the same time that the dogs did.

Then, once Draig released the trio from his gaze and he gave them another nod, all three rushed over to her, tongues lolling to the side, grinning, barking happily, demanding that she pet them. For just an instant, she had to fight off the sudden unexplained desire to run.

Instead she bent down and rubbed her fingers through their shiny coats, earning grumbles of pleasure for her efforts as well as a few licks.

Having found a willing victim, the three cockerpoos continued to beg for attention for as long as she was willing to give it. Rubbing up against her. Even going up on their hind legs and pushing her with their front paws to make sure that she didn't focus too much attention on just one.

"Butch, Cassidy, Sundance, give her a break." Draig smiled as the three cockerpoos huffed at him, then got in a few more belly scratches from Melissa before heading toward the living room. "They're usually not like this."

"How so?"

"They tend to be a bit more standoffish until they know the person. With you, they didn't display their natural reserve. They accepted you right from the start."

"These are your dogs?" Melissa said softly, pushing herself back to her feet.

"In a sense, yes," Draig confirmed. Melissa gave him a quizzical look, not really understanding his word choice. "You seem surprised."

Melissa shrugged. "After your display against the Berserkers, I have a hard time picturing you with these three cuddly furballs."

"Really?" Draig pursed his lips, eyebrows raised. "What kind of animals do you picture me with?"

Melissa's eyes narrowed as she thought about his question. "Most Teg who could do what you can do," she said with a smile, deciding to offer the outrageous based on her perusal of the first floor of his home, "dragons perhaps."

A knowing smile cracked Draig's visage, his fiery eyes flashing. "I'm not most Teg."

Although not dangerously this time. Melissa took the current display to be one of amusement, which surprised her.

"Yes, I worked that out," Melissa replied with a soft chuckle to hide her nervousness, tilting her head as if she were studying a painting in a gallery that she wasn't quite sure how to interpret. "You've provided an abundance of evidence in that respect."

"I was just doing what was necessary," Draig explained without a hint of emotion.

Melissa's smile turned into a smirk. He was so serious. She couldn't help herself. The need to have a little fun outweighed her good sense.

"When you were fighting against the Berserkers, why didn't you use your rolling pin instead of your walking staff? You say you're just a baker, after all. Yet you took on those giants without a second thought."

"I didn't have my rolling pin with me," Draig replied.

He didn't say anything else, and the silence added to Melissa's unease. Draig's expression didn't change. It was as hard as ever.

Although Melissa believed that his eyes did soften. At least she hoped that they did. If they didn't then she was losing her touch.

"Sorry, I couldn't resist," Melissa apologized. "I really appreciate what you did for me."

Draig nodded. She waited for more from him. When he didn't say anything, she decided to press forward. Maybe a little honesty would help her crack his code.

"It's just that I'm nervous. And when I'm nervous I get diarrhea of the mouth. I just can't help myself. I feel the need to fill the silence. Say whatever comes to mind, no matter how inane it might be." Melissa stopped herself abruptly, realizing that she was doing it right then. "See what I mean?"

"Why are you nervous?"

"Weren't you listening to what I just said?" Melissa wanted to say more, but she held back, not wanting to provide further evidence of what she had just admitted.

"I was. I just assumed that you realized that you had nothing to fear from me." Draig gave her a tight grin and a lift of his eyebrows. "If I wanted to kill you, I would have done that already. I wouldn't have gone to the trouble of making you dinner."

Melissa stared at her host for several seconds, still at a loss as to how to read him. Was he joking or was he being serious? Not knowing what else to do, she smiled. "Sorry." She held up her hands in apology, a slight blush rising on her cheeks. He was making her dinner? She thought that he was making dinner and she just happened to be there at the same time. "I'm sorry. I don't know what to make of you. You're just like your dogs."

"I don't know how to take that."

Melissa's eyes widened when she realized what had just slipped out. She feared that she had insulted her host. She tried to explain. "I mean that how you present yourself is not how you truly are."

Draig nodded, not feeling the need to pursue the issue any further. He understood what she meant. And he understood what she was trying to do. He didn't feel the need to help her. "I really should clarify that Butch, Cassidy, and Sundance aren't my dogs."

"I'm sorry. I don't think I understand. Are you looking after them for someone?"

Draig smiled, even allowing a soft chuckle to escape.

"What I meant is that they're not my pets. Butch, Cassidy, and Sundance," he motioned to each one as he said their names so that she would know which dog was which, all three having found a comfortable spot on the blankets he left there atop the leather couches for just that reason, "they're my friends. Well, actually, more than that."

"How so?"

Draig looked at her for quite a long time, sensing that she was getting nervous under his scrutiny. Also sensing why she wanted to know.

He could explain the bond between him and the trio of dogs. How they were really connected. He chose not to.

He didn't know this woman well enough to provide her with such sensitive information. They still had a great deal more to discuss before he did that.

"A good question, but not the one that you really want to ask."

"How do you know that I'm not asking the question I want to ask?" Melissa challenged.

"Because I frighten you. You're worried about how I'm going to react if you ask the question you really want to ask me."

"You're really full of yourself, aren't you?" Melissa laced her words with a touch of sarcasm that was right on point, trying to wriggle out from a situation that was quickly becoming more uncomfortable than it already was.

Draig shrugged. "I'm just calling it like I see it."

"That's not true," Melissa protested, the words sounding false in her own ears. "I'm not frightened of you."

"Then you really should be," he said in a very soft, dangerous voice, his eyes burning like a wildfire.

For just a second, she was fixed in place, frozen, the desire to run rising up within her, dominating her instincts. Doubting that she'd even get to the door if she tried.

Then Draig's expression softened. He offered her a gentle smile. "Sorry, but I couldn't resist."

Melissa opened her mouth in surprise then closed it just as quickly. He was playing with her. She scrunched up her face, fighting off a smile. "You really are difficult. You know that?"

"I do, but thank you for reminding me."

"And just to be clear," said Melissa, crossing her arms, "I'm not frightened of you."

"Then my mistake," Draig replied. He turned away from her. "I need to take out the bread for dinner. Don't forget the salad."

Draig left Melissa standing there as he returned to the kitchen. Giving Draig's broad back a questioning stare for just a heartbeat, she followed him. Using the ingredients he had left on the counter, she quickly put together the salad.

They finished making dinner in a comfortable silence. In part because the entire time Melissa was stuck in her own head.

She was trying to figure out how Draig knew that she wasn't asking him the question that had been bugging her ever since he had told her to grab the groceries from the galley.

Melissa smiled as she walked over to the table, salad bowl in hand. Apparently, the very large steak wasn't for them.

The three dogs leapt down from the couches and rushed over to their bowls when Draig placed several juicy slices of meat in each one.

"I don't eat a lot of red meat," Draig explained when he saw the probing look Melissa gave him. He went back to the kitchen and pulled out from the oven the homemade vegetarian lasagna that he had spent a good bit of his time crafting, placing it on the table. "My mother's recipe. Hopefully you'll enjoy it."

"I'm sure I will," Melissa replied as she sat down. "It smells wonderful."

Draig nodded, then returned to the kitchen, coming back with a loaf of Italian bread, made just that morning, of course, that he put on the table next to the lasagna. Gluten free, Draig explained.

When she took a bite, Melissa was surprised even though she shouldn't have been. It was light and fluffy. Not stodgy as she had anticipated. Then again, he had made gluten-free cinnamon rolls that morning, and those were the best she had ever tasted.

For the next several minutes, neither Melissa nor Draig felt the need to talk. Oddly, Melissa found that she was hungry, almost famished, even after eating at Renzetti's.

"Why did you help me?" Melissa finally blurted out when she was almost done. She had so many questions, and it had taken so much effort to keep them in check while they ate dinner, but she couldn't contain herself any longer.

She also hoped that if she took the initiative, she might be able to keep the focus on him rather than him trying to do the same to her.

Throughout the meal, she had been waiting for him to start in on her. To give her the grilling that she had been dreading as soon as she realized he knew that she had stowed away on his boat.

But he hadn't. And that, in part, was why she felt so much nervous energy surging through her.

He had left her in peace. Allowing her to enjoy her meal. To relax. To permit the stress of the day to drain out of her.

It was his restraint and his understanding that she needed time to decompress that was driving her crazy.

Because she was still stressed. Even more stressed actually as her worry intensified.

And maybe that's why he did it. He knew what effect his approach would have on her. It wasn't compassion or understanding. It was just a tactic.

He was putting her at ease, or at least trying to, so that when he finally started asking her questions, it would make it easier for him to extract the information that he wanted.

Although even as she thought that, a small part of her mind, the more rational part, not the part prone to look for underlying motives or a person's hidden weaknesses, was telling her that she was fooling herself.

That Draig wasn't the type of person that she thought he was. That he was just giving her a good meal and a place to stay until it was safe to return to town.

The less rational part of her mind had won out because she had assumed that her host would be angry with her. That he would lose his temper because of what she had brought to his door.

That's what she was ready for. For him to confront her and demand that she answer whatever question he put to her.

She wasn't ready for this.

This ...

This kindness. This compassion. This humanity.

And not treating her like a suspect on one of those TV crime shows that her mother liked to binge watch.

In fact, to an outside observer, the way they were sitting there eating dinner and talking made it look like they were on a date.

The reality was anything but that. For a second she thought how much nicer the perception was to the way things actually were.

She refocused. She had a job to do, and she wanted to make sure that he wasn't going to get in her way.

Perhaps he could even help her out with the task she needed to complete. Unwittingly, of course.

That rationalization made Melissa feel better about what was happening right then.

"Because you needed help," Draig replied in a strong, quiet voice.

Melissa didn't know how to respond to that. She had thought that more would have gone into his decision making than just that. That he would have spent more time thinking about the consequences of getting involved.

After all, no one willingly got into a fight with Berserkers.

And no one did what he did without hoping to get something out of it for himself.

Yet he had. Without a second thought.

Or at least that was what he was claiming. What he wanted her to believe.

Melissa was too cynical to give Draig the benefit of the doubt. Her host wanted something from her. She just hadn't figured out what that might be yet.

Admittedly, Draig had handled himself quite well. Not only with respect to the Berserkers, but also in terms of how he interacted with her.

Even so, there had to be more to his decision than just her needing help. There had to be, because if there wasn't, then the sketch that she was creating of him was hopelessly incorrect.

Eventually, she assumed that he'd show his cards, just like everyone else she knew. He wanted something from her, and he would reveal what it was when he was ready.

She just needed to be patient. If she was, she could probably figure out what he wanted before he revealed it.

Because no one she knew was as selfless as he had demonstrated himself to be. If you were, you didn't survive very long among the Teg.

"So you just make it a habit of showing up at the exact right time to save the damsel in distress. And against Berserkers, no less. Teg that are best avoided."

"Yes," Draig replied, leaning back in his chair. "Lucky you."

He said it with a straight face and without a hint of condescension or sarcasm. She was looking for a crack in his expression. For the tell that would reveal that he was lying or putting her on or teasing her.

Nothing.

Who was this guy?

Still, she wasn't entirely convinced.

"Seriously? You saw that I needed help and you rushed in against my kidnappers? Without a second thought?"

"Yes," Draig repeated, his eyes never leaving hers, "and let's be honest. You're not a damsel in distress. Far from it, in fact. I know you're more than capable. It's just that the numbers were against you. If not for that, I'm sure that you would have managed quite well on your own."

Melissa stared at Draig for a little longer this time, an expression of disbelief creeping onto her visage. Once again, she didn't know what to say.

Had he just complimented her?

Was this another tactic to soften her up before he asked her what he wanted to know?

"That's probably the nicest thing anyone has ever said to me."

"You're welcome. I do what I can."

For a few heartbeats more they stared at one another. Then they both smiled, Melissa enjoying Draig's dry humor. It seemed as if they had reached a truce of some sort.

For the first time since she had taken her current job, she didn't feel as if she was carrying the weight of the world on her shoulders.

Here, on this island, with a man she barely knew, for whatever peculiar reason that she had not yet deciphered, she felt safe. Comfortable. More like herself.

Maybe he wasn't a psycho.

Still, she reminded herself that she needed to be wary. Draig clearly wasn't all that he seemed to be. He was much, much more. She just hadn't determined what exactly.

"You're not what I expected. Just when I think I have you figured out, you throw me for a loop. Time after time."

"You're welcome," Draig replied drily.

Melissa tried not to laugh, her effort to do that only forcing out a snort that brought her hands to her mouth in an attempt to hide her embarrassment. She finally allowed herself to chuckle softly when she saw Draig's smile.

Open. Honest. Not judgmental.

She liked it.

"I thought you would be angry with me."

"Why?"

"For the Berserkers." She decided not to mention what else was hunting her. "I didn't mean to drag you into any of this. It's just that I was trying to escape, and you got pulled into it."

"Well, that was true for the Berserkers," Draig agreed with a nod. He then leaned forward, placing his elbows on the table.

"Not so much for the Weres. You did stow away on my boat. So I really didn't have much choice in terms of inviting you to dinner."

Melissa's face turned white. "You know about the Weres?"

Draig's reddish-orange eyes flashed. "I know about the Weres. That's the only reason I didn't throw you overboard."

Melissa stared, her eyes wide like a deer caught in the headlights. "I'm sorry. I had no intention of getting you or anyone else caught up in all this."

Draig's expression suggested that she had failed to convince him of that fact. "And what is all this?"

The question hung between them for quite some time.

"All right, all right. You have me there." Melissa held up her hands by way of an apology. "I just didn't have any other options. I tried to get away -- I even used the Grym -- but I couldn't. I was stuck between a rock and a hard place. You and your boat were the best and only option I had. Otherwise, they would have killed me."

Draig didn't respond right away. Instead, studying the very powerful Teg sitting across the table from him. Clever on her part to ignore his question. But he would get the answer that he wanted. When the time was right.

"I understand. I probably would have done the same thing in your shoes." He shrugged, then gave her a nod. "Of course, as you said, you do seem to be caught between a rock and a hard place ... quite often in fact."

Draig didn't bother to tell her that he disagreed with her. At least in part.

He didn't think the Weres were there to kill her. At least not immediately. Rather, he believed that they were there to kidnap her. They wouldn't have killed her until whoever hired the pack got what they wanted from her.

"Thank you," Melissa said, never anticipating that he would be so understanding. And rather than challenging his last comment as was her wont, she tried to be conciliatory instead. "And yes, getting stuck between a rock and a hard place is a recent habit that I'd like to break."

"A worthy goal," Draig agreed. "One request, however."

"What would that be?" Her eyes narrowed, her smile giving way to a worried frown. This was what she had been waiting for. What she had feared.

His demand for a quid pro quo.

He had done her a favor. Twice.

Well, more than a favor, actually. He had saved her life both times.

She closed her eyes and took a deep breath to settle herself. Preparing for what he was going to ask of her.

She really hoped that he wasn't a psycho.

She was used to working with some of the less savory of the Teg, and with that guiding her thoughts, she could only imagine what he would require of her. Here, on an island, with no means of escape, she wasn't in a good position to refuse whatever he might want from her.

"Next time, just give me warning. I'm happy to help so long as I know what I'm getting myself into. Fair enough?"

"Fair enough," Melissa whispered, her eyes locked onto his. She was stunned. She had never anticipated that as his request. No one ever did something for nothing. "Wait. That's it? That's all you want for risking your life for mine?"

"That's it."

"I don't know if you're for real," Melissa grumbled as she slouched back in her chair. What was that saying her mother liked to throw at her from Winston Churchill, the former British Prime Minister using it to describe Russia. *"A riddle, wrapped in a mystery, inside an enigma."* In her opinion, that fit Draig to a tee. "I'm not used to interacting with someone who is straightforward and who doesn't seem to have an ulterior motive."

"I didn't know that you needed to deal with me. I thought that we were just having dinner and talking."

"You know what I mean," Melissa replied, still not quite believing that Draig was going to give her a free pass. Two, in fact.

"Do I?" He gave her a look that made her scrunch up her lips even more.

She couldn't determine if he was angry or curious. She didn't care if he was either or both. That didn't bother her. Rather, she hated the fact that she couldn't read him like she could read everyone else.

"Are you always so difficult?"

"Yes, I tend to be."

"Why is that?"

"It's just who I am."

"And who are you?" Melissa asked, her voice adopting the tone of the therapist she had been seeing for the last few months. The gentle prod that worked so well on her had no effect whatsoever on her dining companion.

"You don't know that by now?" asked Draig, giving her a look of surprise. "From what I can tell, you have a knack for evaluating people. Their desires. Their intentions. I assumed that you would have completed your profile of me and filed it away minutes after meeting me."

"Why would you think that?" she asked, believing it odd that he'd use the word profile. Did he know all that she could do with the Grym?

"Just a feeling," he replied vaguely. "What about you? Who are you?"

She decided that difficult was a kind word to use when describing him. "I feel like I don't know you at all even though we just had dinner together." She laughed. "You first. Then if there's time. Me."

He shrugged, then offered another grin and a quick lift of

his eyebrows. "I'm your knight in shining armor, of course. What more do you need to know?"

They both laughed at that, Melissa shaking her head in mock disappointment, the tension that had been building between them dissipating thanks to the joke.

"You're just like your dogs. You're not anything at all as I expected you would be."

"You've heard the expression don't judge a book by its cover?"

"Of course."

"It certainly applies to Butch, Cassidy, and Sundance. You don't want to get on their bad side. They've got mean streaks."

"And you?"

He leaned back toward her again. Those fiery eyes of his, which made her slightly uncomfortable, blazed even more brightly. "They're nothing compared to me."

Melissa began to laugh, thinking that it was another joke. She stopped abruptly. Draig wasn't smiling.

"So what's with that walking stick of yours?" She nodded toward the shillelagh leaning against the wall by the door, seeking to change the subject. "It was just as effective as the rods the Berserkers used." She placed her arms on the table and leaned toward him. "There was even a time when it didn't look right."

"How so?"

"You're going to laugh."

"Try me."

Melissa gazed shrewdly at Draig, then smiled. "It almost looked like a sword. A blazing sword."

It was Draig's turn to smile. "Probably just a trick of the light."

"Right." Clearly, she didn't believe him.

"It's a long story."

"I'm not going anywhere. Besides, until you get me off the island, I'm your prisoner."

"That's how you're looking at this? A free ride out to a safe, warm place, to say nothing of a good meal, and you believe that I'm holding you prisoner?"

"The night is still young. And I'm still here. We haven't talked about how I might be leaving or when."

Draig stared at her, his eyes flashing.

"So what am I? Your knight in shining armor or you're warden?"

"If you don't like either of those characters, I'm sure that we can come up with one that works for both of us," she responded. "If you're into roleplaying."

Draig didn't respond, though his eyes tightened.

"I'm just kidding." Melissa laughed softly, leaning back in her chair when she realized that he didn't seem to appreciate the innuendo. "Really. It's been a stressful day, and being difficult helps me to relax."

Draig stared at Melissa, his expression unreadable. He was really beginning to wonder if he had made the right decision. Life certainly would be simpler if he had left her to the Berserkers or the Weres.

That was a useless thought, however. He knew that he couldn't do that.

It wouldn't have been the right thing to do. And he had been trained before he was even out of the crib to do the right thing. Always. Even when some might say doing the right thing was the wrong thing to do.

Besides, she had raised a whole host of questions that continued to plague him. He was certain that she was connected to the matter that Cerridwen had mentioned when they had last spoken. And that meant she had drawn Kraken Cove into the political machinations that inevitably riled up the

Tylwyth Teg from time to time. Something he'd worked hard to prevent.

"There are other ways that two consenting adults can have fun with one another. Blow off a little steam."

"Like I said," Melissa finally replied once she started breathing again, needing some time to gather her thoughts as she shook her head slowly, her eyes shrewd as she strangely enjoyed the banter between them. "I can't get a read on you."

"That's how I prefer it."

"Is that so? Why?"

"If you're predictable, you're ceding the advantage right from the start."

"With that perspective, you make it seem like every interaction is a combat."

"More often than not, it is. At least in my experience."

"Thus your blazing sword." She smiled. "And you thought that I had forgotten about that. You didn't really answer my question."

"Why do I have it?" He didn't bother to deny that his shillelagh actually was a sword.

Draig could make up some story, but he got the sense that she was almost as good as he was at smelling a lie. So better just to give her the truth. Or at least part of it. He was willing to be honest with her ... up to a point.

"The sword chose me," he responded, ending the long stretch of silence.

"The sword chose you?"

"Yes, the sword chose me."

"And that's a normal thing with swords? They choose their owners?"

"With this sword, yes," Draig said as if it was no big thing. "And I don't own the sword. It chooses who it will allow to wield it."

"Don't tell me the sword is your friend just like your dogs are."

"No, it's nothing like that."

"I'm glad to hear it," Melissa replied. "I was beginning to worry about this relationship you have with your sword. If you're not friends, then what is it?"

"We bonded."

"You bonded with a sword?"

"Yes. Look. You obviously know more than you're letting on. And we keep playing this game. But why is it so hard to believe?"

Melissa decided to keep her cards close. "You do know how weird that sounds, right?"

Draig smiled then. "I do, but it's the truth. When I was younger, we bonded. We both agreed that we'd prefer to be together rather than apart. That we needed to be together."

"I repeat, you do know how weird that sounds, right?"

"I do."

"And that doesn't bother you?"

"No. That's just the best way that I can explain it. There's really not much more to say."

"So with the Grym you bonded with the sword in much the same way you did the dogs."

"In some ways, yes. In some ways, no."

"Did I mention how difficult you can be?"

"You did."

She waited for him to say more. He didn't.

"Why a baker?" she asked finally, realizing that she needed to take a different angle.

"I like to bake."

"I gathered as much. Who taught you to bake?"

"My mother."

"Is that why you like it?"

"In part. It's how we first bonded."

"We're back to the bonding," Melissa sighed in frustration. "Can we get away from the bonding?"

"You brought it up. You started it with that joke of yours about the prisoner and the warden."

Melissa stared at him for several heartbeats. Speechless. He had caught her. She couldn't believe that he had just turned that back on her. Then she laughed. "Funny. Very funny."

"I try."

"So you're not just a baker?"

Draig smiled. "I'm whatever I need to be."

"Mysterious. Somewhat unsettling. It makes me think of a chameleon."

Draig shrugged, done with her questions. "What about you?"

"What about me?"

"In some ways we're the same."

"How do you mean? I don't have a flaming sword."

"You're whatever you need to be," Draig said, his eyes sparking in challenge when he said it. "Much like a chameleon."

"That's a big assumption based on the fact that you have known me for less than a day."

"Just a feeling."

"Just a feeling." Melissa leaned back, deciding whether she should be offended. "You say something like that based on a feeling?"

"Am I wrong?"

That question stopped her short. She heard the challenge in his voice. "Well, I don't know ..."

"Why are the Renegades after you?"

Her breath caught in her throat. "The Renegades?"

"The werewolves hunting for you. The Renegades. Although I'm sure you already know who they are."

"How do you know who they are?" Melissa challenged.

Draig gave her a smile, but it wasn't really a smile. More of a warning. "I haven't always lived in Kraken Cove."

"Why do you think that the Weres are after me?" she asked softly, knocked slightly off balance and struggling to regain her footing. "Another feeling?"

"No, I saw it on your face before you snuck onto my boat. You knew what was coming behind you."

"You saw me?"

"I did."

"Even though I was using the Grym?"

"Yes."

"Who are you?" demanded Melissa, almost losing what little patience she had left, although she was careful not to raise her voice.

"A baker," Draig replied simply, wondering if his reply was going to push her over the edge. It might be productive if that happened.

It didn't, although she did pretend to kick him under the table. "You really are a pain in the ass. You know that?"

"I do," he confirmed. He wasn't going to allow her to distract him. "Why are the Renegades after you?"

"Why would you think that they're after me? Maybe they're after you."

"Pretty obvious, don't you think?"

"Not to me," she said, realizing immediately that her attempt to throw him off the scent had failed.

"Don't waste my time, Melissa."

She was about to reply, to attempt to deflect, but she stopped herself. She could sense that he was becoming aggravated with her, and she had witnessed firsthand what happened when he got angry.

"I don't know why they were after me," she finally replied, refusing to give him what he wanted, hoping that she could tell him just enough to satisfy him, although she doubted the strategy before she even applied it. "And if I did, I wouldn't be able to tell you."

Draig studied Melissa for quite a long time. He nodded, then abruptly pushed himself up from his chair. He knew that she was lying. But there was no point in pushing her. Not yet.

Besides, the fact that she was lying told him a great deal and confirmed some of his suspicions.

"I need to do a few things before it gets too late. Leave the dishes in the sink. I'll clean them later." He headed toward the back door. "A room is ready for you just up the stairs, first door on the right. I'll get you back to town tomorrow morning."

She nodded in thanks. She could tell that she had disappointed him. Nevertheless, she wasn't willing to reveal all that was going on.

She wanted to trust him. She really did. She was beginning to understand that she was in over her head. But she still wasn't certain that she could. Even after he had saved her life twice.

That realization made her feel even worse. Still, she kept her mouth shut.

"I'd suggest leaving town tomorrow. The Renegades know you're here. They won't give up. Better you leave now while you can."

Melissa watched him walk through the back door with the dogs in tow.

She should feel bad about how things had just ended between them. She probably would have felt worse if she didn't know what was really at stake.

But the truth was, she got the sense that he was less concerned about her and more interested in getting her out of town fast for his own sake.

Her knight in shining armor?

She doubted it.

No one did what he had done without wanting something in return.

He just hadn't told her what that was yet.

13

THE NEED FOR MEDITATION

Shillelagh in hand, Draig stalked across the steel and wire bridge that swayed slowly from side to side, the gusty wind coming off the Atlantic Ocean having picked up. When he stepped onto the larger island, he shifted his gaze to the south.

His cabin cruiser rested comfortably against the dock. All was as it should be. Nothing to worry about. Yet.

Closing his eyes, Draig took a deep breath.

Interacting with Melissa was exhausting. Just having a conversation with her more resembled a combat than a dialogue, each opponent looking for an opening. The goal not to drive a sword through the other's gut but rather to dig out whatever tiny nuggets of information that might be of use.

He much preferred the other form of combat. It was more straightforward. Simpler. With a clear and definitive result.

When he was younger, Draig might have relished the challenge Melissa presented. Now, he didn't have the patience for it.

He had done it too often in the past. Cutting through schemes and subterfuges to get to the truth. And usually a truth that only served to make his life more difficult.

Although he did have to admit that there was something

about Melissa that intrigued him. What it was, he wasn't quite sure.

Whether he wanted to put in the effort to find out what it might be ... well, he wasn't sure about that either. Because he felt other strings pulling on him.

Opening his eyes again, he looked up at the full moon shining down brightly upon him. There was a common misconception that werewolves and other Werebeasts couldn't transform unless there was a full moon.

Those who believed that usually obtained their knowledge about lycanthropes from movies and dime store novels.

Skilled Weres could change into their natural forms whenever they chose. The only distinction was that when there was a full moon a Were gained greater strength, agility, cunning ... it was based on the primary traits of their species. Whatever the unique characteristics of the Were, the full moon enhanced those characteristics.

As was the case tonight, the Renegades, all of them werewolves, would be even stronger and faster than usual, and they were already incredibly fast and strong to begin with.

Werebeasts were dangerous. That couldn't be denied. But there were more terrifying monsters slinking about in the shadows of the Teg world.

He had come up against monsters -- and killed those same monsters -- that would have made every single one of the Renegades empty their bladders right before they lost their heads ... literally.

He hoped that would all wait until tomorrow. Although he knew just how much hope was worth.

All was quiet now. Exactly the way he liked it.

Just to make sure that he had nothing to worry about, Draig reached for the Grym. He began his search on the larger island and then expanded from there until he was several miles beyond Kraken Cove and well out into the Atlantic Ocean.

Nothing yet.

However, he had no doubt that was going to change. It was just a question of when.

If he had learned nothing else since meeting Melissa, she was a magnet for trouble.

And he was sure that the morning would give him a different problem to solve. It always did.

Satisfied that all was well for the time being, Draig walked away from the dock and toward the north, making his way through the wood. He didn't see Butch, Cassidy, or Sundance, but he could sense where they were, stalking through the darkness, staying close to him, just as they had done since he was a young man.

His mother had told the trio of dogs that it was their responsibility to keep Draig safe. Against any danger. Whether presented by friend or foe.

They took that responsibility seriously. Even when they were close to home.

Draig was more than just a ward to them. More than just a friend. They viewed him as a brother.

As Draig hiked through the wood toward the northern shore, he used the Grym to check the tripwires and other magical defenses he had set along the island's perimeter as well as deeper inland. He also inspected those that he had placed out in the ocean that gave warning when anyone approached through the few narrow channels that allowed access to Raptor Bay and the lighthouse that was Draig's home.

All appeared as it should.

Still, a faint hint of unease nagged at him.

His father had been incredibly demanding when Draig was growing up. Always wanting the best from him. Always expecting him to pick up a new skill on the first try. Always requiring that he master that skill.

Mistakes were never permitted. Because his father didn't believe that Teg like them made mistakes.

Mistakes were beneath them.

Mistakes were a sign of weakness.

And his family was anything but weak.

As a result, even though that perspective wasn't necessarily the best approach for building a healthy relationship between them, his father had taught him a great many useful things while applying a very rigid hand. Training him to look at the world in a certain way. In particular, to never accept what he first saw as what was there when that little voice in the back of his brain was telling him to be wary.

Listen to that voice, his father liked to say. If you didn't, then you had no one to blame but yourself when you were stabbed in the back.

With that lesson guiding him, he stopped looking for the obvious. He looked for the less obvious. Not for what was there, but rather for what had been there.

He took his time, using the Power of the Ancients to search around his island again. Not rushing. Not really knowing what he was looking for.

Until he found it.

There wasn't a break in his defenses. There was a repair. Several in fact.

He followed that string of repairs, tracking the path the intruder had taken.

It was faint. But the residue of the intruder's passage was still there.

A trace with which Draig was all too familiar.

The Twisted Grym.

The evil stench of that corrupted power still lingered. It would linger for a little while longer, then fade entirely in just a few hours.

He would never have known it was there if he hadn't decided to check now.

What he had identified was delicate work. Skilled work.

Only a few of the Teg to turn to the Twisted Grym could evade his traps and hide so well that they had been there.

He worked his way through the forest for a few minutes more, taking his time, following the fading trail.

It ended exactly where he thought it would. At the very edge of the small beach that gave him a view of where the Atlantic Ocean met Raptor Bay.

As he stared out across the water, watching the moonlight play off the surging waves, he doubted whoever had visited had come for him. If someone wanted him dead, they would have made the attempt where he would be less protected.

The intruder had come for Melissa. That was the only answer.

Not knowing who lived on this island. Likely wondering what kind of job their employer had sent them on when they realized what was waiting for them.

Not willing to take him on.

That was a good thing and a bad thing.

Good because it meant that Melissa was still alive and would remain alive. At least until tomorrow.

Bad because the secret that he had been hiding for more than a decade might not be a secret any longer.

He would need to assume that was the case.

He had lost his anonymity.

And if he hadn't, it soon would be lost because whoever had come ashore would report what they found to their employer.

Understanding that, Draig concluded that he had some decisions to make.

As he stared out at the water, he began to think of that very short list of Teg with great skill in the Twisted Grym.

The names were associated with people he had little desire

to deal with again. But it seemed like he might not have a choice.

He closed his eyes, pushing his worries to the side as he took several deep breaths. He had been attending Brigid's yoga and meditation classes the last few months, trying to reduce his stress and clear his mind. He put some of what he learned into play.

When he opened his eyes again, he felt calmer. More centered.

His concerns could wait until tomorrow because there was nothing for him to do about them now.

With that realization, he looked up at the full moon and the stars blazing in the sky.

It was a beautiful night. It made him think of a similar night when he had been forced to make a decision that he didn't want to make.

That beautiful night had a terrible conclusion.

Whether that would be the case this evening would be determined soon.

Gripping his walking stick a bit more tightly, he studied the grain of the wood as the memory flooded him.

His father had sent him and a good friend out on a job. Or rather Draig thought that he was a good friend.

He would learn otherwise by the end of the night.

They had been sent after a woman his father said was trafficking in stolen magical items. His father had said that the artifacts were dangerous. That the woman's dealings were dangerous, and they were bringing unwanted attention to the Teg.

His father had sanctioned her removal.

It was a hit.

There was no justice involved.

Removing those Teg his father deemed as having crossed his line.

Another skill that he had acquired thanks to his father.

He was young then. But he had done it before.

More times than he cared to remember, in fact. So it was just another job to him.

A task that needed to be accomplished. No more than that.

But he had begun to wonder.

In the beginning, when his father sent him out after a Teg who was doing something that he or she shouldn't, he hadn't bothered to ask any questions. He had trusted his father. And with good reason.

His father held an exalted position among the Teg. Deservedly so, or so he had thought.

He believed that his father was telling him the truth. That he always told him the truth. Until he started to realize that his father's truth wasn't always the entire truth.

His father offered him bits and pieces of the truth so that he would get the job done. So that Draig believed that he was doing the right thing.

After a while, Draig realized that the details that his father gave him didn't always add up. He started doing some research on his own.

It had been a scary moment. A defining moment.

Draig concluded that his definition of doing what was right differed from that of his father.

Even worse, that perhaps his father's definition of what was right was being twisted by what his father needed.

This was the first job his father sent him on where he had questioned the assignment beforehand, although not enough to raise his father's suspicions. Even so, his doubts plagued him.

He told himself that he wouldn't do what he normally did when he was supposed to kill one of the Teg. He would talk to her first. Get her side of the story. Then he would make a decision on what to do next after that.

All well and good in theory. Not in practice.

Draig believed that he was being circumspect with his questions, but he hadn't been.

His friend had been sent with him to make sure that he killed the woman and had been watching him closely.

Because not for the first time his father had doubted his loyalty.

Draig didn't kill the woman.

After doing some research, he had determined that the reason his father sent him to kill the Teg was a lie. She didn't deserve to die.

He was glad that he didn't kill her for another reason as well. If not for her, he would be dead.

He had saved her life. She had saved his.

If not for her, his former friend would have killed him.

He hoped the woman was well. He hadn't heard from her in a very long time. And he viewed that in a positive light.

No word from her meant that she was still safe. Because he would have known if she had been killed. And he would have sought vengeance on those who committed such a crime. Even his father.

His former friend was still alive as well. Draig could have killed him, but he hadn't. He still wondered whether that was the right decision.

Draig had been working to build a new life and escape the blood and death and revenge that had been the foundation of his previous existence. Instead trying to focus on more productive topics.

Sometimes he succeeded. Often he didn't.

Still, at least he was trying.

Why did that memory come up right now?

Draig didn't know. He hadn't thought about all that since he had come to Kraken Cove.

What was it that pulled that experience up from the depths?

Then he had it. He knew how the werewolves had gotten so close to Kraken Cove before he discovered them. Who had helped them.

At that moment, one name came to mind.

And it was the name that he feared the most.

Because if he was right, and he had no reason to think that he wasn't, then this was just the starting play in a much larger game.

A game that he had tried to leave long before.

A game that he had known he could never escape forever.

A game that only had one ending.

A bloody one.

14

TOO CURIOUS

Melissa kicked the last of the covers off her bed. She had been tossing and turning ever since she had lain down not long after dinner, unable to sleep.

It wasn't because of the accommodations. The four-poster bed, an antique that had been meticulously maintained, was incredibly comfortable. She had sunk down into the mattress as if she was meant to be there, burrowing beneath the comforters piled atop it. At least for a little while.

And the room itself was charming. Just like the living space below, Draig had modernized the rooms on the second floor. In addition to her king-sized bed, she had a private bathroom and a small sitting space that allowed her to look out the window. It was still dark since it was the early morning hours, the stars gleaming in the cloudless sky, the glow of the moon reflecting off the water of the bay.

She couldn't sleep because she was still wired after all that had happened since she left the Safe Haven.

Yet Berserkers and werewolves had nothing on the real cause of her discomfort.

She was on edge primarily because of her host.

Draig made her uneasy. And it wasn't just because of that sword he concealed as a walking stick.

Melissa shook her head in frustration for what seemed like the hundredth time that night. She didn't want to admit it, but if not for Draig, she likely would be dead. Either because of the Berserkers or the werewolves.

He had saved her life and he had yet to ask her for anything in return. Maybe that was why he made her feel so uncomfortable. In her world, tit for tat was commonplace.

Or perhaps it was because his strength in the Grym exceeded her own, an unnerving thought since there were few members of the Teg who could make use of more natural magic than she could.

No, she was just fooling herself. She had been in difficult situations before. Too many to remember, in fact. And she knew how to take care of herself. Even when faced with Teg who enjoyed advantages that she didn't.

Melissa grumbled in displeasure. This was what had been keeping her awake. Why her mind wouldn't stop working. Searching for some reason, any reason, as to why she felt as she did.

She couldn't lie to herself any longer. The cause for her restlessness wasn't Draig so much as the feeling that he generated within her. It would be so nice to trust someone. Especially after the hell that she had lived through a year before.

Growling in irritation, she pushed herself up from the bed and slipped on the robe she found hanging on the door to the bathroom. What she felt terrified her. So instead of allowing herself to think, she decided to just do something.

Melissa walked over to the window, looking out toward the east. Right below her was the back door to the lighthouse.

The stars and moon illuminated the sawgrass and rocks below, the waves crashing softly against the shore with a soothing repetitiveness.

She leaned her forehead against the glass so that she could look down toward the back porch.

A shadow detaching itself from the darkness caught her eye as it moved around the base of the lighthouse toward the bridge.

Draig.

Where was he going?

That question left her in a flash, replaced by another thought.

She had the lighthouse to herself for a time.

She didn't give a second thought to what she was about to do. She had sticky fingers after all, and she would be the first to admit that she was more curious than a cat. Besides, she had learned it was better to heed her instincts rather than fight them.

Yet even with Draig gone, she needed to be careful. She didn't know how long he would be away.

Wanting to make the most of however much time she had, Melissa opened the door on silent hinges, taking a peek before stepping out into the hallway.

Nothing but shadows on the landing and a kitchen light. She didn't hear a noise. Not even the scrabble of paws on the wooden floor down below.

Had the dogs gone with Draig?

Melissa stepped along the floor to the staircase without making a sound, then worked her way down slowly. She really liked the metal staircase, and not just because it was original to the lighthouse. She didn't have to worry about creaking boards.

When she reached the bottom of the steps, she stopped, surveying the living space. She didn't see the dogs.

She walked toward the kitchen. The cockerpoos weren't sprawled out on their favorite couch. They must have slipped out with Draig.

Melissa grinned. She did indeed have the lighthouse to herself.

She never thought that she would get this chance.

Wanting to make the most of it, she took hold of the Grym and sent wispy constructions of energy that resembled spiderwebs sparking out from her fingers. The webs drifted throughout the lighthouse, rising to the second floor and into the bedrooms as well as up to the light at the very top of the tower. The tangles moved as if they had minds of their own, fizzling out slowly in rhythm to the ticking of the grandfather clock in Draig's office.

She was disappointed, although she couldn't say that she was surprised.

Nothing.

She had used this same spell many a time to find a target's hidden treasures. It had always worked before, but it proved useless to her here.

Her brows furrowed in thought. Either Draig had nothing to hide or his skill in the Grym was even greater than she had anticipated.

She didn't want to admit to the latter, but she couldn't ignore that possibility either.

Melissa stood in place for several minutes. Biting her lip. Thinking.

He was stronger than her in the Grym -- she still didn't want to admit that, although she had to -- and he was more skilled than she was. That bothered her. It also played off the emotion that she was attempting to suppress in a way that she had not anticipated.

To quell the impact of the uncomfortable feeling that had taken up residence within her, she returned her focus to the problem she faced.

He was hiding something from her. She was sure of it. But where would he keep it?

With no good ideas on what else she could do, she slowly spun around in a circle.

Nothing that she ran her eyes over seemed like a good possibility.

Wait!

Her lips curled ever so slightly into the beginnings of a smile.

Her gaze kept coming back to the shield hanging from the wall. She walked over toward the door so that she could get a closer look.

Three red dragons on a field of green. Welsh dragons, she corrected herself. She knew at least that much because of the distinctive design.

An old shield as well, dents and scratches marring its length. As if it had been used. Quite a lot.

Why did she feel like she was missing something? Like she should know what three Welsh dragons, one atop the other, meant, but for the life of her she couldn't remember. She should have brought her phone down with her so that she could do a quick online search.

She studied the shield for a few seconds more. It was in a place of prominence. Clearly important to Draig.

She decided to try something different since what she had tried first hadn't worked.

Melissa placed her hand on the metal.

A bright flash greeted her touch, blinding her, a blast of energy sending her stumbling back a few steps, her fingers tingling painfully as if she had placed her hand in an open flame.

Melissa reached out to the side with her other arm to steady herself. She felt dizzy and nauseous, close to passing out.

Bending at the waist, she took several deep breaths. Slowly she came back to herself. When she didn't feel like she was going to spill her guts, she stood straight again.

Thankfully, her sight was coming back, the large black spots becoming small ones that gradually receded to the edges of her vision. No longer lightheaded, she lifted her hand and studied her fingertips.

They still tingled with pain. No burns, however. Her skin was fine, not cracked and oozing as she feared.

She hadn't kept her hand there long enough for any real damage to occur. In addition to the curiosity, she liked to think that she had the reflexes of a cat. She was certain that her fingers would have been burned to a crisp if she hadn't pulled them back so swiftly.

She was certain as well that she had found Draig's hiding place. Why else put such a powerful ward there? Could it be protecting the item that she had failed to find in the bookstore? The item that was so essential to her continuing to draw breath?

Melissa shook her head in irritation. She could try to circumvent the magical defense that he had put in place, but that would take time that she likely didn't have. Worse, she wasn't certain that even if she had the time that she could actually find a way past the ward. If she made a mistake ...

Well, she didn't want to think about that. A charred hand might be the least of her worries.

Before she did something that she regretted, she thought about her host. A baker. A lighthouse keeper. A man with a great deal of strength and skill in the Grym. A man with a blazing sword.

None of that added up. Why would someone like him live in a lighthouse just off the coast from Kraken Cove?

A man she knew nothing about.

She had returned to the Teg world less than ten years before, plying her trade in its more shadowy circles.

She felt certain that she would have heard of someone of

Draig's strength and skill, and of course that sword. A whisper at least. But she hadn't.

Another mystery. Usually, she enjoyed solving enigmas such as this. But not now.

She had more pressing concerns, yet she found it difficult to focus on them because she believed that she was missing something important. She didn't want whatever that might be to come back and spank her at the worst possible time.

Putting all that to the side, once again she shifted her attention back to the task that was most important to her. Having hit a roadblock, she realized that there was only one way to find out if he had the artifact that she needed.

She needed to learn more about him. She needed to stay close to him.

That decided, going against her better instincts, Melissa concluded that she needed to follow him. She understood the danger involved if he caught her, but she wouldn't allow that to happen.

Clearly, Draig had a strength and skill in the Grym that she had rarely if ever come across before. In fact, other than her mother and perhaps her current clients, he was probably the strongest Teg with whom she had ever crossed paths.

Yet even knowing that, she allowed her curiosity to get the better of her.

Turning the knob silently, she opened the back door an inch at a time. Once she stepped through, she made sure the door wasn't locked before closing it behind her.

Melissa then crept off the porch and headed toward the steel bridge that would take her over to the larger island.

She couldn't stop the smile that quickly spread across her face. What she was doing was dangerous. Perhaps even more dangerous than when she pilfered the item that was the cause of all of her current problems.

Melissa couldn't help herself, however.

She was a thief after all.

Of items. Information. Even hearts.

She was in her element now as she moved through the moonlight. Exactly where she preferred to be. Digging up secrets.

About to set foot on the bridge, a voice from the darkness stopped her cold, draining the energy and excitement coursing through her. Replacing it with a shiver of fear.

"Out for a stroll at this hour?"

Draig stood on the center of the bridge, the three cocker-poos, barely visible in the brush of the larger island, sitting quietly behind him.

She found it strange that the dogs weren't looking at her. Rather, they were focused on the beach a few hundred yards to the south.

"Something like that," she replied, giving him her best smile. "I couldn't sleep."

Draig's expression confirmed that he had little patience for games. Maybe it was because she was wearing a terry cloth bathrobe and pajamas.

"We need to talk."

"About?" Melissa asked innocently.

"You."

"Me?" Melissa fought hard to remain calm. She didn't think his interest came from any attraction he might have for her. There was a hardness to him that kept him shielded from others.

Draig nodded ever so slightly, his reddish-orange eyes blazing brightly in the darkness. "You."

"Now? It is kind of late."

"No better time than the present."

Melissa offered him another smile, one that had dazzled more than one man in the past, fairly certain that it would have little effect on Draig but still worth a try.

"How about tomorrow morning? I really should get some sleep."

She turned away from Draig, taking her foot from the bridge, wanting nothing more than to get back to the lighthouse and her room so that she could think about how she was going to deal with him when the sun was up.

Before she could take another step, Draig was right in front of her, less than a foot away, his furious eyes capturing hers.

"How did you ..." Melissa began, shocked not only that he had moved so quickly, but also that he had gotten past her without her even realizing it, crossing the channel somehow in the blink of an eye.

"Now." His voice was soft, cold ... insistent. Not to be ignored.

Melissa realized that the friendly baker and lighthouse keeper was no longer with her. This was the man who had taken on the Berserkers with a remarkable, dominating ease.

"Look, I'm sorry. I don't ..."

Draig's eyes flashed dangerously, cutting off Melissa's words. He didn't move. He simply spoke in a quiet voice devoid of emotion.

"They'll be here any second. There is no time for games."

"Who's going to be here?" Melissa was confused. She was also frightened. Draig hadn't made a move toward her, yet his very presence froze her in place, filling her with a dread that made it hard for her to think.

"You know who's going to be here," he replied, clearly losing patience.

"I don't really ..." She held up her hands quickly. "I'm sorry, I'm not trying to be difficult. I really don't know."

Draig stared at her for a few heartbeats, then whipped his head down toward the beach. Butch, Cassidy, and Sundance were already moving in that direction, staying out of sight as they did so.

"You have the artifact on you?"

Melissa's eyes widened in shock. "How did you ..."

"Do you have the artifact on you?" Draig repeated, biting off the words so that her attention wouldn't wander.

Melissa didn't reply right away, trying to comprehend how he could have known. Having no choice, realizing that she couldn't lie because he would know in an instant, she nodded.

"Head back to the lighthouse and stay there," Draig ordered. "There are wards in place that will protect you." He stepped past her and began to walk across the bridge. "We'll talk after I've greeted our visitors."

15

A POOR STRATEGY

"You sure you want to do this?" Seamus asked. His eyes flashed with a mix of disbelief and resignation. Why had he agreed to Draig's request? "You could just call him. Makes my life easier. I can give you his number. I doubt he'd be very concerned about meeting with you."

"He'll be concerned, believe me."

Seamus considered the obvious conceit laced within that comment, then shook his head. "Sorry, I don't see that happening. Better just to give him a call. He really doesn't like surprises."

Seamus stood with his arms crossed, leaning back against the helm, seemingly at ease despite the dozen men who stood aboard his craft. None of them invited. None of them a paying customer.

Those were two immediate strikes in Seamus' book.

All of the men were staring at him. All of them were giving him hard looks. All of them were trying to intimidate him.

They were wasting their time and his.

Seamus was bored. There was other business that he wanted to take care of that evening. Not this.

But it didn't look like he was going to get out of this mess that Draig had dropped in his lap anytime soon.

Admittedly, he was curious now. He had a sense of how all this was going to play out. Still, he wanted to see it for himself.

In large part because he didn't like these thugs stomping onto his boat like they owned it.

It hadn't taken Seamus very long to figure out who the men were or what they were. It was obvious the instant the first of the giants jumped onto his boat from the dock, ignoring the ladder.

He recognized the golden eyes that he had spotted the night before. They were unmistakable. The leathers they wore only strengthened his belief.

They were dressed as bikers with patches on the back of their jackets that identified them.

The Renegades.

He knew them by reputation. And their reputation wasn't a good one.

He had never sought the pleasure of meeting these louts. But some things couldn't be helped. And now he wasn't going to get the quiet night that he had been hoping for.

"We're doing this my way, *matey*." The leader of the group stood in front of Seamus, giving him a broad grin, his voice filled with disdain. "Take us across to the lighthouse."

"You're going to have to be more specific," Seamus muttered in a tired voice.

"I wouldn't recommend trying to be smart with me," growled the heavily bearded fellow. He took a step closer to Seamus, leaning down, actually getting so close to him that their noses were almost touching.

"There's more than one lighthouse in the cove, *Sparky*," Seamus replied through gritted teeth. Not out of anger, however.

He appreciated the biker's attempted intimidation. It was to be expected in a situation like this, although it wasn't very effective.

It took a great deal to intimidate Seamus. In fact, there was only one Teg who could do that, and that Teg was actually this gang's target.

Seamus rarely backed down from a conflict, but in that moment he felt the need to retreat, the man's bad breath threatening to do him in. The stench of rancid meat that wafted out from his broken teeth was almost too much for him, his eyes beginning to water.

"You need to be more specific," Seamus clarified, worried for just a moment that he might pass out because of the overwhelming stench. "There are many lighthouses along the coast."

The biker took a step back then, which Seamus almost thanked him for.

"Raptor Bay Lighthouse."

Seamus nodded. "You sure you want to go out there? This time of night the currents are tricky. I'm just as likely to get you there as beach you somewhere along the way."

"Just get us there, *matey*."

"There's a reason why no one ever goes out there but him."

"Yeah? What might that be?" asked the leader of the gang.

"I've been told that's where he buries the bodies."

"Buries the bodies?" scoffed the biker. "So the town baker has a shady side, huh? The story I was told was that he's a grump and prefers to live like a hermit."

"Well, he is a grump," Seamus agreed. "And he is a baker. But have you even considered what it is that he likes to put in his pies?"

Silence descended on the boat.

"You're saying that the baker lives out here because he kills people and then puts them in his pies?" snorted the leader in disbelief.

"I'm not saying it," Seamus clarified. "It's just a story. No more than that. I'm just telling you a story."

"If it's just a story, then why are you wasting our time with it?"

"I just thought you'd like to know. There's a reason no one ever goes out to the Raptor Bay Lighthouse," Seamus said with a shrug. "Those who do rarely if ever come back."

"Nice try, *matey*," the biker scowled. "You're feeding us a load of bullshit. Now get this boat out of the harbor. If you give us any trouble, you're a dead man. Got it?"

Several of the bikers, long hair trailing well down their backs, their beards extending almost to the large shiny buckles on their belts, crowded around him again, emphasizing their leader's point, putting him into shadow, only the full moon providing any light.

It was in those shadows that Seamus saw what these men truly were. What they were hiding from him.

Seamus almost wanted to laugh. This might not be a wasted night after all.

Fools one and all. Trying to intimidate him on his own boat. The nerve.

Seamus shrugged as he turned the key and the engine rumbled to life.

"Your funeral," he muttered under his breath.

"IS THAT IT?"

Seamus barely glanced at Derrick, the leader of this band of miscreants, knowing the danger of taking his eyes away from the narrow channel he was motoring through for more than just a few breaths. The risk of running aground on the shallow sandbars that extended along both sides when the tides were like this was too high to begin with.

If he made a mistake like that, then he wouldn't be able to get his boat back into the water until the early morning.

He nodded to himself, his brow furrowing.

After thinking about that for a few seconds, maybe that wasn't such a bad thing. It was certainly a better option to consider than the one he had fixed on the moment these losers had hijacked his cabin cruiser.

He had learned the name of the Renegades' leader because the man had introduced himself as if he and his friends were coming aboard Seamus' boat for a charter. Just a bunch of big, bewhiskered guys heading out to fish for tarpon, tuna, and swordfish.

They had no clue that they were hunting a much more dangerous animal.

Even the great whites that frequented these waters didn't compare to what waited for them on the dark island that was gaining clarity just ahead.

Seamus had no doubt that when these hoodlums finally came face to face with the lightkeeper, they were going to regret it. He almost wanted to be there when that happened.

Almost.

He looked over his shoulder at the eleven other men lounging around his craft.

Not a care in the world. They believed that they had taken on an easy job.

Clueless fools he snorted to himself.

That lack of understanding set his temper burning, and he worked hard to keep it under control. Because now wasn't the time to let go. Not yet.

He needed to be careful.

If Derrick and his friends figured out who he was, he didn't stand a chance unless he got into the water before they grabbed him.

They hadn't felt the need to reveal their true selves,

thinking that he was nothing more than an old, craggy boat captain. He needed to keep it that way, because he knew what they were capable of. And he understood the lengths to which they were willing to go and the things they were willing to do when they took their true, more savage form.

What was really setting his butt burning, though, was the fact that as soon as Seamus had taken the wheel, Derrick hadn't left his side.

In just seconds Derrick acted like he was Seamus' new best friend.

The thug had a new captive audience, and he was making the most of it. The bearded giant spending the last hour regaling Seamus with his adventures as one of the leaders of what he described as the most notorious and dangerous biker gang in the country.

Seamus didn't really care what Derrick had to say. He could brag all he wanted.

But he was really getting tired of the constant prattle, which had become an irritating buzz. If Derrick had been an insect, Seamus would have swatted him away.

Seamus had stopped listening as soon as Derrick started talking. He just grumbled now and then to make it seem like he was actually paying attention.

That's what almost got him into trouble.

"Is that it?" Derrick asked again with more heat, pushing Seamus on the shoulder with a large, meaty hand.

Seamus didn't move an inch, though he did look over his shoulder, catching how Derrick's golden eyes flashed in the darkness.

Derrick was strong. The muscles that made his t-shirt look five sizes too small for him supporting that conclusion. But appearances could be deceiving. Something that Seamus knew quite well.

He didn't give in to his natural inclination to throw a punch at Derrick for having the temerity to touch him. He couldn't risk angering the biker while he was still aboard his cruiser with so many of his friends.

"Did you see any other lighthouses on the way here?" Seamus asked in as calm a voice as he could manage.

"No," Derrick replied, giving Seamus a hard look.

"Do you see that lighthouse there?" Seamus worked hard to keep out of his voice the pique rising within him.

Derrick stared in the direction that Seamus pointed. Both watched as the bright light swept through the darkness toward them, flashed across the boat, and then continued on its way. A constant loop until morning.

"Yes," Derrick replied with a confident grin. "I do."

"Then that's it," Seamus grumbled tiredly.

The longer he spent with Derrick the more aggravated Seamus became. It reminded him of the time that he had made the mistake of agreeing to babysit his former girlfriend's eight children. All at the same time.

That had not ended well. He doubted that this would either for Derrick and his pack if Seamus played this the right way.

Derrick seemed to think that he was in control of the situation. He was anything but.

"Are you making fun of me, old man?" demanded Derrick.

"No, I'm not," Seamus replied, the bad taste of loathing working its way into his voice. "There'd be no fun in doing that. No challenge at all. It would be too easy. So why even try?"

The massive biker leaned in close to Seamus, acknowledging the insult. More than happy to intimidate their skipper with his great size.

"Are you cruisin' for a bruisin', old man? Because I haven't beat on someone for several days, and I'm getting crabby."

Seamus' immediate impulse was to jab the biker in the throat with his elbow. Crush his windpipe and the shifter would die a slow and painful death.

It would have been such an easy thing for him to do. Less than a second. Scarcely any effort.

But he didn't. It was too much of a risk.

If he struck true, Derrick's friends would change in an instant and rip him apart. If he didn't, Derrick could remove his head from his shoulders with a single swipe.

Besides, his mind was elsewhere, stuck on what Derrick had just said as well as the reality that he'd need to finish off eleven more interlopers to have any chance of getting out of this mess in one piece.

"Cruisin' for a bruisin'?" Seamus mused.

"You heard me," Derrick challenged, clearly irritated by the fact that Seamus wasn't frightened like he was supposed to be.

"Cruisin' for a bruisin'?" snorted Seamus, no longer able to contain his amusement. "What are we? Sharks and Jets?"

When Derrick didn't respond, his hard look becoming one of bewilderment, Seamus continued. "Sharks and Jets. Come on." Seamus stared at the thug, waiting for him to get it, realizing that as the seconds passed, and Derrick's expression didn't change, that this biker clearly was culturally inept. "You don't know about the Sharks and Jets?"

"You need to quit your yapping."

"Clearly not a fan of *West Side Story*." Seamus shook his head at Derrick's clear lack of understanding. "One of the best-known and most loved musicals in the history of theater?"

The only response that Derrick offered was a hard-eyed glare.

Seamus kept his eyes on the channel. Even if he was looking at his unwanted passenger, the overgrown biker's expression wouldn't have bothered him in the least.

Seamus had faced off against a great many more stares in the past that had actually scared him. Even though Seamus knew what his new best friend could do when he got angry, biker boy just wasn't doing it for him. Now, he kind of felt sorry for the leader of this pack of mongrels.

"That phrase originated in the 1940s, maybe even before that," Seamus explained once he realized that Derrick wasn't going to say anything else. "It made me think of *West Side Story*. It's the kind of phrase that they used back then. It's from where your reference originates. You had no idea? Really?"

"Why should I care?" Derrick growled.

"Because right now we're cruisin'."

Derrick's glare didn't waver, not comprehending why the boat captain was telling him what was so obvious. "What does that have to do with anything?"

"Well, we're cruisin', and now we're getting to the bruisin'," Seamus explained.

"What are you talking about ..."

Derrick never got out the rest of his question.

Seamus turned the wheel hard to port, the cabin cruiser lurching then surging through the shallow water and right up onto the sandbar.

Seamus held tight to the wheel, so he weathered the impact quite well. Derrick and his friends not so much. Caught completely by surprise, they were thrown forward in a jumble of arms and legs when the *Kraken* ran aground and came to a jarring stop a few hundred yards from the island.

Seamus didn't hesitate. With a surprising sprightliness, he ran past the large tangle of bodies and limbs in his way, ignoring the cries of anger and howls of pain, several of the bikers suffering from broken bones that Seamus knew would heal faster than a great white gobbling up an elephant seal.

Reaching the aft deck, Seamus studied the water. Perfect.

His cabin cruiser was two thirds of the way up on the sandbar, and it would remain there until the tide turned. Best of all, he had shut off the engines before he made his escape and taken the key with him so the Weres had no chance of restarting the cabin cruiser.

"I'm going to kill you, old man!" Derrick cried as he struggled to extricate himself from his fallen friends.

Seamus laughed, then gave the biker a one-finger salute.

"Come and get me, Were!" he called as he dove off the deck and into the deep water of the channel.

16

THE HUNTING GROUND

"Faster, damn you!"

"We're going as fast as we can," grunted Donnie, paddling his way through the choppy water as best as he could. It seemed like for every yard he swam forward, the current pushed him back two. He couldn't get away from the sandbar no matter how hard he tried, a challenge for all of Derrick's gang. "I've never experienced a current this strong."

Derrick ignored Donnie's complaints, struggling just as much as his brother.

Only a few years apart, Donnie and Derrick had grown up together. And though they rarely had gotten along when they were younger, they were inseparable now. When Derrick had a job, Donnie was always there with him. Protecting each other's backs.

For the most part, the jobs tended to be easy money. Robbery. Carjackings. Kidnappings. A little rough stuff on occasion just to keep things interesting and prevent them from getting bored or rusty. This job should have been no different.

Except now Derrick wondered if perhaps he and the other

Renegades had gotten into a mess that it would have been better to stay out of.

When he took the job, something felt off. He had shrugged away his concern. No one refused his current employer, not if they wanted to continue breathing. It had gone downhill shortly after that.

Finding the Witch had been easy with the help that they received. But the town set his fur bristling. It didn't feel right to him. And now this. An old man actually having the balls to challenge him?

The Renegades instilled fear wherever they went. Always. Yet in Kraken Cove, he and his men had felt distinctly out of place. As if they had reason to worry.

It was the strangest feeling. An unsettling feeling.

He had never experienced it before, the sense that he had wandered into a bigger, badder predator's territory.

He didn't like it.

And now he and his men were dogpaddling in the ocean, the current shifting in ways that didn't make sense.

Derrick was used to exercising a power among the Teg that few others could. But now that sense of power was greatly muted as he swam through the increasingly choppy water. The island was only a few hundred yards away but had grown no closer ever since he and his brothers jumped off the grounded boat almost an hour before.

Derrick didn't understand why this swim was so difficult. When they started out, the current actually was pushing them toward the cay, helping them on their way. After just a few strokes, however, the current changed, pushing them away from the lighthouse and toward the far side of the island.

He didn't understand how that was possible. After leaving the cabin cruiser, they had run along the sandbar in a foot of water, finding themselves only five hundred yards from the shore where the sandbar ended.

Derrick even had joked that to get to the island, all they needed to do was walk on water. The rest of his pack had laughed.

Then everything soured in an instant. The current and the waves started nudging them away from their objective, keeping them in the deep water.

"We're not getting anywhere!" roared Derrick, hoping that his rising anger would urge his pack to pick up the pace. "I'm going to kill that old man!"

"Who cares about the old man?" spluttered Donnie. "Let's get the girl, do what we were paid to do, and then we can get out of here. You've already mucked things up enough as it is."

Derrick snarled, his natural reaction to being challenged. He did no more than that, however. Not bothering to explain that the old man had taken the key with him when he left them stranded on the sandbar. Without the key they had no way off the island except for the lightkeeper's cruiser, assuming it was there.

This job was turning into one of the biggest mistakes Derrick had ever made.

He twisted in the water toward Donnie, a snarl in the back of his throat, about to order him to shut his trap. But he couldn't get the words out.

For just a heartbeat he locked eyes with his brother, Donnie's going big, as if he didn't quite understand what was going on.

Donnie looked down toward the water, then back at Derrick. With a gulp and a gasp Donnie disappeared beneath the waves with barely a splash.

"Donnie? Donnie!" Derrick couldn't comprehend what was happening. "Donnie! Donnie!"

The other members of Derrick's pack turned toward him.

"What happened?" asked Markie.

"I don't know," Derrick sputtered, his words mixing with a

wave that smacked him in the face. He spun around, dipping his bearded maw into the black water, trying to find his brother, hoping that Donnie's head would pop above the surface. Hoping that it was just another of his brother's endless parade of jokes. Knowing as soon as he thought it that it wasn't. "He was there. I was talking to him. Then he was gone."

The rest of the gang swept their eyes across the rough surface, looking for the missing member of their pack.

"It's not one of his pranks, is it?" demanded Curly. The golden-haired biker, who's hair was perfectly straight – at least when he wasn't swimming through the ocean, hated it when Donnie did one of his stunts.

"No. No. It's not." Derrick continued to spin around in the water, looking for any hint of his brother. Even with the full moon lighting their way toward the island, he saw nothing but choppy water. His brother was gone. "He was there and then he wasn't. Something must have taken him."

"You're not in on it as well, are you, Derrick?" demanded Curly.

"No, I'm not. It's not a prank! Donnie! Donnie!"

With that admission, a few of the bikers dove beneath the surface, looking for any sign of their missing friend. Only a few seconds later, those who had gone below were back above the surface. They couldn't see a thing in the dark water. The bright moon couldn't penetrate the increasingly angry ocean.

"Where is he?" Derrick demanded.

"I don't know," came the reply from several of his pack.

"I can't see him anywhere," Curly replied. The burly biker had kicked himself at least fifteen feet below the surface, but there had been nothing to see. Nothing but shadows at the edge of his vision.

"He's got to be here," Derrick pleaded. "He can't just disappear."

Then with no more than a gasp, another biker who had

been staying afloat only a few feet to Derrick's right disappeared beneath the waves.

"What the hell?" Derrick wheezed.

"Where did Ricky go?" demanded Markie.

"I don't know," replied Derrick. "The same thing happened to Donnie."

"Is it a shark?" asked Curly.

"It can't be a shark," replied Markie, a hint of fear in his voice. The biker was the worst swimmer out of the entire pack, and he was tiring. So much so that he was having a hard time keeping his head above the surface, oftentimes just bobbing there before kicking himself back up for a breath. "Could it?"

"Are there sharks in these waters?" wondered Curly, a similar thought coursing through the minds of the other bikers.

A shark? Derrick remembered the boat captain saying something about sharks.

The old man had dove into the water like he belonged there. They had never seen him surface. And they had looked. For several minutes. But no sign of him.

Derrick assumed that he had drowned. That the crusty old bastard had misjudged the depth and cracked his neck on the sandbar, his body pulled out to sea by the current.

But maybe that wasn't what happened.

Maybe the old man wasn't what he appeared to be.

For just a breath, Derrick was torn. He wanted to keep looking for his brother. That desire warred with the small voice in the back of his brain that told him that Donnie was gone and that he was never going to find him. Because of that an even stronger instinct began to take hold.

Donnie was his brother. Derrick would do anything for him. But he couldn't do anything if Derrick joined him in the darkness of the deep.

"Make for the island!" Derrick shouted, spluttering as a wave slapped him in the face. "As fast as you can!"

Before he had even finished spitting out his order, another of the bikers vanished. Teddy managed a brief scream that was cut short when his head vanished beneath the surface.

Shocked by the latest loss that was all the incentive the bikers needed.

They forgot their friends. They thought only of themselves as they swam as fast as they could for the shore.

They found the going even harder as they tried to escape. They had to fight more and more against the waves that had grown in height and now were smashing down onto them, almost as if the ocean didn't want to let them go.

Still, they persevered. Driven by terror. Knowing now for certain that there was something in the water with them.

Derrick took the lead, head down, fighting against the ocean, pulling himself through the water with an almost manic energy that infused the rest of his brothers with a newfound strength.

They had about a hundred yards left now before they reached the island. They were almost there.

Derrick didn't feel any relief. It was still slow progress. Much too slow.

The dire nature of the situation threatening to crush him, Derrick put his head down again and swam for all that he was worth. Forgetting his friends. Not caring about them. Caring only that he got out of the water before he was dragged below to join his brother.

Fifty yards left. Maybe less.

He was exhausted and losing quickly what little strength he had left. He dug deep within himself, his terror driving him onward through the water.

He could hear the splashing and cursing right behind him. Curly, Markie, and the others were doing all that they could to stay with him.

None of them were good swimmers. But that didn't matter

now. Their instinct for survival had taken hold. Most floundered more than they swam, their fear taking hold. Even so, they managed to close the distance to the cay.

None of them knew what was swimming in the water with them. They didn't want to know.

Derrick stayed at the head of the group, freestyling through the water, the rocks on the shore growing bigger with every stroke, his panic giving him the burst of energy he needed to momentarily burn away his worsening fatigue.

When he heard another scream behind him, knowing that another of his pack had been dragged below, he pulled himself through the water at an even faster clip. He didn't bother to look behind him. He never even gave a thought to stopping and seeing if he could help whoever had been pulled beneath the surface.

He didn't care about his men. He didn't care about his brother. He only cared about himself. He just wanted to get back onto land.

Finally, after several more endless seconds of desperate struggle, he felt the sand beneath his feet. Pushing himself out of the water, he ran the last few yards onto the rocky shore.

Placing his hands on his knees, he turned away from the ocean and spent the next few minutes puking out saltwater, his entire body shuddering with relief.

With his stomach empty, Derrick turned back around. He caught Curly's eye first. Then Markie. Both of them were only then standing up straight again, having gone through the same exercise that Derrick had just completed. The same exercise that his other men were still working their way through, the rest of them on their hands and knees, a few pressing their heads in thanks against the rocks jutting out of the sand.

He had boarded the old man's boat with twelve. Now he was down to eight.

He had lost a quarter of his men in less than half an hour.

Worse, he had lost his brother, and there hadn't been anything that he could do about it.

To a shark?

He didn't know. He didn't want to think about that now. So long as they were on this island, they were safe.

They could worry about what might be lurking in the water once they found the Witch.

One thing was for certain. There was no way any of his pack was going back into the water to reclaim the old man's boat.

And, thankfully, he didn't think they would need to. He could see the lightkeeper's cabin cruiser tied up to the dock on the other side of the small breakwater.

Derrick would mourn his brother later. Now, he had a job to do. And he was going to do that job no matter what it took.

He was going to find the woman and take her to his employer.

If the lightkeeper got in his way, then Derrick would kill him. Quickly and without a second thought.

And if they found the old man, then Derrick would take his time with him. He would make the boat captain hurt until he begged him for death. And then he would make the old man hurt even more before he finally killed him.

Or maybe he would assign the task to Curly. It would give the rest of the boys something to smile about. They always enjoyed it when Curly ripped a man's head from his neck with his bare hands.

WATCHING Draig disappear into the darkness, Melissa took a few steps toward the lighthouse before she stopped.

Why was she hesitating? What was bothering her?

She could do as he asked. Ordered more like. Hide in the

lighthouse. The easy path. But when had she ever taken the easy path?

The fact that she was stranded on an island certainly proved her point.

She bit her lip, irritated with herself.

This wasn't like her. Usually, when she made a decision, she went with it.

Confident. Committed.

But now, she was doubting herself.

All because of Draig.

Digging her fingernails into her palms, she steeled herself for what she needed to do.

Draig was likely her best bet.

She needed to tell him what was going on.

She couldn't put this off any longer. The more she delayed, the angrier the *baker* was likely to be and the angrier she would be with herself.

Not just a baker, she corrected quickly.

Definitely not just a baker.

So much more than that. Although she wasn't certain that she wanted to discover what that so much more could be.

Enough!

She couldn't avoid this any longer. She needed to tell Draig. And she would.

Just not at this very moment. Tomorrow morning. After she got some sleep. When she was ready.

She walked up to the lighthouse's back steps and reached out toward the door handle. She pulled her hand back just as quickly.

She was still hesitating.

Why?

What was bothering her?

Her preternatural sense of warning that had saved her time

and time again was making the skin along the back of her neck prickle.

Was it the thought of confronting Draig? Of spilling all that she was hiding?

She didn't think so. Not this time.

Then what?

Melissa took a few deep breaths. She wasn't going to find the answer to that question hiding here in the dark.

She was about to pull the door open, her fingers finally on the knob, when she heard a series of loud curses back on the beach and then a few low growls broke the silence that had wrapped itself around the island.

What in all the hells?

Quietly, she stepped away from the door and trotted back to the bridge.

When she saw the large shapes stalking along the dock and the rocky beach next to it, her eyes widened in fear.

They had found her.

HIS LONG HAIR matted to his head and water still dripping from his beard, Derrick stood on the dock, his mood becoming fouler with every breath he took. The forced swim hadn't helped. Losing a quarter of his men made it even worse.

The real kick in the gut?

Donnie being pulled to the bottom.

This was not how this was all supposed to go down. It should have been a simple snatch and grab job, yet somehow she had evaded his hunters.

Taking in everything around him with a single glance, sniffing the air, he started to think that maybe this job was finally getting easier. He had no doubt that she was here, and she couldn't hide from him.

Not now.

He had her scent.

And she had nowhere to run.

Curly and Markie joined him just a few seconds later. The others followed more slowly.

All of them swept their gazes around in every direction, trying to get a feel for the island.

Or rather two islands. They hadn't noticed it while they swam through the cove, focused instead on surviving whatever it was that stalked them from below. But they could see their hunting ground clearly now.

They had come ashore on the larger island, a small wood just a few hundred yards farther up the shore from the dock. From where they were standing, there wasn't much more to see.

The lighthouse was to the north on a smaller, rocky knoll that was connected to the cay by an old steel and wire bridge. In addition to the slowly rotating light atop the tower, they could make out a few dim lights shining through the windows of the cottage built right up against the beacon.

Nothing that they saw worried them. Nevertheless, that didn't satisfy them.

After what just happened, they wanted to make certain. They didn't want to deal with any more surprises.

The bikers began to sniff the air more carefully. Smelling the salty spray. The evergreens. Something dead and rotting just a little farther to their east that had washed up onto the shore. Probably not one of their friends. Not yet.

They were searching for any scent that could be a potential threat. Though there were several interesting smells on the island that caught their attention, there was nothing that worried them.

"Check out the boat," Derrick ordered.

Curly and Markie nodded to each other and then moved toward the ladder so that they could climb aboard. They stopped after only a few steps, frozen by a cold voice coming from the path that led away from the dock and toward the bridge.

"I don't think so." Draig walked casually out of the gloom, shillelagh in hand.

"Who the hell are you?" demanded Derrick.

He didn't know what to make of the man who used a walking stick to navigate the narrow trail in the dark. Especially with those eyes of his flashing orange red.

"The owner of the cruiser that you're about to board. No one steps onto my boat without my permission."

"Really?" asked Derrick, unable to contain a smile and a deep laugh. After what had happened during the last hour, he needed a little fun. Preferably in the form of spilled blood. And he believed that he had just found the perfect target for his rage. "I'll do what I want, little man. Best that you stay out of my way."

"You'll do what I tell you to do, you furry bastard." Draig stepped onto the dock, the full moon picking that moment to break through the drifting clouds and shine down on them. He didn't stop until he was only a few feet away from Derrick. "Besides, I don't listen to men who smell like wet dogs."

Derrick's eyes, a golden yellow, flashed with the promise of a painful death as he stared hard at this new arrival. He was not used to being insulted. He didn't like it. And he wasn't going to take it.

He was primed for a fight. Rather than try to suppress his rising fury, he reveled in it. Having lost his brother and three of his men, there was no point in trying to control his temper. Still, he needed to take care of business before he released his rage on who he assumed was the lightkeeper.

"Where's the woman?" Derrick demanded in an angry growl.

"What woman?"

"The woman! The Witch!" Derrick shouted, giving full throat to the emotions roiling within him, his rage now mixing with his grief.

Draig stared hard at Derrick, clearly not affected by the man's outburst. He knew what the intruder was. What he could do. He didn't care.

"You mean to tell me that you came all the way out here looking for a woman?" Draig chuckled softly, his expression hinting at amusement. "You're looking in the wrong place, puppy. There are easier ways to find companionship these days. A bunch of different apps you can choose from."

"We're not here to talk about apps," growled Derrick, losing patience quickly, definitely not appreciating the lightkeeper's insults.

"Although taking a look at you, I don't know that eHarmony or Match or Hinge would be of much use to you," Draig continued, tapping his shillelagh on the dock in a numbing rhythm as if he were giving Derrick's need for female companionship serious consideration. "Maybe dumbasses.com."

"There's a dating site called dumbasses.com?" asked Curly, who clearly wasn't the sharpest tool in the shed.

Draig gave the gigantic biker a sad look, shaking his head slowly, almost as if having fun at the biker's expense wasn't worth the effort.

"There is no dating site called dumbasses.com, you dumbass," growled Derrick. "He's wasting our time."

Curly looked at the lightkeeper then, his brow crunching together, fingers flexing into fists.

Draig simply gave the angry giant a sardonic grin and an arch of his eyebrows, understanding that his reaction would only make the blonde-haired beastie even more furious.

Derrick sought to regain control over the conversation, having little interest in more insults from the lightkeeper, only wanting to rip him apart. But he couldn't do that yet. Not until the job was done. "You know the woman I'm talking about."

"You'll have to be more specific," said Draig. He wasn't tapping his walking stick on the dock anymore. He held it with both hands now, leaning it against his shoulder.

"The woman from the town."

"There are a lot of women in the town. As I said, you need to be more specific."

Derrick sighed and grumbled at the same time, looking down and pinching the bridge of his nose with his fingers. He could feel a headache coming on. "I'm really beginning to tire of you, lightkeeper."

"I was tired of you before I smelled you, Were."

Derrick lifted his head upon hearing that. He gave Draig an appraising look. "You know what we are?"

"I do," Draig replied with a brief nod.

"That doesn't frighten you? Knowing what we are? Knowing what we can do? Knowing what we will do?"

There was a glint of anticipation in Derrick's golden eyes, as if he was finally getting to the good part of this encounter with the lightkeeper. When the conversation became a confrontation.

"Sorry," Draig said with a shrug. "I'm sure that disappoints you, but there's nothing that you could possibly do that would frighten me."

"You shouldn't be frightened, little man," growled Derrick, taking a step closer, flexing his long fingers as he did so, his golden eyes flashing even more brightly. "You should be terrified."

"Actually, I'm a little bored with this show you're putting on for your brothers."

"Brave words from a little man who is about to die."

"True words, nothing more," Draig replied matter-of-factly. "I've faced your kind before."

"I find that hard to believe," Derrick chuckled. "If you had, you'd already be dead."

"Believe it, Were. I'd tell you to ask your brothers sent against me about what that experience was like, but they'd have little to tell you."

"Why is that?"

"Because they're all dead, dumbass." Draig shrugged again, his hands flexing on his shillelagh.

There was a long silence on the dock following that proclamation and insult, all the bikers staring at the lightkeeper. Not sure whether they should believe him.

Derrick broke the building tension when he snorted out a laugh that his brothers joined him in. They had to give the lightkeeper credit. He certainly had a pair.

"If you came up against my kind before and survived, then you probably came up against the weak and infirm," Derrick argued. "I'm not weak. My pack isn't weak. The Renegades are the most feared pack on the East Coast."

A chorus of growls rang around the breakwater. The bright light of the full moon gave Draig an excellent view as Derrick, Curly, Markie, and the other Weres all transformed into the monsters they truly were.

Already large. Already broad. Already towering. They all became more so. Their bodies stretched, muscles bulging, expanding and tightening, transforming. Hands and feet becoming claws, faces shifting into large snouts filled with gleaming teeth. Clothes replaced by thick fur. Though the eyes remained the same. Flashing gold.

In seconds, a pack of werewolves stood where a biker gang once had been, several of the beasts lifting their snouts to the full moon and howling.

Draig wasn't impressed. He had seen it all before.

"Afraid now little man?" Derrick asked in a raspy voice, the monstrous werewolf cracking the knuckles on his massive claws as he stalked toward Draig.

"No, I'm not." Draig's orange-red eyes, once simmering like smoldering embers, now burned with the heat of a forest fire. "I haven't had a good fight in days. I'm looking forward to this."

"This is going to be fun, little man. I'm going to eat your ..."

Draig didn't wait for the Were to finish his threat. Instead, he seized the initiative just as he had been taught to do.

Lifting his shillelagh off his shoulder, with a bright flash his walking stick instantly assumed its true form.

With a single slice of his sword, a white fire blazing along its length, Draig cut through Derrick's thick, muscled neck. But he wasn't done. He was only getting started.

Curly and Markie, staring dumbly at their leader's head as it bounced and then rolled off the dock and into the surf, never expected the lightkeeper to do what he had just done. Nor did they expect him to be on them so swiftly.

It was that lack of anticipation that guaranteed their speedy deaths. Curly raised a meaty paw, attempting to block the flaring steel slashing toward his neck.

It didn't work.

Eyes flaming brightly, Draig cut the Were's claw off at the wrist and continued with his swing, taking the beast's head just as he had done Derrick's.

Before Curly's still snarling maw hit the pier, Draig drove his blade through Markie's belly. The Were's snarl became a sad whimper when Draig pulled his sword free, the flesh around the wound charring. The fire spreading, burning the lycanthrope from the inside out.

Not bothering to watch the dying werewolf as the monster slumped onto the dock, Draig turned to face the rest of the pack, sword held comfortably in his hands.

His hard gaze froze the werewolves in place. They had

never seen three of their brothers killed so quickly and with so little difficulty. Usually ferocious predators, they hesitated. They had no idea what to do in a situation such as this. When one Teg demonstrated a power that was well beyond them.

Yet at the same time, they realized that they still enjoyed an advantage. There was only one lightkeeper, admittedly a lightkeeper with a blazing sword that obviously he knew how to use. Even so, there were still five of them.

The Weres bent their knees and dug their claws into the sand and rock, preparing to launch themselves at the man who had the temerity to kill three of their pack.

They hesitated again when three cockerpoos ran out of the darkness and up onto the dock, placing themselves between them and the lightkeeper.

None of the dogs came up to the lightkeeper's knees. Yet they growled angrily in a deep rumble. Then, wanting to make their point, they let loose loud barks that didn't match their size.

After taking in the sight before them, one of the Weres began to laugh. The others quickly followed his lead.

"This is the best that they can do?" the Were closest to the dock asked in a gravelly voice, the words out of place coming from the long muzzle of a wolfman the size of a giant.

It was Draig's turn to laugh then. And he did. Softly. Though not for long. There was no point in continuing to delay.

"No, they can do so much more."

Draig looked down at Butch, Cassidy, and Sundance, making sure that he had their full attention as he issued his instructions. "I need one or two alive. It doesn't matter how damaged they are. Just breathing and able to speak."

Butch nodded. Then in a flash the three dogs leapt off the dock.

The werewolves stopped laughing, watching in horror as the three cockerpoos transformed into three dragons that were half as big as the cabin cruiser.

Clawed feet dug into the sand and rock. Maws gaped wide with teeth the length of a man's forearm. Razor-sharp spikes ran from their foreheads down their backs. Wings held tight to their sides as powerful tails swished behind them much like a shark's through the water, giving them even greater speed as they raced toward their prey.

One was red. Another gold. The last green.

But their coloring was lost on the Weres, the lycanthropes having eyes only for those teeth and claws that were about to slice into their flesh.

A few of the smarter furry shifters tried to escape. But they didn't stand a chance. Nor did their brothers who tried to put up a fight.

The dragons were too fast.

Too determined.

Too vicious.

Too hungry.

Draig didn't bother to watch what was happening on the beach. He started walking down toward the end of the dock. He knew how the fight was going to end, and he had other business to take care of.

MELISSA HAD a ringside seat to the entire encounter on the dock as she peered from her hiding place among the rocks.

She couldn't believe her eyes.

She had been right when she watched Draig fight the Berserkers. That walking stick of his was a sword, just as he had confirmed during dinner.

The more she learned about this supposed baker, the more confused she became. Who was he?

And those dogs of his? Three sweet, little cockerpoos turning into dragons?

She wouldn't have been able to wrap her mind around that if she hadn't seen it with her own eyes.

Werewolves were bad enough. But shapeshifting dragons?

Holy crap!

That was absolutely ridiculous.

Next level, in fact.

Although it certainly was proving quite useful right at that moment, all at the expense of the werewolves.

When the fight began, she thought about rushing out and helping Draig. She realized almost immediately that there was no need.

The clash was over before she would have made it down to the beach.

Who the hell was this baker who was so much more than a baker?

Melissa had been frightened before. Now she was terrified.

Not so much of the man with the blazing eyes and the blazing sword that once again resembled a walking stick.

No, what really terrified her was her own intense curiosity.

She needed to find out who this baker really was.

"SUNDANCE, LEAVE THAT FOR BUTCH," Draig called in a chiding tone. His blazing sword was once again a blackthorn shillelagh that he leaned against his shoulder. "You already ate your fill. You need to stop doing this. What's yours is yours and what's his is his." Sundance had crept over toward Butch on silent claws, ready to snatch the werewolf legbone that the dragon was happily gnawing on. "What's his is not yours."

The dragon who sought to steal the tasty prize from his brother gave Draig a disappointed and disapproving look. Not because of what Draig said, but rather because Draig had sniffed out his intentions.

"Cassidy, keep those two under control," Draig ordered.

Cassidy snorted, not bothering to acknowledge Draig as he turned his broad back. The dragon had claimed a carcass of his own and he had no intention of sharing, dragging it closer to the shore and the only werewolf still breathing on the beach.

His terror dominating his natural aggression, the badly injured Were couldn't walk, his legs mauled in a dozen places. He didn't want to watch the dragon eat what had once been his friend, but he couldn't pull his eyes away from the terrible and sickening spectacle.

Draig walked down to the end of the pier, the full moon lighting his way. The howling had died on the beach just seconds before when Cassidy finished off the last of the Weres.

Leaving the three dragons to enjoy the remainder of the spoils, when he was no more than a few feet from the end of the pier, he stopped, waiting for the rush of water coming toward the dock.

Just seconds later, a surge of brine pushed up out of the ocean. Atop it stood Seamus, dripping wet, a huge smile breaking his craggy countenance.

When he stepped onto the dock, the pedestal of water dropped back down into the sea with a splash.

"The others?" Draig asked.

"Davy Jones' locker," Seamus replied with a shrug. "They got what they deserved. They hijacked my boat after all."

"I'm not arguing with you, Seamus," Draig replied. "I'm just asking."

Seamus nodded an apology. "What are you going to do with him?"

Draig looked back over his shoulder. The werewolf who

was huddled against a large rock was bleeding badly, but he was still alive. Butch, Cassidy, and Sundance had listened to him … for the most part.

"Use him to send a message."

"Smart," Seamus agreed with another nod. "You might want to hurry though. Those monsters of yours still look hungry."

17

MAKING A DEAL

"What are you doing with three dragons?" Melissa demanded. Right from the start she hoped to gain control over the conversation that she didn't want to have but that she knew she couldn't avoid. And she believed that she was already beginning at a deficit.

"I'm not doing anything with them. Like I told you, Butch, Cassidy, and Sundance are my friends."

"Friends who eat werewolves?" Watching the three dragons scour the beach for any tasty morsels that might remain, her stomach began to protest. She feared that she was going to hurl.

"Useful, don't you think?" Draig offered her a grin that appeared to be almost predatory.

Melissa had heard stories about dragons that were able to shapeshift, but that was supposed to be a rare trait. So much so that she believed they were no more than stories now.

That specific talent supposedly had died out centuries before. Moreover, dragons tended to keep to themselves. Staying in their hereditary mountains.

What in Hades were three of those beasts doing here? And running around most of the time looking like cockerpoos?

Most Teg stayed away from dragons whenever possible, because when they didn't it never turned out well for the Teg.

Only those Teg who were ...

It struck her like a bolt of lightning streaking down from Mount Olympus. Melissa put her hands out to steady herself, losing her balance as a white noise filled her ears for just a flash.

She had been a fool. Not seeing what had been right in front of her the entire time. So consumed by her own issues that she missed the warning signs.

Her mother had kept her isolated from other Tylwyth Teg when she was younger, telling her and her sisters that it was safer that way after their harrowing escape from New York City.

When she was older, Melissa asked her mother why they remained at the fringes of Teg society. Her mother never answered despite her constant prodding.

Melissa had only become more a part of the Teg world during the last few years. Even then she worked hard to stay off the radar as much as possible. Doing so was one of the keys to her not only thriving, but also surviving in her profession of choice.

She planned on having a long discussion with her mother when all this was over. Assuming, of course, she got off this island, escaped her pursuers, and finished the job.

Why had her mother kept such crucial information to herself?

Admittedly, her mother had been more open when she decided that Melissa required a better sense of the bigger picture. Because if she didn't know what she needed to know, it might put Melissa at risk during one of her heists.

But this was a massive fail. There was no way Melissa's mother could argue otherwise.

Her inability to identify Draig upon seeing him for the first time proved that her mother had not told her everything that she needed to know.

Melissa had listened in rapt fascination to everything her mother was willing to share with her and her sisters about the Tylwyth Teg. One story in particular had captured her interest, and rightfully so.

It was almost too much to believe, but when she deigned to open up, her mother always told them the truth. Even when she didn't want to.

How an assassin had come for her mother one night.

Arthur Pendragon had decided that she needed to go, and he had sent his best killer after her.

An assassin who never failed in his work.

His very name whispered into the ear of most Teg was enough to make them piss their pants.

Yet, shockingly, rather than kill Melissa's mother when he had her dead to rights, he let her go. Helped her, in fact, and Melissa and her sisters as well though they didn't know it at the time.

The killer gave them an avenue for escape and what they needed to start a new life, making sure that they wouldn't have to worry about Arthur and his Knights coming after them so long as they didn't draw any unnecessary attention to themselves.

An assassin named the Dragon.

An assassin named Draig.

Dragon in Welsh.

Of course he had three pet dragons. It only made sense. With a name like that, how could he not?

Draig could challenge her perspective all he wanted. That the dragons who had finished their meal and were now stalking up and down the beach, reclaiming their territory, were friends and not pets.

But that wasn't relevant. It only confirmed who he was and what he could do. What he was capable of. Because only the ...

Melissa didn't want to think about what completing her thought meant. It was hard enough just gazing into those blazing eyes of his.

She did, nonetheless. Forcing herself. Refusing to look away.

Even though he was the Fallen Knight.

The Dragon.

And his sword. That had to be ...

"You good?" Draig asked. Melissa had gone from pale to green. She looked like she was going to be sick.

"You're the one," Melissa whispered.

Draig tilted his head to the right, his brow furrowing, not quite understanding. "The one what?"

"The one who helped my mother," Melissa replied so softly that Draig had to lean in to hear.

She didn't want to start with all the horrible stuff she knew about him. If she did, she definitely was going to hurl. Better instead to start with the one good thing she knew about him.

He smiled at that. "I didn't think that it would take you this long to figure it out. Your mother said you were the sharpest of the four."

A flash of shock crossed her face. "Wait! You still speak with my mother?"

"Of course I do," Draig replied. "I like to keep tabs on all the Teg I've worked with."

"To make sure they're still safe?"

Draig nodded. "That, yes, and also to make sure that I don't have to worry about anything I did to help them coming back to blow up in my face."

"A good bit of self-interest there," Melissa grumbled.

Draig ignored the barb. "I wouldn't be alive otherwise."

"My mother said I was the sharpest of the four?" Despite

the precariousness of her situation that statement had stuck in her mind. Seriously? She couldn't quite believe she uttered the words. Conceited much?

"She did, but don't let it go to your head," Draig said with a wink. "After I tell her about this, she might change her mind."

"I certainly don't feel like it," Melissa admitted. "Not after having no clue who you were until just now."

"It happens to all of us," Draig offered, trying to ease her disappointment in herself.

"I had other things on my mind," Melissa replied.

Draig nodded. "I can understand that. You're in a bit of a mess."

"That's an understatement. Berserkers. Werewolves. And now you."

"I feel as if I should be offended," Draig murmured, but seeing how Melissa's eyebrows rose with concern, he raised his hands to ward off her concern. "But I'm not. I've been compared to worse than Berserkers and Weres."

"You seem quite proud of that," Melissa offered.

"It hasn't hurt," Draig admitted. "But enough of that. You need to leave."

"I need to leave?" Melissa asked, her mind requiring a few seconds to catch up to what he was telling her. "What do you mean I need to leave?"

"You're a threat to the Teg living in Kraken Cove. You need to go before your problem becomes our problem."

Draig said it without a hint of emotion. He was simply stating a fact.

For Melissa, his declaration was something more. Possibly a death sentence. And not just for her.

Melissa opened her mouth to protest, then she closed it just as quickly. She needed time to think. "You're supposed to be dead."

"I am dead," Draig replied, "or rather the people who I want to think I'm dead believe that I'm dead."

"But why would you ..." Melissa nodded, beginning to understand. "You helped more Teg than just my mother."

"I did." Draig saw no reason to deny that.

"And Arthur Pendragon wasn't pleased about that."

"About that and a few other issues that came up between us," Draig admitted, offering no more detail than that.

"Are all the people living in Kraken Cove of the Teg?"

"Yes."

"And they're all hiding away here like you are?"

"For the most part, yes. Although we're not hiding away."

"Then what would you call it?" Melissa challenged him, once again seeking to take the initiative that she had lost upon realizing who Draig really was.

"Living our lives without having to worry about someone plunging a magical knife into our backs."

"I'll give you that. How did you do this?" Melissa lifted her arms to the sky and dropped them just as quickly. "I mean, how could you possibly have made this happen without anyone knowing? It just boggles the mind."

"Instead of worrying about me and what I've done, we need to worry about you and what you've done. You need to go."

"I need to go?" A trickle of fear flashed through Melissa. She had hoped that she had moved Draig off this topic, but clearly not. "What do you mean I need to go?"

"You need to leave. Tomorrow at the latest."

"Leave here? The lighthouse?"

Melissa was looking for some wiggle room. Draig didn't give it to her.

"Raptor Bay, yes, and Kraken Cove."

Melissa was stunned. She didn't know what to do. And what bothered her the most is that she usually knew exactly what to do. "You're throwing me out of your town?"

"It's safer for the Teg I'm trying to protect if you're not here."

"I'm not a threat to anyone," Melissa protested, grasping for any argument that she could make.

"You brought the Berserkers here."

"How was I supposed to ..."

"And you brought the werewolves here," Draig cut in, not allowing Melissa to stoke her protest.

"You knew I was on board your boat and what was after me," Melissa shot back, her anger rising. "You knew they would follow."

"You're right, I did," Draig acknowledged. "I wanted them to follow. I wanted to deal with them here rather than in town."

Melissa opened her mouth several times, though nothing came out. Each of the arguments that she wanted to offer in her defense fell flat, and she had no choice but to condone his strategy. "That makes sense."

"I'm glad you agree," Draig said, although clearly he didn't care if she agreed or not. "Why didn't you tell me what was going on? You had several opportunities."

Melissa snorted in disbelief. "You can't expect me to take you into my confidence without even knowing who you were."

"You're right. I don't. But I would think that you would be more open with me and have a better sense of my intentions after helping you against the Berserkers."

"I did not need your help with the Berserkers," Melissa objected.

Draig didn't bother to respond. Staring. Waiting.

Finally, after shaking her head in annoyance, she growled, "All right, I needed your help. Are you happy that I finally admitted it?"

"I'm glad that now we can have a real discussion."

"You stuck up ..."

"Show me," Draig ordered, cutting off Melissa once again so that she couldn't build up a full head of steam.

"Show you what?"

Draig's eyes flashed with irritation. "We don't have time for this, Melissa. Not after all that has happened. Show me *The Book of Whispers*."

"How could you possibly know that ..." Melissa began, unable to contain her shock.

"I know. You've had it on your person ever since you came to town."

"You can sense the artifact?"

"Among other things." He didn't bother to offer any more detail than that, instead reaching out with his hand.

Melissa stared back at him defiantly, even crossing her arms, pleased that she had done so.

She didn't want to accede to his request. No! It wasn't a request. It was an order. And she didn't do well with authority. But what was she to do? She was facing off against the Dragon.

The more she stared into those eyes of his, the more she realized that her natural stubbornness wasn't going to help her in this situation.

Muttering a few curses under her breath, she reached beneath her robe and extracted a package that was all the way around an inch larger than a paperback book. She pulled the item out from its protective cloth case, then reluctantly handed it to Draig.

"Why did you take it?" His eyes locked onto hers.

"I didn't have a choice," she grumbled in resignation. "I was caught between a rock and a hard place. Two Teg I couldn't stand against."

Draig didn't push. He didn't need to. She had told him everything that he needed to know. "You know the power contained within this book? What it's purported to allow the user to do?"

Melissa didn't respond right away, realizing that no matter

what she said wouldn't matter. She could lie, but that was just as bad as telling the truth.

"I do."

"Why did you do it, then?" Draig asked. His eyes hardened just a little bit more, his disappointment plain.

"It's what I do. I procure items that others can't. And like I just said, I didn't have a choice." Melissa tried to add some heat to her voice, but it was no more than a tepid warmth.

Draig snorted in disbelief. "There's more to it than that."

"Believe what you want." Melissa crossed her arms again and placed all her weight on her back leg. She refused to give Draig the information that he was seeking. He didn't need to know everything about her.

"You examined it?" he asked, letting his last question go.

"How could I not examine it?" Melissa growled. "Any self-respecting procurer of ancient items would do as I did just to make sure." She shrugged. "I couldn't make heads nor tails out of it."

"You don't think you stole the right item?"

"I *acquired* the right item," Melissa hmphed. "I've never made that mistake." She chose not to add that a few times she had *agreed* to acquire the wrong item, like the one Draig held in his hand.

Draig smiled. "You couldn't crack the magic shielding the book."

Melissa shook her head in annoyance. There was no point in trying to hide her failure. "No, I couldn't."

"And that's driving you crazy."

"It is, all right. You don't need to have fun at my expense."

"I'm not," Draig replied, smiling gently, not laughing. "There's only one Teg who can get past the Grym protecting this book."

"Who?"

Draig gave her another wink. "Me."

Placing his hand on the front cover of the text, Draig murmured under his breath, the artifact beginning to glow softly then flashing dimly before doing so with greater intensity.

Melissa had to look away. When she turned back around, she gasped.

Draig held the artifact that she had taken from Mordred. But it looked nothing like what she had been carrying with her ever since she escaped his castle on the cliff.

An ancient red leather that appeared to be the skin of a dragon had replaced the ratty and worn cover that most resembled human skin. Inscriptions written in a language that she couldn't read ran along the cover and the spine. And the inside appeared to be vellum. Maybe even papyrus.

She couldn't tell for certain. She would need to take a closer look, but she doubted that was going to be possible. She didn't think that Draig was going to give the book back to her. Which created another problem for her.

"You have the primer," Melissa murmured. That's what she had been looking for in Kraken Cove.

Without the primer, there was no way to unlock *The Book of Whispers* and make use of the priceless knowledge it contained.

"In a manner of speaking," Draig admitted, but he said no more than that, shifting to a more pressing matter. "I want you out of Kraken Cove."

"I get that," Melissa admitted. "But if I leave without the book ..."

"You're not getting the book back," Draig explained in a deadly quiet voice.

"Then you're putting a price on my head." She couldn't bear to think about the other cost that would have to be paid. And not solely by her.

"There was already a price on your head," he replied without a trace of emotion in his voice or his expression.

All business, Melissa realized. This was likely what he looked like when he showed up to help her mother.

Melissa didn't know how to respond. Because Draig was right. And she assumed that he already knew who she was working for.

It could be her current client who was trying to kill her. Or the client she had double-crossed. Or both. Probably both if she was being completely honest with herself.

She sighed, deflated. "I'm dead."

"Not yet," Draig replied. When Melissa looked at him, the book was nowhere to be seen. Her one piece of leverage was gone.

"What, you're going to help me like you helped my mother?"

Draig didn't respond right away, clearly thinking about the question. "I'm going to help you, yes."

"Why?" Melissa demanded. "Because of my mother?"

"No, my debt to your mother is paid. I'm going to help you because helping you helps me."

Melissa's eyebrows furrowed. What debt was Draig talking about? And how did his helping her help him? "I don't understand."

"I'm going to help you disappear like I've helped other Teg disappear."

"That's great, but that doesn't mean my hunters are going to leave me alone."

"They're not, you're right," Draig agreed. "But they'll be less interested in you if they can't get the artifact. They'll focus on that fact instead of on you. And as you've experienced once before without knowing it, I'm very good at protecting Teg when they need to be protected."

"You're not just a killer?" Melissa blurted out, more a statement than a question. Her face turned white. Better to have kept that last thought to herself.

She breathed again when she realized that Draig wasn't offended.

"Only when I have to be."

Melissa stared at Draig for several seconds. Then a smile broke out followed by a melodic laugh. She had no choice. If she didn't try to inject some humor she was going to cry. "What are you going to do? Hide it in the Book Nook?"

Draig laughed as well, although his eyes weren't smiling. "No, I'm going to return it to the Dragon Vault. And you're going to help me. Because if we do this right ..."

"I get out free and clear?" Melissa asked. The hope in her voice was almost palpable.

"We can try," Draig replied, "but let's not get ahead of ourselves."

18

UNWELCOME NEWS

"Where is she, Lucius?"

Two large bikers dragged the injured Renegade through the entrance, a trail of blood following him across the floor of the bar.

The Renegades had taken over the Red Moose, the dive located just off the interstate and a few miles north of Portland, Maine.

This wasn't the gang's normal place of business. They didn't usually come so far north. They worked closer to Boston.

But their primary benefactor required their services. With the amount of money he put on the table, they were more than happy to do his bidding.

Besides, what was required of them was right up their alley. They specialized in abductions among a variety of other violent crimes.

"She's with the Lightkeeper."

"The Lightkeeper?" asked the figure hunched over in the booth at the very back of the bar, shadows hiding his face. "Who's the Lightkeeper?"

The two bikers dropped Lucius into a chair that was just a

few feet away from the bar. The trail of blood quickly became a pool, seeping through the bandages wrapped around his severely mauled legs. One of his arms was strapped to his chest, broken, the ligaments in his elbow ripped from the bone, that bandage crusting and ripe. His face was swollen, black and blue. His lips cut, covered in dried blood, hiding his many chipped and broken teeth.

"Who is the Lightkeeper?"The large shadow in the booth finally moved, pushing himself up and walking the few steps to crouch down in front of Lucius. His face was barely visible, covered by a beard that extended all the way down to his belt, his hair resembling a tangled rat's nest.

The only distinguishing characteristic were his eyes. Golden. Blazing brightly. Perhaps even a hint of madness in the very back.

"I don't know who he is, Raik. I don't." The injured man spoke slowly, clearly exhausted, his blood loss making it hard for him to concentrate. "I just assumed that he's the Lightkeeper because that's where we were when we came upon him."

"Where did you meet this Lightkeeper?"

"At the lighthouse," Lucius grimaced, bending at the waist, a surge of pain tearing through him.

"The lighthouse? What lighthouse?" Raik reached out with one of his massive mitts and pushed Lucius back in his chair so that they could look each other in the eye, not caring about the additional pain his action caused his pack member. "And why were you at a lighthouse?"

"That's where the trail led. She took a boat from Kraken Cove to the lighthouse in Raptor Bay." Lucius gasped, another bolt of pain shooting through him. His injuries weren't healing as they should. Not unexpected considering what used him as a chew toy. A few seconds passed before he could continue. "We commandeered another boat and followed the Lightkeeper to the island. The boat captain who took us there called him the Lightkeeper."

"The woman was with him?"

"No," Lucius hissed, a third bolt of pain trying to double him over. Raik's strong grip preventing it.

"Then why are you so fixated on this Lightkeeper?" demanded Raik, his voice a growl of menace.

"The woman's trail stopped at the lighthouse. She was there. I'm sure of it. Although we didn't see her. We just came up against the Lightkeeper. The Lightkeeper and his three dogs and also the boat captain."

Raik slapped the injured man across the face. Not so hard as to knock Lucius from his seat, but hard enough to clear the cobwebs from his brain. "You're wasting my time. You're talking gibberish, Lucius."

"I'm not. It's true, Raik. It's true."

"Start at the beginning."

Through fits and starts, Lucius took Raik through the events of the last few hours. Raik had a difficult time believing much of what he heard.

Lucius finished with the three little dogs who turned into dragons, killed the rest of his brothers, and left Lucius in his current state.

Lucius the only one to survive.

Not because he fought his way free, but rather because the Lightkeeper allowed him to live.

To deliver this message.

To show Raik what he was up against if he persisted in his quest to take the Witch.

"Why did he pick you?"

Raik looked at Lucius with a measured expression. One man killing three of his? Three dogs turning into dragons?

Little fazed Raik. He had seen too much of the world. Done too much. He was rarely surprised anymore.

But he was now.

None of what Lucius told him made sense, assuming that Lucius hadn't hallucinated it all because of his injuries. Or because he'd fallen off the wagon again.

But those injuries. Clawed flesh. Bite marks. And none of his wounds had begun to heal. Strange and more than just a little concerning.

Could it be dragons? Dragons rarely left their mountain enclaves. Unless ...

His thoughts awakened an emotion within him that he hadn't felt in quite a long time.

"I don't know," mumbled Lucius. "I was lucky."

"Were you? Because this all sounds quite fanciful. It sounds like you've been drinking again, Lucius." Raik leaned in close to the Renegade, their noses no more than a finger apart. "Have you been drinking again, Lucius?"

"No, I swear. I haven't. I'm telling you the truth."

"So I'm supposed to believe that I lost one of my packs to a sea monster and this Lightkeeper with a blazing sword and three little dogs that turned into dragons?"

"Yes, it's the truth, Raik. I swear it." Lucius was nodding slowly, desperate for Raik to believe him. "I swear it. That's what happened."

Raik leaned back then, still on his haunches, nodding to himself. He couldn't detect a lie in what Lucius was telling him. And he was very good at identifying lies.

Was Lucius telling him the truth? Or was it what he believed was the truth, his many wounds clouding his perspective?

"It seems that you're in quite a pickle, Lucius. By all rights you should be dead, but you're not."

"I know. I should. You're right, Raik. You're right."

"And these stories. We talked about what was going to

happen if you started drinking on the job again, Lucius. What I would be forced to do to you."

"Raik, I'm telling you the truth. I didn't ..."

Raik rode right over his lackey. "You know this better than anyone, Lucius. You've been with me the longest. The pack comes first. Always."

"I know, Raik. I know." His words came out quickly, his fear becoming real. He knew what usually happened when Raik's eyes sparked as they were now. "I haven't been drinking. I swear. I'm telling you the truth."

"A Lightkeeper with a flaming sword?"

"Yes."

"You're certain?"

"I am, Raik. I am. It looked like a staff and then when he went after Derrick it changed. It was a sword, truly, and it was on fire. I swear it, Raik. I swear it."

Arms crossed, eyes fixed on Lucius, Raik didn't say anything for quite a long time. Lost in his memories. More like nightmares.

"I knew a man once with a flaming sword," he said finally. "His eyes ..."

"Burned like the fire of his sword. I saw it, Raik. I saw it when he took Derrick's head."

Raik had planned on killing Lucius. With the loss of a pack, he needed to make an example of the Renegade. If he didn't, he'd appear weak, because Lucius had demonstrated his weakness. By surviving when all his brothers were dead.

But what Lucius said stopped him. He stepped back into the shadows. Back turned. Thinking.

His benefactor had hired him to find the woman and deliver her to him. A simple task he had believed. Witch or no.

He and his crew had taken many Witches in the past. They knew how to deal with those cursed women so skilled in the Grym.

Derrick and his pack in particular, as they had never failed to bring in a mark before.

The fact that the Witch had escaped capture multiple times in just the last few days bothered him. But he could deal with that. He would deal with her himself.

She could wait for a little while longer, however.

If Lucius was speaking the truth, and the Lightkeeper was who Raik thought he was, then he just struck gold.

"Bring me a map," Raik ordered, turning back around and giving Lucius a hard look. "You're going to show me where all this happened."

19

THE DRAGON VAULT

Melissa was geeking out when she walked through the Dragon Door.

She didn't care.

One moment she was standing in front of the innocuous door hidden in shadow on the lighthouse's third floor. The next she found herself on a windswept crag, staring at a wall of rock.

She had a feeling about that door when she had searched the lighthouse while Draig was out. The wood didn't look like anything special when she first studied it. Not until Draig applied the Grym, of course, the Power of the Ancients surging in a bright light across the surface, revealing the intricate carvings and scrollwork hidden beneath the glamour.

She was amazed. Exhilarated. And just a touch frightened.

"I thought that Dragon Doors were just a myth."

"Not a myth." Draig stepped up next to Melissa, the wind ruffling his hair. He pulled the door shut once they both exited, the door still there right on the ledge, waiting for them. "We just don't talk about them all that much anymore."

"How did you acquire one?"

"A gift," Draig replied cryptically.

Melissa arched an eyebrow, having learned that this was Draig's standard practice when he didn't want to offer much in the way of information. "From whom?"

"My mother."

Your mother, she mouthed. Melissa desperately wanted to ask Draig about her. She was certain that there were a host of issues there for her to delve into.

She decided not to, choosing a safer course since he had agreed to help her. At least up to a point. "What exactly does a Dragon Door allow you to do?"

"Thinking of *acquiring* one?" Draig asked, Melissa not missing his sarcasm.

She ignored it. "No, smart guy. I'm just curious. Although I get the sense it could prove useful on certain jobs."

"It likely could," Draig admitted. "The Dragon Door allows me to go wherever I want in the Teg world whenever I want. I just need to have the location fixed in my mind. As soon as I walk through, I'm there."

"Very useful indeed."

"It is."

"Including to the Dragon Vault?" asked Melissa. She had expected something grander. Like the entrance to a bank or a museum. Not snowcapped mountains and a ledge with barely any room upon which to stand.

"Yes."

"This is it? You're certain?"

She thought that they were somewhere in the Alps. Switzerland? Austria? She didn't know for sure.

She did know that it was frigidly cold, the gusts of wind scraping across her body, snowflakes cutting across the face of the mountain and blinding her every few seconds.

He nodded.

"What do we need to do?" she asked.

Melissa assumed that a magical ward blocked their way, and she had no desire to try to force her way through it, remembering the pain that she experienced when she made the mistake of touching Draig's shield.

"Stand here," Draig said, motioning for her to join him when he walked closer to the rock. Once she did, he explained what was required. "Next, we need to recite an ancient rite still performed by Celtic Druids."

"We do?" asked Melissa, her expression both curious and questioning. "You're serious?"

Draig laughed softly, enjoying himself. "No. We don't." He gave her a wink and then walked right through the stone facing them.

There one second, gone the next.

Melissa stared after him. Initially, because he teased her, which caught her by surprise and was distinctly out of character for her companion of less than a day.

Then because she couldn't quite believe what she had just witnessed. He had walked through stone. She had never heard of an illusion as strong as that.

Melissa took a step toward the stone, about to follow him. But she hesitated. Should she take the risk? Or was this just an easy way for him to get rid of her permanently?

Before she could make up her mind, Draig poked his head back out from the rock. "Come on," he urged. "You're with me so you can get past the magic in play."

"And if I wasn't?"

"You wouldn't be able to get through. And if you tried to use the Grym to break through, the magic would respond by pulling you into the stone and leaving you there to suffocate."

"Pleasant," Melissa grumbled, a shiver of cold running down her spine that had nothing to do with the wind buffeting her and chilling her to the bone.

"I can think of worse ways to go," Draig countered. "Now come on."

Closing her eyes, steeling herself, she walked toward the stone, not bothering to stop even though every sense told her she was about to collide with an unbreakable barrier. She opened her eyes again when she felt the temperature rise, the chill leaving her.

Draig stood a few feet in front of her. Melissa's eyes widened and her mouth opened, her surprise getting the better of her. "Holy crap!"

They had entered a massive cavern that seemed to have no end, spheres of light hovering far above them and extending off into the distance. She couldn't believe what she was seeing, so many treasures of the ancient and supposedly mythological world welcoming her.

She recognized many of them, her mother making sure that they were a part of her education. The Armor of Achilles, said to be impenetrable, the metal shining brightly. Tarnhelm, a magic helmet that gave the wearer the ability to become invisible or change form. Duban, the shield of Cu Chulainn. The Shield of Ajax, seven cowhides stretched over a layer of bronze.

Aphrodite's Magic Girdle, a garment that made others fall in love with the wearer. Fjaorhamr, Freyja's cloak of falcon feathers. Why those were there with all the weapons she didn't quite understand.

Fragarach, the sword wielded by Manannan mac Lir and Lugh Lamfada. Hrunting, one of Beowulf's swords. The Sword of Damocles. Dozens of swords. Clearly way too many swords, more than she could identify from where she was standing.

Heracles' club. The Caduceus, the staff carried by Hermes. Cronus' scythe, used to castrate his father Uranus. Odin's spear Gungnir. Poseidon's trident. Ogmios' whip. The Axe of Perun.

Everywhere she looked, another weapon with a long history that many of the Teg likely had forgotten.

It seemed that this first section of the Vault was all weapons, extending back for as far as she could see. She could only imagine what else was kept here.

Truly remarkable.

Her fingers beginning to itch as they always did when valuable items appeared before her, she clenched her hands into fists, squeezing for a few seconds, working to control her professional instincts.

"And who is this vision of loveliness who graces the Dragon Vault?" A man with shoulders that were wide enough for two people walked out from the dark recesses of the chamber, his legs slightly bowlegged.

"Just a humble servant seeking to return an item."

"Humble my ass," the man snorted, "and you know I didn't mean you."

"She's helping with a matter that has come up in the last few days," Draig replied. "Fafnir, allow me to introduce you to Melissa."

Fafnir walked right up to Melissa, offering his hand. They shook briefly, and as they did, she sensed the strength in the man. An ancient strength that reminded her of Draig.

"Are you the custodian?" she asked.

Fafnir and Draig looked at one another, then broke out into a laugh at the same time. Clearly amused by what Fafnir had every right to take as an insult.

"I didn't mean it like that," Melissa corrected as quickly as she could, "it's just that ..."

"It's all right," Fafnir replied, his laughter over but his smile remaining. "I am a custodian of sorts for all that is stored in the Dragon Vault. A guardian as well."

"I'm going to use that against you in the future," Draig warned. "Custodian. Several of our friends are going to enjoy that."

"Do so at your own risk, brother," Fafnir warned. He was still smiling, although now his eyes weren't.

"A challenge," Draig responded, his eyes burning just a little more brightly. "You do know how I like a challenge."

"I do, brother," Fafnir replied. "That got us into a good bit of trouble when we were younger."

"It did," Draig agreed. "A good deal of fun as well."

"I'll give you that. Now what do you need? You rarely come here, so I can only imagine it's a matter of some urgency."

"It's not what I need," Draig corrected. "It's what I need to return. In that I was speaking truthfully."

"Return? What are you talking about?"

Draig reached beneath his jacket, holding up the artifact that was only slightly larger than a paperback.

His expression hardening, Fafnir's eyes flashed dangerously, becoming the same color as Draig's. "*The Book of Whispers*? How could you have ..." He was clearly upset. "Did you ..."

"No," Draig said, cutting Fafnir off, knowing how quickly he could lose his temper. "My sister, perhaps?"

Fafnir thought about Draig's suggestion. He didn't understand how an item could have been taken from the Dragon Vault without his knowledge. Nevertheless, Draig's sister had visited a few weeks ago. Ostensibly to examine another artifact.

Fafnir took hold of the Grym. An instant later, a book that looked exactly like the one that Draig held in his hand shot through the air from some place deep within the cavern, Fafnir reaching out and snatching it before it flew past. He examined the text, turning the book over and back again. Then he applied a stream of the Talent to the artifact.

That wasn't right. No response whatsoever.

A fake!

"I am in your debt, Draig," Fafnir nodded, clearly angry, his eyes burning brightly. "I hope you understand that I will be having a conversation with your sister. Likely a very unpleasant one ... for her. She has much to answer for."

"Do what you need to do, Fafnir."

Fafnir nodded. "Now, for the book you've acquired ..."

Before Fafnir could complete his request, a commanding voice sounded from just behind Draig.

"You really should have stayed dead, Draig. It would have made life so much easier for everyone."

20

BAD BLOOD

Melissa stepped back several feet, moving closer to Fafnir, struggling to control the anxiety and fear rising within her.

Normally she would have been disappointed in herself for allowing her emotions to affect her in such a way. Not now. She was proud of herself for not having bolted already.

She couldn't believe that he was there.

Arthur Pendragon.

The King of the Teg.

With him came a half dozen of his Knights, swords sheathed on their backs. They were dressed in their famed leathers that allowed them to fade into the background no matter what the background might be. Ensuring that you were never quite certain they were there ... until they were.

A trick of the light some claimed. A trick of the Grym she knew.

Last through the magical ward was an old man. His long, wispy white hair and ragged, unkempt appearance, along with his corduroy pants and cardigan sweater, made Melissa think of an absent-minded professor.

She knew that he was anything but, unavoidably sensing the power that he radiated.

Merlin.

One of the most powerful users of the Grym among the Teg. Perhaps the strongest depending on who you talked to.

"Good to see you again, lad," Merlin said with a broad smile, as if he were making a social call.

Melissa noticed that Arthur was less than pleased by Merlin's greeting. The cold, hard look in his eyes that made her think of Draig for just a heartbeat told her that the King of the Teg was used to being obeyed. Always. And Merlin had crossed the line, if only briefly, by speaking first.

In that instant it was quite clear who was the more dangerous of the two.

~

DRAIG IGNORED THE KNIGHTS, his gaze never leaving his father as he put together the last few pieces of the puzzle that had been troubling him.

He had heard through the more nefarious channels of the Teg that his sister had started working for Arthur. Doing various jobs that once had been his ... before he died.

Arthur's appearance confirmed for him who had stolen *The Book of Whispers* from the Dragon Vault. Because only a Draca could enter the Vault ... or someone invited by a Draca.

"She didn't have the courage to show herself?" Draig asked.

Arthur's lips curled into a less than welcoming smile. "She's working on other matters for me." He stopped when he was ten feet away from Draig, his Knights spreading out behind him in a semicircle.

Merlin halted just a few feet behind the King Teg's right shoulder, a position he had held ever since Arthur had drawn the sword from the Stone, advising, doing the work that others couldn't ... or wouldn't. Much like Draig, until Draig decided that he had had enough.

"You better be careful," Draig warned. "She'll steal you blind."

Arthur didn't respond right away. Instead, he studied Draig. Taking his time.

The way he was nodding suggested that he might actually be pleased to see him.

Draig knew better.

"You're right, she will. Just as I expect her to. So, unlike you, she will never disappoint me."

Before Draig could offer the smart rejoinder that was on the tip of his tongue, Arthur shifted his focus to Melissa.

"On the other hand, my dear, I expected better of you. If for no other reason than I believed that you understood the consequences of crossing me." He shook his head sadly. "How very disappointing. I will deal with you when I am finished here."

"Why don't you do something?" Melissa whispered. She had crept back a few more feet so that she was standing right next to Fafnir. "He shouldn't be here."

"Arthur Pendragon is here rightfully. He has done nothing wrong." Fafnir smiled sadly. "This is not my fight unless the King Teg makes it so. Until then, I must remain neutral. I must follow the Code."

"The Code ..." Melissa began to ask, but she gave it up when she saw Draig square up to the King Teg, stopping only a few feet away from him.

That quick movement didn't earn a reaction from Arthur, but it did make the Knights nervous. Their hands touched the hilts of their swords, some actually pulling free a few inches of steel.

Her eyes widened with worry. She couldn't quite believe what was happening. Worse, she saw no escape route when the crap hit the fan. And she had no doubt that it would.

Watching Arthur and Draig was like watching two dragons staring the other down, preparing for the clash that would determine who was dominant.

Did Draig really think that he could challenge the King of the Teg -- Knights at his back, Merlin at his side -- and survive?

"It's been a long time," Arthur said finally, his flinty eyes locked onto Draig's.

"You mean since you tried to kill me?" Draig asked casually. "Not long enough for me."

"I didn't kill you, Draig," Arthur laughed, although there was no mirth in the sound. "Besides, I knew you were alive."

"Then why do you seem so surprised to see me?"

"Because I never thought that you'd be stupid enough to become a part of all this."

"And there's the pep talk I haven't missed in the least," Draig said with feigned humor.

Arthur didn't appreciate the sarcasm. "Still a smart ass, I see."

"Some things don't change," Draig replied, then he shook his head, a mix of disappointment and resignation. "You weren't satisfied with all that you have so you felt the need to take *The Book of Whispers*? Knowing the power it contains, you would risk releasing it into the world? Even after all I had to do to put it here for safekeeping?"

"That's exactly why I made a play for *The Book of Whispers*. With the power it unlocks, all that we've fought for over the years will come to fruition. We'll be able to change the Teg world as we need to."

"All that you've fought for," Draig corrected.

"You were there right by my side for much of it, Draig," Arthur said, offering him a brief nod of respect. "Give yourself some credit."

"I'd prefer not to."

Arthur shook his head, his turn to be disappointed. "I never thought it possible that you would turn soft."

Rather than getting angry, Draig laughed. "Believe what you want. It wasn't a matter of going soft. It was a matter of finally seeing the world for what it is and realizing what we were doing for what it was."

"We were doing good for the Teg," Arthur argued in a strong tone. "You know it just as well as I do."

"You're still the same," Draig snorted, although he couldn't say that he was surprised.

"What do you mean?" A look of confusion briefly crossed Arthur's face. A rare emotion for him because usually he was certain in everything that he did.

"Still masking your desire for more power by doing what you say is right, not what is right," Draig clarified.

"Who are you to judge me?" demanded Arthur, his face turning red with anger.

"After what you did to me, I have every right to judge you, father."

Melissa couldn't stop herself from covering her mouth, although it did help prevent the gasp that wanted to leak out. That unexpected revelation shocked her.

"Draig is Arthur's son?" she asked Fafnir in a whisper.

"You didn't know that?" he replied, more than just a little surprised.

Melissa opened her mouth to reply, then closed it just as quickly. Why hadn't she put it all together sooner? Draig playing with a sword. The Sword, she realized, her breath catching for just a second. And he had three pet dragons, which meant ...

She didn't allow her thought to complete its natural course, caught up in the drama playing out before her.

"What I did to you made you stronger. It made you what you are today. You should be thanking me."

"And what did you make me, father? A killer?"

"I made you one of the strongest, most capable Teg to ever serve me," Arthur grated out through clenched teeth. "Because of who we are, because of what you are, sometimes you were required to handle tasks that others couldn't or wouldn't."

"And there's the rub," Draig said sadly.

"What?"

"For you, it's all about service."

"There's nothing wrong with that."

"Service to you, father," Draig continued. "Not to the Teg. There's a big difference."

"You're making a distinction without a difference. I am the Teg."

"And that's why you want *The Book of Whispers*. To ensure that no one else can take your place."

"Exactly," Arthur confirmed unapologetically. "I am the only one who can lead the Teg. You know that. And if I don't do what needs to be done, if I don't do what others don't have the courage to do, we die. Whether because of the Daemons or some other threat that's more than happy to wipe us from the face of the earth, the Teg cease to exist if I am not leading them. If I am not making the decisions that need to be made."

"I didn't miss this part at all."

"What are you talking about?" demanded Arthur, his tone making it clear that he was losing patience. Rapidly. "You sound like a spoiled child."

"Your efforts to rationalize why you do what you do. Just admit it."

"Admit what?"

"You seek power for yourself, father. Any claims you make with respect to the Teg are nothing more than an attempt to hide that truth. A smokescreen."

Arthur stared at Draig, his eyes turning cold, calculating.

"I can't say that I've missed these conversations of ours."

Arthur's countenance suggested that he had made a decision. "Still, seeing you again has put me in a magnanimous mood. Are you ready to return to me?"

"Return to you?" Draig was incredulous. The last time he had faced off against his father, Arthur had almost killed him. And now he wanted him to serve again?

"Now that you're back among the living, I'll forgive your previous transgressions and we can get back to work. It will make what needs to be done that much easier."

"My previous transgressions?"

"Do we need to go through all those? The missions you said you accomplished yet never did?"

"You mean the innocent Teg I didn't kill on your orders?"

"Those Teg were far from innocent," Arthur growled. "They were threats. They needed to be eliminated."

"Threats to whom?"

"To ..."

"Do we really need to go through all this again," interrupted Merlin. He didn't want Arthur to finish his thought, knowing what the result would be. "Without our host, our time here is limited, Arthur. The invitation will not remain open forever."

"Good point, Merlin," Arthur growled, using the interruption to reign in his anger. "I'll take the artifact."

Draig stared hard at Arthur. Almost no one said no to the King Teg. He did.

"No."

The silence that descended seemed to last forever. Arthur returning Draig's stare much like two prize fighters waiting for the bell to start the first round.

Arthur had other ideas, however, deciding to begin with the undercard.

"Rufus, Brutus, retrieve the artifact."

The two Knights, twin brothers, didn't hesitate. Striding forward, they pulled their swords from the scabbards on their backs. Grinning with a malicious intent, confident, they didn't appear to be concerned about their opponent.

Draig shook his head as he watched them approach.

Fools.

"Faster!" roared Arthur, cognizant of Merlin's warning. "We don't have time for this."

The Knights broke into a sprint.

Draig stood his ground calmly, clearly unconcerned. Tapping his blackthorn shillelagh in a slow rhythm against the stone floor.

Ten feet away.

Five feet.

The Knights pulled their swords back, gleaming blades past their shoulders, swinging their Grym-infused steel, about to cut into their target, when Draig finally moved.

Ducking, he darted right between Rufus and Brutus. Their wild swings sliced through nothing but air.

Draig didn't miss, however. Swinging his walking staff in a quick, compact movement, he caught them at the knees and sent the pair sprawling to the floor.

When Rufus and Brutus regained their feet, Draig stood there waiting for them. Although there was one significant change. His shillelagh had taken its true form.

Excalibur.

The longsword shimmered brightly, a white flame dancing along the edges of the blade.

"Care to try again?" Draig asked.

Rufus and Brutus didn't say a word, their scowls turning into sneers. They didn't like being embarrassed.

"You're going to pay for that, traitor," Brutus hissed.

"Traitor?" Draig mused. "A bit harsh."

"And a coward," Rufus added, "since you don't have the courage to stand against us."

"Now I'm offended," Draig admitted.

Then he was moving, a blur of motion, only the white streak of Excalibur visible.

In a flash, Brutus was down, sword broken, the Knight lying on his back, unconscious from a hard rap to his head.

"Your turn, big boy," Draig said, turning his attention toward Rufus.

The Knight looked at Draig in a new light, the first signs of fear visible in his beady eyes. He had heard of the traitor.

The Fallen Knight.

They all had. Yet he had listened to all the stories with a grain of salt. They were too fantastic to be real. Or so he had assumed. He was beginning to realize that he should have listened more closely.

Rufus took a step back. Telling himself that he was creating more space so that he could better defend himself. Not willing to admit what he was actually doing.

In a blur Draig was on him before he could take another step.

Rufus raised his sword, only succeeding in getting it parallel with his hip.

The next thing he knew, he was on his back, sword knocked from his hand, Draig standing above him, the tip of his shining blade pressed against his throat.

"Coward, you said?"

"I didn't ..." Rufus tried to apologize, seeing death in the Fallen Knight's eyes.

He was too slow, Draig kneeling quickly and twisting his blade so he brought the hilt down on the Knight's head.

Rufus and Brutus were now blissfully asleep.

"You've gone soft," scowled Arthur. "The Draig I knew, the Draig I raised, would have killed those men."

"I'm not that person anymore."

Draig pushed himself up and turned around. Arthur, Merlin, and the four remaining Knights stood across from him.

"A pity," Arthur grumbled, obviously disappointed. "Get me the book."

The four Knights standing behind Arthur pulled their swords. They only took a few steps before they stopped cold.

Not because of Draig's blazing reddish-orange eyes. Although those were more than just a little alarming.

They stopped because Arthur held up a closed fist, his hard gaze fixed on the artifact that appeared once more in Draig's hand.

"Fafnir, I believe this belongs to you."

He tossed *The Book of Whispers* over his shoulder, his eyes never leaving his father's, smiling thinly when he saw how Arthur's pupils grew bigger with alarm because of his action.

"Thank you, brother," Fafnir said, snatching the artifact out of the air.

Then, giving Melissa a wink, the Guardian disappeared along with the Dragon Vault. One minute he was standing right next to her, thousands of priceless artifacts at her back. The next it was all gone. Only the spheres of light remained, illuminating what was now just a large empty cavern.

"Go home, father," Draig said in a tired voice. "*The Book of Whispers* is back where it belongs. You will never get access to it again. Not after what you've done here."

For almost a minute, Arthur didn't say a word, staring at Draig, not a single emotion revealed on his handsome, craggy face.

"I will take the thief," Arthur said, his voice barely above a whisper yet thick with authority. "She owes me a debt."

Hearing that, a shiver of fear ran down Melissa's spine, and she stepped a bit closer to Draig, keeping him between her and the King Teg and his Knights.

"She owes you nothing, father. You tried. You failed. The balance is restored. Go home."

Arthur stared at Draig a few seconds more, then grunted

out his disapproval. “I did so much for you, Draig. Gave you so much. And this is how you repay me?”

“Everything you did for me, everything you gave me, came with a steep price, father. A price that I had to pay. That I still pay every day.” Draig’s eyes blazed with an unquenchable fire. “Stop playing the victim. It doesn’t become you.”

“You are stronger now than when you left me,” Arthur said, seeing his son for what he truly was now. “I’ll take credit for that as well.”

“Of course, you will,” Draig snorted in derision. “You can take all the credit you want.”

“Remember who you’re speaking to, Draig. I will not tolerate your insolence now as I did then.”

“Then to avoid that,” Draig said in a helpful tone, “I suggest that you and your Knights leave.”

“We will leave. But we will take the thief as I said, and I will take my sword back.”

Draig smiled. “I didn’t pick Excalibur. Your sword picked me.”

“The sword,” Arthur commanded, biting out the words that followed. “I will have my sword.”

“As you wish.”

Draig looked at the shining blade briefly, then tossed it in the air so that his father could catch it by the hilt.

The steel traveled no more than a few feet when it stopped, hanging in the air for a few heartbeats, before it flew right back into Draig’s palm.

“What was the saying?” Draig asked as he admired the blazing blade, his hand flexing on Excalibur’s hilt. “When you pulled the sword from the stone the first time?”

“To be drawn by the one worthy to be king,” Merlin murmured softly, although everyone in the cavern heard him.

Draig turned his gaze toward his father, smiling when he saw that Arthur’s face was red with rage. Embarrassment mixed in as well. "As I said, I didn't take Excalibur. Even your sword doesn't believe in you any longer. Excalibur chose me."

Arthur's hands became fists, his knuckles turning white, his face now matching that color. When he spoke, his voice was chillingly cold.

"You should have stayed dead, Draig." He nodded over his shoulder to the old man just a few feet behind him. "Merlin, kill him."

"You want me to kill, Axel? Arthur, this really has gone too far. It will not play well with the other Teg if …"

Arthur turned his furious eyes to Merlin, then let his rage out, his shout echoing down the length of the chamber. "I don't care! Either you kill him, or I will!"

Merlin opened his mouth to protest, but he closed it just as quickly. When Arthur was in a mood like this, there was nothing to do other than obey. Besides, this might be the opportunity he had been hoping for.

Merlin stepped forward then, squaring up to Draig. "I'm sorry, Axel. I don't want to do this. But you know how it is."

Draig smiled and nodded. "I do know how it is."

"Draig," Melissa whispered from almost right behind him, "what do you want me to do? How can I help?"

Draig looked over his shoulder. "Hold onto Excalibur for me. This is my fight." He reached back and handed her his sword, which had once again taken the shape of a blackthorn shillelagh. "And be ready."

"Ready for what?"

"To play the possum."

Draig turned back around before Melissa could ask any more questions, flexing his fingers, his expression hardening.

"Shall we, Merlin? My father is an impatient man."

"I'm sorry, Axel." The mild-mannered Merlin wasn't so mild-mannered anymore, his gaze narrowing, his expression hardening, his long strands of wispy white hair sticking out in all directions as the Grym filled him. "But this is for your own good."

Merlin lifted his hands quickly, a surge of energy blasting out, streaking right toward Draig.

His arms spread wide, Draig brought his hands together with barely a thought, mimicking the prayer pose. As he did so, a circular shield of swirling energy formed right in front of Draig, rising from the floor to several feet above his head.

When Merlin's blast struck the shield, Melissa ducked and cringed, worried that Draig's barrier wouldn't hold.

It did.

Just as quickly as Merlin crafted the stream of energy, it disappeared, the rush of noise created by the two powers meeting fading away, only a soft echo remaining in the cavern.

"I'm glad to see that you were paying attention during our lessons, Axel."

Draig nodded appreciatively at Merlin's comment. "I paid attention when I thought it was important."

It was Merlin's turn to nod. "Then let's see how you do against this."

Merlin sent another blast of energy toward Draig, the Grym's impact on his shield setting the entire chamber rocking.

But this time Merlin wasn't done.

Maintaining the flow of energy with one hand with the other Merlin threw a dozen glowing spears that arced over the barrier.

Draig deflected those with the Grym.

Spinning bars of energy that resembled boomerangs came next, curling around Draig's shield. Then a surge of power that blasted into the floor and ripped the stone apart, creating a trench twenty feet deep except for the small, circular tor upon which Draig and Melissa now stood.

And so it went. Merlin shifting from one attack to another. Draig defending against each one, whether with a shield or a swirling mist of white or some other magical tool constructed of the Grym that Merlin had taught him when he was learning to make use of the Power of the Ancients.

Nothing that Merlin did worked. He was proud of his student, though he knew he needed to keep that hidden. He could sense that right behind him Arthur was growing more and more impatient. It was time to end this before Merlin lost control of the affair.

"You have done well, Axel," Merlin called. "I'm sorry that I have to do this."

A spark of energy that was no larger than a nail sped through the air, hidden within the stream of energy that Merlin continued to direct toward his former student.

Draig held onto his shield, but unlike Merlin's other attacks, against this one, for some inexplicable reason, the nail didn't play itself out against the barrier. Instead, when it struck the sliver of magic stayed there, pushing in on the shield, Draig watching in amazement as the energy he was using was pushed back toward him.

For just a second, he held his breath, fearing what was to come as the shield he built more resembled a cone. A heartbeat later his construction reached the limit of its elasticity, the nail piercing the energy and blasting through Draig's barrier.

Reacting instinctively, Draig pivoted, the tiny bolt of energy speeding past.

Draig looked behind him upon hearing the gasp.

He had been fast enough to avoid the attack. Melissa hadn't.

She looked up at him, her eyes pleading. Then she dropped to the ground, Excalibur still cradled in her arms.

Everything stopped in the chamber then.

Draig let go of the shield that had failed. Merlin released the Grym.

There was a heavy silence until Merlin finally broke it.

"I'm sorry, Axel. Killing her wasn't my intention."

Draig didn't reply. He didn't even bother to turn around.

His gaze stayed on Melissa.

Shaking his head sadly, Draig leaned down and picked her up, holding Melissa gently in his arms. Then he turned toward Merlin and Arthur.

His words were intended for his father. "You never knew when to stop. Even now, you can't help yourself."

In a flash, the Dragon Door appeared right behind Draig.

"Your thief is dead."

"A fate she deserved," Arthur said forcefully, believing it. Unmoved by his son's stricken expression.

Draig's eyes narrowed then, refusing to waste any more energy or emotion on the man who had turned him into a tool to be used as he deemed most appropriate.

"I'm dead as well, father. To you. We're done."

Draig turned toward the door and was about to walk through when Arthur's voice stopped him.

"Get me *The Book of Whispers*, and I'll allow you to stay dead, Draig."

Draig didn't bother to turn around. As he stepped through the doorway, he called over his shoulder, "Take it up with the Queen, King Teg. I'm sure she'd love to speak with you."

In a flash, the Dragon Door vanished, and with it Draig.

21

AN OFFER

"They can't stop talking about it," Cerridwen said.

She sat on a stool watching Draig as he carefully placed in a pan the rolled dough for his gluten-free cinnamon rolls. Three other pans were already done and waiting for the oven.

Once word got out that Draig was in the kitchen at Tia's Bakes, they would be gone seconds after he drizzled the frosting over them.

"Already?" Draig asked. That done, he wiped his hands on his apron. "I wouldn't think Arthur would want what happened to get out."

Cerridwen shrugged, agreeing with him, yet at the same time suggesting that he was being naïve. "You know how it is among the Teg. Word spreads swiftly, especially when you don't want it to. Of course, it didn't help Arthur that Fafnir was there. If he wants to, the Draca can cause quite a stink."

"He can," Draig agreed, his tone suggesting that he didn't think Fafnir would make the effort. There would be little need.

Draig was already mixing the dough when Cerridwen

arrived at the bake shop at the crack of dawn. He had told her all that had happened. Arthur hiring a Draca to steal *The Book of Whispers*. And then the series of events that followed. The drama coming to a head in the Dragon Vault.

"Do you really think your sister was involved?" Cerridwen asked. She had met her once. Truly a piece of work. In so many ways so different from Draig.

"I wouldn't put it past her," he confirmed as he placed the four trays in the commercial oven, shut the door, checked the temperature, and set the timer. "I doubt she's any different now than she was when we were growing up."

"And our new friend? Clearly, she has some unique skills."

"That's an understatement. She's still alive after acquiring *The Book of Whispers* from Mordred. That says it all right there." There was a hint of admiration in Draig's voice that Cerridwen didn't miss.

"And Arthur was behind her involvement?"

"She confirmed that's who hired her." Draig leaned back against the counter, crossing his arms over his chest.

"You don't believe her?"

"I believe her," Draig said, although his eyes flashed. "Arthur gave it away in the Dragon Vault as well."

"But ..." Cerridwen prodded.

"But I don't think she's telling me everything."

"Another client perhaps?"

"That was my thinking," Draig confirmed with a nod.

"You think Melissa would do that? Take that risk?"

Draig considered Cerridwen's question. "I do. Although she might not have had a choice in the matter. You know how things are between my father and his sister. It's been going on since before I was born."

"Why would Morgase hire Melissa to steal the artifact from her own son after her son hired Melissa to steal it from Arthur? That's the part that I don't understand," Cerridwen mused.

"My guess?"

"I'll take a guess."

"I think it all comes down to power."

Cerridwen was quiet for a time, thinking, then she nodded. "She doesn't want her son to become more powerful than she is. If Mordred has *The Book of Whispers*, he overshadows her."

"That seems like the most reasonable explanation to me," Draig agreed.

"And do you believe that giving *The Book of Whispers* back to Fafnir will bring this conflict to an end?"

Draig gave her a look, his turn to suggest that she was the one being naive. "The conflict between Arthur and Morgase will never end. Not unless one of them puts the other in the ground."

"We can always hope."

"We can always hope," Draig agreed with a soft chuckle.

Cerridwen pushed herself off her stool. It was getting busier by the register. Word had spread and the vultures were descending. "Even dead, you caused quite the stir, Draig. Berserkers. Werewolves. A confrontation with your father and Merlin. And managing to fall in with a Witch who happens to be an excellent thief."

"I didn't know all this was going to happen."

Cerridwen laughed at that. "You never know what's going to happen. That's the problem. Instead of thinking before acting, you act. You have the incessant, almost unstoppable, quite irritating need to help a Teg when there's no one else who can."

"I can't tell if you're angry or disappointed?"

"A little bit of both," Cerridwen replied, "because when you do that, you put Kraken Cove at risk." Then she gave him a broad smile. "But I'm also proud of you. Because it means you care. And I'll never fault you for that." She placed her hand on the swinging door, about to exit the kitchen, but stopped, needing to ask one more question.

"Do we have anything to worry about beyond the obvious?" Cerridwen was concerned, and she believed that she had every right to be. "Now that the Dragon is awake once more."

"That wasn't my intention," Draig protested.

"Yet still we can't escape it."

"Thanks to Merlin we should be fine," Draig finally said.

Cerridwen gave him a hard look, then grinned. "Do you really believe that?"

"Do you really want me to answer?"

"No." Cerridwen laughed then. "So best to keep an eye out."

"Just as we always do."

At that moment, the door swung into the kitchen. Cerridwen pressed herself against the wall, getting out of the way just in time.

"Oh, I'm sorry, Cerridwen," Melissa said. "I didn't see you there."

"No apologies needed," she replied, walking out to the front of the shop. The line was getting longer. Almost out the door. "I shouldn't be here. I should be out there."

When the door swung closed, leaving just Melissa and Draig in the kitchen, an uncomfortable silence descended.

Draig was the first to break it. "So how does it feel to be dead?"

"Not how I anticipated it," Melissa replied with a smile. She stepped up to the table that separated them. "Before I go, I wanted to thank you. For everything that you've done."

Draig nodded. "You're welcome."

"Will you ever tell me how Merlin did what he did?" she asked. "Or why?"

Melissa had observed over his shoulder Draig's combat with the Sorcerer. Frightened. Worried. Trusting him, which was a rare thing for her.

When she allowed the energy to strike, she lost all control

over her muscles, collapsing like a marionette dropped by its puppeteer. A very convincing death if she did say so herself.

She was awake, but she couldn't move. She hadn't enjoyed the experience, but she had gone with it. Knowing that it was her only chance of escaping the Dragon Vault.

What had made her most uncomfortable was that anything could have happened to her when Merlin's Grym hit. Draig could have given her up to his father, in fact. But he hadn't. He had taken her out of what had been the Dragon Vault and returned her safely to her room at the Safe Haven.

And now, she had one less threat to worry about since Arthur believed that she had passed to the other side. Or so she hoped.

"Sorry, but I can't give away all of my secrets."

"I thought as much," Melissa replied, her gaze locked on those reddish-orange eyes of his. Muted now. She had never seen him this way. Almost relaxed.

There were several things she wanted to say to Draig, but she couldn't do it. She couldn't take that risk.

Pushing off the table, she turned to go. His voice stopped her before she pushed through the swinging door.

"I was thinking that since you are dead, you have a choice now."

Melissa turned back around slowly. She studied Draig. She didn't notice anything different about him, other than the fact that she detected a hint of hope in his voice. Faint, admittedly. But still there.

"A choice?" she asked hesitantly, not wanting to get ahead of herself. "I thought you wanted me gone. You made that quite clear before you took me to the Dragon Vault."

"I did, didn't I," Draig admitted. He pushed himself off the counter then leaned on the table with his hands on the edge. "I can still help you relocate. That's not a problem. I'm just saying that after all that's happened, you don't need to rush into that decision."

"What are you suggesting?" asked Melissa, her lips curling into a small smile.

"You're enjoying this, aren't you?" Draig asked.

"I am."

"You want me to say it?"

"Just so there's no confusion."

Draig looked at her, his eyes beginning to simmer. Because of her. She liked that.

"If you would like to stay a bit longer in Kraken Cove, you're more than welcome."

Melissa nodded, then pushed through the door, calling over her shoulder, "I'll think about it."

Melissa waved to Cerridwen as she exited the bake shop, having to slip through the crowd as more customers came in, all of them knowing that Draig was working in the back.

She walked across the street and then along the border of the green, not stopping until she stood at the fence at the top of the cliff. She looked out at the ocean. Calm this morning.

The salty smell pleased her. Although not as much as Draig's offer.

She liked Kraken Cove. She liked her room at the Safe Haven.

She needed to decide if it was better to keep moving or stay in one place for a time.

Even more important, she needed to decide about Draig.

She knew who he was now. What he had done. What he could still do.

One of the most feared of all the Teg.

King Arthur's assassin.

Also his son.

A killer.

A baker.

A lightkeeper.

A man who saved her mother's life.

And a man who had saved her life more times than she cared to remember in just a day.

She smiled.

The Dragon.

She knew what she was going to do.

22

BEWARE THE WITCH

Draig stood on the beach, lost in thought, still not seeing the distant shore of the mainland that was several miles away, the sun just beginning to peek above the horizon behind him.

He hadn't slept well, only getting a few hours. His brain just wouldn't turn off.

Primarily because of his guest. The woman who had complicated his life in ways that he never thought possible.

There were questions upon questions running through his mind, none of them with any easy or good answers. The most prominent that he kept coming back to?

Why in all the hells did he decide to help her?

He had recognized that she was trouble the second she walked into his bakery. He could sense it. And not just because of who she was. Not just because of the power that she could call upon.

No, there was more to it than that. A hint of trouble radiated from her.

And he had avoided trouble for more than a decade. That's why Kraken Cove had flourished ever since he settled here. Yet in just the last few days all that he had worked for was now at risk.

All because of Melissa?

He would have liked to have blamed her for all that had occurred, but he couldn't. He understood that there was more to his growing sense of unease than the Witch who had required his assistance. There had to be after he came up against a fist of Daemons in Williamsburg.

There was more going on here than met the eye. Little of it good.

In the world of the Teg, those with power were always seeking to obtain more power. It was in their nature. He understood that better than most.

That was why he had avoided playing that game for more than a decade, seeking to put his past behind him. Seeking to create a refuge for those Teg who wanted the same as he did. Who wanted to evade the eyes of those seeking to use them for their own purposes.

But he also knew that in the world of the Teg, often no matter what you did, you couldn't escape the machinations that rippled unbidden through the lives of those who employed the Grym, the Power of the Ancients giving them a great many benefits along with a great many more responsibilities.

Draig had learned quite a bit from his father about those benefits.

He cursed under his breath. He had known that this day was coming. Still, that didn't mean he had to like it.

He needed to decide. There was no way around it.

He just didn't like his choices. That was why he was delaying.

He was hoping that he could come up with a few more options. But after spending the last few hours staring out at the ocean, no other solutions had come to mind.

His mother had taught him that it was better to decide then

do when faced with a difficult choice or one that didn't appeal to him. Then, if his decision didn't work out as he wanted, he could adjust. He could make another decision.

Because that's what life was. A series of decisions. Some good. Some not so good.

Decide then do.

And as his mother had explained to him, better that he decide then do rather than someone else deciding for him.

His mother's advice had worked for him in the past. But now?

Now he feared the larger consequences if he made the decision that he wanted to and became involved in what had already become a huge mess.

Catching a hint of movement, Draig lifted his eyes to the sky. A few hundred yards away from him, he saw a black speck coming his way, steadily growing larger. He squinted so that he could get a better look, the rising sun aiding his effort.

A huge raven was winging her way toward him, flying faster than any bird had a right to.

He shook his head in aggravation. Now? Of all times?

Draig ducked to the side, the raven swooping just past his head, talons outstretched.

The raven wheeled tightly in the air, clearly undeterred. Draig ducked again, rolling out of the way and across the sand.

When he was back on his feet just a heartbeat later, the raven was gone. In the large bird's place stood a tall, beautiful woman with very pale skin and long, straight black hair. She wore a leather bodysuit, the necklace of raven feathers circling her neck her only adornment.

"It's been a while," Draig said, leaning on the shillelagh that was never far from his grasp.

"Not long enough," the woman replied in a sharp voice. She gave Draig a wicked smile when two short swords took shape, holding one in each hand. She sliced the black blades through the air, the steel singing crisply.

"Do we really have to do this?" asked Draig. Knowing the likelihood of his opponent walking away from the combat was close to zero, in a flash the illusion disappeared, his walking stick transforming into Excalibur, the fiery blaze that usually ran across the edge more muted this morning.

"We do," the woman confirmed with a nod and a suggestive wink. "You know how much I enjoy foreplay."

"There's no other way?" Draig asked, a trace of disappointment in his voice. "I thought we had gotten past all this, Riga."

The beautiful woman shook her head no. "After all we've been through, Draig, I'm disappointed that you're not as excited to cross blades as I am."

In a blur, Riga closed the distance between them, the short sword in her right hand slicing toward his neck, the blade in her left hand just a heartbeat behind the other and cutting for his hip.

Draig didn't bother to block either strike. Instead, he pivoted to avoid the first and then in the same motion jumped over the second blade, flipping through the air and turning his body so that he landed in the sand right behind Riga. It was his turn to give her a grin and a wink.

That only made Riga smile all the more as she lunged for Draig with one sword, the other sweeping in a wide arc for his knee.

Draig turned sideways to avoid the lunge, then parried the slash. He stepped in close to Riga, holding her one blade in place with his sword while gripping her other wrist with his free hand.

They were so close together that their lips almost touched, chest pressed against chest. Rather than being worried by the skill of the other, Draig and Riga both felt a surge of exhilaration racing through their blood, their eyes flashing with pleasure as they stared at one another.

"There are other ways to get close to me, Draig," Riga whispered, leaning forward and giving him a quick peck on the cheek. "You should know that by now."

Draig leaned in close to Riga, making her think that he was going to touch her lips with his. Something that she wouldn't mind in the least. "I do know that. And I also know what happens if we get too close to one another."

Draig pushed her backwards, putting some space between them. "Do you remember what happened the last time that we got close?"

Riga snorted out a laugh. "How could I forget. It was the most fun I had in years."

"It was for me as well," Draig admitted.

"Then why the concern now?"

"Because we also almost burned that hotel to the ground."

Riga smiled, then rushed toward Draig, so fast that she closed the distance between them in less than a heartbeat. Just as swiftly as she started, she stopped, Draig catching both her blades with his. "That's what made it so much fun."

Draig's eyes flashed, sending a jolt of electricity through Riga. Oh, how she loved it when that happened. Only Draig could make her feel this way. "You're right about that."

Riga pushed off of Draig this time. For the next few minutes both gave into their instincts, gliding across the sand with an almost inhuman grace, their movements mimicking those of a dancer across a Broadway stage but so fast that they were barely visible to the naked eye. Their blades slashed through the air, flashing when caught by the sunlight, the clash of steel on steel muted by the pounding of the surf on the beach.

The combat came to an end abruptly, stopping where it had last started, Riga pressed in close to Draig, his sword keeping her blades from slicing into his flesh.

"I heard about what happened in Williamsburg." Riga leaned in and gave Draig another kiss on the cheek, this one lingering for a few heartbeats before she pulled back from him, taking her swords with her.

"I thought that might be why you decided to visit." Draig took a few steps back himself. He knew just how dangerous it could be for him if he stayed close to Riga, her blades, which faded away into nothingness, the least of his concerns. Riga having decided that the combat had come to an end, Draig used the Grym to conceal his sword once more, the blazing steel again taking on the appearance of a shillelagh. "She told you about that?"

"Just last night when I stopped by to take her to dinner," Riga confirmed. "She watched it all from her house."

"I didn't intend for that to happen. I didn't know that it was going to happen."

"I know you didn't, Draig. But you need to remember what she can do. What she can see. And there are certain things that she doesn't need to see about you. Not yet anyway."

"I'm sorry," Draig sighed, more angry with himself than anyone else. Riga was right. He should have been more careful. "She was never in any danger. I promise you that."

"I know," Riga replied, giving Draig a gentle smile. She knew him better than she knew anyone else. He was speaking the truth. "That's not why I'm here. You'd as soon as cut off your own arm as place her in danger."

"Then why come here, Riga? It puts us both at risk, and I haven't seen you since ..."

"We don't need to reminisce about that," Riga replied, a hint of color appearing on her pale face. "That was a mistake."

"It didn't seem like it was a mistake at the time. Actually, it seemed quite ..."

"It was a mistake, Draig," Riga repeated, a hint of steel

entering her voice. "We agreed on that. We also promised that it would never happen again."

"And it hasn't."

"I know, and it won't happen again," said Riga, although it seemed as if she were saying that last part more to convince herself than Draig.

"Then why are you getting so worked up about it?" Draig's expression was one of innocence. His flashing eyes were anything but.

"I am not getting ..." Riga stopped herself, needing to find some calm. Draig had an effect upon her that no one else did, which thrilled her in a way that she couldn't explain. But he also was an expert at pushing her buttons, even when he wasn't doing it intentionally. Although she had no doubt that at the moment he had every intention of pushing her buttons, the spark in those fiery eyes of his that almost always took her breath away suggesting as much.

"I came here to warn you," she continued.

"To warn me? Why?"

"Because despite all that's happened between us, I still love you, Draig."

Draig offered Riga a sad smile. "I love you too, Riga."

She was quiet for a moment. "He knows."

"He knows?" Draig repeated in the form of a question.

"He knows."

Draig closed his eyes for several seconds, fighting to restrain the many curses that he had the immediate urge to expel. He should have expected this. "Crap!"

"That's a good way to describe it," Riga admitted.

"Does he know exactly where I am?"

Riga stared at Draig, a small smile playing across her lips. This was another reason she loved him. She had just told him that arguably the most powerful of all the Teg had not fallen for his trick and was likely coming for him, but there wasn't a hint of fear in his voice. Only resolve. As well as a touch of resignation, as if he expected that this day would come.

"Not yet," she replied.

"But he will."

Riga shrugged. "You know him better than I do."

"He'll figure it out then." Draig shook his head in aggravation. Just another major complication to what was already becoming a much too complicated situation.

"He probably will," Riga agreed. "Sooner rather than later." She reached up, caressing his cheek with a calloused hand. "So the Dragon has awakened."

"Not by choice."

"That doesn't matter. Word is already spreading among the Teg."

"I'm sure many of the Teg will not be pleased to hear that."

"Probably not," Riga agreed, giving him a sly smile. "Then again, some will be pleased to hear of your resurrection."

"I don't know about that," Draig challenged.

"They know what you did, Draig."

"I didn't have a choice."

"That doesn't matter," said Riga. "But you have a choice now. You will need to decide what to do."

"I already know what I'm going to do."

"What's that?"

"Stay in Kraken Cove, of course."

Riga laughed. "Don't play the fool, Draig. It doesn't become you. You will do as you did before."

"I don't want to do that. That's why I left."

"And I'm proud of you for doing that. But now when you do what you do best, you can decide what's right instead of your father."

Draig didn't reply at first. Thinking. Allowing her words to simmer. "Thank you, Riga. Truly. I appreciate you coming to warn me. And the advice."

She nodded. Then, against her better judgment, she pulled him into her arms and gave him a long, lingering kiss, both savoring the heat rising between them.

"One more piece of advice?" Riga said when she released her grip on him.

"I doubt that I could stop you."

That brought the twist of a smile to her lips. "Beware the Witch."

Here ends *The Dragon Awakens,* Book One of *The Fallen Knight Series.*

~

Axel Draig's story continues in *Duel With the Dragon*, Book Two of *The Fallen Knight Series.*

Keep reading for the first two chapters of Book Two.

BONUS MATERIAL

If you really enjoyed this story and if you have a few minutes, consider writing a review.

Keep reading for the first two chapters of Book Two of *The Fallen Knight Series, Duel With the Dragon.*

Order Book Two on my author website at PeterWachtBook s.com or on Amazon.

AN URBAN FANTASY FICTION SERIES

DUEL WITH THE DRAGON

THE FALLEN KNIGHT SERIES BOOK 2

PETER WACHT

Duel With the Dragon
By Peter Wacht

Book 2 of The Fallen Knight Series

Cover design by Ebooklaunch.com

Published in the United States by Kestrel Media Group LLC.

ISBN: 978-1-950236-56-5

eBook ISBN: 978-1-950236-55-8

Library of Congress Control Number: 2024920388

Created with Vellum

1. LATE-NIGHT VISITOR

Draig stood in the shadows, leaning his blackthorn shillelagh against his shoulder like it was a baseball bat.

He stared at the Book Nook. He had been for the past quarter hour. Still as a statue, just another piece of the darkness.

Not a sound to be heard. Not a whisper of movement. Not even a breeze, which was strange with the ocean just a few hundred yards to the east.

He was alone but for the smothering shadows, the street-lights reminiscent of Victorian London few and far between on Market Street.

Well past midnight, all was as it should be in Kraken Cove.

Although it wasn't as it should be in his bookstore.

Draig hadn't been planning on leaving his lighthouse and piloting his cabin cruiser back across Raptor Bay until later in the morning. When the sun was up.

He hadn't had a choice, though. A common theme these last few days. Ever since his adventure in Williamsburg, in fact.

Not having a choice.

He wasn't enjoying feeling as if he were one of the main characters in an online game, being moved this way and that.

Reacting, not acting.

Just like it had been when he served his father.

That was one of the reasons why he had come to Kraken Cove. So that he could make choices that had an impact on his life rather than allowing someone else to make them for him.

His displeasure at the sensation of being played with like a marionette on strings would have to wait.

The alarm for the Book Nook had awakened him, drawing him across the water. The alarm that would alert him, not Cerridwen or Seshat.

From where he was standing, all looked as it should in his bookshop. Just a few lights on toward the back and the front light on to counter the night.

He knew the truth, however.

He knew who was waiting for him.

Just to make sure that he wasn't in for any of her frequent surprises, he used the Grym to examine the store and its environs. Seeing what was obvious and not so obvious. Looking for what might be hidden. What might be lurking.

Draig pursed his lips, thinking for a moment.

All clear, which was out of character for her. She usually left a small gift at the very least.

But nothing this time.

He could wait a little longer, just to irritate her. But what was the point? She was hard enough to deal with as it was when she was in a good mood.

Draig walked across the street and stood in front of the door. Still wary, he sent a strand of the Grym beneath the frame, allowing the Power of the Ancients to slither its way through the shop like a snake.

Just because he knew who had decided to make a late-night

visit didn't mean that he trusted her. She had given him little cause to do so in the past.

Especially since more often than not she tended to work against him. Taking a unique pleasure from doing so, in fact.

Once the stream of magic completed its circuit, working its way over every inch of the store, Draig's eyes tightened.

Definitely out of character for her. His use of the Grym confirming that there were no surprises or traps waiting for him, Draig placed his hand over the door lock.

He didn't have the key with him. He didn't need it. Because though the lock resembled a deadbolt, it was much more than that.

Murmuring a few words under his breath, the palm of his hand glowed softly for just a heartbeat, and then the lock snapped free, at the same time disarming the several nasty surprises that Draig had woven into the wards set at all the entrances and exits to the store.

Pushing the door open on silent hinges, he stepped through and closed the oak slab just as quietly behind him.

Then he waited. Extending his senses. Wanting to check again. Examining every nook and cranny of his bookshop. Gaining a feel for what waited for him.

He smiled. He had to give her credit. She was good.

She had broken into his shop, avoided all the traps, and then reset all of his wards.

No one else of the Teg, except perhaps his mother, could have done the same. Then again, she did have an advantage that few others could claim.

There was just the one snare that she had failed to avoid, and he assumed that wasn't an error on her part.

Draig sensed her passage. Where she had walked. Where she had trailed her fingers across the covers and the spines. Where she had hesitated.

Draig followed the same path, coming to a stop after a

meandering journey through the aisles right where the two steel staircases that resembled the caduceus met at the very back of the shop.

He waited there for almost a minute. Still cautious. Then he decided that he was wasting his time. If she wanted to do something to him, she would have already tried.

Placing the tip of the shillelagh in the center of the circle he was standing within, almost invisible runes carved into the floor that had been worn down over the years flashed to life.

When he opened his eyes again, he still stood in the circle, although he was no longer in his shop. Or rather the shop reserved for most of his customers.

"It's not here, Eris," Draig said.

"I didn't think it would be, brother dear."

Eris didn't turn around. Her eyes were fixed on the almost transparent wall to her front. What looked like glass but wasn't, the slight shimmer giving it away.

Her reflection revealed that she was smiling. Draig wasn't surprised. His sister had a penchant for the unique. The hard to acquire. Just like someone else he had met recently.

"I always enjoy coming here," Eris murmured, transfixed by the packed shelves staring right back at her. "It's so ... relaxing. Enticing as well."

She licked her lips, thousands of priceless books and artifacts teasing her. The knowledge protected by that gleaming barrier that gave off an almost imperceptible hum. The power that could be obtained by anyone able to acquire and make use of just one of those items.

It was beyond imagining.

She and her brother were quite different from one another. But in this respect, valuing knowledge, understanding how it could be used ... in that respect they were much alike.

"You did well getting into the shop. You won't be able to break through the barrier, however."

"I'm aware of that, because I've tried, more times than I care to mention, and I'm quite disappointed by my failure to do so." Eris snorted in amusement, then turned around. "You're quite proud of yourself, aren't you? A unique construction combining two distinct powers over which only you can exercise control. Not even mother has the strength or the cunning to do what you did here."

Draig shrugged. "Not proud. Just telling you the truth is all."

Eris' snort of laughter became a low chuckle. "And there's the brother I know." She shook her head in disappointment. "Always telling the truth. Always doing what he believes is right. Even when doing so could cost him in the end."

Draig's expression soured slightly. He had no desire to relive the argument that they had engaged in ever since they were children.

Draig always doing what was right. Always so boring. Never having any fun.

Eris doing what she wanted to do. Ignoring the rules. Always having fun.

To curb his rising irritation, he studied his half-sister. She seemed little different than when he last saw her.

In appearance, they were very similar. Taking after their mother. Tall. Lithe. Wiry. Dark hair.

The primary difference being the color of their eyes. Draig's an orange red that burned as his anger intensified. Eris' eyes an icy blue that only got colder.

Draig lifted his chin just a hair. There. In the back of Eris' sea-swept orbs. A hint of concern?

Strange and slightly worrisome.

Because it was out of character for her.

Usually she was only concerned about herself.

"You wanted to talk."

"I did," Eris confirmed with a nod, her smile turning into a smirk.

Even though she hadn't come here of her own volition, Draig knew that she wasn't going to make this easy for him. If only because she so enjoyed trying to get under his skin. "You didn't want to talk in the Dragon Vault when we had the chance?"

"I thought it best not to interrupt. Besides, father-son reunions tend to make me emotional." She crossed her arms and shifted her weight, her right hip sticking out, left leg extended. "Did you enjoy seeing the King Teg again? It must have been quite a shock for dear old dad, particularly since you're still alive."

"You wanted that to happen." It was his turn to shake his head in disappointment. "Even after I helped you out with that paramour of yours. What was his name again? The one who threatened to reveal your relationship to mom?"

She laughed softly, a hint of condescension radiating out from her. She sought to hide her discomfort by provoking him just as she had done when they were younger.

He had helped her, unexpectedly so. Draig had told her that he had done it for the reason he offered. To ensure that Eris' boyfriend couldn't reveal the relationship to their mother.

She knew the truth, however. Her lover at the time had gotten aggressive, and she was having a hard time dealing with that. She thought she was in love, ignoring the fact that he was abusing her, emotionally and in other ways.

Draig had ensured that her former lover would no longer be a problem for her ... or anyone else for that matter.

"I was quite curious about how he reacted when the son he believed he killed was instead standing before him, holding his favorite sword no less," Eris said, ignoring her brother's questions, refusing to allow him to knock her off track. "He wants Excalibur back, doesn't he?"

"My father has wanted Excalibur back ever since the sword

chose me instead of him. I had nothing to do with it. And even if I wanted to give Excalibur back to him," Draig said, lifting the shillelagh off the ground, "it doesn't matter. It's up to Excalibur, not me. That's the way it's always been."

"What is it with boys and their swords?" mused Eris, shaking her head, as if slightly mystified, also clearly amused as revealed by the sparkle in her eyes. "I never understood the attraction. Very Freudian."

"You're losing focus again, Eris."

"Right, sorry about that," she replied, although she didn't sound the least bit contrite.

"Why did you bring my father and his Knights to the Dragon Vault?" he asked, trying to bring their conversation back to the primary topic. "Why did you want that to happen? Just so my father knew that I was still alive?"

"I didn't want that to happen," Eris replied. "In all honesty, I really didn't care. I had other plans that evening, but I had to change them."

Draig nodded, understanding dawning. "Mom."

"Mom," Eris confirmed.

"Why?" She had been the one who granted him sanctuary after Draig faked his own death, giving him the time to put in place the final pieces necessary for him to start again in Kraken Cove without needing to bear the chains thrown upon him by the King Teg.

"You know mom. She does things for her own reasons." Eris raised her arms to her shoulders, revealing her exasperation. "She doesn't tell me everything. In fact, she barely tells me anything at all. No more than I need to know."

Draig nodded. Their mother was tight-lipped to begin with, always keeping her cards close to her vest. He could understand why considering the demands placed upon her. "What did she tell you?"

"That you couldn't hide anymore. That your sabbatical was coming to an end. That you were needed once more."

"Why would she say that?"

"How long is this inquisition going to last?" Eris wondered. "I've got better ways to spend my time than serve as our mother's messenger."

"Eris!" Draig demanded sharply, his eyes flashing as his aggravation became more tangible. He took several deep breaths to calm himself, knowing that if he lost his temper with his sister, it would serve her purposes and not his.

"You'd have to ask her," Eris replied, giving him a shrug that suggested she had little interest in her mother's designs. Seeing how Draig's eyes flashed again, she realized that continuing to push her brother when he was like this was a bad idea. She did like to tease him. But she had no desire to make him angry. Because she knew what could happen if she did. "As I said, she doesn't tell me everything."

"That's all she had to say?"

Rather than reply right away, Eris examined her brother. Ignoring her better instincts, just as she usually did, she spoke in a voice normally reserved for a mother speaking with her young child. "Do you miss your mommy, Axel? Do you need a hug?"

In a flash, Draig stood right in front of Eris, no more than a blur as he shot through the twenty feet that separated them.

Eris tried to step back, her eyes widening slightly, having forgotten just how dangerous he could be, but she couldn't. The shimmering barrier behind her prevented it.

"Do you really want to test me now, Eris?" he asked in a very quiet voice that made her entire body prickle as if she had been struck by an icy gust. "Do you really want to push me?"

"Look, Draig, I was just having a little fun," Eris stuttered. Hating herself for demonstrating such weakness. She couldn't look away from Draig's eyes, which burned even brighter as he leaned in toward her. "Really, I didn't mean to ..."

"I know what you did, Eris," Draig said oh so softly, the timbre of his voice chilling her to the bone.

Eris gulped. "Like I said, Draig, I only brought your father to the Dragon Vault because mom wanted me to. That's the only reason ..."

"And was it mom who told you to steal *The Book of Whispers* from the Dragon Vault?"

Eris' eyes bulged even more, her shock complete. She had planned that job to perfection. No one could have figured it out. "How did you ..."

Draig didn't let his sister complete her question. "Fafnir wants to see you, Eris. He'd do almost anything to see you, in fact. And you know how he can be when someone steals an item from the Dragon Vault."

"Fafnir knows?" Her voice broke when she asked the question, her initial concern becoming something more akin to fear.

"Do you remember what he did when Felix snatched the Shield of Achilles?"

Eris didn't reply, simply nodding at the memory. It wasn't a good one.

Felix had asked Fafnir if he could borrow the artifact so that he could perform a test on the metal. Fafnir had refused because Felix didn't have permission from the Queen. Felix had taken the artifact anyway.

No one really knew what happened when Fafnir caught up to Felix. Nevertheless, Felix was never quite the same afterward. Jumping at shadows. Having nightmares. A trace of fear always in the back of his eyes. Worried that Fafnir might decide to come after him again and finish what he started.

"I suggest you find Fafnir and apologize. Don't wait for him to find you. You know how he is."

"But if I do that ..."

"It will be worse if you wait, Eris," Draig explained. "He will go easier on you if you demonstrate the courage to face him."

"That's all well and good," Eris protested, "but I don't have the book to return to him. With it still missing, he's not going to be very understanding."

"You have nothing to fear in that regard. Much to my father's chagrin, I returned the book for you."

Eris smiled then, beginning to think that what her brother was suggesting just might work. Although she was still unwilling to commit to it. "I'll think about it." She should have assumed that he had gotten his hands on the artifact.

"Do more than think," Draig suggested. "The longer you wait, the angrier Fafnir will be."

Eris nodded, then slid along the barrier behind her until she was free of Draig. "My job is done here. I'm going to head home. Anything you want me to tell mom?"

Draig answered in a tone that was more bite than bark. "Tell her that my decisions are my own. She doesn't need to make them for me."

Eris chuckled. "I will tell her word for word, but it's your funeral."

Eris walked toward the circle carved into the floor. She stopped and turned back when Draig called to her.

"Here is what you were looking for."

Eris scrunched up her brow in confusion until she saw what he held in his hand. The book materializing out of a series of distorting waves that reminded her of the heat rising off a desert highway.

"How did you know?" Her eyes sparkled in delight, temporarily forgetting her problem with Fafnir.

"It's what you were searching for, isn't it? *The Song of the Sirens*?" He flipped the book to her.

Eris snatched it deftly out of the air. "Yes, but how did you …"

"We all have our secrets, Eris, you know that," Draig replied mysteriously.

Eris realized that there was little point in pushing her brother for a more in-depth explanation. Because he was right. He had given her the book she was looking for.

Since her mother had forced her to make this trip, Eris was hoping to do a little shopping while she was here. But she couldn't find the volume, and she had no clue as to how to get past Draig's barrier.

"I'll return it when I'm done."

"Don't make promises you can't keep," he said with a playful smile as she stepped into the circle. "Eris?"

"Yes, brother dear?" Her usual smirk once again gracing her wily countenance.

"Do you agree with mom? Do you think that I've been hiding away?"

Going against character, Eris gave serious consideration to her brother's question before replying. Usually, she spoke from the cuff, trying to infuse her dissatisfaction with the world whenever she could. But not now.

"I can understand why you needed to step away. If I was in your position, I would have done the same." Eris didn't use the word *hide* as their mother did. She knew that her brother never hid from anything. Doing so was antithetical to his very being. "After everything your father required of you, all that you had to do that no other Teg should have to do, I can understand. But when mom sent me here to talk to you …"

Eris hesitated, needing a few seconds to gather her thoughts. "I could tell that mom was worried when she told me to come here. Why, I don't know. But I don't think she would send me here unless there was a good reason to do so."

"What would that be?" Draig asked, wishing as soon as the

words left his mouth that he hadn't. Not wanting to deal with another sarcastic response from his sister. Surprised when she once again went against her own nature.

"I don't know," Eris replied in a sad tone. "I do know that whether you like it or not, the Teg need you. And not just the Teg in Kraken Cove."

2. AN UNLUCKY BREAK

"A winery?" Gregor demanded. "We're infiltrating a winery? You can't be serious. I thought our target was in prison." He huffed in disappointment. "I was hoping that we'd at least have to breach a wall. Maybe blow something up. This is no fun at all."

Gregor and a squad of Knights hiked along the path, avoiding the creepers and prickers that reached for them. Out of habit, they stayed close to the trees at the top of the ridge so that they wouldn't be visible to anyone who might be looking up from below.

Despite their caution, they believed that they had little to fear in that regard. Their leather armor had been modified with the Grym so that it blended into their surroundings, whether the forest at their backs or a cityscape. For all intents and purposes, they were invisible unless a watcher knew exactly where they were and what to look for.

"Keep your voice down," ordered Jonas. He and his ten Knights of the Round might be well camouflaged, but voices tended to carry atop ridges. He had no desire to be discovered because of a novice mistake.

"I'm just saying," Gregor said in a much quieter tone that was close to a whisper, "a winery? Really?"

"What did you expect?" Jonas murmured, pushing out of the way a long vine that hung down from a tree growing close to the ridgeline.

"Certainly not this," Gregor grumbled. From where he was marching along the crag, every so often he glimpsed the fields upon fields of grapevines running up the slope that began at the base of the ridge and ended close to a large home made of steel and glass. Several barns and warehouses were just off to the west within easy walking distance of the mansion.

Peaceful. Bucolic. Idyllic, even.

And where one of the Knights' most dangerous enemies had been forced to take up residence.

"A Supermax prison," Gregor murmured. "A mine, maybe, with a cell three miles down. Or a steel tube runed with the Grym dropped into the Mariana Trench. But not this."

Jonas shrugged. He didn't want to waste his time arguing with Gregor. Because much like all the other Knights with them, he had thought much the same as the disenchanted Gregor. He just didn't feel the need to give voice to all that ran through his mind.

Somehow the Fallen Knight had bested the Daemon King more than a decade before. And somehow the Fallen Knight had imprisoned him.

But why a winery of all places?

It didn't make sense.

Jonas sensed the Grym surrounding the large estate, the shield of energy that was only visible to those of the Tylwyth Teg.

Admittedly, the barrier served its purpose just as effectively as would any of the other options Gregor had mentioned, the Daemon King restricted to the property that extended several acres around the knoll in all directions.

Even so, it was a strange solution. And Jonas couldn't fault Gregor or the other Knights for questioning it.

He understood why Draig had not destroyed the Daemon King when he had the chance. The politics and realities involved that stayed his hand.

No one could fault him.

Draig finishing the job when he had the Daemon King under his blade would have caused more problems than it would have solved and led to a period of unrest among the Teg that was best avoided. That had been avoided thankfully.

Still, this was the solution?

Locking away one of the greatest threats to the Tylwyth Teg at a winery that also had a large open-sided barn near the lake on the other side of the tor that on the weekends was used to host bands and other entertainment while food trucks rolled in? The Daemon King couldn't leave but others could enter the property?

It seemed more a vacation for the Master of the Abyss than a prison term.

It didn't make any sense to Jonas, and he didn't like it when the facts didn't make sense.

Of course, did all that really matter? He had been given an assignment, and he would complete that assignment just as he had completed all the others given to him ever since he joined the Knights of the Round three decades before.

"I just don't understand," Gregor grumbled again, shaking his head in disbelief.

"When the Fallen Knight defeated the Daemon King, he granted leniency," Jonas said, hoping that a brief explanation would stop Gregor from asking more questions and get him to focus on their assignment. "Instead of imprisoning the Daemon King in some other place like those that you suggested, Draig locked him away here. From what I understand, it was the best decision that the Fallen Knight could make at the time."

"But a winery?" Gregor whined again. "King Arthur actually agreed to it?"

Jonas closed his eyes for just a moment as they trod along the path, pinching his nose between his thumb and forefinger. He was losing patience with Gregor. He was a good Knight. He had served well for almost ten years. But sometimes, as he was doing now, Gregor didn't know when to keep his mouth shut and just concentrate on the task at hand.

"King Arthur said as much," Jonas explained in a weary tone, "although from what I heard he didn't have much of a choice."

"Didn't have a choice?" Gregor scoffed. "The King Teg always has a choice."

"Not this time. The Fallen Knight did the deal with the Daemon King and Merlin ratified it before King Arthur could stop them. Rather than spending his sentence in the deepest hole in Tartarus, just as he deserves, the Daemon King gets to spend it here instead."

"From where he could continue to cause problems for the rest of us," Gregor muttered.

"From where he is continuing to cause problems for the rest of us," Jonas clarified. "Otherwise, we wouldn't be here."

Although Jonas actually was more than pleased that this was the setting for his current assignment. Better this than some dreary cavern three miles belowground.

Scout the Daemon King's property and identify points of infiltration.

Simple.

No muss. No fuss.

Once that was done, Jonas would develop a strategy for when the Knights came back in force.

"If the Daemon King is locked away, why are we wasting time doing this?"

"Because we follow orders, Gregor. It's as simple as that."

"I understand that, Jonas, have no fear. And I understand as well that the Daemon King is still doing business from what looks to me more like home detention rather than a prison cell. But why make a play for him now? He hasn't bothered anyone since the Fallen Knight took him off the board. From what I understand, for the most part he's left us alone ever since Draig put him here."

"Gregor, how long have we known each other?" Jonas asked with a weary sigh.

The narrow game trail they were following along the edge of the wood was wider here, becoming more of a path as they entered a copse that would keep them out of sight for the next quarter mile before they curled around the far edge of the cliff and headed down, approaching the winery from the west.

When King Arthur had given Jonas and his squad this charge, he hadn't been able to provide much detail about the property. What magical wards and other defenses were in place. How many guards there were. How many points of ingress and egress. He couldn't really tell them anything at all.

That lack of intelligence had worried Jonas, and for good reason. In the past when he had been sent out on a mission, he had been briefed thoroughly. But for this, he knew virtually nothing. Not even Merlin could provide any useful details beyond the bare minimum.

Not only strange. Also alarming.

Maybe that's why King Arthur was so interested in learning more about the property that served as the Daemon King's prison. He didn't know all that he needed to know in order to put his larger plan in motion.

Although Jonas did know that he was getting tired of

Gregor's unending questions and complaints. If he didn't shut up soon, Jonas would shut the Knight up himself.

"Ever since I became a Knight."

"And what was one of the first lessons I taught you?"

"To always put on a clean pair of underwear before a mission because you didn't know how long it would take and you wanted to avoid chafing. I did that this morning, so no worries there." Gregor's grin, which set Jonas' temper to a simmer, was both one of pride and good humor, knowing that his response would get under his commander's skin despite its truthful nature.

"That, yes, although it's not relevant to our current conversation," Jonas replied with a hiss of exasperation. "The first thing I told you when you joined my squad."

"When given a mission, do the mission. Never question it."

Jonas nodded and continued quickly, worried about what else Gregor might decide to spout if he was given the chance. "Excellent. Now stop asking questions. King Arthur sent us here to scout the prison. He sent us here to prepare the way so that the Knights of the Round could come in force and eliminate the Daemon King once and for all. So that's what we do."

"You think King Arthur is ready to do that?" Gregor wondered.

Jonas shrugged. He couldn't really answer that question. It wasn't like the King Teg confided in him. Still, he had his suspicions. "The Daemons don't want to be in their world. They want to be in ours. They want to take over ours. Kill the Daemon King and the Daemons will no longer be able to leave the Daemon Realm until a new King is selected and gains the power necessary to send them out into our world and the many others where they can wreak their havoc. It could take centuries for that to happen. That helps us now. It wouldn't have ten years ago when Draig fought the Daemon King. Thus, the change in strategy."

"I understand all that, Jonas. You don't need to sound all high and mighty."

"I was simply explaining so that you would stop asking questions," Jonas replied through gritted teeth, his patience at the breaking point.

Gregor didn't seem to notice his commander's rising irritation. Either that or he didn't seem to care. "You believe all the PR crap they're feeding us about what the Daemons want?"

Rather than berating Gregor, Jonas snorted out a laugh. "You actually expect me to answer that considering who we work for?" He shook his head in mock amusement, failing to notice how some of the shadows in among the trees that lined the path were moving in opposition to the leaves that obeyed the wind that blew south to north. "In the last few months, King Arthur has done everything short of declaring war on the Daemons. Why? I don't know. Does he have good cause? I don't know. And I don't care. As you said, when given a mission, do the mission. Never question it."

"Yes, but Jonas ..." Gregor began, wanting to continue to argue with his commander.

"Whether the Daemons actually want to take over the Teg world or it's just a ploy that's part of a larger strategy isn't relevant," Jonas cut in, seeking to prevent Gregor from going off on another tangent. "Whether we're being fed the truth or the truth as King Arthur wants us to know it doesn't matter. What the King Teg wants, the King Teg gets. And it's clear that he wants the Daemons gone. For good. Now stop asking questions and concentrate on the mission."

Jonas halted abruptly, almost running into Horatio's broad back, the Knight walking a few yards in front of them stopping. Rather than cursing at Horatio, he cursed himself for being a fool.

The other Knights, who had been doing their best to ignore his conversation with Gregor, noticed it well before he did.

They had turned outward in response, forming a small circle with Jonas and Gregor in the center.

They weren't alone in the wood. They never had been. They just hadn't noticed until now.

But what could it be?

Guards this far from the property? He didn't think there were guards, Draig's magical barrier enough to contain the Daemon King.

Jonas didn't have long to ponder those and the many other questions that ran through his mind. Several large shadows detached themselves from the trees, a few even dropping down from the branches above.

When those shadows materialized in the dim light that illuminated the trail, Jonas' eyes widened in shock, a trickle of cold sweat running down his spine.

He reached for the sword on his back, pulling it free from the scabbard, all the Knights with him doing the same.

"There's no need for that," growled the Daemon who stood opposite him. "We are not here to harm you. If we were, you and your Knights already would be dead."

Even Horatio's large form couldn't block Jonas from seeing the creature. At least as best as he could, because the Daemon and its ilk blended extremely well into their surroundings. Just as they were designed to do.

The Knights of the Round were quite familiar with Daemons, having come up against these creatures a great many times in the past.

That only stood to reason.

King Arthur butted heads with the Daemon King frequently, the Master of the Abyss a constant annoyance. A threat to his rule if Arthur let down his guard. Just as Jonas and the Knights had done then, never thinking that these creatures could take them by surprise.

The weaker Daemons were made of spirit, not yet having

earned the gift of substance that only could be bestowed upon them by their master. To survive and serve the Daemon King when these lowest of the Daemons came into the Natural World from theirs, they had to claim a human body.

Alive or dead these creatures rarely cared. Male or female didn't matter either.

These lesser Daemons simply needed the flesh so that they could move through the Natural World as they needed to. The only real limitation if they chose someone who died was how badly decomposed the body was.

The Arch Daemons were stronger. They had their own bodies, having earned the trust and the good will of the Daemon King. They could appear as humans. As animals. A mix between the two, such as a centaur or a shifter. Or they could take some other monstrous shape.

The only limitation was that Arch Daemons could not change their shape once they selected it. To do that, they had to return to the Daemon Realm.

Because they could leave their home plane for only so long.

How quickly they needed to return depended on their strength. The tremendous energy required to enter and then remain in other worlds weakened all Daemons.

Therefore, they had no choice but to return to their own. To do otherwise put their very existence at risk.

Once back in the Abyss, they would need time to recuperate. To take in the sustenance that only could be obtained in the Daemon Realm. Then, once they had regained their power, they could decide what form to assume when next they left their own world on another task for their master.

These creatures who had slipped out from the shadows of the forest and surrounded the Knights without them even realizing it clearly were the more powerful Arch Daemons.

The five had taken the same form.

Some Knights of the Round believed it was their most lethal form.

Claws.

The hunters of the Daemon King.

Manlike creatures that were covered in greyish black scales who stood seven feet tall if not a head more. Small fangs hung over their lips, and their noses were broad and wide, almost as if they had been punched in the face one too many times. Their eyes were a deep black that appeared to glow. And spikes ran down their shoulders to their forearms, their claws larger than catchers' mitts. Thus, their name.

And, perhaps most worrisome for the Knights, a natural armor shielded their chests, arms, and thighs, which meant that it would be that much more difficult for them to cause injury with their swords. Even with their steel infused with the Grym, cutting through an Arch Daemon's hardened flesh would be a challenge, taking several strikes in the same place to breach it.

"Why should I believe you?" Jonas asked.

The Claw considered his question. The Arch Daemon understood why the Knight was hesitant to take him at his word. Knights and Daemons had been enemies since the Knights came into existence more than a thousand years before. If their positions were reversed, he would be just as skeptical.

"You shouldn't," the Claw replied, shrugging his broad, spiked shoulders. "I assume that because of your grey hair you have served as a Knight for a long time."

"I have," Jonas confirmed.

Jonas' mind worked furiously for a solution to his dilemma. Twelve Knights against five Claws?

Not good odds.

For the Knights.

The Knights were excellent warriors. Few other Teg could match them when blades were drawn.

But against this many Arch Daemons?

They would be lucky if any of them survived.

"Then you know that I and my brethren have no love for you or your companions."

"The feeling is mutual."

The Claw actually smiled at that, if it could be called a smile. The creature's sharp teeth, perfect for ripping into flesh, were revealed for just a heartbeat.

"But you also know that I and my brethren obey our master. And our master does not wish for us to draw blood. He wishes for us to take you to him."

"You want to take us to the Daemon King?" Jonas asked, not quite believing what he was hearing.

"Yes, that is what our master has charged us with," the Claw confirmed.

"Why?"

"We do not question our master, Knight. We simply do as he commands."

Jonas nodded, lips pursed as he did so. It seemed that the Daemon King and Arthur Pendragon were the same in that respect. They both required unquestioned loyalty.

And perhaps this was the fix that he was looking for with respect to their dilemma. Perhaps he could get his squad out of this mess without any or all of them dying.

But he would need to handle matters delicately. Because he had little cause to place much faith in a Daemon's promises.

Jonas' concerns in that respect proved unnecessary, as Gregor took his ability to decide their next step out of his hands.

"Die, Daemon scum!" the Knight shouted. His sword raised above his shoulder, Gregor was poised to slash down with his glowing steel as he charged toward the Claw just a few yards to his front.

When Gregor attacked, all of the Knights followed. Listening to their instincts. Not thinking.

Jonas had no choice but to join them, although he did so with a deep foreboding tightening his chest.

He knew how this skirmish was going to end.

The Knights fought well. Although they met with little success. Their Grym-touched blades did nothing more than chip off a few pieces of armored flesh from the Claws the few times that they actually struck their adversaries, and even then it was more luck than skill.

The Claws were too fast. They used the shadows around them too well. There, then not. Appearing and disappearing on a whim. Evading ...

Jonas' mouth opened in surprise while he swung his steel in a wide arc, seeking to slice across a Claw's throat.

His blade missed by a hair, yet that was all the Claw needed. Sensing his momentary vulnerability as he left himself open to an attack, Jonas believed that he was about to die.

Shockingly, instead of punching his daggerlike fist into his chest, the Claw held back. Shouldering into Jonas and knocking him backward instead.

His Knights were fighting to kill.

The Claws weren't.

At least not at the beginning of the clash.

Not until they lost patience with the fight, which happened only a few heartbeats later, the Daemons' natural instincts becoming too strong for them to resist.

Once that happened, the clash ended swiftly, one Knight after another dying a painful death, the Claws' razor-sharp digits colored in blood.

Gregor first, his head removed from his shoulders. Horatio next, much of his chest missing thanks to a Claw ripping through his ribs. Then all the others. None of his men lasting for more than a few seconds.

Until only Jonas remained.

His Knights dead all around him, he gave in to his own impulses. He knew that he stood no chance against a Claw, much less five, so he did something that he never expected that he would.

He ran.

Scrambling off the trail and into the wood, Jonas allowed his fear to guide him. His terror taking control. Leading him to he didn't know where, only caring that it took him away from the Claws.

Jonas skidded to a stop when he broke free from the trees, the edge of the cliff just a foot away from him, the large vineyard stretching out below and the mansion shining brightly in the waning sunlight.

The sounds of pursuit drawing closer, Jonas turned to face the Claws who sprinted out of the shadows. They skidded to a stop right in front of him, only a few yards away, the space along the ledge narrow and tight.

Gulping in fear, Gregor took a step backward, bringing his sword up, preparing to defend himself from the Claw who was reaching toward him.

"Stop, Knight," hissed the Daemon who had spoken to him before all hell broke loose. "We did not want this. We did not want to fight. Come with us now. Our master waits. You need not die."

But despite the Claw's remarkable speed and agility, he was too late.

As he pivoted around, Jonas' back foot slipped off the edge of the cliff. His balance lost, instead of reaching for the claw the Daemon offered to him to prevent him from falling, Jonas tried to swing his steel one more time.

Jonas sliced through nothing but air. Before he even

thought to scream, he was dead, a broken bag of bones on the rocky ground far below.

The Claw looked down in puzzlement, not understanding why the Knight persisted with his efforts despite the perilous nature of his circumstances. Nevertheless, he couldn't say that he was saddened by the Knight's death or those of his companions.

He was disappointed, however. And he was worried. "The Daemon King will not be happy."

"We didn't do anything," the Claw standing next to him said. "The Knights started this clash. We were just defending ourselves. Trying to disarm them until it became too much."

"That doesn't matter. We failed. Our master wanted to talk with Pendragon's Knights. That was all. And now he can't."

"He will understand," the other Claw said, although the Daemon didn't sound like he believed his own words.

"There are a dozen dead Knights on the fringe of our master's property. That's all the incentive that the King Teg needs. Arthur will say whatever he must to get what he wants. And it will be as the Knight said. Pendragon wants to destroy us. We have given him the reason to do so."

The other Claw had no response to that, the terrifying creature seeming to deflate as the reality struck him. "You're right, the Daemon King will not be happy."

THE END OF CHAPTER TWO

~

I hope you enjoyed the first two chapters. To keep reading *Duel With the Dragon*, Book Two of *The Fallen Knight Series,* order your copy today at PeterWachtBooks.com or on Amazon.

MORE BY PETER WACHT

THE FALLEN KNIGHT SERIES

The Death of the Dragon (short story)*

The Dragon Awakens

Duel With a Dragon (Forthcoming)

Beware the Dragon (Forthcoming)

The Dragon Returns (Forthcoming)

THE REALMS OF THE TALENT AND THE CURSE

THE TALES OF CALEDONIA

(Complete 7-Book Series)

Blood on the White Sand (short story)*

The Diamond Thief (short story)*

The Protector

The Protector's Quest

The Protector's Vengeance

The Protector's Sacrifice

The Protector's Reckoning

The Protector's Resolve

The Protector's Victory

THE TALES OF THE TERRITORIES

Stalking the Blood Ruby (short story)*

A Fate Worse Than Death (short story)*

Death on the Burnt Ocean

Monsters in the Mist

The Dance of the Daggers

Bloody Hunt for Freedom

A Spark of Rebellion

Shadows Made Real

Shadow's Reach

Storm in the Darkness (Forthcoming 2025)

THE SYLVAN CHRONICLES

(Complete 9-Book Series)

The Legend of the Kestrel

The Call of the Sylvana

The Raptor of the Highlands

The Makings of a Warrior

The Lord of the Highlands

The Lost Kestrel Found

The Claiming of the Highlands

The Fight Against the Dark

The Defender of the Light

THE RISE OF THE SYLVAN WARRIORS

*Through the Knife's Edge (short story)**

* Free stories can be downloaded from my author website at PeterWachtBooks.com. My books are also available on Amazon and other online retailers.

YOUR FREE SHORT STORY IS WAITING

THROUGH THE KNIFE'S EDGE

This short story is a prelude to the events in my epic fantasy series *The Sylvan Chronicles* and is free to readers who receive my newsletter.

Sign up and get your free copy at PeterWachtBooks.com

Made in the USA
Columbia, SC
23 June 2025